THE BOLD THING

Also in Arrow by Mark Daniel

UNDER ORDERS

Mark Daniel

THE
BOLD THING

ARROW BOOKS

Arrow Books Limited
20 Vauxhall Bridge Road, London SW1V 2SA

An imprint of the Random Century Group

London Melbourne Sydney Auckland
Johannesburg and agencies throughout
the world

First published in Great Britain by Barrie & Jenkins Ltd 1990
Arrow edition 1991

Printed and bound in Great Britain by
Cox & Wyman Ltd, Reading, Berkshire

ISBN 0 09 984670 5

In memory of Captain Robert Nairac, my schoolfellow, and Giuseppe Conlon of the Maguire Seven, both men of honour and intelligence, who died abused by damned fools.

November

Sansovino came home on 9th November. It was a clear bright evening of sugar colours, Fragonard colours; and the sun was white and all alone. All sounds – the cawing of the rooks, the thuds and thumps from inside the horsebox – were very sharp and clear.

Screech Reagan the stud groom it was who shot the bolts. He and Michael Ryan slowly lowered the backboard. Michael was a big fellow with a long, white smock face and plenty of muscle. He took the greater part of the strain.

Screech was a full head shorter, a good twenty years older. What little hair he had was white and wispy, while his skin was the uniform puce of a birthmark. He was the shape of a stubby bullet. He was short one jawbone. His thick face seemed to run directly down into his neck.

Behind them as they walked up the ramp and fastened this or that, Cathy Kramer leaned eagerly forward. The breeze painted her golden hair in streaks across her face. Her hands clutched tight to the arms of her wheelchair. She wanted to be up there with the men.

Then there was Jenny Farlow, the tall girl with blonde cropped hair who sat on her hunkers at Cathy's right. But Jenny showed no trace of interest or anticipation as she watched the men going about their business. Jenny could not give a damn. Her hands hung between her legs. She picked up fragments of grit and flicked them from her. Her pale eyes gave back no more light than soapstone. Her lips were tugged to one side in a calculated expression of scepticism.

It was not so easy to be sceptical about what happened next. Even Jenny's lips parted enough to show spittle-spangled teeth. She had been expecting a horse.

What came down the ramp now was a deal more horse than she had bargained for.

He emerged eager yet stately, a statue come to life. His head was held high, his nostrils dilated and contracted as he scented his new home.

Sansovino was a close-coupled, dark brown stallion with a white blaze. He had an intelligent head, a bold soft eye and big prick ears. Jenny had

3

probably only seen racehorses – young, lean athletes, barely adolescent. This was a mature adult, a pack leader, carrying a mass of muscle and condition and the great arched crest of the stallion.

'Sanso,' murmured Cathy Kramer softly. She blinked and smiled her lop-sided smile. She reached out to the horse in a long distance caress. 'Sanso.'

'Jesus,' Jenny stood. She shuffled back behind the wheelchair. 'That is the most powerful thing I have ever seen.'

'What fuckin' does for you,' Cathy grinned proudly up at her horse, 'ain't it, boy? Well,' she amended after a moment's thought, 'not for you exactly, hon.'

Sansovino's hooves now clattered and scraped on the cobbles of the yard. He looked around the white boxes with their pale green doors. He snorted and rolled back his lips to display an old piano keyboard. He rubbed his eye on his foreleg, then threw up his head, pulling Screech's feet from the ground. 'Whoah, there,' Screech croaked.

'That's my boy.' Cathy slapped her thigh. She wiped away an invisible tear. Her right hand beat a palsied time. 'Welcome home, you old bastard.'

'Say that was born here?' Jenny shrugged.

'Yep. Old rogue. Eight years ago in February. Bed him down, will you, Screech? We'll lunge him tomorrow morning first thing, OK?'

'Right,' Screech nodded. He clicked his tongue at the horse and led him off down the yard.

'Ed would have liked to have seen this,' Cathy sighed, 'Sanso was his favourite . . . Ah well, there you go. Nothing to be done about it. Crack on. Come on, Jen, push me back to the car, would you? I want to see those damned yearlings.'

Fergal Doherty arrived soon after dark, and with him his woman Margaret and the biggest dog you have ever seen.

They appeared at the black bush at the foot of the hill and trudged in silence up the moonlit mud-track.

It was a cold night, nigh freezing. Steam trickled from their lips like milk into water. The booted feet of the humans crunched on the deep ridges of crusted clay.

And now as they neared the five-bar gate, you could see them more clearly. Fergal was a giant, six foot six, maybe more. His head was a black stormcloud of curly hair and beard. Margaret was thin as a lily and pale as the moon. Her hair was swept up beneath a shapeless tweed hat. The dog, a grizzled, loping wolfhound, was a worthy partner for its master. Its shoulder was as high as Fergal's hip.

Fergal gestured with his left hand. He made a small hissing sound. The dog dropped onto the track and, with an impatient little yawn, unfolded its long legs. It laid its nose between its forefeet. Fergal pulled the canvas bag from over his shoulder. He laid it on the ground and pulled out a fine black net. 'Here,' he spoke softly to the girl.

She took one end of the net, and together they played it out and slung it loosely over the gate. For the next five minutes, they worked silently and methodically, weighting the net until Fergal was content.

'OK,' he nodded. He clicked his fingers once. The dog bounded over the gate into the darkness of the field.

Fergal and Margaret retreated into the shadows of the trees and bushes by the track. They crouched, and they waited.

Below them, some two miles down into the valley, lights still burned both in the house and in the yard of Ballysheenan. 'She's got a stallion in,' Margaret murmured, 'you hear that?'

'Yep,' said Fergal absently. He was listening intently for sounds from the field.

'Means they'll have to send someone in, pay her a call.'

'What?' Fergal's eyes swivelled this way and that, the better to hear. 'Not her. She's an American, not a Brit.'

'Still,' Margaret shrugged.

'Ah, hell. She's only a little old lady, Jesus sakes.'

'Still.'

'Ah, well,' he sighed, 'Seems all wrong, but . . .'

'Think of the money she'll be raking in!' Margaret yapped.

'Sh!' Fergal clutched her arm, then, 'OK, OK, if that's the way of it. Listen now.'

You could hear it clearly, the rapid patter of footfalls on the hard ground. It came nearer, receded, came nearer, receded. Then a shadow streaked at the gate. The shadow slipped under, but the creature that cast it hit the net, tangled and frantically kicked. It looked enormous in the pale grey light. The net bellied and twitched, but whatever it was was caught fast.

Fergal was on his feet and moving towards it almost as it hit, but the trapped animal still had time to recognise the futility of struggle, to give itself up to despair. It had just set up the terrible shrill wail of the hare's farewell when Fergal's left hand swiftly plucked away the net. The scream was cut short as he straightened with the big red hare hanging twitching from his fist, but the echo seemed still to shiver across

5

the valley long after his right hand had chopped sideways to snap the spine.

'So that's it, then,' Margaret still whispered, 'she gets the treatment.'

'Who's that then?'

'The Kramer woman.'

The dog returned, panting, and banked the gate. Fergal reached down to scratch behind its ears. He shrugged. For the first time he spoke out loud. 'S'pose so,' he sighed, 'no choice, is there?'

Micky parked the Peugeot down in the Highflyer car park because the valets up there by the sale-ring would recognise him.

He twisted around to pick up a tweed cap from the back seat and pulled it down over his forehead. For a moment then he just sat there, staring through the charcoal dust dusk at the stableyard ahead. Then he breathed, 'Oh, fuck it,' and, quickly now, gathered the clipboard and the leaflets from the passenger-seat. He opened the door.

His stomach whimpered like an eager dog. His right hand flapped off drops of excess nervous energy. He locked the car door and turned away to trudge up the hill. He had stopped for a piss five miles back. Already his bladder was straining.

He hunched his shoulders and forced his chin deep into the corduroy collar of his Barbour. There was little wind, but the moist evening mist seeped through his collar and cuffs. For now, he was safe. In this light, his face was mere smoke.

At the top of the rise, he swung left through a gap in the white railings into Park Paddocks. The lamps were already lit. They drew evening in close. Scattered groups of people in Puffas and Hermès headscarves, British Warms and trilbies, sheepskins and flat caps, stood talking in the cones of warm light. A familiar machine-gun rattle came from the loudspeakers on the big octagonal sales building to his left: Ed Mahoney strutting his stuff. '. . . fifty-four fifty-four bid again yes sir? At fifty-four a great walker fifty-four fifty-six thank you sir? At fifty-six fifty-eight he says fifty-eight yes sir?'

A frisson shook Micky's shoulders. He was home again. He wished that he were not.

He walked on with as decisive an air as he could contrive. Through the windows of the restaurant ahead, he saw faces, familiar faces many of them, their mouths opening to laugh, to gossip, to bite on cream cakes or smoked salmon sandwiches. It was too bright in there, too confined. Every eye would swivel as he entered. The same applied to the bar beneath the sales-ring. It would have to be the ring itself. At least there he would only be a secondary object of interest. First, though, he headed for Tattersall's offices.

The light was bright in here.

If you had seen the old press photographs from way back, you might still have recognised Micky, except that in those days he had always looked drawn and emaciated, a bit like the young Sinatra in a portrait by Van Gogh. He had filled out now. His frame had grown into his swagger.

A girl with amber hair and a nice pale pink and pearly smile said, 'How can I help you, sir?' Micky liked her because she smiled and because he did not know her and she did not know him.

'A catalogue, please, love.'

'Part two?'

'I suppose, yes.' He grinned at her *corps de ballet* teeth. 'You wouldn't have any part ones going cheap, you know, seeing as it's Saturday evening?'

'Afraid not, sir. All gone.' She slowly rocked head, considering. 'Tell you what. Why don't you borrow mine? I'll not be able to get back to the ring tonight. I'd like it back though. Keep them, you know; souvenirs.'

'OK,' Micky nodded, surprised and happy. Perhaps this was not going to be so bad after all. 'That's very kind of you, thanks.'

'Ah, nothing.' She tossed the big grey hardback onto the counter. 'You can fill in some of the prices for us.'

'Sure.' He paid her for the one catalogue and picked up both.

'Sorry,' said the girl. 'You're . . .?'

'Micky.'

'Micky?'

'Micky Brennan,' he said quickly. He turned away.

'Right.' There was no discernible trace of coolness in her voice, so he turned back and smiled. Perhaps she was new. 'See you later then.'

He pulled open the plate glass door and his face was still distended in a broad and goofy grin. Hell, he had been blowing this thing out of all proportion. People weren't so bad.

And he walked into Ted Bolus.

Ted was a lean, snipy little fellow with a twisted grin and a left cheek like a solitaire board. He was four, five years Micky's senior, but where the tarnish was fading on the hair above Micky's ears, there was no trace of grey on Ted's flat, mushroom-gill head.

Ted had been a pretty hard rider in his time. No technique, but as a trainer, a little surprisingly, he had done OK, particularly with sprinters and sharp two-year-olds. Once he had asked Micky to find him a good animal. On a trip to Kill, Micky had picked out a little darling called Hampton Court which had only won the Vernons and a small packet for his connections before breaking down.

Ted used to drop in on Micky after the sports sometimes. He would drink his whiskey and tell him how impossible were his wife and his life. This never served to cheer Micky vastly. At the time, his life and wife had not been so possible either.

It seemed that Ted had recently acquired some rich-in-unsaturated-oil Arab owners, which would explain the camelhair, the Rolex Oyster, the gaunt, wispy blonde on his arm. She, unlike the former Mrs Bolus who was called Yvonne and had looked like a walnut, looked really quite distinctly possible.

'Hello, Ted,' Micky stood back to let them pass.

Ted frowned. He said, 'Micky.' He walked straight past him at speed.

Micky's chum at the counter had disappeared into an office at the back, so Ted and his fox-wrapped floozie had to wait, becalmed. Micky gritted his teeth, took a deep breath and strolled back. He leaned on the counter beside him.

'So, how's it going then?'

Ted stared straight ahead. Nelson, seeing no ships. His fingers played a quick arpeggio on the counter, then curled into a loose fist. 'Fine, thanks, Micky,' he sighed.

'Great. Listen, Ted. I'm in a new line of business. Got this feed supplement, see. Vitamins, minerals, trace elements, you know. The Glendale Champion range. It's bloody good stuff, actually. There's a syrup you can add to the feed, or there are these halibut liver granules, all sort of tasting of molasses . . .'

'I don't think so, Micky,' Ted hummed. He did not turn towards him. His fist now lightly struck the counter.

'The syrup'd be great for your sprinters,' Micky persisted. 'Glucose and all. Ideal for glycogen-loading. Oh, and there's a mares and foal compound too: calcium, vitamin D, you know?'

'Ah,' Ted straightened as the amber girl emerged from the back. 'Good evening.'

Something hot pushed at the back of Micky's eyes. He had to blink a couple of times. His right hand arose of its own accord as though to wipe his brow. He thought better of it. It dropped again.

'Evening, Mr Bolus. Can I help you?'

'Yes, er. Yeah, my wife here. She hasn't got a catalogue. I was wondering.'

'Of course. No problem.' She smiled.

Micky resented that smile. It bore a distinct resemblance to the one that she had given him a mere minute ago. It had been precious to him, but it seemed that she had them to throw around ad lib. She ducked down behind the counter.

Every muscle in Micky's arms was taut and trembling. Something small and cold clambered hand over hand up his spine. Absurdly, embarrassment and anger had brought tears to his eyes.

'Oh, damn it,' he growled, 'take the bloody leaflet anyway.'

He slammed the Glendale leaflet on the counter and swung away, barging through the smoked glass doors.

Outside now, he leaned against the brick wall and looked up at the lights on the sales-ring walls. They were fuzzy as thistledown until he had blinked a bit more. He gratefully swallowed the fresh air and waited for his lungs to stop puffing like bellows, the hubbub of his heart to subside.

Somehow he didn't reckon he was cut out for this salesman lark.

'It just won't do, Micky,' Mr Birtwhistle had intoned mournfully a couple of weeks back. Birtwhistle showed Micky the top of his iron-grey head. He told his genitals, 'It really won't, you know.'

Birtwhistle had a thin, reedy voice for his cottage loaf-bulk, a precise, mincing trick of speech. The vowels cringed, flat and conciliatory. Micky's name came out as 'Meekee'. Birtwhistle liked to use it a lot.

'I mean, we are trying to do our best by you, Micky. You know that, don't you? But you really have to pull your weight, Micky, do your bit too, you know? Your sales figures, well, they're not exactly impressive, now are they? They really don't justify the car. To date. You know?'

He cast a quick glance over his shoulder at a large grey graph on the pale blue wall behind him. GLENDALE PETCORPS, it said in crimson upper case, then, in black copperplate, *Putting Your Pets First*. Micky could not distinguish his name at that distance, but there was a sort of limp, drooping line near the bottom which inspired a whole lot of fellow-feeling.

'Yeah, well, sure,' he shrugged fetchingly. He leaned forward over jauntily crossed legs. With his hands, he framed the attractive picture that he wanted Birtwhistle to see. 'But thing is, there'll be orders coming in. I've got some big yards have taken samples, you know. It takes time.'

'Racing yards?' Birtwhistle's eyebrows shot up. His dewlaps jumped an inch or more.

'Sure.' Micky flapped away his scrutiny. 'Sure!' Then, 'Well, one or two.'

Birtwhistle sighed. He slapped the partners' desk and pushed himself to his feet. 'Now come along, Micky,' he was stern, 'come along, come along.' He lumbered over to the grimy window. He told it, 'You know why we took you on. If we had just wanted any old hunting or showing people taking our product, we could have employed any number of professional salesmen. Persons. We took you on because of your contacts, Micky. We want the big yards, the prestige yards. Stoute, Cecil, you know, that crowd. We want the Classic winners. And all that you've brought us so far is – what? Two small orders for Halibut Liver Ultragrains from Ronan Byrne and . . .' he clicked his fat fingers.

'Jack Carlton,' Micky supplied. 'Yeah, well, that's not too bad. They're mates. They'll get the word around.'

Birtwhistle turned away from his perusal of the sky above Doncaster. He lurched back to the desk and leaned on his fists. 'But Micky, Micky, come on now. Let's be honest, hmm? Straight down the line time. Have you even tried the big Newmarket yards yet? Have you? Have you even visited them? Truthfully now, Micky?'

Micky thought for a moment in hope that the answer might change in the meantime. It remained resolutely the same. So he looked down at the floor and up at the ceiling and said, 'No.'

The word seemed a little cold on its own. He gave it some company, 'No, but thing is, I was thinking as how, if the word got about first, you know, from the smaller boys . . .'

'No, no, Micky,' Birtwhistle flagged down the flow, 'We'll make the marketing strategy decisions, thank you. Your job is just to go and see these people, talk to them, persuade them to give Glendale Champion a try. That's all.' He slumped back into his chair which puffed under his weight. For a few seconds he just sat there, recovering from the unaccustomed exercise, then pulled himself forward, picked up a red plastic ballpoint and hit the blotter hard.

'I'm going to have to be hard on you, Micky. I don't want to be, but. I've got to insist. I can give you . . . what? Another month? Two at the outside. Me, I wish you all the best. You know that. But I'm answerable to Mr Glenn, and it isn't easy, you know, explaining why we're shelling out for your car and so on ... You're going to have to go back to Newmarket, Micky, and really push the boat out. Sell and sell hard. It's the December Sales soon, isn't it?'

'Yup,' said Micky glumly. Suddenly he felt as though he had eaten a great deal of raw pastry. 'End of the month.'

'Well, then. That's fine! Splendid! So, we'll expect to see a sizeable upturn in your December sales figures, all right, Micky? Remember, you're in charge of racing because of who you were – who you are – and racing's important to us, hmm? You've got a great chance here, Micky. Make the most of it, or . . .'

He gave a big wet grin and extended a hand across the desk.

'Yeah.' Micky stood and took it. It was soft and dry as a bitch's belly.

'Go to Newmarket, Micky,' Birtwhistle beamed, 'see your old pals. Have fun, Micky, have fun!'

Have fun.

So far, he had been cut by three people. A further six had said hello, looked at their feet a lot, enquired after his health and seen someone behind him whom they had been earnestly seeking all day. Of course they would read the leaflet. Thanks a lot. Be in touch.

A few of the dealers seemed genuinely glad to see him and had gone out of their way to shake his hand. A very lovely marchioness had kissed him fondly and fragrantly and had made him promise that he would call.

That was the score as at last he pushed open the sales-ring door and walked wearily up the stairs.

And there it all lay beneath him, unchanged.

Tattersall's is a pale blue octagon with eleven tiers of seats fanning out from the central ring. As Micky entered, a washy foal was being led around beneath the big Chinese lantern which hangs from the centre of the cupola.

Even as he emerged in the light, a pretty redhead down by the ring hurled her catalogue up at him. Luckily she remembered to keep hold of it.

Micky stopped. He took an uncertain step backward. Then he realised that she was one of the girls appointed to pick out bidders. She was pointing at a chubby Middle Easterner just two tiers down on his left.

Well, he was here now. May as well put a bold front on it.

11

He squared his shoulders and sauntered casually down the aisle. Over in the gate, where most of the dealers stood, a couple of heads arose. Timmy Hyde, king of the pinhookers, nudged his neighbour and pointed up at Micky.

'Is that a bid?' Ken Watt, who had taken over the rostrum, peered down over his bifocals in his best myopic dominie manner. 'No? Oh. Two, then. Two thousand ... two two ... two four. Own brother to a winner and a smashing pedigree, you know. Two six? Two six. Come along now ... And I sell him. I give him away. You'll regret this, you know, ... Two eight. Two thousand, eight hundred ... Three thousand ... His bid, his bid. It's against you on the top. Is that all? I sell outside, and value, I think, at three thousand guineas ... three two ...'

Micky shuffled sideways to a seat halfway down and almost immediately opposite the auctioneer. The sales-ring was filling up fast. Something hot must be coming up.

The electronic board above the entrance to the ring said that this was lot 891 and that the bidding stood at 3,800 guineas. The catalogue said that lot 891 was a Hostage colt out of an Exceller mare. Partly from habit, partly because he wanted to look at anything but the crowd, Micky narrowed his eyes and sized up the foal. He was well grown, had plenty of bone – perhaps a tad too much – but he was not straight. He turned out his off foreleg as he walked. Not necessarily a fault, but enough to ensure a low price in today's dealers' market.

He flicked over the page. 892 was nothing special, but 893 ... Ah, since his arrival from South Africa, this was the one: a bay filly by the stallion of the moment, Sadler's Wells, out of a Grade II winning Forli mare. The second dam, Charming Alibi, won sixteen races in the States and had thrown six winners to date, including the great Dahlia. There was a whole lot happening in that pedigree.

Micky hazarded a quick glance over at the bidders' cage. Richard Heron stood at the front, a tall, sleek, plump fellow with gleaming black hair. He was chewing on a gold pencil and frowning down at his catalogue.

He did not look much like a text-book multi-millionaire in his green Husky, fawn trousers and black galoshes, but somehow or other, since his arrival from South Aftica this man had acquired casinos, hotels, pubs, bookmakers' shops, slot-machines, cinemas and Lord knows what else before setting about the establishment of the world's biggest bloodstock empire. He had already had two English, two French and four Irish Derby winners. He owned horses in training or at stud in every continent, bar the Arctic and the Antarctic. He was going to want this filly.

Behind him, his current wife Sabrina stood looking confused and vacuous in black jersey. No one had ever been able to work out why Heron bothered with the costly business of divorce and re-marriage. Each successive Mrs Heron had been a clone of her predecessors. They had all been tall, blonde and impeccably turned out. They had also all been married to other rich men when Heron appeared on the scene. Charlie Vane used to say that that was how Heron got his kicks: 'Stuffs bigger men than he by stuffing their wives.'

Micky returned to the study of the filly's pedigree. To him and his kind it made interesting reading; a delicious amalgam of happy memories and covetous speculation, but he would really sooner be looking around, checking out the faces. The trouble was, he might catch a furtive eye or an eye might catch his and he would have to cope with the hurt as a supposed friend looked away, the embarrassment of a nervous half-smile, the pang of rejection as this or that person suddenly took an earnest interest in his neighbour.

'Evening, Brennan,' barked a stentorian voice behind him. Micky jumped and frowned. He slowly turned. And there, just taking his seat, his pink and white face spread in a wide carefree grin, his black hair as ever splashed and splayed like storm-smashed hay, was Charlie Vane.

'Charlie,' Micky risked a smile. He turned quickly back to the ring. 'Hi. How's it going then?'

'Fine,' Charlie leaned forward. Micky felt the warmth of his breath on his ear. 'How's the old jailbird, then?'

Micky swallowed. A treacherous warmth suffused his body like a blush. 'Surviving.' He shrugged, then he had to clear his throat and say it again.

Charlie's hand clasped his right shoulder. It quickly squeezed. 'Tell you what, let's just see this Sadler's Wells animal, then go find a jar, OK?'

'Sure,' Micky nodded. 'Yup. Great. Thanks, Charlie.'

Lot 892 was led out unsold at 7,000 guineas, and here she came: the belle of the evening. The sales-ring stirred.

Oh, yes. She was a looker all right. She reared as she came in, startled at first by the loudspeakers and the lights, but the girl who led her easily brought her down, and steadied her.

'Put her in fifty . . . forty, then . . . There should be a show of hands! All right, put her in thirty . . . I have thirty thousand . . .' From here on the bidding bounded up. At fifty thousand, it started to go up in units of two thousand at the time, at one hundred thousand in units of five thousand.

Micky listened and watched and admired the little doll and coveted her faintly fiercely, but all the while, the greater part of his mind was on Charlie Vane, his schoolfellow, patron and, for reasons best known to himself, his constant friend.

'One hundred and sixty . . .' Things were slowing now. The bidding was crawling upward. 'One hundred and sixty thousand . . . are you all out on top? Are you all out in the gate? And I sell her . . . One hundred and sixty-five thousand . . . one seventy. One more, sir? All done?' The auctioneer's eyes flickered over the bidders' cage. He found what he was looking for. Richard Heron raised his black eyebrows. He nodded once. That nod represented one hundred and seventy-five thousand guineas sterling.

The competition – a Swedish rock star down on Micky's right – gave it one more desultory try, then shook his bearded head and folded his hands in his lap. The foal raised her tail and crapped. A little old man in granny glasses and brightly polished brogues shuffled promptly forward. Dolefully he swept up the droppings.

'At one hundred and eighty-five thousand guineas . . .' The hammer rapped. 'Richard Heron.'

'Crap,' said Charlie.

'Hmm?' Micky stood.

'Crap one hundred and eighty-five thousand guineas Richard Bloody Heron. One nomination to Russian Dancer and about fifty grand if that.'

They were side by side in the aisle now, in a burbling current of humanity. Micky had to raise his head and tread people. 'What are you on about?'

'Heron bought half that foal privately on the Curragh a couple of nights ago, that's all,' Charlie shrugged, 'so, win or lose, he wins. What's Russian Dancer stand at now? Seventy, eighty grand? That covers most of the little bugger's expenses for today, and meantime he's successfully inflated the price of this foal and of all the other foals on the market. That man is a particle of skunk-smegma.'

'Mean he was buying from himself?'

'Yup. Yes. Damned near always does these days.'

Charlie held open the door. Micky stepped out into the chill darkness.

''Parently, his fifty percent only cost him thirty grand, so he's out – what? Forty? Fifty? Canny, huh?'

'Mildly bent, I'd say.'

'Mildly!'

'Nothing's improved in that department, then?'

'Not a jot. Jesus, Micky,' Charlie walked over to the paddock and leaned on the rail in the lamp-light. 'I mean, I'm happy to believe that leopards change their spots. I've known sneaky little shits at school have turned out to be really nice guys, but that man . . . I mean, he behaves like that, then he expects me to welcome him with open arms to my clubs and things. Tried for the Travellers' the other day.'

'You blackballed him?'

'Sure. What am I meant to do? But there's no sense of justice in that man. He can't come up to me and say, 'Look, sorry I was a right shit, but it's all a long time ago.' Not Heron. He resents *me*, for God's sake. He spreads the word that my mares are barren or my yearlings are unsound, so they fetch a tenth of what they should. He gets a whisper I'm in with a squeak in a decent stakes race, he'll interrupt one of his animal's training-programme simply to knock me into second place. The man's obsessive.'

Heron was emerging even now from the sales-ring door. He stood at the centre of a clump of big men, all with the smug smiles and the broad brays of big men on their own territory.

'Bastard,' said Charlie at Micky's side.

Micky nodded. He knew why Charlie despised Heron. No one else did. No one else must.

Back in the sixties, Heron ran illegal poker games, then a gaming club on Mount Street. You scored a big win at the chemmy table, as Charlie's old friend Quentin Naismith once did, and two large persons came round to your hotel the following morning. You 'settled', willy-nilly, or you ended up looking as though you had fallen at Becher's first time round at the head of a tightly bunched field.

Then there was the business with Charlie's sister Victoria.

Victoria Vane was two years younger than Charlie. Micky and she had flirted a bit back in their teens; nothing serious. At twenty-six, she married Guy Allingham, a widowed gentleman farmer in his late thirties. They had two children. After the second one, Victoria became seriously depressed. One of Heron's young men lured her to the Mount Street Club. Soon she was into Heron for seventy-five thousand pounds.

Heron demanded payment. She knew that to pay would ruin her husband, her children and her marriage. She had too much damn fool pride to turn to her father or brother. She pleaded. Heron was gracious. Not to worry, he said. There were always other ways to pay.

15

She had been paying for five years when she swallowed half a bottle of whisky and another half bottle of barbiturates. Micky was staying with Charlie at the time. They were Victoria's first visitors at King Edward VII Hospital. She sobbed out her story. Charlie made excuses to Guy. Victoria was back now with her husband and her family.

Charlie could despise Heron. He could never tell anyone why.

'Ah, well,' he sighed. He led the way over to the building on the left of Park Paddocks, the building which Micky had not dared to enter before. A few heads turned as they strolled into the lobby, but Charlie just said, ''lo, George,' and 'Colonel,' and both men said 'Charlie, Micky.'

Micky's lips curled downward. Whoopee. He existed again.

'So, now,' Charlie deposited an ice-bucket and two glasses on the table, 'tell us the news.'

Micky thought back to trial, sentence and adaptation to prison life. He said, 'Nothing much.' It was almost true.

'You've put on weight. They must feed you well in there.'

'It's all right. I did some weight-training. Circuits.'

'Suits you. So, something must've happened since they sprung you. Spurt forth, Micky. Where've you been hiding? What've you been up to?' He pulled the misted and dripping bottle of Heidsieck from the ice and filled both glasses.

'Well, I've got a job of sorts.' Micky took the glass, sipped and shuddered.

'Yeah? What sort of a job?'

'Selling feed supplements. Don't suppose you'd be wanting some, would you?' He plucked out one of the leaflets and held it beneath Charlie's nose.

'Dunno. Doubt it.' Charlie frowned down at the leaflet. He shook his head. 'Maybe. But hold up, man, what in hell are you doing flogging boiled down Mars Bars, for God's sake? Come on, Micky, you're a horseman! All your life you've . . . And one of the best judges around. You can't just pack it in and become a rep.'

'Charlie,' Micky sighed, 'I'm stony flat broke. The string's gone, the yard's gone. How the hell am I going to deal in horses or set up as a trainer?'

'Problem,' Charlie acknowledged, 'not insurmountable, but a decided problem. If I can help in any way – you know you can always touch me for a bob or two. The good Lord saw fit to give me the stuff in bucketsful.'

'Nah, what's the bloody point? You see the way people look at me? I'm a villain, Charlie boy, *persona non grata*. I've been cut by half the racing world already today.'

'Ah, come on,' Charlie goaded, 'you're imagining it.'

'Oh yeah?' Micky drained his glass. 'Try this for size then.' He had caught sight of Ted Bolus and his new woman standing at the bar. 'Ted!' he called. Ted's eyes shifted quickly towards him, then away again.

'Ted. Excuse us. If I could have a word . . .'

Ted leaned closer to his wife and murmured something into her hair. She rolled her eyes heavenward. Her shoulders sank in a stage sigh.

Charlie loosened his tie. 'Bolus!' he bellowed.

Ted swung round. His bulging eyes were suddenly wide. 'Whassat?' he croaked.

'Come here, Bolus,' Charlie beckoned.

'Well, hello, Charlie boy,' Ted smirked. He readjusted his tie and with it his swagger. He sauntered over to their table, camelhair coat flared and swinging. 'Micky. Hi!'

'My friend Micky was calling you, Bolus,' Charlie oozed autocratic bonhomie. 'Have you had the ears syringed recently? Helps enormously.'

'No, well, yeah.' Ted glanced uncomfortably from Charlie to Micky and back again. 'Thought I heard my name actually. Couldn't be sure in the crowd, you know? So, then, how are you, Micky?'

'Ah, fine, thanks, Ted.' Micky afforded him an ingenuous little smile which flashed on and off again like a torch.

'Hear what happened to Micky, did you, Bolus?' Charlie cocked his head. 'Sent to jug. Hear that? God almighty, it's not as if he was driving drunk or anything. Bloody unfair, I call it, don't you?'

'Yeah,' Ted swallowed a jagged lump of something, 'Bloody bad luck.'

'Ah, well, it could happen to any of us,' Charlie continued blithely. 'There but for the grace of God, eh, Bolus?'

'Yeah,' Ted looked down at his mulled wine. 'So,' he sniffed, 'what was it, then, Micky boy?'

'Hmm?'

'What was it you, you know, wanted?'

'Ah, just wanted to say hello, you know. It's been a while.'

'Oh, yeah. Right. Well, good to see you, Micky. Come and see us sometime. Done the place up a bit. Oh, and I'll be in touch with you about this feedstuff. Promise.'

'Great,' Micky let him off the hook. 'You do that.'

Ted nodded and shuffled back to his wife.

'See?' Charlie waved. 'It's not that bad.'

'Oh, sure,' Micky pulled the bottle from the bucket and filled their glasses. It felt good to do a simple thing like that. 'Sure, it's fine if I happen to have the stinking rich son and heir of one of the senior stewards and one of the biggest owners in the land at my side. Sure. No problem.'

'Did you know Bolus got disqualified a couple of months ago? Driving over the limit.'

Micky smiled. 'No, you bastard, I didn't.'

'Well, there you go. Bloody ridiculous, far as I'm concerned. If it had been good old lethal, socially acceptable booze, everyone'd said, 'poor old Micky. Good chap. Jolly bad luck,' and welcomed you with open arms. As it is, you're instantly top of the floating shit list. Burks.'

'Maybe, Charlie,' Micky told him sadly, 'but that's the way of it. I'm just not going to be the most sought-after trainer in the land, even if I could afford a yard, so let it be. Buy this muck from me – well, that'll be an end on it.'

'You seen Cathy Kramer yet?'

'Nope. Look, there's the basic feed supplement syrup. Molasses, glucose, full of vitamins, minerals . . .'

'Pity. She was here earlier. Wheelchair entirely now, poor old love. Can't remember, was she still hobbling the last time you saw her?'

'Bit of both . . . and the calcium, selenium, Vitamin D supplement; you could really use that with your mares and foals. . .'

'Yes, yes, Micky. You're getting to sound like Barbara Cartland, you know. Listen. She'll want to see you. Cathy, I mean. Tell you what. She'll be delighted to see you back in action. You know she's moved Sansovino over to Ballysheenan?'

The mention of his old home made Micky look up sharply. 'Yeah?'

'Yup. He's done two seasons in Kentucky. Fertility high. *On dit* is, he's thrown a good first crop too. Anyhow, yes, so now she's got the whole shooting-match in Ireland. She'll tell you all about it tomorrow.'

'Charlie, I told you,' Micky moaned, 'I've got nothing to do with this game now. I just want to sell this stuff and head off home.'

'Ach, balls, man! This is your game. You're good at it. Tell you what. You come to Reader's Hall tomorrow and I'll promise you so many orders for this – this Glendale thing – that you'll be promoted to managing director in the field.'

'I'm not even invited,' Micky told him. 'Forget it.'

'Course you're bloody invited, man,' Charlie snapped. He turned his head, leaned back in his chair and called, 'Henry!'

'No, Charlie . . .' Micky pleaded. He reached forward, but the Marquis of Garswood had already turned from earnest conversation with a sleek young lady in ranch mink.

'Charlie,' his smile drew a big diamond on his scrubbed pink face, then he saw Micky and almost bounded forward, hand extended.

'Micky, so good to see you. This is a surprise. How are you?'

Micky stood and shook his hand and mumbled fine, thanks and how's yourself, sir, and Garswood said doing well, and one way or another Micky was so tongue-tied and embarrassed that he did not even remember to flog him Halibut Liver Ultragrains.

'I was telling Micky he should come to your binge tomorrow,' Charlie said casually.

'Course he must come! Course you must, Micky. Help you get back in the swing of things. Really bad luck, all that business. No, absolutely, I'll expect you.'

'Well, thanks,' Micky muttered, 'but I really ought to be thinking of work, you know, and . . .'

'Rubbish,' said Charlie shortly, 'think of, er, Glendale Petcorps, Micky. Do your duty. You'll be there, my boy, if Henry and I have to drag you there ourselves.'

'Oh,' Micky said glumly. Then he said 'Um.' It was the best that he could manage, just then.

Once, home had meant Ballysheenan. It had meant the big white house, the white-railed pastures, the rabbit-grazed lanes and those deep green bogs. It had meant the ruined abbey on the banks of the Barrow and the constant scribble of rooks about the rooftops and the trees. It had been inconceivable then that it could mean anything else, but all that had gone out the window when he was sixteen.

For a while it had meant Lambourn and the echoing clattering of a thousand hooves, the rich, acrid smells of soaped leather and Timothy hay, horse-piss and straw. There had been no one building there that really meant home for him – just flats and lodgings and, at the end, a scruffy little cottage out Wantage way.

Another cropper.

Remount, then. Start again.

Then there was the yard outside Marlborough. Once again he had thought that this time he would never need to move. He would bequeath Great Barrow to his son or daughter. But no sons or daughters came, and the place never really felt like home. Nathalie's money had bought the place. Nathalie had decorated it in best *Country Living* and Colefax velvets and voiles. Even the dogs had been banished to the yard.

And last, there had been B Block in Her Majesty's Prison, Ashwell, near Oakham in Leicestershire.

Now home meant this.

It was a cubic, red brick, two-up two-down nineteenth century farm labourer's cottage, set off the main Bury to Haverhill road by a sixty yard dirt track. From the front you could only see the ridged track and the hedgerow which chattered and seethed like a high-voltage cable.

From the back, beyond a narrow strip of garden and a broken fence, you could see a jagged old Dutch barn and flat fields frogged with hedgerows and studded with oaks. It was a mile and a half from the nearest pub, three miles from the nearest village. That suited Micky just fine.

There was no hallway. Micky just raised the latch and walked straight into the living room. It was like breaking a dam. Muddler and Memphis, his two blue greyhounds, burst out and engulfed him. They put their forepaws on his shoulders and lashed his face with their hot tongues.

'Geroff, my old darlings,' he growled, and the dogs spun round and round, kicking up the threadbare Bokharas, claws clicking on the concrete floor. 'Go on,' he held open the door and shooed them out. They grinned and cantered off side by side, clashing teeth.

It was a plain little room. Its white walls were unadorned save for a few photographs of Micky on horses or receiving trophies and a large oil of Billy, Micky's father, on Glenarvon back in 1936. The furniture had the air of beachcomber's gleanings – Globe Wernicke bookcases, utility armchairs and scuffed pie-crust tables picked up at local auctions, a sofa covered with nicotine-stained chintz and a little Sheraton table which, God knows how, had been retained from the old days.

Micky threw the Barbour and the Glendale folder onto the sofa. He grabbed a can of Holsten from the windowsill, sat in one of the armchairs and switched on the television with the remote control. The newsreader was saying something about an RUC man gunned down in the Falls Road area of Belfast. It was a little like *The Archers*, Micky thought. You could sleep for twenty years, turn it on again, and nothing would have changed. Phil would still be complaining about fatstock prices, and stock RUC or IRA men would still be being gunned down, blown up and kidnapped in the Falls or the Springfield.

He ripped the tab off the beer-can and banged *The Sporting Life* open on his knees. Strange. He had ridden against at least half of the jockeys mentioned. He had trained one or two of the animals. He smiled a little wistfully to see that little First Direct had won for Jack Carlton at Worcester. It all seemed a long way away now.

The weather-forecaster said 'cloudy . . . scattered showers . . . some snow and sleet on high ground.'

He did not look up when he heard the car, nor when footfalls sounded on the path. He knew who it was. The latch clicked.

A woman's voice said, 'Hi?' and first the dogs, then Shelagh Meadows breezed in.

She leaned over the back of his chair to kiss him warmly but briskly. He raised a hand to hold her cheek against his for a moment.

She said 'Mmm,' and, straightening, 'you doing anything tonight?'

'Uh uh.' Micky watched her as she reached into a carrier-bag and deposited a large bottle of Italian white wine on the hearth.' Thought just a quiet supper. Good to see you.'

It was good to see her. Shelagh was the local vet's assistant, a trim, full-to-bursting, bright and breezy girl of twenty-six, twenty-seven, with star sapphires for eyes and a figure of the sort which pushed softly but persistently at all restraints. It looked good in clothes, but promised that it would look still better out of them. *Whosoever looketh on a woman to lust after her hath committed adultery with her already in his heart.* A lot of people got to commit cardiac adultery with Shelagh. Micky got to do it more heartlessly too. Today she was dressed in pink angora and a slick of crude denim.

'Good day?' she asked.

'So so. Might've made a few contacts.'

'See any old chums?'

'A few. Avoided most of them.' Micky folded the paper. 'Saw Charlie.'

'Charlie? Oh, the famous Charlie Vane. Good. So how was he?' She walked past him and pushed open the door into the kitchen.

'Oh, fine, fine,' Micky stood. 'Put on a bit of weight, but the same old Charlie. Didn't buy any of my stuff, though, sod him.'

'Don't blame him!' Shelagh called.

Micky sauntered after her into the kitchen. Shelagh was in the little pantry beyond. Tap water galloped on a plastic bowl. 'He wants me to go to the Reader's Hall do tomorrow.'

'What's that?' The tap stopped.

'He wants me to go to this party tomorrow. Reader's Hall Stud. Lord Garswood's place. He's got Bold Raider and Fortis standing there. Has a hell of a party every year, to show off his stallions.'

'So you're going, right?'

'Dunno,' Micky perched on the corner of the table and took a quick swig of his beer. 'I should do, but . . . I dunno.'

'You bloody well should, Micky.' Shelagh appeared in the doorway. She looked very resolute. She polished a wine glass with a blue and white tea-towel. 'You know you should.'

She vanished again. 'Yeah, sure,' said Micky.

'Good binge, is it?'

'Of its kind, sure, the best. Krüg, oysters, everyone there.'

'So you should go.' Shelagh reappeared. She bustled back in with two wine glasses and laid them on the table.

'Hey,' she smiled slowly at him, 'are you really hungry, 'cos I'm on a diet?'

Micky reached for her and pulled her to him. She came easily into his arms, pressing her body against his in all the right places. They kissed a bit. His hands automatically started to explore the contours of her buttocks, her thighs. 'Do we really have to waste time eating supper?' she breathed into his mouth.

'Nah,' Micky growled.

He went to kiss her throat but she twisted from his grasp and stepped back. 'Right. You open the wine and fill the stove. I'll feed the dogs. Chop chop.'

Ten minutes later, they were upstairs and she was warm and naked and wriggly beneath him.

That was what they did, Shelagh and Micky. That was the nature and the extent of their relationship. They liked one another. They liked fucking. They were uncomplicated luxuries each to the other. No need to go looking for other men, women, in search of promise, possession, likes, all that. They had this. Whenever they wanted it. It was better than love. There was no fear in this. So they told one another.

Only later, when they were coated in a slick of silky sweat and the flush of warmth spread through their bodies like sunlight, only then did they fill in time with the less precise medium of talk.

She told him about her day. The junior partner, Hobbs, was a groper. She had told him what he could do with his hands. She had had to comfort an old woman, heartbroken when her cat was put down. The cat was called Snuggles. Shelagh's younger brother Ian had broken his wrist playing rugby. 'Oh and by the way,' she announced languorously, 'Jim checked that horse you were asking about. The hack, you know?'

'Yes?' Micky raised his head from the pillow, suddenly alert. 'And?'

'It's operable, he reckons.'

Martindale.

Ten years old. Ex-hurdler. Bay or brown. Walked on air and jumped like a stag, but had an unfortunate and unpredictable predisposition for flinging himself to the ground and trying to burrow a hole in which to shelter. Also a mild liking for jumping running rails and for galloping in several directions at once. A character, some might say. Others had been known to resort to more vulgar, if expressive, terms.

But if Shelagh's boss were right, there was a physiological cause for Martindale's conduct. And only Micky knew it.

Every enthusiast knew a moment like this, when suddenly the heart stopped its routine Palm Court thudding and started playing *salsa*, and you knew with something approaching certainty that, if the gods were only clement, you could make the big win. The big fin breaks the surface bare inches from your fly; 'Remb . . .' emerges from the filth of centuries on a canvas; you catch a whiff of truffles from a Birmingham café . . . it was like that. Micky's every instinct, his every highly-conditioned reflex, told him that Martindale, a horse unknown, or known only as mad and useless could be trained to win a good 'chase at long odds.

If only he had the purchase price and a little yard somewhere, Micky reckoned he could pull off the gamble of the century. He had been dealt four aces, and he did not even have the ante.

'Jesus,' he murmured, 'that could be a classic. That could be . . . oh, grr,' he thumped the pillow in frustration. 'God, what a cracker that could be. If only, if only . . .' He lay back again.

'You must go tomorrow, Micky.' Shelagh sipped her wine and leaned over to suck his right nipple with icy wet lips.

'I know,' he kissed the top of her head. 'I ought to. I'll regret it if I don't. It's just – mm – I don't know. It's not just the embarrassment, the fear of rejection. It's that too, but – oh, damn it – I've got some sort of damned fool presentiment, you know? Some sort of hunch that it'll all end in tears. Maybe I'm just trying to justify my being wet about it. I don't know.'

'What can go wrong?' she murmured in the hollow of his throat. 'Worst thing can happen to you is some pompous fart is rude to you. Who cares about that?'

'I know,' Micky nodded. Wine trickled down his chin. 'It makes no sense, I grant you. It's just going back into racing . . . I thought I'd said goodbye to the whole business. And while I've been in prison and so on, they've all been doing their things. Changing. Getting older, richer.

23

Growing. Winning. Losing. I've had racing, or it has had me. Dunno which.'

'It's your game, Micky.' She kissed the corner of his lips and drank, then laid the glass upon the bedside table and snuggled down. Her loins started to shift against his thigh. 'OK, so it's given you some knocks, but it's still your game, your business.'

'Sounds more like my Nemesis, you say it like that.' He pushed her upper lip back off her gums with his forefinger.

'Naw, that's just being melodramatic,' she purred. For a while she sucked softly on the finger, then she looked up. 'Or maybe not. Maybe it is your Nemesis, but there you go. No running away from it. Waste of energy.'

Micky shrugged. He stroked her back, her now velvety flank. 'Yeah, you're right of course,' he sighed. 'Probably nothing'll happen. It's just this feeling . . . oh . . .' He groaned now as she turned her lips and teeth to his left pap. Her right hand cupped his balls. His whole body trembled. 'Oh, that's good.'

'More?' she raised her head and grinned wickedly through a peaty cascade of hair.

'More,' he told her decidedly.

She flung back the blankets and laid her head on his thighs. Her tongue-tip tickled. 'And you'll go tomorrow?'

'Yes,' he moaned. 'All right, I'll bloody go.'

All that she could say was, 'Mmmmg.'

The stone said only *Joseph, the Unknown Gypsy Boy*. The fenland wind said only *moo*.

Joseph, it seemed, had made a mistake. He had lost his flock or something and he had thought that no one would ever forgive him or want him again. He had not believed that time would heal. Time was for philosophers. Joseph had known only now. And forever. So he had fetched a rope and, with the skill learned in harnessing and coping, he had made a fine knot. Then he had slung the rope over a branch, put his head through the noose and squeezed the vital juices from his body.

Joseph had been wrong. He had been forgiven. They had laid him here at the unconsecrated crossroads by the Limekilns. And although every day fast horses and lads of Joseph's age thundered past, unthinking, every day fresh flowers were laid on his grave. Today it was pink carnations and yellow primulas, their petals heavy and sparkling with rain.

Micky too had once made a mistake and thought, like Joseph, that no one would forgive him or want him again.

He had had the skill to tie the knot. It just so happened that he did not have a rope.

They had even taken his shoelaces away, just in case.

The mist crept up. For all the tweed suit and Viyella shirt, he shivered. He pulled out the Old Holborn pouch. His fingers fumbled with a Rizla. Although there was no rain, a water drop appeared from nowhere on the paper.

When at last he had rolled the cigarette and lit it, he walked back to the car and sat on the passenger-seat with his legs still outdoors. He drew deep on the cigarette. Atlas tripped. The world lurched. Micky just needed these few minutes to brace himself for what was to come.

Here on the gallops Micky had strutted and fretted his hour like an ambitious potentate. A success story. On the way up. The boy most likely to.

Oh, he was never in a big way of business. Compared with most of the slick, gleaming, high-tech factories in these parts, his scruffy little yard had been a poor thing. He had never had more than forty animals running under both rules. In that last but one year, however, he had had the highest strike-rate of any trainer in the kingdom.

He should have known better. God in heaven, and had he not been there already? In his first year as a pro-jump jockey, he had taken the Mackeson, the Champion Hurdle and the Arkle and ended up just twenty-three winners behind Peter Straker, the champion. In his second season, he had been third in the championship table, then Jack Carlton had taken him on as stable jockey. For two more years all had gone well. Then had come the crash.

To become a successful jockey had been so darned easy. He had claimed success as of right. He was doing better than the other lads because he was just naturally better than they.

It was the same thing with training. The gods loved Micky Brennan. He placed his horses right. He got a lot of good two-year-old winners, he had a lot of good punts on first-time-out, untried animals. He acquired a reputation as a judge of horseflesh. He bought some cheap yearlings for himself, ran them under Nathalie's colours. They did well too.

It had been time for the reminder.

It had come first when his wife Nathalie had left, three days after their sixth wedding anniversary. Micky had not even recognised it.

So it had come again one rainy evening last November. This time it had killed a man.

He barely remembered the sports at Sandown that day. He had trained two winners which would pay outstanding bills, so then he had backed two losers to make it all right.

He had drunk perhaps two scotches, a glass or two of champagne. He had probably gone to the loo a few times. He usually did, and he would try to conceal the sound of sniffing by flushing the bog or tugging at the Izal Medicated just at the right moment. And, of course, he had taken his pills.

DFII8 was a nice friendly sort of pill. Just to look at it made you feel that you belonged. There were no discords in there, just sweet, sweet harmony. Everyone – even family – seemed like family. With alcohol, though, all that nice warmth became a little blurred and confused, as if you had been hit on the head during a massage or something, so than you snorted a couple of lines, took a Tenuate Dospan or three, and you were right up there again, sassy, cogging, ready to show brick walls what you were made of.

That must have been pretty much how he felt as he climbed into the Mercedes in Kew that night and set off homeward.

He had been having a high old time since Nathalie decamped. There was a psychiatric nurse called Susan who supplied the pills, and a coke-dealing fashion designer called Martha who lived out in leafy Kew. That way, he never had to pay much for his goodies, but then, that is always the way. You want it bad enough, you get it.

He had known all along that it could not last. He had even looked forward to the end, whatever that might be. Maybe God would smite him and he would be born again as a fundamentalist rockabilly Christian; maybe a miraculous woman would step from his oldest dreams. Then there was always death . . .

But it came all right, and it took none of those comfortable forms.

His brief had said all the usual things, like jockeys have weight problems, like old injuries cause my client constant pain, like the poor chap depends upon his being able to drive and anyhow he's been receiving treatment, so why does his lordship not play the white man and let my client go to a nice expensive clinic rather than a nasty expensive prison.

The judge sniffed.

The clerks' elastic bands snapped about bundles of Micky. The press scribbled. The judge leaned forward and solemnly meshed his fingers.

His wig had dandruff. He sounded tired: 'Michael Vincenzo McCarthy Brennan . . .'

Micky had been listening to Art Tatum messing about with Dvorak's *Humoresque*. He was looking out for headlight beams. No beams, no cause to worry. He was travelling fast, sure, but it was his business to travel fast. He could control it. He could loot it at will. The world was asleep.

He had swung the car round a left-hand bend. And suddenly there had been a thump at the near wing. A shriek had forced its way from Micky because out of the darkness a giant white bird had stooped at the car and was clinging, wings outstretched, to the windscreen.

He had stood on the brakes. The car had skidded to the right and mounted the bank. It had tilted, and for a moment it had seemed that it must turn over.

It was then that he saw the face of the bird. The eyes were wide. The nose was pressed against the windscreen. The lips were twisted into a sick rose. Then the head turned and a red streak coloured the distorted cheek. There was fuzzy, sandy hair in there somewhere, and a pen in a tartan pocket. Art Tatum kept fooling as the car righted itself and bounced. The thing slithered off, leaving nothing but that streak across the glass.

When he was dreaming, that was always the point at which Micky awoke. In reality however, it seemed that he had just sat there for a while, recovering his breath and blinking at the Jackson Pollock snarl-up of brambles on the bank.

Then he had turned the ignition key and driven on home.

He winced now and swung his legs into the car. It was midday. The party had been going on for an hour. He could slip in unnoticed, have a quick word with Charlie, shake Cathy Kramer's hand and get the hell out. And that, he promised himself, would be that.

He would never go near the racing crowd again. Birtwhistle and his job could go hang. If necessary, he would get a job measuring inside legs or dispensing burgers. He had had racing, or it had had him.

A valet stuck a plastic number on Micky's car. He flicked at the driving seat with his hand before deigning to place his posterior on

27

it. Micky walked with a nervous swagger past the maroon and gold Krüg Rolls Royce van and into the warm sunlight of the white and yellow marquee.

A glass of Krüg was pressed on him. Cocktail sausages and lobster vol-au-vents circled beneath his nose in a miniature Busby Berkeley routine. He grabbed a couple of both and concentrated hard on eating and drinking.

In the far corner, a Dixie band in braces and boaters squirted out 'Bill Bailey,' and all about him, as far as he could see, the great, the good, the bad and the beautiful of racing stood chatting and drinking.

Parties make different noises. Some clink and purr. Some sound like kennels – all yapping and harsh barks. This sounded like a whole load of people roller-skating on bare boards. Micky weaved his way through the crowd with an undirected little smile on his face, and headed for the oyster bar.

It was better than yesterday. Most people smiled or said, 'How's it going?' Robin Nuttall, an old chum who ran a swish stud in Co. Meath, tore himself away from a good joke to clap him between the shoulder blades, punch his arm and generally pummel him about in proof of his affection. Marigold Theodolou, formerly Carlton, formerly Johnstone, formerly God knows, graciously held out a hand to Micky, principally, he suspected, in order to show him her latest engagement ring. The hand was limp and cold as an uncooked sausage. The ring was a daisy of pure fire. He answered her prurient questions about prison – she called it "chokey" and evidently thought it sexy – by showing his teeth and saying, 'Hng.'

The Colonel, a man of medium height with greying black hair and a twinkle in his eyes, laid a heavy hand on Micky's shoulder and said, 'Micky. Grand to see you back,' before moving on. Micky had never known his name. He was just the Colonel, the ubiquitous Irishman, a man of considerable bulk and great presence whom Micky had seen, in his time, at places as diverse as the Dublin Horse Show, a fair at Oughterard and the Palm Court at the Ritz. Charlie even claimed to have seen him at a gallery-opening in New York. Micky had a vague idea that he was a cattle-dealer or a potato-broker. Whatever his business, it sure as hell got him around.

As last Micky obtained his half dozen Whitstables. He turned back to the crowd. Whether because of the champagne or his resolution to kiss the whole business goodbye, he no longer felt like skulking. These people could do or say as they pleased. They could not hurt him anymore.

Then he saw Nathalie.

She had had her dark hair cut short. It was a good move. It made her look plumper, but younger. It drew attention to those flashing, baby-blue eyes. She could use those eyes.

She was using them now, as a matter of fact, on a tall, grizzled bloodstock agent called Sir Maurice Crook and his junior partner Guy Macdonald, an ex-hussar to whom God had denied nothing save a chin and a brain.

Micky watched Nathalie's girlish business. She laughed a light, rippling laugh. She lowered her long thick eyelashes and looked up from beneath them. She shifted her hips beneath the blue silk dress with gauche sensuality. Old men love that sort of thing. It was going down a bomb with Crook.

Micky's heart did not change pace. It refused to leap. It just kept on doing its job in a workaday style. That startled him. He had shared his bed and his work with this woman for six years, yet here he was watching her with a deal more detachment than he would have felt with a stranger. He recognised each gesture. He felt a little protective. She was, after all, inalienably of his clan. But otherwise, there was nothing; no twinge of jealousy, no twitch of lust, no pang of resentment or nostalgia. Nothing.

He drained the last oyster-shell and laid down the plate, accepted a refill of champagne from a passing waitress and sauntered over.

'Hi,' he said to Nathalie's back.

She spun around. She was sweet. She really was. 'Micky!' She threw her arms around his neck and kissed a tactfully chosen spot about an inch from the corner of his mouth. 'Good to see you! How are you?'

'Ah, fine.' He stepped back. He shrugged. 'What about you, then?'

'Oh, frantically busy. You know I'm back with the NBA?'

'Nope.'

'Yup. That's what I'm doing with these two rogues. I'm pretending to be a wheeler-dealer and getting nowhere fast.'

Crook and Macdonald smiled approval. Crook said, ''lo, Micky.' Macdonald, having received his superior's sanction, burbled, 'Yes. Jolly good to see you, Micky.'

They then talked tactfully among themselves.

Nathalie took Micky's arm. 'So, darling, you've got to tell me all your news. How are you really? What have you been up to? Was prison really gruesome?'

Oh, she was adorable all right. He just did not happen to adore her.

'Ah, it wasn't that bad. Frustrating, that's all. Bloody boring. Otherwise just like public school, only the facilities weren't so good. Closed nick was pretty filthy. You'd be prosecuted if you kept animals like that. But that was just five days. After that – just infernally bloody boring.'

'Poor you. And now. What are you up to now?'

'Oh, this and that, this and that. Feed business. Doing OK.'

'You're not far away, are you?'

'No, no. Just down the road. Got a little cottage, you know. Nice. Bit of a relief to be out of – all this.'

'I can imagine,' she lied graciously. She took his hand and squeezed it. 'And you're off those filthy pills?'

'If they were quite that unattractive . . .' Micky started. He relented. 'Yup,' he sneered, 'you see before you a Clean Machine. Glory Hallefuckinlujah.'

'Oh, Micky, I am glad. It wasn't your fault. And you're such a nice person when you're not . . . you know.'

'Ah, me I was born "you know",' he grinned. 'And you, you're OK?'

Behind her a group of lads 'got' a joke. Nathalie shouted above the clatter of their laughter, 'Oh, yes, of course! Fine!' And then her words became inaudible.

'What?' Micky leaned closer.

'Bit lonely at times!' she bellowed in his ear. The laughter behind her suddenly subsided. 'But . . . oh, well,' she blinked and looked away. 'Can I come and see you sometime, Micky?' The words burst from her suddenly. 'We could – I don't know – have a meal, have a good talk, you know?'

'Sure,' he smiled. Her eyes were very wide, very shiny, very beautiful. He wanted to hug her. Instead he looked at the jazz band and sipped champagne. 'Sure. I'm not on the phone, but if you call the Three Crowns, they'll always get a message to me. Let's do that one day.'

'Please.' She reached up then and kissed him. For a moment she just stood there tiptoe, her cheek cool as apple-skin against his. 'I'll see you before I go, won't I?'

'Oh, sure,' he squeezed her tight, then released her. There was moisture on his cheek.

'Good,' she said briskly. 'Right. Oh, I am glad to see you. Micky. Um . . .' she scanned the crowds. 'Right, see you later.'

Still his heart showed no inclination to leap about. It ached too much for that.

The Marquis of Garswood made a brief speech of thanks and optimism, then asked everyone to step outside where the stallions were to be paraded. Micky joined the crowd. Charlie caught him as he emerged into the weak and watery sunlight. 'Good,' he said, 'come with me.'

Micky limped meekly after him. Charlie made good speed, despite greeting everyone that they passed. He even deigned to nod to Richard Heron and murmur, 'Heron.' Heron scowled.

Cathy Kramer sat in her wheelchair at the end of the long semi-circle of guests. At sixty, her cheeks were a sight closer to the roses of song than the half-baked or golden-roasted beauties all around. Her golden hair was swept back in a wispy bun. Only the weary sagging of her lower eyelids gave her age away.

'Here you go, Cathy,' said Charlie briskly.

Those mournful eyes swung round. 'Micky Brennan,' she said slowly in a deep voice like a belch. 'Well, about goddamned time. Where the hell have you been, damn it?'

Micky bent and kissed her. Her cheek was soft as a half-deflated balloon. 'In nick, Cath, in case you hadn't heard.'

'When'd you get out then?'

'Couple of months ago. Three.'

'So, whyn't you get in touch? You may have time to waste. I haven't. You met my niece?' She jerked her head towards the girl who stood behind her. 'Name's Jenny. She's a mess like you.'

'Thanks a ton,' Micky laughed. The girl's eyes did not so much as smile. She said, 'Hi.'

'Hi.'

Cathy raised her glass to her mouth. Her hand shook worse than Micky's father's had, the year before he died. She tipped up the glass, wiped her chin and made a noise like a satisfied astronaut. 'What's this Charlie tells me? You flogging pep pills or something?'

'Got to do something, Cath. Got no cash. Reputation blown to hell.'

'Ah, the hell with reputation,' she slapped the word away. 'Life's too damned short. Look, there's that Bold Raider.'

Micky turned. He whistled. 'God, he looks great, doesn't he?'

The glossy dark brown stallion looked as mighty as any TV wonder horse on the prairies. He knew it too. As if on cue, he reared and struck out with his forefeet, apparently inches above his handler's head. Jenny gasped. Cathy, Charlie and Micky just laughed.

'Damned old ham,' Cathy cackled. Charlie shook his head. 'Never fails, does he?'

31

'But he could hurt someone.' Jenny's American accent was more pronounced than Cathy's. She was confused. 'Couldn't he?'

'He could,' Micky told her. 'But he won't. He's just a big show-off.'

'Oh. Is he really good, then?'

'You better believe it, Jen,' Cathy nodded. 'You boys remember the St James's Palace Stakes?'

'Do I ever,' Micky shook his head. 'He ran 'em ragged.'

'So how much does he cost,' Jenny asked, 'per screw?'

'£15,000 a go.'

'Jeez.'

'Yup. What wouldn't I give for a slice of that,' Cathy sighed. 'Still, I haven't got that sort of cash. Buy me a mare tomorrow, Micky.'

He blinked. 'What?'

'I said buy me a mare tomorrow,' she frowned fiercely, 'What's the matter with you? Got a problem with your ears? Go to the sales tomorrow and buy me a mare.'

'What sort of mare?' he croaked, incredulous.

'Hell, I don't know. The usual. Not too old, great bloodlines, perfect confirmation, bit of compensatory bone, fit to get a champion miler who wins at two. That's all. Maximum ten thousand. OK?'

'Oh, thanks,' Micky snorted. 'Make it easy for us, why don't you? A bargain basement champion. Sure.'

'Don't bug me over how difficult your job is,' she flapped a hand. 'Just do it. You hear I brought Sansovino over to Ballysheenan?'

'Yeah. Charlie told me.'

'Yup. I gotta be ill, gotta be ill proper, you know? Nice respectable clinic, die on the doctors' say-so. Solicitous, sanctimonious, self-important shitheads. You tell me, Micky. We're meant to know something about breeding, so how'd Ed and I produce two anal-retentive Ivy League nerds, huh?'

'Nerds is right.' Jenny's lips twitched once.

'And those wives of theirs . . . The clockwork mice, Ed used to call them. Won't even let me mix with their milksop kids, fear I might corrupt the little bastards, say "fuck" or something, traumatise them, sometimes I get the feeling even infect them, you know, like MS doesn't happen to decent people. People Like Us. Shit, I got out of that. Ballysheenan and Sanso are all I got on God's earth. Do me. So,' she suddenly bellowed. She rocked herself forward in the chair. 'You gonna come and run the place for me, Micky?'

Micky gulped. He looked at Cathy to ensure that she was talking to him. She gave nothing away. She just stared straight ahead at Fortis, the stud's second stallion. A small ironic smile turned her lips downward. Micky turned to Charlie. He was grinning happily. Jenny's eyebrows were raised as though she thought Micky an idiot.

'I . . . what did you say?'

'I said why don't you come over and run the fucking place? Jesus, I mean you know the place. None better. You were born there. You got nothing better to do and I need a man who knows his business running the show. You know old Sanso better'n anyone else too. And Screech. He's an idle old bugger, and I can't get around enough to check up on him. And don't think I'm doing you any favours. You'll have to work hard and I'll be paying you doodle-squat. Say twelve grand, the cottage and a nomination to Sanso. So, what do you reckon, Micky Brennan?'

'I, er, I don't know,' he said stupidly. 'I mean, I don't think . . .' Shock and uncertainty made him fumble blindly for the handle of Cathy's chair. His hand touched warm skin. Jenny did not move her hand away.

'Come on, Micky,' Charlie urged, 'you'd be crazy to turn it down.'

'Yeah, but. Thanks. It's just . . .'

'Just what?' Cathy snapped. 'Come on, Jen, let's get back to that darned tent. We're wasting good drinking time.'

Jenny tipped up the wheelchair and pushed Cathy towards the marquee.

'I'm staying at the Garden House. Going back Wednesday, Micky. Give us a call, if you're interested.' Cathy's voice shook with the jolting of the wheelchair on the turf. 'Oh,' she called over her shoulder, 'and don't forget that mare.'

He watched her until she reached the tent and had vanished inside. 'Ballysheenan,' he said slowly.

'Yup,' Charlie was still at his side. 'Home is the sailor, home from sea, and the hunter home from the hill. It's a great chance, Micky.'

'I know.' It came out as a husky whisper. 'But . . . I'm not ready to go back, Charlie. It's too perfect, too final.'

'Ah, come on, Mick!' Charlie chided. 'Leave out the high drama, would you?'

'No,' he said sadly, 'I'm serious, Charlie. You leave Ireland, you win your battles, you go back triumphant or not at all. Or to die. Me, I'd crawl back. And it'd be even worse than here. Everyone knows everyone there. At least here – this crowd may look through me like I was a dirty window, but at least I can walk into a post office or a bar without nudging or whispering and all that. Over there . . .' he shrugged.

'I do not believe I'm hearing this,' Charlie snapped brusquely. 'Of all the mealy-mouthed, pusillanimous, self-pitying crap!'

And he strode away.

Micky told Shelagh of Cathy's offer in the lounge bar of the Three Crowns.

She said smoothly, 'You're going, of course.'

'Ah, now, I'm not so sure about that,' he sniffed, 'it won't be so easy, you know.'

He was hoping for sympathy. He was looking in the wrong quarter.

'Nor's anything worth doing, Micky,' she crossed her stockinged legs. 'Come on, for heaven's sake. The whole thing's just – so obviously right, you know? I mean, this is your home we're talking about. It's what you do best. And you've got damn all to do here and bugger all money. I don't see the point in discussing it, really, personally. You're going.'

Micky shook his head sorrowfully. 'Well,' he looked up, clutching at straws and hoping that he looked fetching, 'what about you?'

'What about me?' She looked casually about the bar. 'I've got a job, thanks, Micky.'

'Yeah, but . . . won't you miss me?'

'Oh, for God's sake,' she sighed.

He shrugged. 'Well, all right, but . . .'

'Yeah, fine. So suppose I miss you sometimes. Suppose one day my insatiable yearning for your beat-up body gets the better of me. What then? Not very difficult actually. I get off the corner of the washing-machine and I get on a plane. I could be there in – what? A couple of hours? Three? Anyhow, as things stand just now, I think I'd prefer the washing-machine. Nothing like a tender bio-pre-wash following by a fast and frantic rinse and spin. And at least it doesn't whinge and feel sorry for itself. I need a drink.' She stood up and walked briskly to the bar. Were it not for the carpet, she would have clattered. She was exceptionally chummy to the barmaid.

'Yeah, OK, OK,' Micky said ruefully when at last she returned. 'I understand what you're saying. But it's like when I was riding. I used to think, 'Oh damn I've got to go to Kelso or Carlisle or something today. A major bore, you know?' And I'd hear on the wireless Kelso or Carlisle had been called off due to bad weather, fog or something, and I'd be furious. I'd've geared myself up for the trip by then. Well, it's like that here, in some ways, I've just succeeded, all those years of racing and injuries, victories, defeats, just managed to adapt to something like a normal life, like normal people. Boring, OK, sure, but. I can do a job, go home, grow old peacefully. No ups, no downs, off the Vanity Fair roller-coaster for the first time in my life, you know? And I've just about got to like the idea, and now . . .'

'Yup. It's called resignation,' Shelagh said crisply, 'Making do. Wholly admirable when there's nothing better to do. Nothing short of bloody wetness when there's another way open.'

'But I know everyone over there!' he cried. 'I've known them since I was a baby.'

'Yeah, sure, and then you were the bright boy from the big house and you went off to England and everyone thought you were bloody marvellous. And now you have to go back a failure and an ex-con, living in the little cottage. Boo bloody hoo.'

'That's not it,' he growled. 'It's just . . .'

'It's just that you're funking real life, Micky,' she was scornful, 'and, as far as I'm concerned, you do that, that'll make a real hundred percent rock bottom failure.'

So he got tetchy, and Shelagh became the second person that day to give up and walk out on him.

Frank Despard swept the lank, colourless hair from his eyes. It fell back at once. He rested his cheek on the stock of the gun and he waited.

He was in a child's bedroom. Behind him where he knelt at the window there was a little bed with a duvet adorned with cows and clouds. A mobile of pink and blue fish bobbed in the breeze from the window.

Frank knew that he would only get the one shot. He would make it a headshot. Riskier, of course, because the head was a smaller target than the back or the gut, either of which would kill as surely, but Frank liked to see the moment of death. That for him was real power, true pleasure. He enjoyed the build-up, the anticipation, he enjoyed – once the first depression had passed – the recollection, but it was that moment which counted. The moment when he, Frank, turned infinite potential into finite fact.

Frank had no politics. He had no religion to speak of. He had not even the justification that he had been brought up in the squalor and indignity of the Divis Flats. He had been born on a Donegal farm. He hated Brits because you had to hate someone, and he was good at this side of things. He stayed cool and undistracted by impulses or desires. His chosen work was pure and fulfilling precisely because it was done at long-distance, precisely because it was a one-way traffic. He did the shooting. The other man just did the dying. The other man never got to touch him with his hateful, hairy hands or grasp him in his sweat-slicked arms. His function was simply in one moment to be alive, in another, to be meat.

Frank simplified life.

Frank was twenty-three. With his fine sharp features, his narrow shoulders; his sunken chest and arms and legs just so much macaroni, he looked younger. He resented that.

The patrol was late. They should be here by now. Frank sighed. He let his shoulders droop for a second. He wriggled a bit. He liked to be comfortable on a job. That was why he favoured boxer-shorts and trainers and suits as sharp as he could afford.

He could afford precious little. For all his good work, for all his hints and pleading, he had never been asked to make the oath or to join an ASU. It bemused him. There were so called *bona fide* boyos down the pubs in the Ardoyne or Turf Lodge had never so much as seen a shot fired in anger, yet they were on four hundred quid a week and the whores fawned over them as heroes. Frank – all he got was an occasional commission for the leaning business. Frank had to work in a shoe-shop.

Oh, sure, they had helped him out when he had needed them. First time, he had gone over to England as a football fan accompanying his team. He had burgled a big bastard house on the Wirral, got away with some silver and a hunting rifle – walnut stock, fixed sights, the works – and thirty-six rounds.

His age and his physical slightness had got him through Customs with no problems. On his own initiative, he had picked off a squaddie chosen at random from a patrol, at the junction of the Falls and Springfield. The man – a little Welshman, Frank had later learned – had blossomed blood and jerked a lot against the graffiti–covered wall before sliding down the wall. Frank had been so engrossed that he had barely made it down the stairs and over the garden fence before the rattle of kit and the thudding of boots sounded on those same stairs.

He had learned fast. That one gun had injured three soldiers – paralysing one – and killed a second lieutenant and an UDA bastard before at length Frank had received a visit from someone from Belfast Brigade. The man had been coarse, revolting. He had said, 'Leave the war to the men, kid. We pick the targets. We run the show.' He had confiscated the gun. Frank had hated him.

After that, from time to time, they had called him, but never for a proper job, never for the real thing, just occasionally extracting money or services from businessmen or women by threats or work with the blade. Thing was, you did a job, you wanted to do it properly.

You've seen hard-core, no way can you get off on *Emanuelle* any more.

So Frank had taken another trip to Britain. This time he had broken into a public-school's firing range and had extracted an old Martini action, .303 and fifty big, dog's cock bullets. He had sawn the rifle in four parts and hidden them in presentation whiskey boxes which he carefully re-sealed. He had had colleagues at work bring them in as duty free. The stock had had to remain in England, so he had carved a new one and nailed it on. It hurt his shoulder, but it served.

Now. They came in little sudden, scampering runs, like toads in their dowdy battledress. Frank took a deep breath.

They were well spread out. Just let it be the officer he got this time. A People's Taxi – one of the Provies' fleet, juddered past with its light on, a fat cruising shark, and suddenly, under its cover, the first two squaddies were gone. Another two soldiers ran up, took their place in the doorway. That would be the officer, there in the shadows. The squaddie behind him walked backward, guarding your man's back.

Frank steadied his breathing. He could not get the officer, unless, perhaps ... The .303 had power enough, if the angle was right. Frank leaned hard against the window frame. He hummed a fanfare. He smiled.

He squeezed the trigger and saw the squaddie's young, fat face explode, the man behind him stagger, lurch. Then came the bang and the smell of cordite, and, as the sound ripped back through the tiny room, Frank was bouncing on his knees, 'Go on,' he urged, 'Go on ...'

The man in the shadows fell. A crumpled leg, a booted foot emerged into the lights. 'Yay!' Frank whispered.

There was a volley of shouting out there. The clatter of rifles, the splashing of running feet on the wet pavements.

Frank threw himself back through the child's room, across the landing into a flaking pink bedroom with a stained pink candlewick counterpane. He clambered through the open window, still carrying the gun, and slithered down the corrugated iron lean-to roof. He jumped down into the fallen window-box they called a garden in these parts, ran for the garden gate, through, out onto the dark street.

Holy God, there was a police car up the Glenalina end. What he'd planned was to run up there, just twenty yards, cut through Sean Macdonough's, drop the gun in the water-butt and be clear and away before the unwieldy army could spread out that far.

No bloody way. Not with the gun. Not now.

Frank said, 'Fuck it,' threw the gun as far as he could down the street to his left.

He walked briskly towards the junction. The gun was fair crawling with his prints. He was in trouble.

'Name Francis Pius Despard,' the Brigade Intelligence Officer intoned to the meeting. 'Fucking embarrassment Fucking maniac. Unaffiliated, but he's done a job or two because he's a nasty little sadist. Even his small knowledge could be dangerous. Sort of filthy little punk would crack in two seconds they get him down Castlereagh. Goes around shooting Brits on his tod, just for fun.'

'So? Let him,' the Brigade Adjutant shrugged. 'Quickest way for us to get rid of him.'

'Yeah, but they've got the fucking gun with his dabs all over it, haven't they? They'll pick him up tomorrow, the next day, we turn him out on the streets. And his sort's no fucking good for PR. We've got him safe for now. Thing is, we've got two options. We slot the little bastard or we get him out. Well?'

'Get him out,' the Adjutant advised. 'No point in wasting your man's peculiar talents. Might as well sell him dear. Send him down South. Give him to the Colonel to play around with. Tell him Despard's dispensible. Tell him to use him once then chuck away. Jesus, when will these little bastards learn? We don't get compulsive gamblers to manage our investments, so what do we want with compulsive killers when it comes to Operations? Get him out of our hair.'

'OK. Settled?' the Intelligence Officer raised his eyebrows to the Chief of Belfast Brigade.

'Settled.' The Chief nodded. 'Send him down to the Colonel. And good riddance.'

It was a burly red brick house with white windows and an ornate white porch. Mock Regency, with lots of pale flannel lawn in front but none of the mighty trees normally associated with the real thing. The yard looked big and swish enough though, and the post-and-rail fencing around the paddocks spoke persuasively of money.

Micky threw his cigarette from the window and changed down into third to negotiate the narrow downhill lane. He had first seen this place a couple of weeks back. He had marked it down as a possible.

Polo players, perhaps; breeders of Arabs, show people.

He had studied the sales catalogue this morning over breakfast. All that he had wanted was coffee and milk and Alka-Seltzer. Nothing approaching Cathy's specifications would come up this morning, but he had put a large question mark by the names of three mares to be sold this evening. He might do something about it. He might not. Depended.

The car rocked over the ramps on the tarmac drive. A sign on the verge said *Dead Slow Children and Horses*. For the benefit of the hard of hearing, there were green silhouettes of two children and a horse. He cruised very slowly past the house and into the yard.

It was modern and slap-up and somehow depressing. The concrete was spotless, the disc of grass at the centre encircled by dahlias which died without breaking ranks. There was a dovecote undirtied by doves, and where, in a racing yard, the box doors would be painted in bright livery, here there was only uniform creosote black.

He unclipped his seatbelt, picked up the bumf and stepped from the car. He strolled over to the nearest box. A bay hunter. Horse of the blood. Classy. Strong. The next one: a big liver chestnut fellow with a Roman nose, again a hunter, this time a heavy-weight, again good news. Then a stocky detergent-advertisement Welsh Montain pony stallion with a Brigitte Bardot mane. He would look great in harness or in the circus. A dun Welsh Mountain mare, an iron grey Welsh Mountain mare, a grey mare and foal . . .

Right. He had them sussed. Rich people, probably professional, certainly not farmers. One big man and his wife, possibly his daughter. Hunted a bit. Bred and showed little grey ponies as a hobby.

Micky called, 'Hello?' His voice made the open boxes buzz. No one answered.

He walked through the archway beneath the clock tower and onto the thick rinsed gravel of the carriage-sweep. The wind was soft and fresh. It felt good on his hot eyes. Ahead of him, on pasture that looked like lawn, a girl rose to the trot on a showy flame chestnut animal with a white snip and a lot of Arab in it. The girl was probably in her twenties. Her almost white blonde hair was swept up in a net snood beneath a blue riding hat. She wore a blue jacket too, and stretch breeches. Micky leaned on the gate. He watched the breeches stretch.

The horse, a colt, was playing up. The girl wanted it to move in figures of eight. It wanted to go sideways instead. She wanted it to trot. It wanted to canter or to stop altogether. Above all it wanted to be alone. Once it put in a quick buck in a bid to attain this end. The girl held on, but only just.

Micky's first thought was that she was not bad and had a fair seat. Then he turned horseman and concluded that she was not good and had a moderate seat. She was too weak and indecisive for her mount. Her legs flapped uselessly. And she was windy.

She looked frankly relieved when she caught sight of Micky. She set the horse to walk over to the gate. It preferred to hop like a nervous firewalker.

'Hi,' she said when she was within six foot. Her voice was that of a confident schoolboy. 'Can I help you?'

'Hi, nice animal you've got there.'

'Yah, he's all right, isn't he? Aren't you, boy?'

The nice animal turned his head and tried to bite her kneecap off.

'Thing is,' Micky said, 'I was wondering if you'd be interested in this feed supplement I've got here. You may've heard of it. Glendale Champion. A lot of the big showing and racing yards are using it now for muscle-development, speed, condition and growth of bone in young animals.'

'Sounds interesting,' she drawled, only she actually said sharnds intereshting. She talked like a fart in the bath. 'So, what's in this stuff?'

'Well, now, I'll leave you the leaflet of course, so's you can read all about it, but basically what you've got is, there's the Glendale Ultravite Syrup – that's full of vitamins and minerals, glucose and dextrose, all in a palatable molasses medium. Real high performance stuff. Formula one, high octane, you know? Then you've got your Halibut Liver Ultragrains. I feed them to my dogs, matter of fact . . . Whoops!'

The girl's mount, having given the subject serious thought, had decided that Micky was quite the most shocking thing that he had ever seen. He whipped around in one swift movement and gave two two-footed back kicks and farts in Micky's general direction.

'No!' yapped the girl. 'That's very naughty! No!'

She tottered but recovered her balance. She set her hat straight on her head, her strained smile straight on her face. With cheeks like Victoria plums, she steered the colt back to the gate. 'Sorry about that,' she yawned, 'he's a bit wicked at times.'

'Hmm,' said Micky. 'Anyhow, yes. These grains. You'll see from the leaflet that they contain all the requisite vitamins and trace elements for even the hardest working horse, together with, oh for God's sake what's the bloody point?'

The girl's white eyebrows jerked upward. 'What?'

'Well, look at you,' he said equably, 'there you are, completely overhorsed, on an animal that needs a damned good sorting-out from a pro, and all you can say is "naughty boy". Drop-noseband, standing martingale, every bloody bit of restraining tack, bar hobbles, and here I am trying to flog you muck that'll turn this pig into a wild boar. Just forget it, OK?'

He turned away with a wave of his clipboard. Behind him, the girl burbled. 'I say! Just a minute! Who the hell do you think you are?'

'Name's Brennan,' he called happily over his shoulder, 'Micky Brennan!'

'Well, just you wait . . . Daddy . . . swearing at me . . . Brennan . . .' the words followed him on sporadic puffs of wind.

Back in the yard he opened the car door. He had just put his left foot inside when he paused. He looked down at the clipboard and the leaflets in his hand. 'Ah, sod it,' he muttered. He grinned and flicked them away from him. The clipboard slapped down on the concrete. The papers ran away cackling and doing somersaults. He reckoned he knew how they felt.

When he re-entered the sales-ring that evening, David Pym, the flamboyant Irish exponent of "eyeball to eyeball" auctioneering, had taken over the gavel.

Of the three mares which Micky had picked from the catalogue, one had proved on examination simply not to have been his type. The second fetched eighteen thousand guineas without Micky's assistance. For the mare beneath him, however, he was in with a squeak.

Her name was Barbauld. She was a deep-girthed, long-backed washy bay. She had been covered by Caerleon, and with her looks and pedigree, she would have gone for maybe five, maybe six figures if that covering had taken. As it was, the bidding had stopped at just seven thousand. This mare had a problem. She had been well – and expensively – covered four times. And she remained barren.

'You've made all the running, sir,' Pym was raucous. 'She's altogether too cheap, you know. She'd be well bought at this money. In any money she's still cheap, sir.' With the heel of his hand he smoothed the yellow hair above his ears. He fondled the gavel. 'You're out on top, sir. No . . .?'

In the bidders' cage, Micky chewed on a blue BBC ballpoint that he had picked up somewhere. Now he raised it.

'Seven-four, thank you, sir, and welcome back. It's good to see you. Seven-eight, is it? Seven-eight . . .' Pym turned back to Micky. 'Come along now, sir. You very seldom let me down, sir. I need you now! Ah, there you are. I knew you wouldn't. Fill her up then, fill her up. Do I see eight-four? You're out in the gate, you're out on top. Eight thousand for a winning daughter of a stakes winning mare. Are you all out? All done? Eight thousand . . . eight thousand . . . and I sell her this time at eight thousand guineas.' He brought the gavel down with a crack, then spun it like a Western gunslinger with his Colt. He pointed. 'Mr Michael Brennan. Thank you, sir,' he smiled, 'and good luck with her.'

Micky nodded and winked and turned away The other bidders and spectators stepped back to let him pass. He trotted down the steps, rapidly signed the purchase chit held out to him and walked out into darkness sequinned with rain.

He turned towards the car-park. The wet ground sounded like tinfoil beneath his feet. He walked fast because he was nervous. He had often bought more expensive animals, but that had been in another life. He had taken one hell of a flier on this Barbauld, and he had some explaining to do.

'Micky? Micky!' A woman was calling his name. It was no more than a split second before he knew the voice to be Nathalie's. He heard her running footfalls behind him. He turned slowly, reluctantly, and waited.

She ran out of darkness and into lamplight, her hair and eyelashes spangled with rain, and rain ran down her cheeks like tears. Her wide eyes reflected the light with a pale blue arsenic flush. 'Micky,' she panted and swallowed. She grasped his forearms. 'Where are you going? You left the party without . . . I wanted to talk to you. Is it true you're going to work for Cathy? Charlie told me, but . . .'

He sighed. 'Let's get out of the rain. The car's just over there.'

She held onto his hand. Her touch angered him. He walked faster than she. She had to trot to keep up. Micky opened the passenger-door and almost pushed her in before walking round to the other side. He inserted the wrong key, then the right one the wrong way up. He was hopping in irritation before at last he contrived to open the door and climb in.

'Well,' he slammed the door. The car rocked. 'So what was it? What did you want to talk about?'

He could see no more of her face than a slick of light outlining her profile, but he could feel the tension in her. He knew too well the aggressive crispness and tightness of her tone as she protected herself from hurt.

'Are you going to work for Cathy?'

'Looks like it. She's offered. Why?'

'Why?' she turned to him, then as rapidly back to look at the rain on the windscreen. 'I'd have thought . . . I am your wife, Micky. It concerns me.'

'Yeah, OK, but . . . Yes, all right. I think I'll go back to Ballysheenan. It's a job.'

She said softly, 'I'll come with you, Micky.'

His mouth was suddenly very dry. He swallowed several times. His lips crackled when at last he spoke, and all he managed to say was, 'I . . .' then he stopped.

'I've thought about it a lot, Micky,' she spoke in a careful monotone, 'and now you're back to normal . . . We're married, Micky. For better or for worse and all that. I'd like to give it a try. Wouldn't you?'

'Well – I mean, of course,' he said hoarsely, 'but . . . see, you say I'm back to normal, right? But you never knew me – normal, as you put it. Aren't you afraid that – I mean, you could get an annulment from the Vatican, you wanted it. The guy you married wasn't – isn't – well, the same person. I may be a monster, for all you know.'

'You aren't a monster, Micky,' she laid a cool hand on his. 'I know you well enough to know that. You're a gentle man. Even when you were out of it. Oh, you were argumentative and bloody-minded, but you were never . . . You're a nice guy, basically.'

'Thanks.' He took the hand and quickly squeezed it. 'So why'd you walk out on us, then?'

'Oh, come on, Micky. You know why. I was lonely, for God's sake. You'd sooner be with a bottle or those women than me, and anyhow, it gave you a chance to sort yourself out. You had to be made aware . . . It could have gone on forever.'

'OK, so sure. I'm off all that stuff, but shit, I mean, why now? All the time I was in the nick . . .'

'I did write, Micky.'

'Twice.'

'No. More than that actually, but I did write. You were the one who didn't.'

'Yeah, well. Not much to say. Anyhow, you're allowed only three letters a week. And there was a girl who had been good to me . . .'

'What girl?'

43

'Doesn't matter.' Micky's leather jacket rustled. His lighter clicked. He puffed out smoke. 'She was called Susan, as a matter of fact. She just . . . she just helped me out when I was on bail, that sort of thing.'

'The bitch that got sent to gaol?'

He closed his eyes. 'No bitch,' he muttered, 'but let it pass. Yes. The girl who got me the pills.'

'Oh. She still around?'

'Nah. She was married anyhow.'

'Thank God for that. How can you defend a woman like that . . .?'

'Leave it.'

There was a pause then. The water on the windscreen turned red in the light from a Rolls Royce which started up ahead. It purred away. Now they gazed forward into a dark gap.

'You don't sound too keen,' Nathalie said, double-tongued.

'No. No, sure I am!' he waved both hands like a nigger minstrel. 'It's just – I don't know. We've not made too good a job of it up to now.'

'*You* haven't,' she corrected. 'No, sorry, darling. That's not fair. It wasn't you. It was all those things. But – I know I'm short-tempered . . . God, darling, anyone would be, you know – but you can't say . . . I put up with those tarts, everything, and Micky, I hate to say it, but the business, everything. It was you that lost it, wasn't it? Not your fault, OK, but . . . At that time anyway, it was me putting in – and daddy, my friends – and you taking out. Is that not fair?'

'Maybe, yes, and I'm grateful, love. Very grateful.'

'I'm not talking about gratitude,' she cooed. 'I'm just saying, well, I think now you've got a job, you're straight, I think we should give it another try.' Another pause, then, in a quavering half laugh. 'Or perhaps you don't love me anymore.'

'Oh, God, love, I do.' Micky clasped the bridge of his nose between his forefinger and thumb. He knew that she was crying now. 'I do, but . . . It's just – I don't think I'm very good at being married. I'm not good at being faithful. I'm not good at sharing my space, I'm not good at having anyone know everything about me, being able to use the knowledge, being dependent. I like work and being alone and . . . Oh, Lord, I'd like to be good at it. I love you and I hate being lonely. It's just . . .'

'I know, darling,' she breathed, and suddenly her cheek and hair were against his and her arm was pulling him close. 'I know,' she kissed his cheek. Sobs turned her breathing into a stage whisper giggle. 'But we should give it a go, Micky. Please. You owe it to me – to us. And I will try and control my temper. I can't guarantee, but I will try.'

He found his arm slipping about her shoulders. The smell of her, the shape and touch of her, were warm and so frustratingly familiar that he shook with anger. He could tear her apart. Instead he kissed her salt eyes and muttered against her lips, 'Oh, God, damn you to hell,' before his lips closed on hers and she groaned for sheer happiness.

'*No!*'

It was as though a bomb had burst in his cerebellum. He knew that he had shoved her away from him because he felt the shock as her back hit the car door and heard the click as her teeth jolted together. Now she stared at him, her eyes and lips wide and glistening. Her breasts rose and fell. She mouthed, 'Micky . . .?'

'No, no, no. Sorry. No. I can't sacrifice my whole bloody life on the altar of politeness. You found me when I was down – a cripple. You liked it that way. You kept it that way. Sure, you looked after me, sure, you were oh so tormented and hard done by because I drank and took those bloody pills and spent as long as possible away from home. You know why? Because I couldn't sit there wondering just what I was allowed to say without having you scream and spread hatred like . . . Because when we married, we agreed we'd try for children in eighteen months, and six years later, nothing. Limbo with occasional spurts of flame from hell. No, Nathalie. No, Nathalie. No.' It was he who was crying now. She had recovered her breath and just sat and stared, preparing her withering response. He knew it. He had seen it many times before.

'No,' he went on, and he wiped away the tears on his sleeve. 'No. This is a chance for a clean break. A new start. Away from – all this. I'm going home. To Ireland, do you understand? Ireland, which you so despise. My place. And I'm sorry, sorry. OK, so I'm a shit, but I'm going alone. D'ye hear me?'

'I hear you, Micky.' She spoke like pan-pipes. 'And I suppose I could expect nothing more from you. Yes, Micky. You are a shit. I've given and given and given . . .'

'So *take* for once in your life,' Micky roared. 'Be someone other than a cypher, a dependent bloody vampire. Go on. For God's sake. Just go.'

He reached over her. He pulled up the door handle and pushed the door open.

'Micky,' she said.

'Go.'

'Micky . . .'

'Go!' He turned the key in the ignition. The car awoke with a shudder.

Even when the door had slammed shut and the car was bobbing over the turf towards the gate, Micky was repeating through his tears as though to overwhelm the persistent whisper of her pain in his skull, 'Go, go, go.'

He rang the Garden House Hotel from the Three Crowns. He asked to speak to Mrs Cathy Kramer, but it was Charlie's voice which demanded, 'Explain yourself, Brennan.'

'Hi, Charlie. What's to explain?'

'Cathy and I are having dinner together. I'm having difficulty finding hiding-places for the kittens she's been dropping since she heard you bought her a barren mare.'

'What'd she expect for eight grand?'

'A moderate mare. Even a bad mare. You may have forgotten this in stir, Micky, but the basic ideas with mares, their *raison d'être*, one might say, is that they have babies. What the hell got into you? I thought you got rid of a mare if she didn't take after four seasons!'

'Three, actually, and then it's off to the Burger Bar.'

'Well?'

'Yeah, but did you see her feet?'

There was a long silence. Charlie seemed to be having some trouble with his breathing. At the Garden House, a pianist was tinkering with 'Misty' throwing in a lot of grace notes and capricious chords which Errol Garner had somehow omitted in the printed score.

'Look, Micky,' Charlie returned at last, 'I know it's been a long time since you had anything to do with the distaff side, so just let me run through a couple of points. You see, you don't have babies with your feet. Fact is, feet have precious little to do with it. Several people, I am told, have had bouncing bonny bairns while racked with verrucas, bunions and athlete's effing foot. Same thing with mares, old chap. Have foals with other bits.'

'Yup,' Micky grinned, 'and they're all in perfect working order. I've checked. Her feet aren't. You see the way she stood? What's it mean to you when you see an animal with her hind feet brought forward till she's on her heels and her back's all arched?'

'I dunno, damn you, Micky!' Charlie was exasperated, 'Tell us, will you?'

'Laminitis.'

'So? So she's got bad feet. Someone's been giving her too many carbohydrates, right? Big deal.'

46

'Yup, or she's had toxaemia from colitis x or fatty liver syndrome or she's hyperthyroid or . . .'

'OK!' Charlie barked, 'OK! Leave out the gobbledygook, will you, Mick? She's got laminitis. So we've got a barren mare with bad feet, just as a bonus. Why's that good news?'

'Ah, just an idea,' Micky smiled. 'Call it a hunch. Something Dad told me once. What you reckon she'd be worth in foal?'

'Depends in foal to whom?'

'Try – King's Lake.'

'Anything. A hundred and fifty? Two hundred grand?'

'Well, now, just suppose she hasn't been taking because her feet are in agony and she can't take the extra weight, so she's covered, but some instinct prevents her from conceiving or she absorbs the foal, right? Now, I take her, give her acetyl-promazine and shove her in big surgical soft shoes of sorbo rubber and leather. No more pain, right? Then she's covered, gets in foal and we've got one hell of a mare at a bargain basement price. How d'ye like that scenario?'

'I love it!' Charlie whooped. 'About as plausible as *National Velvet*, but I love it. Just wait until I tell Cathy. She'll either throw a fit or she'll swear you're a bloody genius. I take it that I can tell her you accept her offer?'

'I dunno,' then, 'yeah, go on. S'pose so.'

'I should bloody well think so too. Never heard such prattishness as you yesterday.'

'Yeah, well. Look, tell you what. You've done me a favour on this one. You want to hit the bookies really hard?'

'Do sharks eat flesh?'

'So what are you doing tomorrow?'

'Nothing. Well – hanging about the sales in the morning, then setting my watch back a hundred years and flying back to Waterford. Why?'

'Go down to Sussex instead. Place called – you got a pen?'

'Hold it. Yup. OK. Hold on. OK. Tell me.'

'Myerstone House, near Rye.'

'Got it. Speak on.'

'There's a Mrs Fitzwarren down there, owns an animal called Martindale.'

'Martingale?'

'No, Martindale. D.'

'Never heard of it.'

'No, you won't have. He's a show hack. Buy him, would you?'

'What?' Charlie almost whimpered.

'Buy him.'

'Oh, God, now I'm to buy hacks for your man. He's gone. Barking. Potty. Total bloody fruitcake. How old is this – this – hack?'

'Nine.'

'Has he ever raced?'

'Yup. Tailed off both times over hurdles. Anything else?'

'Yeah, I met a man runs a charming little place near Camberley, deals with shell-shock, nervous strain, that sort of thing. I'll drive you down.'

'Just go and buy him, Charlie. Bring him back to Ireland. Oh, and by the way, don't pay too much. You don't know anything about it, but the good Mrs Fitzwarren does. The animal needs an operation. He's got a brain tumour.'

The echoes of Charlie's howl could be heard ringing around the restaurant. The pianist even stopped his tinkling.

December

Micky Brennan was born in the year Ambergris won the Epsom Derby. It was also the year Vicenzo won the Stewards' Cup at Goodwood.

Billy Brennan had bred Vicenzo. He had also had two hundred pounds on him, each way at thirty-threes. In consequence, Micky, who saw the light at 1.40 am on 30 July, was christened Michael Vicenzo McCarthy Brennan and his attic nursery at Ballysheenan was entirely decked out in the scarlet and silver of Vicenzo's silks.

Such memories as Micky would later have of these early years at Ballysheenan were all of his parents; days at the races with them, children's parties at which they presided, a trip to see pantomime at Dublin's Gaiety theatre and to lunch at the Shelbourne, one notable holiday aboard the *Serena* in San Remo, his first day's hunting on a stubborn grey pony, impatiently urged on by his mother . . .

Serena and Billy Brennan ran like the hounds of hell snarled at their heels. They sped back to Ireland for a day or two at the time between Newmarket and Deauville, Ascot and Longchamps, London, Hong Kong, New Orleans, Nassau . . .

Micky soon came to hate racing. Every conversation was about horses, odds, training and breeding – and occasionally sex – none of them, at the time, engrossing subjects. Days at the races meant smoky bars, races that he was too small to see and too young to understand, more smoky bars, more sweat and wet tweed and stale beer.

Oh, there were high and heady days and memorable encounters. Sir Gordon Richards and the Queen Mother always spared the time for a smile and a chat. Gregory Peck once slipped him a ten bob note. Rita Hayworth scared the hell out of him. She was married to Aly Khan at the time, and for some reason or another had given up washing. She had, in consequence, turned quite orange. Micky found his hand clasped by a bejewelled kipper with a copper cloud of hair. He yelped and ran and hid.

Of the many long days without his parents at Ballysheenan there were no specific memories; just a blur of scarlet and silver, a nanny who looked by Popeye's Olive Oyl, Latin lessons and catechism classes from the portly and dogmatic Father Fitzgerald, riding lessons from old Pat Reagan, and the rough, tender chiding of Louella Flynn, the housekeeper.

At eight, he was sent off to Farleigh House, a Catholic prep-school by Basingstoke in England.

Self-conscious and uncomfortable in ribbed grey stockings, grey corduroy shorts and grey shirt, a blue knitted tie constricting his working throat, Micky climbed into Lord Kilcannon's Silver Shadow. Charlie, Viscount Vane, already sat there, clad in an identical miniature suit of armour. His thick black hair was imperfectly flattened with water. His eyes were red.

Charlie had done his crying. Micky had to bite his lower lip and stare rigidly ahead as the car swept quiet as a breeze down the drive.

'Your father and mine were in the war together,' announced Charlie.

'Yes,' Micky blinked as Louella Flynn and young Annie waved from the front door of the lodge.

'Your father's a major, isn't he? My father's a brigadier.'

'So?' Micky gulped.

'Have you been on an aeroplane before?'

'Yes. Of course. Lots of times.'

'So've I.'

'We go to England often, actually. Well, quite often.'

'So do we. And to Switzerland.'

'Oh.'

'You've got a stallion here, haven't you?'

'Yes,' Micky was bullish. 'He's called Horatian. He won the Irish Derby. He's brilliant.'

'My father says he's pretty old. Past his prime.'

'You haven't even got a stallion,' Micky wiped his eye on his grey sleeve. He sniffed and blinked out of the window at the ruined priory on the banks of the river. 'So what do you know?'

'My father knows. He won the Queen's Vase at Ascot this year. Now Voyager. Really good horse.'

'So. We've won that.'

'Oh, yes? When?'

'Oh, I don't know,' Micky was dismissive. 'We just have.'

Micky was twice sick on the way to Dublin. To this day the smell of leather and the cushioned floating of a Rolls Royce makes his stomach turn.

He and Charlie continued to trade experiences and achievements on the flight to Heathrow. They were met by Claridges' representative at the airport and shown to a taxi.

On the way down to Hampshire they were quieter. Fellow strangers, their common qualities now bound them closer. By the time that the taxi shuddered in through the gateposts and the two boys saw the great flint house at the end of the drive, the many bigger boys playing French cricket on the playing-fields, their mouths were dry and their stomachs whimpered. Ireland seemed many days away. Had they not been boys and taught to be brave, they would have clung to one another.

Charlie received a long letter from his father instructing him to look after Micky. It was no longer necessary. Already they were fast friends.

Micky returned to Ballysheenan for the holidays.

Left, if anything, still more to his own devices, Micky made the most of his parents' carelessness. He spent his holidays down in the yard. He lunged, groomed and long-reined. He walked the yearlings. He hacked his cob around the hills of County Carlow. In season he fished. In season he hunted.

It was on one autumn evening's ride that he met Fergal Doherty.

Micky was twelve. Fergal was just thirteen. Micky was smallish, strong and slight. Fergal was big and coarse-boned, with a well-sucked mottled gobstopper for a face and big muscles which barely showed beneath his thick white skin. He was crouched on a steep bank just above the Leighlinbridge road, cramming newspapers into the rabbit-holes. A leggy black long-dog with a white front lay beneath him, watching with bright eager eyes.

Micky emerged from Mill Wood. He narrowed his eyes. With *Laramie* or *The Virginian* on his mind, he squeezed his mount with his knees and clicked his tongue. The Connemara broke into an easy rocking-horse canter across the tussocks of scrub.

They clattered across the road. Fergal heard them. He turned, half-smiled, shrugged and resumed his work. The horse grunted and lengthened his stride to climb the bank. Micky drew in the reins and called, 'Whoah.' At the horse's feet, the black dog did not move. Its shoulders were tense. A deep growl seeped from between its teeth. Its upper lip wrinkled.

Micky was disconcerted. The big boy gave no impression of trepidation, no sign, even, that he knew Micky to be there. He just kept on cramming pages of the *Irish Independent* and the *Kilkenny People* deep into the rabbit-holes. This was not in keeping with the deference which Micky had counted on as equestrian, heir apparent to Ballysheenan and Western hero.

'Um, hello,' he said.

'Hi.' Still Fergal did not look up.

'What are you doing?'

''S it look like?'

'Yeah. But why?'

'Catch rabbits,' the boy droned.

Micky's curiosity got the better of him. 'How d'ye do that, then?'

'Rabbits are out grazing.' Fergal nodded towards the brow of the hill. 'I get all these holes blocked, go off, rest a while, keep quiet, come back, put the dog in amongst 'em, shoot one or two maybe. What they do? All come running back here, don't they? Go down the holes, can't go in, too bloody scared to get out again. Just reach in, grab 'em by the legs and Koh!' He drew a saveloy finger across his throat.

'How many d'ye get?'

'Twelve? Fifteen?' Fergal shrugged. 'Enough. Not as good crack as ferreting, but.'

'You got ferrets?'

'Yup.' The boy gathered up his newspapers and moved on to another hole. He knelt. 'Jill. Beauty.'

'You got a gun?'

'Yup.'

'Four-ten?'

'Peashooters. Twelve bore.'

'You haven't.'

'I have, and why wouldn't I have?'

'Oh.' This was not going as Micky had planned. 'Well, you got permission? To hunt rabbits here?'

At last Fergal showed some sign of animation. He raised a black eyebrow. He laughed. 'Permission, is it? And what'd I be wanting with the likes of that?'

'Well,' Micky frowned. 'It's just normal.'

'Ah, is it, now?' the boy grinned up over his shoulder. 'You a Brit or something, are you?'

'No,' said Micky hotly, 'I'm Irish, same as you.'

'Don't sound it.'

'I do too. Anyhow, so I go to school in England. What's it to you.?'

'Ah, nothing.' Fergal stood and scratched. 'Nothing, nothing. Just wondered why you was after talking like a damned Brit is all. Permission, all that.'

'Well, it's just . . . they're our rabbits, aren't they?'

'Dunno. Axed 'em have yez?'

'Don't be stupid.'

'Ha,' Fergal barked cheerfully again. 'S'pose the salmon down the weir-pool, they're yours too?'

'Yes.'

'But then they neither know nor care,' said Fergal. He added slyly, 'Know I don't. Had plenty out of there.'

'Salmon? On what?'

'Ah, now, there's telling.'

'You've never caught one on a fly, I'll be bound.'

'And why'd I want to?'

'It's fun,' said Micky simply.

'And you've never caught a hare in a lamp-beam, right?'

'No.'

'Know how to set a snare?'

''Course. Everyone knows that.'

'Tell you what,' Fergal sauntered up to Micky's horse. He raised a confident hand to the snaffle. 'You're so clever, you show me what you know, I'll give you a lesson or two. Like to learn some of that fancy stuff, anyhow.'

So Micky and Fergal became partners in murder.

There was Irish life and there was English life. To be Irish was no advantage in England, nor to be English in Ireland. Micky quickly learned to keep the two elements distinct. On the three occasions on which Charlie and Fergal met, Micky was jumpy and anxious to speed the encounter.

On the English side of the coin, Micky went to Ampleforth in Yorkshire while Charlie was sent to Eton. Micky lived amidst black-cowled monks and the constant throbbing tone of plain-chant. He sang soprano, then bass with the choir. He hunted with the beagles on the heather-plush moors. He played cricket ineptly and rugby fiercely. He fished for trout on the school's three lakes. He kept pigs in the farmyard. He played guitar and wrote songs. He was gregarious and idle, but somehow contrived to win eight reasonable 'O' levels.

As for Charlie, he strutted about Windsor in his high collar and tails. He rowed a bit, played polo, poker and the trumpet. He backed a lot of horses. If Micky was sharp and feckless, Charlie gave the impression of being an amiable dolt. He too, however, passed his exams.

One rainy evening when he was fifteen, Micky returned from hunting cold and drenched. His parents were at Newmarket for the sales, so he helped himself to a shot of whiskey from the sideboard and padded upstairs in stockinged feet. His mother had a beautiful cornflower blue bathroom with a large sunken tub and a white fur rug on which it was pleasant to masturbate or just lie naked allowing tired muscles to relax. As usual in her absence, he headed for her room rather than for one of the more spartan bathrooms.

He opened the door and was halfway across the bedroom before he noticed that there were people on the bed. He jumped. He said, 'Oh.'

A man lay flat on his back on the candlewick counterpane. He was naked. Micky could not see his face because Serena was sitting astride it. Her left hand, on which her emerald engagement ring glistered, clasped the large penis which thrust upward from between his white legs.

Serena gasped, 'Micky!'

Her hand flew from the man's cock. She raised her trunk from his startled face. She twisted around, reaching for a pillow, for anything with which to cover herself. There was nothing.

She closed her eyes. She sighed. She shook her head. Resignation tugged her lips into a thin straight line. 'Oh stuff it,' she said sadly.

The man said 'Wha . . .?' but the word was cut short as Serena lowered herself once more onto his lips.

'I'll see you later, Micky,' she said softly, and again her hand moved forward.

Micky just nodded and left the room.

An hour later, Serena came down into the drawing-room. She had showered, and her long blonde hair dangled in springy brown ringlets about her fresh and pretty face. She wore a large white towelling bathrobe.

She said, 'I'm sorry, Micky.'

Micky didn't bother to get up. He flicked over a page of *Country Life* and said, 'Doesn't matter. Don't worry about it.'

'It's a good thing in some ways,' she said dreamily. She sat on the arm of his chair. Her fingers twiddled his hair. She smelled good. 'It couldn't have gone on forever. Something had to give. It's just . . . I hope I haven't – I don't know, you read all these stories in magazines and so on, I hope I haven't traumatised you, turned you off sex or something.'

'Hm,' Micky's shoulders arose and fell. 'Fat chance.'

'I hope you're right,' she said gently. 'I am sorry.' She bent down and kissed the top of his head. 'Well now,' she was brisk and bright. 'Looks like I'm on the move again. You come and see me in America?'

'American, is he?'

'Yes, 'Fraid so.'

56

'Huh,' Micky's shrug expressed his views of Americans in general. 'Well, just have to see, won't we?' he mumbled. He laid down the magazine. 'Going out for a while,' he said.

'OK,' she nodded. Micky looked up quickly. Her eyes were wide and sad and loving. He looked away. 'You know, I'm really bloody proud of you, Micky,' she said. She kissed him again and stood. 'Oh, well, goodbye Ballysheenan,' her voice quavered. 'Better be getting myself dressed, be on my way.' Her laugh was like a distant whinny. 'Bye love,' she sang from the door. 'I really am sorry.'

Now Billy Brennan spent most of his time at home, filling his days with the switching off of lights and the gloomy reading of obituaries and stock-market quotations. The joys of the chase were now subsumed in the quest for a bar or a bookie who would allow him credit.

Ballysheenan was going down the tubes.

It took time for the end to come. Billy could no longer afford to pay Micky's school fees, but the monks at Ampleforth declared that what they had started, they would finish. Micky started to work.

Ballysheenan was sold to Ed and Cathy Kramer, Bostonians of Irish stock. Billy moved out into the lodge. Micky got his three 'A' levels. He had planned to busk his way to the Marquesas, to go to Cambridge, to make a living with his music. All that was now a frayed fantasy. He cut his hair. He knew only one job. Through his father's introduction to Major Herbert Gosse, a Lambourn trainer and tartar, he enrolled as a stable-lad.

Whilst Charlie partied at Trinity Cambridge, Micky was "doing his two" in a Lambourn yard. Their paths had diverged, and then some.

Micky returned to Ireland when he could – at Christmas-time, for a week in the summer. Fergal was now at teacher-training college. His republicanism had now become – or appeared to have become – less purely theoretical than before.

'Ah, sure, and you know all about it, don't yez?' he snarled at Micky one night as they argued on the way down to O'Brien's bar. 'You down here and over in Britain with your high and mighty racing chums. What do you know about living up there? You should just try, you venture out the Falls or the Ardoyne, it's "Fuck off, Mick," or "Fuck off, Taig,". You go down a bar, the bastard Brits come in with their big boots and their clattering smug voices, turn the place over, smash the place up. You should try it one day. Living in a little scrubby two-up, two-down, shithouse in the yard, bath in the kitchen, and there's no work, no way out. You just bloody try it is all.'

'Ah, come on,' Micky taunted. 'You've never even been there.'

'Oh, haven't I just?' Fergal gave a sphinx's grin, 'Haven't I just?'

And another evening while Billy was away drying out, Micky visited Fergal down in his little cottage in the valley. He found him in shorts and singlet, weight-training in the front room while watching the RTE six o'clock news.

The television was saying '. . . gunned down while on patrol in the Turf Lodge area of Belfast. Sergeant Watts, 31, who leaves a wife and two young children, was described by colleagues as "a cheerful chap, always laughing and joking". Last year he took part in the interservice Row Round Britain for Leukemia Research. The Provisional IRA have claimed responsibility for the murder . . .'

And Fergal whooped.

Micky was tired. He said, 'Ah, come on, man. Right or wrong, you can't be glad the man's dead, Chrissakes. I hope they get the bastards.'

'Ha!' Sweat trickled down Fergal's brow and glued his hair to his temples. Each time he raised the bar-bells, he sounded like an outboard failing to start up. 'They'll not get 'em. You try pursuing a man knows his streets, you're lumbered with a bloody great Macron shield and all that. No way. Anyhow, what's the silly fucker want to come here for?'

'So – look, you got a drink in this pit?'

'Sure. Over there. Help yourself.'

Micky squatted down at the white-painted kitchen unit which served as a sideboard. He fished out a can of Smithwicks. 'So you're saying, you disagree with someone, you shoot him, right? All I can say is, I hope for your sake you never run into a member of the Flat Earth Society thinks the same way as you . . . Christ!'

'Ah, rubbish,' grunted Fergal, 'I'm not going to get into all that. What's up?'

Micky had closed the cupboard door before he had realised just what he had seen inside. He reopened it now as though the thing might jump at him. He was used to seeing instruments of death about Fergal – snares, shotguns, rifles, nets – but this was altogether different. You would not pick this to kill any animal. Not that it could not, at short range and if the animal were confined. 'What the fuck . . .?' Micky breathed. He turned the cold heavy gun over and over in his hands as though it were too hot to hold still.

'Pistol,' Fergal grinned. 'What's it look like?'

'Yeah, but . . .'

58

'Know what that is?' Fergal rolled onto his back. He linked his head behind his hands and started to do sit-ups. 'That is – a Stormont Road special, that is. Walther – PPK – came – from an RUC – Special – Branch – bastard – got no – use for it any – more.'

Momentarily impressed, Micky said, 'Jesus.' Then he thought. He said, 'Yuk.' A slow shudder abseiled down his spine. He replaced the gun almost with reverence. He wiped his hands on his jeans. He straightened. 'What the hell you want a thing like that for?'

Fergal lowered his arms. He jumped to his feet, grabbed a towel which looked like a pocket handkerchief and wiped sweat from his eyes. He said idly, 'Sure and everyone's got one, haven't they? Man never knows.'

Micky winced. 'You're mad.' he shook his head, despairing. 'You're stark staring crazy.' Suddenly anger warmed his blood. 'I mean, c'mon, man, you could end up in real trouble with one of these – these *things* around. Is that what you want? Is it? Is it, Fergal?' Now he glared at him. 'Look, man, you've got a brain. You can go places. You don't have to stay in the goddamned bog all your life, fighting battles with – with ghosts, for God's sake. You don't have to stay a ignorant bloody fool stubbornly perpetuating the saddest, stupidest Irish joke of the lot. Playing bang bangs, for God's sake, with a dead man's gun in a dead man's battle. Is that what you want out of life, is it? Another wasted Irishman stuck in the past, doing the bidding of the fucking Libyan terrorists with American money convinced that it's an Irish fight? Jesus. You make me sick!'

'Hell,' Fergal blinked over the towel. 'I mean, it's only a gun . . .'

'Sure, same as a Doberman's just a dog. It's a gun with only one purpose, Fergal: killing human beings. Whatever happens – it stays here, gets sold, handed on – one day that's what it's going to do. It's the thing's nature. It's going to kill someone, and you're going to be at least in part responsible. Does that not worry you?'

Fergal now stood stock still. The towel was slung around his neck. He looked down at his feet. When he looked up, his cheeks were very red. 'Doesn't seem to worry the Brits, does it?' he mumbled in defiance. 'You don't care. You're on their side.'

'I'm not on any bloody side, Fergal!' Micky yelped. 'I'm – I'd just like to see you doing well. I'd like to see the country doing well, people respecting it, investing in it, coming here on holiday, treating us like adults, not like petulant peasants haven't got the nous or the balls to call a halt to a blood-feud. "It's his fault! He hit me first!" It's pathetic, man. Oh, Christ, I don't know,' Micky slammed the unopened beercan onto the formica table-top. 'I can't believe you could be so *stupid*!' His shoulder hit Fergal's, spinning him round, as he stormed to the door.

Two days later, Fergal sheepishly approached Micky down at O'Brien's. 'Got rid of it,' he told the table at which Micky sat.

Micky grinned up at him. 'Good,' he slapped the table. 'Sorry I lost my rag, but, God. Ah, come on, mate,' he stood. 'Have a scoop with me.'

Micky was just twenty when he next saw Charlie Vane. He had charge of Clairmont, second favourite for the 2,000 guineas that year. He was leading him around the Newmarket paddock when he suddenly heard that familiar voice.

'Brennan, you old bastard. And what are you about, then?'

And there was Charlie leaning on the rails, surrounded by all these buffed and burnished girls and beaming young men with raspberry-fool faces. Micky blushed easily, which only served to increase their barracking each time he passed them. He sort of smiled and muttered 'Shut up, will you?' or, 'Come on, leave it out,' which just made them jeer and cheer the louder. Bastards.

When Clairmont had come in fourth and been bedded down, Charlie appeared in the racecourse stables with two incongruously beautiful things. One was a bottle of Bollinger. The other was a walking traffic-hazard with hair the colour of pigskin and eyes clear and green as tourmaline and a whole load of undeclared assets. She was an undergraduate, an aspirant actress. Her name was Eledi; Eledi Donovan.

The three of them sat down in the straw. They chatted and they giggled and they guzzled smoked salmon sandwiches, and somehow that turned into one the most memorable days in Micky's life.

From then on between them developed – perhaps it had always been there – a different unspoken and easy sort of friendship. They saw one another only occasionally. Sometimes Charlie would turn up out of the blue at Micky's place. Sometimes Micky would doss with Charlie at Cambridge or in London.

Micky started to ride races, and he would find Charlie lined up alongside of him at the gate. Charlie was a lousy coachman, but he rode for the crack and bounced up to his fences with all the reckless acceleration of the baby grand the removal men let go. Luckily, he was the sort who bounced on the ground too.

When Micky had problems, like whether he should turn professional or no, he would talk them over with Charlie. When Charlie had problems, like why wouldn't Eledi marry him or what should he do about his drinking – which became excessive one time – he talked it over with Micky.

Micky was the one who got married, and Charlie was somehow just the obvious best man. Micky set up as a trainer, and Charlie brought him some good horses. He could not abandon his family trainers, but he sent him the hunch animals, the problem animals, the ones who had something against running. Micky did well with them too.

For sixteen years now, Micky had not returned to Ireland or seen Fergal Doherty. All that was about to change.

The rooks were everywhere, scraps from a bonfire twisting and floating about the trees. They lay dead in the verges too, sudden silky black splashes in scrub the colour of bones. The rooks announced that he was back in Ireland, so did the potholes in the road, so did the ruined towers, the roofless Georgian houses, the grey one street towns with their 7-Up and Guinness signs, the braided little green fields, the constant smell of rain despite a high yellow sky.

Micky smoked a lot and chatted to the dogs in the back. His stomach sounded like an amusement arcade. He was apprehensive of ghosts – the ghosts of his parents, of lovers and friends – of his own ghost, principally, the ghost of the long-haired boy who had hunted and fished in these hills. In his certainty, his freedom and his Irishness, that boy now seemed at once enviable and absurd – a ghost which yet had power to accuse and to make his accusations tell.

Little had changed. Micky made his way up to Enniscorthy with the broad grey sheepskin of the Slaney at his left, then up to broad Bunchody and on to Fighting Cocks. He found his way without thinking and without the usual dismay on returning home after sixteen years. There were a few new bungalows, a bigger meat factory; that was all.

At Fighting Cocks, he turned left to cross the Barrow at Leighlinbridge. The Barrow was a slower, silkier river than its frilly sister. He turned right then, and followed the car upstream for a mile and a quarter, a mile and a half, and suddenly he was passing through the granite ruins of a priory on the very banks of the river. He looked to his left then, as he had always looked to his left then, because there, some two miles up the shallow valley, you catch your first sight of Ballysheenan House.

Ballysheenan was pink these days. By the time that the Brennans had ceded it to Ed and Cathy Kramer, its once white façade had been streaked with greyish yellow like an old urinal, but Micky remembered it best in the old days, before, when it was white as a cow's back before a storm and gilded by the eternal bright sunlight of memory. Important people and important horses had come to stay. The food was good and plentiful, and in the evenings, after a day's fishing or hunting, they would sit on the huge ranges in the underground kitchen, play cards and pick at carcases and drink Horlicks and whiskey and tell stories well into the flush of dawn.

That was how he chose to remember the old place, but the image turned to sepia, grew dog-eared and faded. The games became more desperate, the consequences more dire. 'Divorce', 'alcoholism' and 'suicide' crept into the conversation. 'Dear old so-and-so' became 'poor old so-and-so'. 'Great gases' became 'old farts'. Ballysheenan started to crumble.

The car now inhaled and exhaled angrily as it jolted up the ilex avenue, up the rough gravel drive. It drew up outside Ballysheenan's front door. Micky unfastened his seatbelt, clambered out and stretched. He hummed something vague. He looked around him with eager wet eyes. He said 'Yes. Right. Now . . .'

From the car he caught a brief glimpse of Cathy through the drawing-room windows to the left of the flaking porch. She frowned her stubborn determination as she wheeled her chair towards the door.

A minute later, the front door swung inward and Cathy appeared on the stoop in pink and fawn tweed. 'Micky,' she blinked out at the fading sunlight. 'Welcome home. Journey?'

'Fine. Fine,' Micky called, 'no problems, none at all.'

He trotted up the steps, tripped on the top one and nearly landed sprawling in Cathy's lap. 'Good to see you, Cathy.' He kissed her cheek. It gave like an old pillow.

'Yeah, well, now. Listen. You talked to Annie while I was away at Kill, right? She told you you've got the old groom's cottage at the bottom of the yard. All fitted out, only I'm told they've been having stove trouble or something.'

'Great, Cathy.' Micky grinned, and sniffed the air. 'Well, I'd better be getting down there.'

'You want to come up here for supper?'

'Thanks, Cath. I'm too whacked. Let's meet up first thing tomorrow, you can show me round the yard, OK?'

'Yep, sure. Eight do you?'

'Fine.' Micky nodded. He jumped down the steps as though he had never left Ballysheenan.

Jenny Farlow was washing up. Micky saw her through the steam-misted window as he backed the car up to the white bungalow at the bottom of the yard. She looked up as she waved a yellow plastic brush and pulled off her rubber gloves when she saw him and the dogs which cantered by the car.

By the time that she appeared in the doorway, Micky had the hatch-back up and his salmon-rods propped against the car. Jenny wore a white man's shirt, a black waistcoat and bleached jeans tucked into tan boots. She must have been nigh exactly the same height as Micky, but the slender tapering of her body made her seem taller. She was dusty and dirty. Micky reckoned she looked great.

She said, 'Hi. Glad you made it. I'm a mess. Been trying to get the place clean for you. Feels like my hair's been used for a broom. Should've seen the place this morning. Something wrong with the Hamco or whatever it calls itself. There was oily soot everywhere. Shit. Annie and I were black come lunch-time.'

'Hey, thanks,' Micky grinned at her. 'No need for you to do all this.'

Her lips twitched. Micky frowned as he turned back to the car. It was as though his grin had caused a frosted glass window to slam shut before her eyes. 'Yeah, well,' she said, 'I quite enjoy it. Here,' she leaned into the car, 'let me give you a hand.'

She pulled out the two biggest suitcases. Micky said, 'Hold up,' but she just shrugged and turned towards the house. At that moment, Muddler abandoned his exploration of the yard and cantered up to say hello. He shoved his nose upward at Jenny's crotch. She had time to say 'Hey!' before he sprang up and put his paws on her shoulders. Then all she could manage was something like, 'Plpf' and, as she turned her head, she squeaked, 'Off!'

She staggered backward, propelled by the weight of the dog, dragged by the weight of the suitcases. She sat heavily on the flags which surrounded the cobbled yard. 'Hell!' she spluttered. She pushed the dog back. It came back for more. 'Get off, will you?'

'Off, damn you, boy!' Micky growled. He shoved the dog to one side. He bent and held his hands out to Jenny. She looked at them. Her eyes were hard, her mouth a thin straight line. For a moment Micky thought that she would reject his offer of assistance. Then a giggle bubbled up from somewhere deep inside her and those eyes curled deliciously. 'Oh, damn,' she said. 'That's all I bloody need.' She took his hands and jumped nimbly to her feet. 'Goddamned rapist dogs. My cup runneth over.'

'Serve you right for showing off, wonder-woman,' Micky looked away. Already he was learning. She was not to be invaded with easy smiles. She must be – what? Thirty-two, thirty-four. She had been burgled too often. Now she preferred to keep the windows locked and the alarm-systems active. Tough nut. Micky quickly erased the facile erotic romance which his mind had predictably and automatically sketched. Nice girl, but about as sexy as Mike Tyson. 'Tell you what,' he said, 'Whyn't you bring in the most important piece of luggage?'

'What's that, then?' She twisted around to slap dirt off her buttocks.

'Yellow and blue carrier bag in there. Duty-free. Take it in and pull out the bottle of Smirnoff Blue Label. You know where the glasses are. Mine's a large one.'

'You got it,' she said briskly. 'So's mine.'

Micky carried the cases in. The dogs led him on a quick tour of the house. On the left of the tiny hallway, there was a pink sitting-room: television, armchairs, a decent loo-table, an Empire cabinet, prints of fish lying on banks and looking understandably disgruntled, and a lovely library table in the bow-window. Then a bedroom with built-in cupboards and a basin in the corner, then a bathroom with room for precious little more than a bath.

Micky called the dogs back. He made his way back through the living-room and the hall and into a spacious kitchen. Jenny sat at the pitch-pine table beneath a humming strip-light.

'Not bad,' Micky mused. He walked past her and peered through the door at a back hall and the loo off it. He slapped his hands. 'Not bad at all.'

He came back into the kitchen, pulled out a bentwood chair and sat astride it. 'Not exactly palatial, but it's sure changed since my day. Used to be dark and damp and full of dead plants and newspapers and mysterious black bottles.'

Jenny pushed a tumbler across the table to him. 'Yeah, well, I'm sure you'll have it back to normal in no time. Cathy's really been pushing the boat out for the return of the prodigal son. Talking of which, there's a fatted chicken, few steaks and so on in the fridge. Don't run to calves. You having dinner with us tonight?'

'Nah. I'm whacked. Thought I'd get an early night and be up with the lark tomorrow. I want to see what's what in daylight.'

You know I'm working for you?'

'You are?'

'Yep. Mornings, anyhow. Secretarial, I suppose. Bit of filing, things like that.'

Micky gulped vodka. He reached for his tobacco pouch. Muddler and Memphis stretched out on the rug by the stove. 'You know the horse business?'

'Not a darned thing. Far as I'm concerned, horse is an expensive and dangerous way of feeding roses. Snorts at one end, farts and kicks at the other. Me, I was in the record business.'

64

'Probably much the same,' Micky nodded. 'Rogues, thieves and toadies and the occasional magnificent crazy moment of genius to justify the whole thing.'

'I thought money justified the whole thing.'

'Uh uh. Not for me.'

She drained her glass and stood. She pulled a cardigan from the back of her chair and slung it over her shoulders. 'So, what is it for you, Mr Micky Brennan?' she asked.

'Just the crack,' he smiled at his glass. 'Just the crack.'

Micky awoke in blood-orange light. He shivered. For a second he wondered where he was. He worked that one out and glanced at the clock by the bed. It said 0817. He cursed. He swung his legs from the bed.

He pulled back the curtains. The light was neon-bright and harsh as a scream. He almost expected to see *Do Not Adjust Your Set* printed across the window. Snow fell deep and fast and skittered on the cobbles.

He squatted down and fumbled in his suitcase for boxer-shorts and twill trousers. He shaved quickly in cold water in the basin. He hopped from foot to foot as he pulled on a polo-neck, thick socks and jodphur boots. The dogs greeted him warmly in the back hall. He opened the door for them and they leaped out to kick up spurts of snow.

Cathy and Screech were already in the office halfway up the yard when Micky arrived flourishing a cloak of snowflakes.

'Where've you been, then?' she croaked.

'Sleeping. Forgot the soporific effects of Irish air.'

'Not up to it, eh, Screech?' Cathy cackled. Screech made a noise like a puncture. 'Still. OK this once. Hope you approve of the decor?'

'Yeah, fine,' he nodded. The walls were the colour of chickenflesh. There was a good big desk. There was a Kenco coffee-filter machine, a good view of the yard and row upon row of Stud Books, Form Books, Directories of the Turf, Ruff's Guides and such lining the rear wall. Everything a man could need.

The black and white photographs of Micky in his riding days which had covered damp patches in the Suffolk cottage were interspersed on the walls with colour photographs of Sansovino racing. In the far right hand corner, a rickety table seemed to hobble like Yonder Peasant beneath the weight of a word-processor and an onyx ashtray, already half filled with buckled filter-tips.

Cathy followed the direction of his glance. 'Yeah. Jenny'll be coming in at nine every morning. Least, that's the idea. Takes a bomb to get that girl up before midday. Still. She'll be no damned good, but kick her a bit. She needs it. Right,' she swivelled suddenly ''s go see these animals. Screech, you go on. Micky, give us a shove, will you?'

Screech moved to the door. He buttoned his tan coat and braced himself to face the snow's roar of applause. He opened the door. For a split second there was a Screech-shaped space in the surge of swirling snowflakes, then the door closed again and the snow settled down like teacher had just walked in.

'So,' Micky grasped the handles of the wheelchair and tipped it backward. 'What's with young Jenny, then?'

'You leave young Jenny alone, Micky Brennan. Not that she wouldn't be good for you after all those vacant available bints you used to hang out with. And that self-absorbed, self-pitying . . . Jesus, open her legs and a little light came on. You rid of her?'

'Yup,' Micky sighed.

'Good thing too. You get babied, you behave like a baby. Yeah, well. Jenny's all right. Just has a stupid cow of a mother spoiled her rotten, clucked over her and Social Registered her half to death. Hugely fat and has a passion for the ballet. Sums her up. So Jenny rebels and who's to blame her. Goes off to LA, works in the music business, does pretty well, all accounts, but you know those guys. Nasty potions. Pumping themselves up with eye of newt and toad of frog – did I just say *toad* of frog? Jesus, I'm cracking up. Yup, so. Jenny has this guy, car gets stopped, both get busted for possession of cocaine or something. And you know what? My two Godforsaken proper sons, they fix it all up. The guy goes down for three to five. Jenny gets put into a nice expensive clinic and she's not even a user, but it looks better that way, doesn't it? A drug problem in the family can even *win* votes, right? So Jen says 'Fuck this, I'm going back to work,' but gloryhallelujah she finds they've fixed that too. No work to go back to. Bastards.'

'So, what's she doing over here, then?'

'What else she do?' She spoke up into his armpit as he leaned over her to pull open the door. 'Whole corrupt thing makes her sick and she's had enough of the self-important shits in the record business. Doctors say – only sensible thing they did say – no way does she go home to Miss Piggy, so she and I're in the same position, really. So I said – Jesus,' she wrapped her sheepskin coat tighter around her, 'Where'd this lot come from?'

'America,' He shut the door behind them. A stable door was open to their left. He steered the chair that way. 'So you said . . .?'

'Yeah,' Cathy called up at him, 'So I said 'OK, I could use a companion. Both escape together, why not?' Right,' she sighed as he pushed her into the warmth of the stable. 'This here's a beast called Fionnuola, some damned Gaelic thing to do with swans. I don't know.'

'Tell you the story one day,' Micky murmured. He was already examining the mare as if by rote. '*The Children of Lir*. How's she bred, then?'

'Holinshed out of that Troy thing won the Irish Guineas. What's her name?'

'Milesia?'

'That's the yoke.'

'Do anything herself?'

'Nope. Ran twice at two. No damned good.'

'So, why'd you buy her?'

'Why'd you buy me a fucking barren cripple? No goddamned cash is why, and I liked her. She's done me well enough. Last foal fetched forty-two grand.'

'Sire?'

'Last one? Double Schwarz. She's in foal to Doulab. Due when, Screech? Mid-March?'

'Somewhere 'bout,' rasped Screech.

'Yup,' Micky slapped the mare's rump. 'Well, I like her too. Reckon you bought well.'

They examined each of the mares in turn. Thirteen of them belonged to Ballysheenan. A further five, three from England, one from France and one from up country, were there with their foals at heel to be covered by Sansovino.

Micky was more than mildly nervous as they approached the box marked *Barbauld*. He need not have worried. She was still in some pain, but she was also the beauty he had thought her back at Newmarket. If he could get her right . . .

'If you can get her right,' Cathy drawled, reading his thoughts, 'you've got the bargain of the decade. If not . . .'

'If not?'

'If she doesn't take this year, Micky Brennan, that's where your nomination to Sanso goes next season. Deal?'

He hesitated. His annual nomination to Sansovino represented more than a third of his annual income. If this mare remained barren, he would be living on nettle soup next year. The mare reassured him. 'Yeah, OK,' he told Cathy, 'I'll back my judgement. Fact, I'll do more. I'll have a little side-bet with you. I'm selling my nomination this year. A grand says she'll be certified in foal before June.'

Cathy's lips wriggled like a caterpillar in a hurry. 'Nah,' she said, 'I'll not take your money. Deal is, she takes this year you get twenty percent of the take for being a bloody genius whether we sell the foal or keep it, right? She doesn't take this year, she's your one service from Sanso next year and we go fifty-fifty on the foal, OK?'

'Sounds fair.' He ran his hand gently down the mare's neck. She hung her head and turned a weary, imploring eye on him. She had been in pain for a long, long time. She needed his help. She was asking for it as clearly as if she had sat up and begged. 'That's my girl,' he crooned softly, 'You will be OK. Don't you worry, girl. You're going to be fine . . .'

When he turned away from her soft gaze with a final gentle pat, he saw scepticism writ large on Screech's crimson face, but Cathy was watching him and the horse with a lopsided affectionate grin. And her eyes were sadder than the mare's.

And so to Sansovino.

They trundled through the thinning static of the snow, past the covering-barn, and so to his Lordship's manor.

He leaned his head put through the gap in the bars and watched their approach with disdainful interest. Micky stroked his snow-spangled nose and peered in over his shoulder. Light streamed through a skylight into the high-ceilinged concrete box, the only new building in the ancient yard. Screech opened the door.

To anyone who did not know, this had little about it of the emotional reunion. Where the mares had politely retreated as the humans entered, Sansovino simply barged forward.

'Get back, you old sod.' Micky shoved the stallion's nose and pushed hard. Sanso stepped back, but tossed his head upward as he did so and took a playful nip at Micky's hand. Had that flashing ivory connected with flesh and bone, Micky's prospects as a concert pianist – minimal at best – would have been nullified, but the man knew the horse. He pushed the stallion's snip back above his teeth and Sansovino just stood there, head held high, grinning absurdly as Micky tickled him.

He knew Micky. Maybe by now he was as shadowy as a figure in a dream, and sure as hell he had more pressing considerations on his mind than the man who, in that distant dream, persuaded him to run his heart out before a hollering crowd, but he knew him nonetheless.

Screech took Sansovino's headcollar. Micky strolled round to examine him. 'Doesn't he look great?' Cathy crowed from the doorway.

'He does,' Micky wiped snowflakes from his lashes and flicked them from his sleeve. 'Too great, far as I'm concerned.'

'What?'

'He's got too much condition on him, Cathy,' Micky pronounced firmly. 'You may like to see him looking like a prize bull, but I want to see some lean on him. This is a gigolo here, not a Sumo wrestler. Ideally, I'd like him ridden.'

'Ridden?' Cathy gaped.

'Why not? All the old stallions in Ireland used to be ridden. Nothing but damned fool vanity, this business of, "My stallion's so big and fat and powerful and vicious that he can't be handled." Jesus, and isn't every circus-horse an entire stallion? We haven't got a good enough boy, more's the pity, but we're going to exercise him all the same. I want him fit and easily handled.'

Screech tutted and looked up at the ceiling.

'Oh, and Screech, I want this straw cleared out now and shavings put in. He's been known to eat his bedding. And that haynet's dangerously low. Take it out. In fact, take all the haynets out. They can eat from the ground.'

'Hmph,' said Screech, habitually eloquent. His eyes slyly swivelled. 'Why not you, then?'

'What?'

'Why'n't you ride him, then? Jockey and all that.'

Micky took a deep breath. He smiled sweetly. 'Because, Screech, I have lost my nerve, that's why.'

Screech smirked. He nodded and grunted, as if to say 'I see.'

All right, so Micky was used to this. OK, so Screech was a silly old fool. It could still rile. Tension scrabbled up Micky's back and shoulder muscles. His fingers flexed. A whole Thesaurus of telling words and forceful phrases declared themselves ready to spring at a moment's notice from the back of his mind to the tip of his tongue.

Cathy saved him. 'Screech, stop asking damn fool questions,' she yapped. She raised her shaking hand in an imperious gesture worthy of Laughton as Claudius. 'Do what Mister Brennan says and mind your own damn business, right?'

'Hmph,' Screech cast a weasel glance at Micky out of the corners of his little yellow eyes. 'Yes'm, you say so.'

'Mister Brennan says so, so get to it.' She turned the chair. 'Micky, let's get back to the office, have some coffee, I'm freezing.'

'Shee-it,' she shuddered as the warmth from the radiators hit. She brushed snow from her hair and her skirt in rapid, almost angry movements. 'I thought you were going to poke him on the jaw.'

Micky grinned. 'And end up fired or without a good stud groom on my first day? Nah. That's *my* horse out there, Cathy, well as yours. I'm going to take good care of him. I can handle the likes of Screech Reagan.'

'Make coffee,' she demanded, then, quietly, 'I'd've poked him on the jaw.'

'Yeah. You haven't had as much practice.' Micky tipped ground coffee into the filter and reached for the tobacco pouch in his jacket pocket.

'Well, I'll say this for you, Micky,' she folded her hands in her lap. 'Thing about you. Always was. You won't be knocked about. You may've lost your nerve on a horse, but you've lost none of your guts. Takes a lot to say something like you said to a guy's gonna be working for you.'

'It's the truth, isn't it?' Micky shrugged. 'Anyhow, what's guts got to do with losing your nerve? One's a virtue, the other a physical disability. You should know, Cath.'

'Funny,' she said, sing-song. 'You play it like your average jockey sort. I keep forgetting you're such a smartarse.'

'You bet I am,' Micky lit the cigarette, switched on the coffee-machine and pulled the swivel chair up to his desk, 'Now,' he told her, 'come and sit here beside me and let's make some smartarsed plans.'

From the hill-road above the house, the man had watched Micky, Cathy and Screech as they made their tour of the stables. He had frequently had to wipe the snowflakes from the lenses of his binoculars. Now Micky and the Kramer woman were ensconced in the office. It looked nice and warm in there. The man pulled his long waxed cotton coat closer about him. He reached for the thermos flask on the passenger seat. He poured himself a plastic mugful of hot whiskey. 'So,' he grunted, 'Micky Brennan.'

He pulled the pad from his coat pocket, flicked over five pages of close script, then drew out a gold ballpoint and wrote at the head of a fresh page: *Brennan M. Stud–manager. Daily routine what? Biographical details what? Character analysis* without *excessive speculation or comment*.

The same man had visited Ballysheenan on the fifteenth of November. From the lane beyond the lawns and the bobbing rhododendrons, he had watched Mrs Kramer's little housekeeper through the car window as she closed the front door, stooped to take an empty tin of Whiskas from the doddering Alsatian on the doorstep and hurried on up the dogleg drive, bobbing like a wagtail.

He had read the details from the pad on his thighs: *Annie Serena Macloughlin, nee Flynn, only daughter of Louella Flynn and Nathan Flynn, Louella's father, would you believe?* The man had pushed a Polo mint into his mouth. He had growled. He had wanted a factual report, not prurient speculation. '*. . . both decd. m. 1971 Tom Macloughlin, labourer. 3 daughters, 2 sons . . .*'

Holy Jesus, and who would have thought that a little birdlike creature like that, – no tits, narrow hips – could get such a brood?

'*. . . cleaner and housekeeper to Mrs Kramer. Hours 0630–1130/1200. Returns 2230 to help the old woman to bed. When sick or indisposed replaced by daughter Theresa, 16.*'

Annie had been on the doorstep of the lodge by now. She had ruffled the long dark hair of the little girl and pushed her in ahead of her.

The man had flicked over a page. *Kramer, Catherine Mary nee Kavanagh*, he had read, '*b. Boston Massachusetts, 1924 Elder daughter of Senator Patrick Kavanagh, businessman (bootlegger, so they say), m. 1947 Edward Delamer Kramer, electrician, racehorse-owner (electrician racehorse owner?) d. 1988. Two sons, Ward Delamer, b. 1948, Jonathan Kavanagh, b. 1950, both residents of Boston. Ward: attorney at law, partner in Roche, Lewis and Kramer, political ambitions. Jonathan: with US Attorney's office. Best horse owned: Sansovino, trained M. Brennan, Marlborough. Won: Festival Stakes, Goodwood, Prince of Wales Stakes, Ascot, Eclipse Stakes, Sandown, 7th, King George VI and Queen Elizabeth Stakes, Ascot and everyone thought he was over the hill, but came with a wet sail in the Arc to finish 1/2 length second to Portfolio. Portfolio!*

So the kid thought he knew his turf history and all.

Sansovino now standing Ballysheenan House Stud, Co. Carlow. 9,000 gns (Ire).

The man had sighed. He had pushed the pad into the poacher's pocket of his long waxed coat. He had grunted as he straightened in his seat and started up the car. He had steered it up to the lodge and into the drive. He hummed 'Always' as he pulled up at the foot of the stoop below the front door.

He had unclipped the seat-belt and pulled himself, puffing through his bulbous nose, out of the car and up the steps. He had scratched the Alsatian behind the ear and reached for the bell-push beneath the thick ivy.

He had turned on the doorstep. He had stamped, flapped his arms across his body, taxi-driver style. He was not a big man, but he had broad shoulders and a big jostling belly and the lumbering presence of a chieftain. His hair was tweedy grey, his face shiny and wrinkled as buffed leather.

The door handle had turned and returned. It had turned again. This time the door had swung inward, thumping against the retreating wheelchair. The man had not moved forward. He had remained courteously smiling on the doorstep. Cathy Kramer had blinked up at him. 'Yeah?'

'Mrs Kramer?'

'Yeah?'

'Colonel Murphy. I am sorry to bother you, but I've been asked to deliver you a message. Damned nuisance, I know, but I hope you'll forgive me.'

'Sure,' Cathy had croaked. 'Come on in.'

She had wheeled the chair backward, then swivelled it around as if to push it towards the drawing-room. Instead she had flicked on the brakes and just sat there rocking slightly backward and forward. He had followed her in, swinging the door quietly back behind him.

'So,' Cathy had croaked, 'what's the message?'

'Oh, it's one of those boring things,' the man had pulled off his gloves and flung them towards the circular walnut table. They had missed, and fallen to the tiles with a soft splat.

'Myself, Mrs Kramer, I'm only delighted, really delighted when someone like you comes over here. Really. God knows, this poor old country needs the employment, the investment. Not to mention, well, the great thoroughbred racehorses belong in Ireland, don't they?'

'S'pose.'

'But I'm afraid . . .' the man had pulled a pipe from his coat pocket. He had looked wistfully down into the bowl. He had raised his head. 'I'm afraid there are those who resent you, your tax-free status, and so on. I mean, I think it's a good thing that stallions should be here tax-free, but there are always bloody trouble-makers, d'ye know? Hotheads. Heard 'em the other night. 'Ireland gives her so much, what's she give to Ireland?', you know? Bastards were talking about coming up here, burning the house down. Of course, it was only the drink talking. I told 'em, 'Go home. Sleep it off.' But I know these people. It'll happen again.'

'Get it the world over,' Cathy had nodded. 'It's all talk.'

'Yes,' the man had agreed sadly. He had put the pipe-stem between his teeth and made a series of little popping sounds. 'But – I wouldn't like you to underestimate this crowd, Mrs Kramer. They see themselves with some justice, as oppressed, deprived. Brits never colonised here, they just used the place as an offshore tenant farm and took the profits back home. So a lot of these guys get really worked up about this sort of thing. That's what happened to Shergar, you know. They asked for some small payment in lieu of tax, and when it was not forthcoming, they got angry and took the horse. That's the sort of people we're talking about.'

72

'Well, fuck them,' Cathy had leaned forward, her elbows on her thighs. 'That's between me and the government, ain't it?'

'I agree,' the man had soothed, 'I agree. That's how it should be. But these people don't think like us. I told you. They're troublesome. Well, I heard them talking like this, and I said, "Hold on. You feel this way, what's the point of damaging a beautiful house or a beautiful horse? Let me put your case." They took some persuading, but eventually they backed down. So here I am.'

'Bastards,' Cathy had sniffed. 'So what'm I meant to do?'

'Well, now, Mrs Kramer,' the man had walked across to one of a pair of hall chairs embroidered with the Brennan crest on a navy blue background. He had sat and intertwined his fingers. 'I think I can persuade them to calm down. I think we can get around them. What I suggest – Sansovino stands at – what? Nine thousand, is it?'

'Nine grand Irish.'

'Yes. And he covers forty mares a season, right?'

'Forty to fifty, if he's full up.'

'Which means three hundred and sixty to four hundred and fifty a year, tax free. Right?'

'I can do arithmetic.'

'So. Normally these fellows would be looking for something like tax would be elsewhere – say, twenty-five percent. That'd be – God, ninety thousand, a hundred and twenty. Yes, well, like I said, I calmed them down. You give me, say, one nomination. Nine thousand guineas. I think I can call them off. That sounds fair, doesn't it? I mean, compared with what these greedy sods want?'

'Sounds to me like nine grand more'n I was intending to spend this year. That value, where you're coming from?'

'No, no. God, Mrs Kramer, I know even that must come as a blow. Thing is, the options are so much worse. These people – well, I hate to say it, but they can be very seriously unpleasant. I can only counsel you . . . well,' he had shrugged and left his counsel unspoken.

Cathy had frowned. 'Nine grand, you say? And that buys me tax-free peace and prosperity in this country, that right?' She had nodded once. 'Not bad. OK. But what can you do to show me there won't be another demand coming along tomorrow, huh? How'd I know you can protect . . .?' She had stopped then. Her mouth had hung open. 'Protect . . .' she had enunciated laboriously.

'It's not that much to ask, I think,' the man had reassured her, 'and I can promise you, there'll be no other demands of any sort. I can see to that. You see, this is an official thing, Mrs Kramer. It happens to all foreign stallion-owners living here tax-free. It's not just a load of opportunistic fellers down a bar. But I've argued with them, and, like I say, you just have to give me nine thousand and – that'll be it.'

Cathy had been panting now. 'Protect,' she had said in a voice like the mummy's from the tomb. 'You know, you nearly had me reaching for my cheque-book? You're good, Colonel Murphy, or whatever your name is. You're fucking good. It's just that word. Protect. I heard it many, many times back in the States, Colonel. Our stores. Protect. Protection. Shotguns behind the counter, dogs big as horses. And you're all the same, Colonel Murphy. You tell yourself you're a nationalist, IRA, Red Brigade, Mafia, you're all nationalists, aren't you? But what you really are, what you've all got in common, you're all bullies, all cheats, all people who believe that having bigger guns or bigger bombs entitles you to steal from ordinary people, isn't that right?'

'None of us likes the methods necessary in this battle,' the man had stood. 'But war is always regrettable. Anyhow, it has nothing to do with me . . .'

'War?' Cathy had flicked off the brakes on her chair and wheeled it a yard or two back from the man. 'War? You looked out there? You talked to the Irish people? They at war, are they? They want blood on their streets, do they? They like having the reputation as violent burks still fighting their great-grandfathers' battles? Shit. They'd like tourism. They'd like peace and quiet. They're not at war, Colonel fucking Murphy. It's just your crowd, not the Irish people. Just Libyan trained bastards exist all over the world trying to undermine capitalism, exploit national grievances, the old songs, the old memories. Well you can fuck off out of here, d'ye hear? And you can tell your fucking friends they'll not get a brass cent out of me. I'll not have blood on my fucking hands and I don't like the stink you make in here. Do you hear?' She had been shaking now, pushing herself forward as though to get up and fling him bodily from the house. 'Get out of my house, and you come back, I'll have a shotgun pointed at your belly.'

The man had pulled himself puffing to his feet. He had replaced the pipe in his coat pocket. He had said sadly, 'Very well, Mrs Kramer, but I am trying to help you. I must warn you, the next people to come won't be like me. Some of them scare the hell out of me, to be honest.'

He had bent to pick the gloves up from the floor.

'Yeah,' Cathy had snarled at his back. 'Well, bullies scare easy. I don't. You tell 'em that.'

The man had pulled the glove onto his right hand. He had flexed his fingers, 'I have tried to help you. I'm afraid – you have made a very rash decision, Mrs Kramer. I wouldn't lay long odds on your still being here this time next year. I'm sorry. But you know how it is. These people demand reciprocity . . .'

'Out!' Cathy had screamed. 'Out, out, out!'

'Oh, I'm going, Mrs Kramer. I'm just sorry to think of who will come here in my stead. Goodbye.' On the doormat he had bowed graciously.

Cathy's fist had pummelled at the arms of her chair. 'Out!' she had shrieked, and her cracked howl had made the windows rattle.

Propose nearly constant surveillance from now on, the man wrote. *Suggest stage one intimidatory action within fortnight.*

The man snapped the pad shut. 'I wonder,' he mused as he started up the car, 'I wonder if young Micky Brennan knows that he's just been recruited into Kramer's private army?'

He hummed 'It Had to Be You' as he released the handbrake and freewheeled down the hill.

February

The mare wore boots on her hind feet to prevent her from kicking the stallion. Jenny thought that that was unfair. Bastard could do with a lesson in manners. Wooing and foreplay, it seemed, were unknown to him. One sniff and he jumped. The direct approach. For a minute, maybe two that huge black thing shuttled back and forth, and that was the old girl's lot.

Jenny had said to Micky, call that value? At – a hundred and fifty sterling per second, something like that, the old girls's been had. She could be the one getting paid, and still get better service.

'Vastly overrated pastime at the best of times,' she had added drily.

Micky had said, 'Oh, I don't know.'

Now Jenny stood in the doorway of the covering-barn. The light from off the snow behind her made a wispy halo of her hair. She leaned back against the doorframe. Her legs were crossed just beneath the knee. Her hands were loosely crossed before her crotch.

Micky stood at the centre of the barn, at the point of the scalpel blade of light which slid across the thick sawdust. He held two fingers beneath the base of Sansovino's cock, making sure that he did not fake it. He had been known to. It was always a problem with the Blandford line, Micky said.

Screech Reagan stood at the mare's head, twisting her snip with a twitch of blue binder-twine. Michael was there too. He held Sanso on a long rope. Michael Ryan was all red-cheeked and grinning like a loon. He was still ill-at-ease in the presence of the Bold Thing itself.

Sansovino pressed shuddering loins hard against the mare's flanks. His forelegs worked uselessly on her either side. His teeth gnawed at the thick ridge of leather which protected her neck.

'And?' said Micky like a bandmaster.

Sansovino's tail flapped upward.

'Got it?' Screech whispered. Screech always whispered.

'Yup.' Micky removed his fingers, dusted off his hands and turned away. 'Right, Michael, that's his lot for today. Wash him down and bed him down, will you?' He walked over to Jenny's side. 'Screech, mate, would you get that Main Street mare in for us, and old Salmagundi? I'll be up at the office if anyone wants me.'

Screech's neck bulged. Micky took that for a nod.

Sansovino, duty done, descended from the mare. His dangling prick gleamed and steamed. Screech pulled the twitch from the mare's nose. He took her headcollar. 'Girl,' he said.

'Good feller,' Michael stroked the stallion's massive neck. 'There's a feller.'

Micky had nothing to contribute to this epithalamium. He simply turned to Jenny and sighed. 'Lord, does it not make fools of us all? Ready? Right?'

She put her fingertips in her jeans pockets, and together they walked out into the dazzling sunlight, he brisk, she shambolic, but then she had a deal more leg to spare, they headed up the cobbled yard. Snow lay like sunlight on the iron hinges of the pale green doors. Snow made the roofs plump.

Micky peered in through the grille on one of the box doors. He told the rustling darkness, 'Reckon she'll foal tonight.'

Jenny rested her forearms on the door, her chin on her forearms. 'How d'you know?'

'Dunno, really,' Micky turned to her. He saw how close she was and turned quickly back. 'She tells you really. She's bagged up of course, waxing, but . . . she's restless. Not usually a box-walker, but look at her. Backward and forward, up one minute, down the next . . .'

'She's been like that for two days. You didn't expect her to birth last night.'

'No, I know,' Micky mused, 'Still.'

'How d'ye get to know all this stuff?'

'Dunno that either,' he grinned. He mumbled into the sleeve of his Barbour. 'It's like a lot of these things – fishing, you know? You do it often enough, there are all these random factors. You don't actually say, 'a salmon is going to take this particular size and pattern 'cos there's a nine mile an hour south-westerly and the sky's high and the light-meter registers . . .' all that. Well, you do say a whole load of things like that because it's consoling, but it's mostly crap. What happens is, somewhere below the rational bits, there's a sort of hunter's repository. All the data of a million casts goes in there; some instinct sifts it all and you come up with a feeling, a hunch which may seem crazy; 'I know, why don't I put on an elver and fish it upstream really fast?' And it works, and then, like with history, you invent a rule to explain it. Same really with horses, though they tell you a lot more than salmon, you spare the time to listen. You handle them enough, ride them enough, produce enough foals, it all gels. I can still be wrong though. Often am. I reckon she's going to foal tonight because she reckons she's going to. May both be wrong.'

'Yeah.' Jenny rested her cheek on her arm to look at him. 'Doesn't it feel a bit weird?'

'What's that?'

'Well, I mean, this yard, these boxes, the house, the land, they were all yours once. Well, your dad's. I just wondered.'

'Nah,' Micky pushed himself back from the stable door. 'Way it goes, isn't it? No point looking back. Anyhow, it's still mine, the bit I'm worried about. I'd not have come back, if Cathy hadn't agreed to that. I have absolute authority in the yard. So watch it.'

'Oh yeah? *Droit de seigneur*, is it?'

'Some hope.' Micky quickly bent to scoop up a handful of snow. He jerked his head back towards the covering-barn. 'Nope, that's his Lordship's privilege. Come on. Work. I could do with a cup of tea and all.'

'Yes, sir, boss.' She put in a quick skip to catch up with him.

Sometimes when she was silent and sullen, Micky wanted to clout Jenny around the ears, tell her we've all got problems, thanks, what'd I want with yours? But happy like this, she was great. He had all sorts of urges at times like these, some of them surprising, like he would like to ruffle her cropped blonde hair or bite her long neck or pick her up and squeeze her until her ribs cracked or . . . Some of them were less surprising, but she was his employer's niece and his employee. That was confusing enough.

Micky pushed the office door open for Jenny. She strode quickly into the Calor Gas heat. She said, 'Brr.' She walked over to her desk in the far right hand corner and stabbed with a stiff finger at the kettle. She sat down. Then she cast a quick glance over at Micky where he stood in the doorway. He was looking down at the snowball in his hand. He tossed it and caught it once. His lips twitched. He threw it to the ground.

He was all business as he bustled in and hung up his snow-spangled Barbour. Jenny thought oh, God, then oh, damn.

At two o'clock that afternoon, Micky, as every day since he returned to Ireland, was steering through the granite gateposts with the greyhounds on top, and the car was wading through deep gravel up an avenue of bare limes. On either side there were snow-spattered pastures smooth as lawns.

Kilcannon House was big; four storeys of eighteenth-century granite surmounted by a balustrade of letters reading *Invictus et Invictus*. The Vane coat of arms – martlets and a boar or something – stood between greyhound supporters above the front door. The two top floors had been sealed up for as long as Micky could remember, and Micky had been coming here for the hunting or children's parties or to catch mumps or measles since he was a toddler. It was necessary to burn two huge stacks of straw every day just to keep the place above freezing-point.

Benet Kilcannon was rich – loaded, even – but his pile did for cashflow what Dracula did for blood pressure.

Micky passed a moment or two in stretching and admiring the parkland, the laden specimen trees, then he trotted up the steps to the open front door. He walked though the high pedimented portico, stepped over a dozing bull-terrier and into the dark and empty hall. 'Charlie?' he called. His voice ran away up the stairs and played hide-and-seek in the rooms up on the landing.

He swung to his left, into Charlie's study. Again, empty but for a big black labrador with a grizzled muzzle which waddled out from behind the sofa.

The sofa was covered with newspapers, the desk with form-books and letters, the mantelpiece with invitations. The labrador growled and wagged its tail at the same time. Micky said, 'Ah, shut up, will you, Magnus?' Magnus said sorry by wrinkling up his eyes and knocking a stack of *Horse and Hound* and *Racing and Breeding Update* off a chair with his tail.

'Hello!' Micky walked back into the hall. There were a couple of nice Raeburns up there amongst the sooty family portraits and the panoplies of swords and spears, and a gigantic study of dead animals by someone who would have liked to be Landseer. 'Where is everyone?' Micky muttered. He strode across to the kitchen door. His heels chimed on the flags.

Since Charlie had taken over, no one dined much in the dining-room save on high days and holidays. All the living was done in the morning-room, Charlie's study and the kitchen.

There was a bit of living being done in the kitchen just now. Charlie's old housekeeper was stirring some potion on the Aga whilst drooling incantations down her hairy chin. Simon White, nigh permanent resident of Kilcannon since he arrived here to work for a week or two a mere three years back, was reading the *Irish Independent* on the table.

'Ah, Micky!' he blinked through thick round glasses, 'good to see you.'

'Eledi? She here?'

'Yes, yes,' Simon chucked back a handful of his rusty curls. 'Lovely as ever, recalcitrant as ever. 'Parently she's off on tour with some Godawful sixties comedy in a few weeks' time and decided to put in a week over here, just to keep Charlie gnawing carpets and climbing up the curtains while she's away. Sweet of her.'

'Ah, come on, Simon,' Micky said, 'That's unfair. She's said no to Charlie a thousand times. It's him never gives up. A one-gal-guy, our

Charlie.'

'Poor fool.'

'So Georgie arrived when?'

''Bout half an hour ago. They've only been gone twenty minutes or so. You are to follow them, as I understand it. I'm not allowed, it seems.'

'Sorry,' Micky shrugged. 'Just a little secret to do with the birds. All will be made clear ere long. Thanks, Simon. See you.' He shouted at the housekeeper, 'Hello, Mrs Halloran!' She turned and nodded. He waved, 'See you later, Mrs Halloran!' She nodded again and resumed her mumbling.

Micky climbed back into the car and drove down to the road again, through a gateway opposite and up a narrow track which climbed through tiny fields to the heath-topped hill. The car rocked and cleared its throat a lot, but the ground was hard and dry.

He saw the rows of jumps first, down to his right. He had ordered them built and supervised their construction – a plain fence with a pole before it, an open ditch and a slightly larger natural. Then he saw the two horses milling about at the start of the schooling ground, then Charlie and Eledi standing some twenty yards above them beneath the old Dutch barn. The gallops were no more than the verge, some ten yards wide, of two large ploughed fields on the side of the hill.

Micky turned the car casually towards the barn. He was humming and smoking as usual. Then what he saw made him say slowly, 'Oh shit,' and gun the engine. He hit the dashboard with the heel of his hand. He sped towards the gateway, regardless of the car's complaints. 'No!' he shouted. He bounced up and down in his seat to urge the car on. He unwound the window and bellowed 'No! No!'

Georgie Blane was the first to see or hear him. He turned his mount, a big brown colt, and raised his right hand to point. Charlie and Eledi turned together. Eledi's hair, the colour of toffee or autumn beeches, wrapped itself around Charlie's crimson and white face. The other horseman, a pallid pixie with jagged bright orange hair zig-zagging from beneath his skullcap, sadly shrugged. He sank in the saddle.

The rider with the flame-coloured hair, Liam O'Connell, was good. That was why they had chosen him. For all his venality, he was unquestionably the best all-round amateur rider in Ireland today.

The other lad, though – ah, now you were talking. Georgie Blane was, quite simply, the greatest stylist that Micky had ever seen taking a fence at speed or riding a mud-spattered hands-and-heels finish.

Micky had ridden against Georgie once or twice, but Micky had just been an amateur and it had been Georgie's last season. He had been hitting the booze a bit by then. Up one minute, down and brooding the next, but just flick him into the saddle and he was beautiful to behold.

He was a cattle-farmer now, a small-time breeder and trainer, but God, just look at the ease of the man, the way he sat into his mount, the beautiful confident long rein crossed right in there beneath his crotch.

This, however, was no time for sightseeing. Micky braked hard and was out of the car before it stopped rocking. 'What the fuck are you doing? Begging your pardon, Eledi.'

He slammed the car door. Charlie sort of wriggled. 'Thought we'd school him a bit. You weren't here, and ground's softened up a bit now. Bit of fun. Eledi hasn't even seen our Martindale in action.'

'Forget it, Charlie,' Micky snapped. 'I'll tell you when I'm ready to have him schooled. Jesus, man, one thing, one little thing goes wrong in schooling, affects his confidence, and we've lost our race.' He turned to Georgie and Liam. 'Boots off,' he commanded, 'Cheek martingales on. Business as usual. God in heaven, man, you haven't even had time to get their backs down. Uphill trotting. We'll give 'em a nice sharp canter after. That's it. God.'

'It wasn't Georgie's fault, Mick,' Charlie said at Micky's elbow. 'He didn't want to school them.'

'So whyn't you listen to him, for God's sake?'

'Just thought – well, we've got the fences up, he's going great and I wanted to show Eledi how he's getting on.'

'Yeah. Well, sorry, Eledi. Not today.'

'Fine,' she shrugged and hugged herself.

'Look, Charlie, we've starved the show condition off him. We're just building up the racing muscle. We're a long way off a hundred percent. When he is ready, I'd like to put him round a loose school. Probably can't find one, but at least . . . Look, perhaps another few weeks, we'll steal him into his fast work, and – Jesus, man, you know Liam. Crazy bugger wants to win his gallop. He'd be blind-heeling all the way. You want to destroy this animal's confidence, that's the right way to do about 't. I want Georgie up on the schoolmaster when we do it. A nice sedate, steady job, OK?'

'OK, OK.' The red spots in Charlie's cheeks were still very livid, but he stroked his thick black hair and said, 'You're the boss, Mick. Sorry.'

Micky said, 'Forget it. Just remember, mate, this may be a game for you, but for me it's life and death. I'm not just in it for the crack. I need that cash. So let's keep it professional, all right?'

'OK. Boring, but OK.'

'Where's the cadge, then?'

'Still in the car. That's the next excitement: chase the new tiercel to Connemara. Great.'

'So,' Micky turned to Eledi, 'Gather you're off on tour, that right?'

'Yup. Back to the dressing-rooms, digs and dahlings.'

'What's the play?'

'*Black Comedy*. Shaffer, remember?'

'I remember. Which are you, the debby bit or what's her name, Clea?'

'Clever clogs,' said Charlie.

'The debby bit, worse luck. All star, i.e. television cast. Dull, but it's a number one tour. Start in Windsor, then Bath, Bradford, Brighton, Richmond, God knows. Three bloody months of it.'

'London?'

'Doubt it, but who knows?'

'So why do it?'

She shrugged. 'Damn fool, the devil drives.'

'That was another R. Burton.'

'You don't say, Micky,' she smiled. It was the sort of smile that tickled your throat and made you swallow a lot. You could have read by that smile under the bedclothes, if you were unable to think of anything better to do with it.

Charlie had the binoculars to his eyes now, watching the horses down in the valley. 'Look, Mick, is this bloody animal going to be ready?'

'Lord knows,' Micky pulled his binoculars from their case. 'I'd say yes, all things being equal, but it's the first time I've ever had to do this, turn a showhack into a racehorse again. I don't know. He's coming on OK. Georgie tell you what he's up to now. Feed?'

'He's doing twelve pounds now he's off the mashes.'

'You arranged the lucerne, the comfrey?'

'Yup. He's getting everything bar the vinaigrette. You should hear this man, Eledi, love. The purest peat water gathered in copper-lined – must be copper-lined – butts, God in heaven.'

'Ah, he'll be ready in time,' Micky murmured. He too was watching the horses through the little Zeiss glasses Nathalie had given him. 'Yup. No setbacks, he'll be fine. He's looking good.'

'Believe in leaving things to the last moment, don't you?'

'Why worry? Once upon a time, that animal could jump. OK, so we're starting over, but all he needs is a reminder. I want him so fit he's busting to do it again. He'll need only the one school, maybe two if he gets it wrong.'

'And on that we invest seventy-five grand? Jesus.'

'It's enough, Charlie. Good couple of gallops, maybe a mile and a quarter, no more. Lots of this. A gentle hunt over the wrong distance at Gowran and he'll be set. I'm speaking sacrilege, but you ask any trainer on truth-drugs, he'll tell you. There's nothing clever about training. Feed 'em, settle 'em, get 'em fit, place 'em well. That's your lot. Him, we know he's got the ability, he's a lovely walker, he's got a pair of breeches on him now. We can get him back on his hocks, get him away from his fences fast enough, we've got a winner. Talking of which Simon's getting suspicious.'

'I'm not surprised. The peregrines take an hour a day out of season. Suddenly I'm out two, two and a half hours every afternoon.'

'So blind him with science. Tell him the tiercel mustn't have too many people around, needs a lot of special handling, something like that.'

'Ah, we needn't worry about Simon. He's safe as houses.'

'Worry about everyone, Charlie.' Micky lowered the glasses with a sigh. 'You're a nice, trusting, open, honest guy. Your friends are all nice people. But nice people go down to bars, have a few jars, can't resist showing off their knowledge. So do you, so do I. If this thing's going to work, you're going to have to think nasty, Charlie. Think mean, untrusting, devious. Think George Smiley. No one, but no one must smell anything more rat-like than roses.'

'God, you can be a pain, Micky.'

Micky grinned.

The horses were returning now. They shook their heads. They strained against the cheek martingales. They wanted to be off.

Liam's mount, Chesterton, was a beautiful big boat of an animal, a veteran 'chaser, genuine as the day was long. He had taken as many pots as Steve Davis in his time on both sides of the water.

His pupil was a very different type. He was small. He was centred, beautifully balanced. Nothing would stop him from pointing his toe at the trot. This was Micky's discovery, the crazy show-hack, Martindale.

And Micky, Charlie, Eledi and Georgie were investing seventy-five grand in this show-hack's ability to jump large obstacles at speed in May.

Micky shuddered. Maybe he could get the animal ready. Maybe he could trust it to do the business, but on this coup depended a whole lot more than that. He also had to trust the gods, and in his experience, the gods were as fickle as felines, and just as savage.

March

It started at one o'clock in the morning with a hammering at the door.

Micky was ready for it. He was instantly alert. He flicked on the lamp and rolled out of bed. The dogs out in the back sounded like a seventy-eight record when the grooves run out. Micky opened the door to the sitting-room. He grabbed a hand-towel from the rail by the basin, wrapped it around his loins and limped through the tiny hallway. He turned on the outside light and Screech's pink stocking-masked face sprang out of the darkness at him, bleared and smeared by the frosted glass. He turned the Yale. The wind came in like Special Branch. Behind him, curtains sighed and paper cackled. A few dry leaves scudded quickly into the warm.

'She's started,' Screech croaked solemnly. 'I thought as you'd better be there.'

Micky nodded. 'Sure.' He left the door open and headed quickly back to the bedroom. He banged his shin on the bloody mahogany cellaret. He dropped the towel and hopped and hissed. What in hell did he want with mahogany cellaret, anyway? He called over his shoulder, 'It's the maiden, is it?'

'Yup. Thought as Main Street be first.'

Micky pulled on a Viyella shirt, Y-fronts, a pair of jeans. He did not bother with socks, just quickly forced his fingers through his hair and strode through the hall again to pull on his boots.

'Right,' he said, 'let's be seeing her.'

The yard was greyish purple in the magic-lantern moonlight. The trees up by the house undulated and hissed like cobras. Screech crouched and scampered. He led the way to the box immediately to the left of the waiting-up room and held open the door. Micky walked briskly in.

Millamant, a bay mare with a hugely distended belly, lay on her side in the straw. Her fast and shallow breathing sounded like a giant outboard just failing to start up. Sweat darkened her coat. Already two slender feet in their tight white membrane wrapping jutted from beneath her tail.

'Come on, old girl,' Micky kicked her rump, 'move it. Up you get. Come on. Screech, get Main Street out, would you? Come on, then, up you get.'

Millamant gave a huge extended grunt. She heaved herself reluctantly to her feet. Micky took her headcollar. He led her out into the yard before she could change her mind. She stood shivering beside him and puffed hot air into his ear.

The doors of the box at the end of the row were also open. A chevron of primrose yellow light slid across the cobbles. First Screech's elongated shadow, then Screech himself emerged. He was leading another mare, also heavy with foal. Her head hung low. Her belly swung. She dragged her hooves as she lumbered towards Micky and Millamant.

Micky clicked his tongue and led Millamant to the newly vacated box. She seemed to reckon one place as good as another just so as she could get some peace. As soon as he released her, she made one quick circuit of the straw, slumped down and resumed her engine imitations. This was the first time for her. She kept raising her head, looking back at her rump. She seemed angry at what was going on back there.

'Should have thought of that before you let your animal passions get the better of you, shouldn't you, girl?' Micky muttered. 'She'll not do here. She's too close to the wall. No room to drag out the foal. Sorry, lass. Come on. Up you get. Up, up, up!'

Again with a shuddering groan of protest at his kicking, she scrambled up. Screech was back now, kicking up the bedding to make it deep and crisp and even. This time the mare selected a more suitable berth, but not for long. A minute passed and she was up again, this time of her own volition. Her ribs and her flanks heaved.

Micky walked round to the back of her. He studied the gleaming vulva around those two white marble feet.

'Have to cut her,' he said. 'Get us the scissors, then just hold her head for us, would you?'

Screech crunched off, breathing like every step was a low punch.

He was back in a matter of seconds.

Micky waited until Screech had a firm hold on Millamant's head. Then he inserted the open blades and cut quickly and deliberately through the palpitating tissue. Waters burst from the enlarged opening. They ran warm up Micky's sleeve.

'Right. Should be OK now.' Micky stood back. 'Come on, my old darling. Lie down. Good girl. Just take it easy now. Attagirl. You just lie down.'

She took his advice, slumped down, and suddenly everything was moving in a higher gear. Once the foal started coming, time was at a premium. It was still breathing through its umbilical. If the cord should become constricted in the process of birth, the foal would die of oxygen starvation in a short time. There was always the risk to the mare too. The foal would be eager to get out. It hind legs could lash out, ripping at its mother's uterus and stomach.

Micky knelt on the straw by the steming rump. He grasped the slippery feet. He leaned back, exerting gentle, even pressure. For now, he could only help the mare.

Nothing happened. Millamant just groaned a lot.

'Come on, girl,' Micky sighed. He pushed hair from his forehead with his arm. 'Give us a hand now, would you?'

'Not coming?' Screech leaned back against the wooden partition. He was putting Micky to the test, damn his eyes.

Micky said, 'Nope. Hang on.'

He closed his eyes and groped tentatively inside the vagina. His hands followed the two legs. No constricted tendons; head where it should be. Perfect racing-dive position. All he needed was a little assistance from the mare.

And suddenly she gave it. Beneath his hands, the foal slid forward. The knees appeared. Micky pulled. One more shove from the mare and the head was out, all enclosed in its white plastic bag.

'OK,' Micky nodded to Screech. 'Give us a hand, then.'

Screech knelt at Micky's side. Each grabbed a leg, and now they really pulled, making those creaking noises which somehow serve to increase strength. One moment there was resistance. The next, the whole foal slipped from its mother and its protective sheath, a damp, dark, steaming creature, ninety percent legs.

Micky plucked the traces of membrane from its nose, checked on the tongue and reached down beneath the belly. He took the umbilical cord between both hands, constricted, twisted and pulled. There was a little splash of blood, no more.

He stood, grabbed the wet forelegs and dragged the foal unceremoniously round to a point just in front of its mother's head. She was not too interested just now. Too busy shuddering and grunting.

But by the time Micky had reached between the foal's hind legs and had established that it was a colt, disinfected the ruptured cord and squeezed an enema up the new arrival's anus just by way of a welcome to the world, Millamant was already leaning forward to lick her son.

Screech turned on the infra-red and the whole scene was bathed in blood.

A nativity, heavy on tempera; the sweat-soaked, panting mare, the gleaming placenta still coiled beneath her tail, the foal, irritably shaking its narrow head as its mother licked and nipped, licked and nipped, soothing, cleaning, building up the body temperature and, above all, urging him to get up, feed, be ready to make a break from the jackals now, now, *now*.

Micky was panting. He threw a companiable sort of grin at Screech. Something twisted once in Screech's left cheek. 'Right, then. Get us the bucket, will you?'

Micky returned to the back end of the mare. He gently grasped the white membrane between his hands, then, twisting and pulling, he eased the yards of warm cleanings out of her. Last came the 'spare tongue', a chunk of brown flesh which looked for all the world like a hearty helping of calf's liver. Micky dumped the skein of flesh in the bucket.

'Nice sort of foal.' Screech sympathetically wiped his dry hands on his kennel-coat.

'Yup, well-found young fellow. Throws to the sire, I reckon. No bad thing. Done, old girl. Reckon we can leave 'em to it. You'll take care of the antibiotics, the tetanus jabs?'

'Course.' Screech nodded.

Micky followed him through the sliding-door in the side wall of the box and down the narrow corridor to the waiting-up room.

It was a cosy little cell lit by one unshaded bulb which always, as though on a ship, seemed to swing a little from the centre of the ceiling. The walls were full to bursting. The cream-coloured paint strained like a body builder's shirt, here and there exposing patches of fleshy plaster.

Micky stood at the back, washing his hands in a shallow oblong sink. There was a wooden draining-board over there and an electric kettle. An overripe leather armchair and a couple of hardbacked chairs surrounded a television in the far corner and, hard against the wall to the right, a plain wooden table stood. There was a threadbare orange rug on the quarry-tiled floor. Kennel-coats and headcollars hung from the hooks on the left of the door. And that, aside from a calendar featuring a bright tan girl with lustreless black hair and tits like wineskins, was your lot.

Now Micky shook his hands and reached for the scrap of pale blue towel. Behind him, Screech said, 'Not bad,' and slumped into the armchair.

'No,' Micky agreed. 'Quite easy in the end. They'd not have made it without us though. Well, best be going up to the house and tell herself. She'll be pleased.'

Micky peered quickly through the little window off the corridor. The mare was up now and urgently licking her foal. They would be fine.

Micky used to play middle-of-the-back. It was as though he were back there now, heeling, shoving and scraping against the milling scrum of the wind. In the boxes at his right, mares grunted contentedly and rustled their bedding. It was light in the centre of the yard. The boxes and the office on the far side cast correspondingly deep shadows.

He was just two boxes from the end of the row when suddenly a bit of the darkness moved.

Micky stopped. He frowned. He said, 'Hello?' He strode with narrowed eyes across the yard. 'Hello? Who's there?'

He did not shout or anything. It could just be a stray dog or a cat turned into a monster by the shifting caul of cloud across the moon. Nothing moved. Micky stepped into the deeper darkness beneath the boxes. A sudden shudder wriggled through him. The downy hairs on the back of his neck slowly climbed, seeking the safety of the big battalions. 'Hello?' he called louder. There was someone there. '*Hello*?'

And suddenly there was an expulsion of breath, a rustle of fabric. The chunk of darkness moved again, not six feet to his left. Whoever it was must have been crouching, hoping not to be observed. Now he was breaking cover.

Yes. He. The rasp of boots on the cobbles, the lung capacity.

Micky's lunge was pure reflex. He jumped at the moving shadow.

His left hand hit cold leather, then wool. It grasped, it pulled. A broken fingernail snagged the wool. His right hand swung around and slapped into thin hair and warm skin. The leather-clad arm pushed back at him. It hit him in the chest. He careened two steps backwards, off-balance. For a split second, the man's hair was against Micky's mouth and the smell of his sweat was in Micky's nostrils. The hair was short and soft. Rodent's hair.

The man breathed, 'Shee . . .'

Something hot touched Micky's left hand. The hand knew something Micky did not. It recoiled like that of a Spaniard playing *staccato*.

The split nail snapped. The man grunted as he gave one more hard shove. The stable hit Micky's back. Hard.

93

This was the moment to shout, 'Hey, you!' above the slapping footfalls which pursued one another down the line of boxes.

Micky gave half-hearted chase. There was little point. With his game leg, he did not stand a chance. As the man took the corner at a run, a dark leg – grey terylene at a guess – and a flailing hand caught the light. The hand held a sliver of water that chucked back the moonlight.

Micky stopped. He was panting more than the running justified. His heart was trying to stage a break-out. He raised his hand to his forehead.

It left a cold sticky trail. He was bleeding.

Micky leaned forward, his hands on his thighs. He panted, 'I mean, what the hell is happening here?' He straightened and called, 'Screech?'

There was no reply. Micky sighed and wearily limped back to the waiting-up room, this time high-stepping, the wind at the small of his back. The little passageway was in darkness, so it was only when he stepped into the room, saw Screech in his armchair with his stubby legs set wide, a mug of tea steaming at his side, a disapproving look in his piggy eyes, it was only then that he could look down at his hand.

A bubble of air forced its way up from his stomach. It came out half laugh, half sob.

'What's up, then?' Screech frowned.

Micky unbuttoned his cuffs as he crossed the room. 'Some gouger out there, Christ's sakes.' He stripped off the shirt and turned on the tap. 'Some yob prowling around. Here. Must've had a blade. I tried to grab him. He did this.'

The water ran pink into the flat-bottomed sink. The wound was deep. It stretched from the junction of his forefinger and thumb back a hand's length along his forearm. Blood spilled from it as fast as he could wash it away.

Screech was at his shoulder now. He said, 'That could do with stitching.'

'Maybe,' Micky winced, 'You do it?'

'Better not. Hold up. I'll get you a dressing, some bandages.'

'Thanks. What the hell the guy'd want?' He stopped. He stared at the plain little mirror in front of him. 'Screech. Go and check the animals. Quick. All of them. Over that side first. Quick.'

Screech nodded. At the door, he picked up an old knobkerrie. He shouldered it and his head sank. He waddled off down the corridor. Micky wrapped the towel around the wound. He followed.

Screech was already on the other side of the yard when Micky emerged in the dim light. The wind wrapped itself like a whip around Micky's naked chest and back. He watched as Screech opened the stable-doors one by one, switched on the light, peered in, shook his head and moved on down.

At the fifth box down, the one just above the office, Screech made a curious little yelping sound and bustled in. He beckoned with his right hand.

'Oh, God, no . . .?' Micky made it sound like a question. He sort of hopped across the yard like a child mimicking a canter. The towel on his hand was already sodden.

'What is it?' he was saying as he swung around the open door. He saw his mare, Barbauld, wedged tight into the corner by the manger pressing her off-side hard against the wall. She snorted and shivered. Her eyes were wide. They showed a lot of cobwebbed white.

Screech was down on his hunkers at the middle of the box. His crimson cranium with its wispy sea-mist covering was shaking as though someone had switched him onto rinse-and-spin.

'What the fuck is it?' Micky stepped into the thick straw, and now he saw.

It was a very old montage. It would have made a choice Christmas card. Micky had read about it often enough, seen it in films and in TV dramas. Still it had power to shock, He knew now why Screech trembled with anger and why his mouth worked uselessly.

There. The peasant's protest. A candle, that was all; a candle wagging a long tail of smoke now that Screech had pinched out the flame.

A candle. On a windy night. In thick straw. In a row of boxes full of mares and foals.

'They put paraffin down,' Screech gasped at last. 'Who'd be after doing a thing like that? To a horse? Mother of Jesus. . . .'

'I don't know,' Micky shook his head. He walked over to stroke Barbauld's neck. The skin shuddered beneath his touch. 'Kids?'

'Kids?' Screech's sparse eyebrows jumped. '*Kids*? You know what you're saying? You see – this – and your first guess is, sort of thing children do. God in heaven save us.'

'Amen,' Micky sighed 'Amen.'

There are worse places to be knifed than a stud. There was antiseptic and bandages aplenty. Micky had even been able to give himself a tetanus jab by the time Screech returned.

Screech said, 'They're all all right, no thanks to them – the fuckers.' It was the first time that Micky had every really heard him swear. It plainly cost him.

Micky shrugged on his shirt. 'This ever happen before, Screech?'

'Nope.'

'Anything like it? People prowling around, I mean, burglaries, anything like that?'

'Videos and things to the tinkers, that's all.' Screech sank into his chair again. 'And who'd be doing a thing like this round these parts? People *like* horses. This place, we've been here how long? A hundred and fifty years? Minimum. People like this place. And you know how it is. Everyone knows everyone. Little Seamus Rourke goes joyriding down in Borris. Father Levy, the gardai, his mum all know about it before he's so much as pressed the starter.'

'Yeah.' Micky spoke distractedly. He was too busy shaking just now.

He had expected this. His body didn't like being hacked about. His mind did not exactly relish it, but his body had a mind of its own, when it came to breaks, shocks and large punctures. For a minute or two he just stood there, trying his best to squeeze the juice from the cement sink and willing his blood to flow rather than jerk through his veins. At last with a deep gulp and a muttered prayer, he straightened. 'OK, I'll be off, then. Just keep an eye open, will you, Screech? I'll not be long.'

'Don't you worry,' Screech said grimly. He waved the knobkerrie. 'I'll watch out. Little *bugger*.'

When Ed and Cathy Kramer bought Ballysheenan, they bought much of its contents. The circular walnut table and the big breakfront bookcase dated from the Brennan days, as did the oil-paintings of the stud's early champions. The pink sofa was new, as, of course, was Cathy's lift, but otherwise the house was much as it had been when, thirty-six years ago, Micky was brought squawking down to the hall as Ballysheenan's heir.

Now its stud manager, he trotted up the stairs and along the cream corridor to Cathy's room. He knocked softly on the door. Cathy groaned. He opened the door and stepped in. It was pitch dark.

'Cathy,' he whispered, 'you've got a fine Elegant Air.'

'Hmm?' she murmured contentedly. There was a moment's rustling, then the bedside light clicked on. She blinked at Micky in its rosy light. She looked very small in the big four-poster.

Cathy pulled herself up. Micky leaned over to pile pillows behind her head. She smelled of talc and antiseptic.

'Sit down,' she patted the bed beside her. She looked down at the gauntlet of bandages. 'What've you been doing to yourself?'

'Tell you about that in a second, Cath.' Micky smiled. 'First things first. Millamant's just had a colt. Good foal.'

'Oh, that's just wonderful.' She rubbed her dry hands. 'He'll pay a few bills, with a bit of luck.'

'He should indeed. Just wait'll you see him.'

'Any problems?'

'Not really. Needed a bit of help, that's all.'

'Why in God's name are we whispering?'

'Dunno. Won't we wake Jenny?'

'Nothing'll wake that girl. Takes a bomb to get her up.' But still she spoke softly, no louder than the creaking of the bedsprings as she moved. 'That's great news, Micky. Your fourth colt, isn't it? Maybe, just maybe, you're going to bring me luck. So. Now. What's the mummification?'

'Strange,' he shrugged. 'Bloody ridiculous in fact. Someone out there jumped me.'

'What?' Cathy started. She made a lot of the 'h'. The eyes which she raised to him now were wide and set and full of concern.

'Yup. In the yard. Some guy hanging around in the shadows. He'd been trying to fire the place. I just happened along, went for him. He must've had a blade, so.'

'Jesus, Micky,' she laid a warm dry hand on his. It suddenly gripped tight. Her face was very pale. 'This is . . . I mean, a knife. Oh, Christ, it can't be. They wouldn't really . . . Oh, God, Micky, this is serious.'

'You're telling me. Could as well have been my gut.' He frowned. 'Hold up, Cath. You said 'they'. You know something? Why someone'd want to do this sort of thing?'

'No!' she said slowly, then, 'I don't know.' Her shoulders sank. Her voice was very small. 'I hope to God I don't. I didn't think they would. Oh, God, Micky,' she shuddered. 'We're going to have to talk about this. I think we're in trouble.'

'Ah, he's all right, Mick,' Kevin Nolan leaned luxuriously back in the Skoda's passenger-seat. He rested his head on his hands, his knee on the dashboard. 'Got a bit snotty once, when he went off to his first posh school in England. Children's party, we flung him in the river, held him down for a while, let the excess bubble out. Jays, but he had a temper on him. You know Terry Roche, has the hardware shop and the Dolomite teeth? You know he's missing the front

97

one here? That was Mick, and Terry's got to be two, three years older.'

Kevin's fingers played a quick scale on his faded jeans. He was young and slight and quick in his movements. He wore a crisp white shirt and a brown leather jacket with the collar turned up.

Mark Morris, the driver, was older and heavier with grey-blond curls and a bulbous nose. His face was an overfilled oblong, a flour sack. He said, 'Yup?' and the Carrolls' on his lower lip wagged, then, 'What's the matter with this feller?'

'Give him a flash,' said Kevin cheerfully. 'You want a bit of siren?'

'You ever grow up, DC Nolan? Nah. He's alright. A trifle fluthered, I make no doubt, but a good boy. Thank you, sir.' He waved. He put his foot down. The car went 'ahem' and tried a new, higher baritone note. The high hedgerows blurred in the swinging headlight beams.

'No, he was very thick, our Micky, would you believe, with Fergal Doherty. You credit that? Micky – Fergal, terror of the valley, they were.'

'So what happened, he ends up in prison?' Mark Morris sounded bored. 'I mean, Mick Brennan of Ballysheenan, who goes to fancy English schools . . .'

'Yeah. But his da blew it, didn't he? Girls and yachts and all that. Last of the Ascendancy playboys. Blew the lot. And the stallion died. What was his name?'

'I dunno.'

'Oh, you know. Famous old sod. What was his name? Ah, you know it as well as I. Anyhow, my God, I remember that. You'd've thought maybe a king, Kennedy something had snuffed it. Not insured or anything, of course. Micky had to leave his schooling, took a job as a stable-lad, then suddenly, you know, you were seeing him in the papers every day. Big jump-jockey. Did all right, then some horse sits on him, smashes him up, becomes a trainer. Whole of the poor sod's life, really, you could say, just false start after false start. Starts out looking grand, then . . . He's not a lucky man, is Mick.'

'No such thing as luck,' said Mark Morris dourly. He turned the car in through Ballysheenan's gateposts. 'You make your own is what.'

'OK,' Kevin Nolan walked back into the hall. He puffed on his cupped hands and kicked backward at the doormat. 'Well, I reckon that's pretty much it for now.'

Behind him, Micky showed Mark Morris in and quietly shut the front door. It was still dark out there. 'Yup,' he said, 'S'pose so. Come on. Drink.'

He led the way into the drawing-room where Cathy and Jenny already sat in their dressing-gowns.

'Micky,' Jenny crossed the room in three strides. She touched his forearm. She was naked but for the long, flaring grey silk gown. Her chest was freckled. 'Are you OK?'

'Yeah, sure. Don't worry.' He smiled. He covered her hand with his. 'I'll be fine.'

She nodded and looked away. She did not remove her hand. 'It's absurd,' she said softly, 'crazy. *Here.*'

'There's no escape,' Micky sighed, 'not even here. Would you do the honours, love? Whiskey all round?'

Micky was weary now. He gave Jenny's hand a quick squeeze and sank into a deep armchair. A blink took him a long time. 'Yup, it's all beyond me.' He shook himself. 'So, how's Sonja, Kev?'

'Ah, fine. Blithe and bonny and good and gay. Needed the baby. Her English is a whole lot better.' Already Kevin strode back and forth over the washed turquoise silk rug. When he perched briefly on the sofa, it was as though he were on his marks. He was up again a second later to take his drink from Jenny.

He gazed up at the picture above the fireplace. 'Stringy looking beast.' He spoke blithe blasphemy of Judgement of Paris, Ballysheenan's foundation sire. He adopted a *paterfamilias* stance on the hearth.

He could not maintain it. Within five words he was prowling again. 'So let's run through what you've got here, see what options you might have. I've taken Micky's statement, and old Screech's. Now, Mrs Kramer, you had your first approach from these people, when?'

'November fifteen.'

Micky frowned. He said 'Hey . . .'

Cathy looked very fixedly at Kevin, or rather, very deliberately away from Micky. She swivelled the solitary ice-cube on her finger. 'I just didn't take it seriously. Everything's so darned quiet here, it was just so unreal. Seemed – fantastic.'

Jenny's dressing gown hushed as she leaned forward, a charcoal and silverpoint curve in the lamplight. 'So, who was it?'

'Dunno. I've seen him around but I can't remember where. Called himself Murphy, but then he would, wouldn't he? Grey-haired chap. Big gut, but not fat. Once an athlete or a soldier, I'd say. Smoked a pipe. Late fifties, I'd guess. Maybe more, maybe less. Difficult to tell.

All creased and leathery. Tweed cap, tweed jacket, looked like they'd grown on him like fungus on bread. Well-educated, I guess. Irish, but sort of lilting like the Welsh.'

'Cork,' said Kevin briskly. 'I suspect I know your man.'

'So. Hello, old friend.' Micky spoke as though tasting something purulent. 'Welcome home, Micky. Our favourite son. Roll out the fatted calf.'

'Come on, Micky,' Cathy growled.

'No, so you see me at the Sales, you think, hell, I'm a little old lady lives all alone and I don't want to pay these people so I'll get in the prison-educated cannon-fodder to fight my battles for me, right?'

'No!' Cathy yelped. 'I told you. I didn't take it seriously. I genuinely wanted you here. Like I said, you belong here, you're good with the horses, and OK, sure it crossed my mind. You're Irish and you don't give in to bullying. People know you. Sure. OK. I thought maybe they'd let up on us if you were around. That's all.'

'But you didn't think to tell me, did you? I could've been gralloched out there, tonight, damn it.'

'Yeah, well. I'm sorry. Like I said, I didn't take it that seriously.'

'You better start right now,' Micky growled. 'This is fucking serious. Me, I reckon you should pay up. Grin, not very broadly and bear it. You, Jen?'

'What's Jen got to do with it?' Cathy was tight as a tennis-ball.

'A great deal, I'd have thought,' Micky kept his eyes on Jenny. 'It's her neck. She'd get brewed up as much you if they chose to fire this house. And presumably she's heiress to this little lot.'

Jenny turned, startled, to Cathy, 'I am?'

'She may be,' Cathy was grudging.

'Oh. Well.' Jenny studied the backs of her outstretched hands, then, 'I reckon, sure. Why not? Pay, I mean. It's cheaper than tax any place else. Sure. Why not?'

'Because these guys are thieves and murderers and shitheads is why not.'

Jenny tutted and rolled her eyes heavenward, 'Ah, come on,' she sighed, 'and the CIA aren't?'

'I'm afraid, I agree.' Mark Morris droned. 'Sticks in the craw, but . . . Thing is, it really is very little, considering what Sansovino can earn. I mean, say he's fully booked, that's what? £360,000 or £450,000 Irish, tax-free, right. Well, nine grand's just a drop in the ocean, isn't it? You ask the other shareholders. Two-twenty quid apiece or something, safeguard a thirty-six grand investment? They'd jump at it.'

'They might,' Cathy drawled, 'but I'm damned if I see why I should tell 'em.'

'I'm not at all sure that's sound business ethics, Cathy,' said Jenny.

'I'm damned sure it's not,' muttered Micky. 'You may have the running of Sansovino, but you only hold what? Five out of the forty shares. That's er . . .'

'Twelve and a half percent,' Jenny supplied.

'Right. Hardly a controlling interest, hmm? So they've got as much right as you to make decisions about their property.'

'Uh uh,' Cathy was emphatic. 'I look on this as a management problem. I manage the investment, so.'

'They'd have more than little reason to object if they lost their capital investment thanks to your idiosyncratic style of management, Cathy,' Micky mused. 'They could sue.'

'Forget "could",' Jenny combed her hair back with her fingers. 'They're mostly Americans. They would.'

'So? Let them sue. I do not think they can do me for refusing to do something illegal. No part of the deal says I should pay extortionists and terrorists. No one can make me do that.'

'You're American,' snapped Micky. 'You're accustomed to making imperialistic decisions, convinced of your own rightness. No room for doubt with the Romans. We have had to learn to compromise. All very admirable, this high certainty, this moralism. We can't afford it.'

'He's right,' nodded Kevin Nolan. 'Nobody likes these fuckers, but there's no Sunday newspaper, no law to protect you here if you offend these bastards. You may wish they didn't exist, but your uncle or great-grandfather got killed back then in the troubles, and you don't want to be thought of as a renegade, so you'll supply the safe house, the word of approval, the odd bob or two. It's what we do. Get by.'

'Yeah, well.' Cathy cuddled herself. 'It's not what I do. They're murdering finks and they'll not get a cent out of me, and that's final.'

Micky exchanged a quick despairing glance with Kevin. He slapped his thighs and stood with a sigh. 'Right, that's unequivocal enough. So, what are the options? First, obviously, you could take Sanso back to Kentucky.'

'Why in hell should I? I'll not be pushed around and that's final too. Someone gimme a drink.' She took a deep breath. 'Anyhow, he's booked solid this season. I can't tell his mares so sorry, go and find another stallion this time of year. I'll be sued from here to doomsday.'

'OK, OK,' Micky soothed. He leaned forward and rested his hands on the arms of her wheelchair. His eyes scanned hers. She looked down at her lap. 'But you just have to understand, Cathy. This is not a big gesture of nobility at a carnival. This is not vote-catching rhetoric. This is the blood and guts of the rhetoric. I know it sounds absurd, all of us sitting here chatting about it over our whiskey, but this is no game. OK. They're not the big nasty professionals up North, but all the same, they can't afford to lose face. One word in the right quarter, and the most expert terrorist force in the world comes down on you and Jenny and me, right here in li'l old County Carlow. It happened to Shergar. It can happen to us. Do you understand?'

'All right. Don't lecture me.'

'You don't know nothing, Cathy. Someone has to lecture you. Just say you choose to stay, keep Sanso here. Jesus, woman, you're going to be under siege. How are you planning to stop 'em? They'll just bide their time, come in when they see their chance. They'll need their pound of flesh. Could be Sanso. Could be this time they'll change their style. Maybe they destroy the yard. Never know, get the right sort of gouger, little Cork boy with delusions of grandeur and a drink or two too many inside him, we get in the way, it could even be one of us. Wasn't that far off, tonight.'

'Dear God,' Jenny shivered.

'Yeah, well,' Micky straightened. 'I'm not sticking around to find out.' He shook his head sadly. 'I'm sorry, Cath, but you should have told me. You should have told all of us. I'll put some – I'll make a few overtures, because I'm not so fucking high and mighty as to assume that our enemy is less than human. But if I'm told sorry, no way, then you pay up and move out or I'm gone. You are not paying enough for bloody mercenaries. Sorry.'

He nodded three times and walked to the door. He said, 'No point in my hanging around, really, is there? Thing is, Cathy. I may not be exactly in demand, but I don't reckon that entitles you to press-gang me into your own private army. You know damn well that any right-minded man would walk out on you, a thing like this. Well, so can I, believe it or not.' He said, 'I'm sorry,' again, then cocked up his exit by trying to pull the door closed with his bandaged hand.

He walked across the hall and opened the front door. Somehow he found his left temple resting against the open door. He gazed dully out at the handkerchief tree at the centre of the lawn. Dawn was coming. The spattered snow phosphoresced palely. Something throbbed above his ears. 'God,' he said. Home had come back him.

Fergal Doherty lived in what most people would call abject squalor. Micky never liked to vote with the mass, but on this one issue he just had to agree. The cottage telegraphed its existence at long range. The smell was bad as Micky walked up the garden path. The smell as Margaret opened the door was downright revolting; a sweet, rich, rotten smell compounded of seedcake, sweat, drying pelts, stale sherry, linseed oil and offal, amongst other things, most of them dead.

Margaret was bent forward. Her hand clung to the giant dog's broad collar. Her dry lips twitched as she saw Micky. 'Oh,' she droned above a chorus of yapping from the rear of the house, 'it's you. Better come in. He's out at the back.'

She tutted and sneered, released the dog and turned away. Micky stepped in. The dog sniffed his hand and seemed to reckon that he had just about earned a fool's pardon. It slumped with a grunt into the rush mat. In the far corner, a leggy black-and-tan hunt terrier lay on a bed of newspapers. Her puppies palpated her tits with their tiny forepaws. Her head was cross-hatched with scars. A Peter Rabbit porringer of rabbit kidneys stood at her head.

Margaret had sloped back to the stove. She was very beautiful, with a long white face and thick dark eyebrows and eyes brown and deep as trout-pools. Only trouble was, no trout swam there. There was no flash of light, no responsive glimmer. Her lips were twisted in a permanent bored sneer. Her skin was lustreless as blotting-paper. Her long black hair hung lank as some coagulated juice from her skull.

When they were sixteen, Margaret and Micky had mingled sweat, breath and spittle in Maggie's Mill, an arcaded ruin down in the valley. She had concentrated hard on what she was doing, pounding with her pubis like a pestle, frowning, eyes closed, sounding as though she was twenty miles into the marathon. It had been fun – God, and was not any life-form higher than a watermelon fun when you were sixteen – and Margaret, if pale and skinny, had been a real-live hippy madonna with freckles on her shoulders and tiny, jiggling, long-nippled breasts and a flat stomach and a scary big black bush which looked like an aerial view of a running horse's tail, but even back then, Micky had thought afterwards, it had been better with Sue. Sue was the English girl he was in love with at the time. He had never got further with her than breathless straining and dark fumbling. It had been better all the same.

Margaret fucked like she had just heard the five-minute warning and you just happened to be there.

Micky had been one of many. With something akin to vindictiveness, Margaret had fornicated with every young buck in Leinster. The more

103

people expressed disapproval or the bucks expressed jealousy, the more resolutely and angrily she fornicated. She despised men and then, needing justification went on to despise her parents, the church, the government. Micky, of course, was despicable because he had once lived in a big house and now lived in England. He was 'privileged' and a renegade. Predictably, if paradoxically, she had picked up a dose of left-wingery and nationalism in the course of her travels.

Still, Micky did not like to have enemies, so he gave conversation a try. 'All well?'

'S'pose so,' she hummed. 'No feckin' money, thanks a lot, but then what'd you expect? S'pose you're rolling in the stuff?'

'Not a brass cent, matter of fact.'

'Huh.'

'No, it's true, Margaret. Thought you'd've heard. Spent eight months in gaol. Not a penny piece to my name. I'm back as a working man. Looking after the stud for a pittance.'

'Huh.'

'You working?'

'What's it look like?' She had picked up a tall plastic carton. She jerked out salt. 'What d'ye call this? Bloody lady of leisure, is it?'

'No, I mean have you got a job?'

'Ha!' Her head rocked backward. 'And where'd I find a thing like that these God-forsaken parts, I'd like to know? Huh.'

The dialogue was scarcely sparkling, but he had given it his best shot. 'I'll be off and see himself, then,' he told her.

She said, 'Himself. Huh.'

Micky stepped over the nursing bitch and her squeaking pups and struggled down the narrow passageway towards the back garden. In the bedroom to his left, a framed roll of honour stood in pride of place next to a tube of spermicidal jelly on the dressing-table. *Bloody Sunday*, it was headed in Gaelic script, *30 January 1972*.

He trampled over an obstacle-course of buckets, purse-nets, newspapers and wellington boots. He pushed at the door. It jammed on something or other. He pushed harder and almost fell out into the garden.

Garden. Call it rather a soggy yeard. Up on the right, on a little fenced knoll, a Toggenburg goat stood with her two kids. Then there were stacks of tea-chests turned on their sides. The lower ones were full of yapping terriers. Ferrets prowled behind chicken-netting above.

The ferrets prowled and their red eyes shifted because their natural prey was just yards away. A beautiful game cock strutted at Micky's feet.

There were white punk Silkies and slick Buff Orpingtons and a huge cock pheasant which seemed bejewelled. At Micky's left, thirty or more finches twittered and fluttered in a jerry-built aviary. An old brindle collie-cross lurcher lay contentedly twitching on the cement path.

'Hello!' Micky called. 'Are you there, Fergal Doherty?'

'I am,' the shed in front of him rumbled. The door opened. Fergal's body emerged stooping. Fergal would have stooped from habit as he emerged from the Acropolis. 'Ah, Micky Brennan,' his beard spread in a broad grin, 'is it you?'

'It is indeed.'

'Well, now, we've not seen much of you. How're you doing?'

'Ah, fine, thanks, Fergal. How's the teaching business?'

'Much the same, much the same. Children are getting stupider by the day. No church, no sit-down meals, just television and videos, you know? Never thought I'd be talking like this. Me, Fergal Doherty, getting all wistful for the mass and all that. Well. Never be a teacher or a farmer doesn't complain.'

'You should try English brats. Anyhow. Listen. What are you about? At the moment, I mean. I'd like a word.'

'Ah, just mixing up some food for the ferrets. I was after taking the young hob out. There's a bank up Michael Doyle's is crawling with rabbits. You care to come along with us?'

'Not this evening, thanks. Another day, sure. I'd enjoy that. Oh, and any time you fancy some lamping up at Ballysheenan, just give us a call.'

'For permission, was it?' Fergal smiled wickedly.

'No. I'd just like to come with you. So. You got the time for a quick jar, then?'

Fergal glanced at his watch. 'Ah, why not? O'Brien's?'

Micky grinned happily. 'O'Brien's.'

O'Brien's was first and foremost a bar. In a few hours' time, it would be filled with men, women and children, all drinking their stout or hot whiskey and telling tales with one eye on *Glenroe* or *Coronation Street*. But you could buy more than drink there. O'Brien's was also a village store and ironmongery. Saws and wellington boots, colanders and kettles hung from the ceiling above the drinkers. The shelves were crammed with corned beef tins and yellow boxes of Sunlight soap. If, at half-past ten of an evening, you felt the urgent need of a four-inch nail or a jar of jam, why, and wouldn't you just potter down the hill to O'Brien's?

At the moment, however, the bar was nigh empty. In the far corner, beneath the videos and the fishing-tackle, two old men sat morosely playing dominoes. At another table, beneath the picture of Arkle and the toothpaste, O'Brien's daughter Brigit, laboured at her homework. A little pale plain redhead with freckles and glasses held together with Elastoplast, she looked up at Fergal, put her tongue-tip away and gave him a nervous half-smile.

'All right, Brigit?' Fergal laid a hand on her shoulder and gave it a quick squeeze. She nodded and squirmed a bit more.

O'Brien pulled stout. Micky deliberately led Fergal to the table furthest from the bar. 'Now,' Fergal said, 'what's up, then?'

Micky said softly. 'I need a word about the-thing-we-don't-talk-about.'

'Oh, shit, Micky,' Fergal punched the foam of the Guinness from his moustaches. 'You know I can't tell you anything. I don't know anything.'

'Sure, sure,' Micky raised his bandaged hand to halt him. 'I know that. It's just, we've had a bit of trouble up at the stud, and I'd like to know where we stand. Thing is, someone's leaning on Cathy, and she's old and ill and . . .'

'Rich?' suggested Fergal.

'No, she isn't, but she's a stubborn old bird and she's stuffed full of high principles. Thing is, I'd heard about this, but I didn't know for sure. Some foreign owners . . .'

'It's been the way for years, Micky.' Fergal sighed. 'The *taioseach* in his infinite wisdom has made all revenue from stallions tax-free, so it's bloody cheap for foreign owners to come here. Their stallions cover – what is it? – forty, fifty mares a season? So it's still good value even if they do have to pay one nomination – one fiftieth of their revenue – to the Irish people. Two percent, for God's sakes. They can't complain.'

'Cathy does. And what if she doesn't choose to pay up?'

'Then she's a darned fool,' Fergal shrugged. 'Jesus God, man, it's not as though they were demanding a tenth of what the taxman would take.'

'That's not the point, Fergal. I know that and you know that, but it's where the money's going gets her goat. What are we talking about here? You say 'the Irish People'. Do you mean that, or do you mean organised crime? Or the people we don't mention?'

'Ah, now. Here we get into the realms of philosophy, old friend. Do the interests of the people we don't mention coincide with the interests of the Irish people? I don't know. I think so, but . . . And then, who's to distinguish organised crime, as you call it, from freedom-fighting? You've got to get funds from somewhere. You know as well as I do that all those Catholics work up North for the building firms, not all of them got their jobs on merit. Bit of leaning had to be done. Is that so wrong?'

'No, no, sure . . .'

'And then you pay taxes. Do you check what the government is doing with every penny? How much is going to slaughter women and children in Nicaragua, how much to polluting the environment, how much to . . . I don't know, murdering suspects up North?'

'No, OK,' Micky nodded, conciliatory. 'OK, but Cathy can choose. She says, if the money's going to murderers and bombers and so on, she's not paying it, and I think she means it. She's got a terminal disease, so she's not exactly desperate to cling to life at any cost. Same time, none of us wants to see Sansovino end up like Shergar.'

'That's right.'

'So. Compromise. Any suggestions?'

Fergal shrugged expansively. 'What the hell? I don't know. How about she stipulates that the cash doesn't go to the military wings? They'd accept that. Boyos in Long Kesh've got families. They need help. She can't object to that.'

'I've already suggested that. She said balls. Money spent on flour is money saved on bullets, she says. She's right too.'

'Sure, she's right.' Fergal glanced over his shoulder. 'I just don't see what other compromise there can be though, Micky. You'll just have to try to persuade the old girl. They could do damage otherwise.'

'You can't . . . you couldn't sort of arrange some sort of meeting, could you? See if I can work something out?'

'Hell, Micky, who d'ye think I am?' Fergal slammed his glass down. 'OK, so I used to give a helping hand, I know a few people perhaps, I'm a sympathiser, sure, but that's just about it. I'm not in there. I don't know who's in charge, who's running the show. These things are organised tight.'

Micky sat disconsolate, frowning sadly at the biscuit-coloured spume in his glass.

Fergal watched him for a moment, then shook his head and sighed deeply. 'All right. Listen.' He rocked from ham to ham. 'I can trust you, so . . . I can make some discreet enquiries, but I really don't think anything can be done, Mick. Just have to bite the bullet and pay up. It's not so much, for Christ's sakes.'

Micky said, 'Thanks, mate. Point is, how do I even know this is – them? Could be just opportunist yobs looking for a bit of cash. Guy I know, barman in London, used to be a guard up in Sligo. He says, he was off-duty, in a post office, and this guy in front of him says to the girl 'OK, this is a gun. Give me all your cash.' So Terry, this guy, he looks at the so-called gun in the jerk's pocket, and the kid's so darned dumb he can't work out if his finger's meant to be the gun-barrel or a trigger-finger. This so-called gun-barrel keeps bending. So Terry comes forward and says, 'OK, Garda, congeal,' or words to that effect. And the kid hisses, 'Don't you know who I am?' Terry goes, 'No. Why?' And he says, sort of out of the corner of his mouth, 'Oy orr ey.' Terry says 'Stuff that for a pastime;' kicks him in the balls and brings him in. Oy orr ey, my arse. The kid's a hard-up student thought every little yob got off scot free provided he said Abacadabra or oy orr ey.'

'It happens. I've heard.'

'So how do I know these are not just that type, like, "I'm a tough guy so I'm Cosa Nostra or SAS".'

'Uh, uh, Micky.' Fergal reached across to take Micky's hand. 'Come on. Don't worry too much. We'll sort it out somehow. But you can take it from me. This is, as you say, them. Look, I'll see what I can do, OK?'

Micky nodded. His smile made deep dimples. He squeezed Fergal's hand. 'OK,' he said. It came out very husky.

Fergal cuffed Micky lightly on the side of his head. He said softly, 'Be seeing you, you old madman.'

There was a whole lot of rolling stock in Micky's gut, shunting at high-speed and whistling as it went. He needed the loo.

When he looked up, it was to see Fergal ambling across the bar towards the street. He waved cheerfully to O'Brien. He stopped for a quick word with Brigit. He stepped courteously back to allow a young couple through the doorway.

Yes, Micky thought, he could take it from Fergal.

Who never once asked about the bandaged hand.

Jenny swung the wheel to the rhythm of the *Thieving Magpie* overture. 'Hold tight,' she told Micky just as his bum left the seat. 'Yeeha!' she whooped, country-style. 'See in the *Independent*? What's the difference between an Irish road and a cigarette? More tar in a cigarette.'

Jenny wore black velvet knee-breeches and buckle shoes and an ivory silk shirt. Her red Loden was thrown over the back of the seat. She said, 'You really did get to her, you know. Punctured her completely. OK, you're right, but I had to feel sorry for her. You can see her point of view.'

Micky wore a grey flannel chalk-striped suit and a blue and white Kingsman. He said. 'I know. Don't rub it in. You like Chick Corea?'

'Dunno. Something cheerful. Road music. Whatever.'

'Wilburys?'

'Sure.'

Micky pressed the eject button, extracted Rossini and pushed in the new tape. He sat back and waited for it to rewind. The hills rolled past like a grey rug unfurling. A grey-faced Simmenthal leaned over a hedge, insultingly disdainful. In a lay-by, children and brindle dogs scavenged around a tinker's caravan filled with glass and bright plastic flowers. Tinkers' clothes hung drying on the roadside hedge.

Micky said, 'Sure, it's hard to justify, abandoning a poor, sick little old lady in a wheelchair, running away from extortionist bastards, but dammit, I mean it's her decision. No one but me has the right to be heroic with my life, certainly not without consulting me. OK, so you don't yield to terrorists. Sure, I know that, it makes more terrorists. I approve of that in principle but – God, there are members of the English Jockey Club, there are American billionaires paying their Danegeld. So Cathy wants to make a stand. Good for her. She's not too worried about dying. She's crippled already. So what if they kneecap her? But it's not her who's in the frontline, for God's sake. It's you, me, Screech, Michael. Don't know about you, but I like my knees. I like your knees.'

'You haven't seen my knees.'

'Haven't I? Yes, I have. At New Year, you were wearing that black lampshade which just about covered your sternum. They're nice knees. Screech's knees I don't care about much but he's probably quite attached to them.'

She giggled. At that moment the accoustic guitars started up and Jenny started to sing quietly along.

'So, what are you going to do?' asked Micky.

'Dunno.' Her fingers kept time on the wheel. 'I'm a little bit like you. Flotsam and jetsam. Don't want to go back to anything. Wouldn't think they'd pick on me. Still, you go, I suppose I go.'

And in a sweet soprano she tracked Orbison's pedal-steel tenor.

Micky grinned. He played bongos on his thighs.

'I worked on a Heartbreakers album once,' Jenny said.

'Yeah? So why'd you go if I go?'

''Cos it'd be boring. OK, she's got no chance, but if you go she has absolutely no chance. I wouldn't want her hanging on because she thinks I support her.'

'Ah, well – left here – I don't suppose it'll come to that. Hope not. I'm hoping we can work out some sort of compromise. I mean, it's such a tiny sum of money.'

'You got it?'

'Nope. You?'

'Uh uh.'

'Yeah, well, "tiny" is relative.'

'Must be a dirty joke there.'

'Don't bother.'

She sang along a bit more. 'You know, perhaps I think you were a little unfair.'

'Unfair? to Cathy?'

'To Cathy. To yourself. I was talking to her yesterday. She really did want you because you know the business, you know. Not just 'cos you had nowhere to go or she thought you'd had a crash-course in street-fighting inside. I mean, she's talked about you before. She rates you. And she likes to have her boys around. You, Charlie; surrogate sons, I guess. And you trained Sansovino. I mean, sure, she should've told you about this business, but she'd have offered you the job either way.'

'You reckon.' The way Micky said it, it did not sound like a question.

'I know. She's lonely, Cathy. She likes to have her old friends about, and she respects your judgement. I was asking about you as a jockey. Hear you were pretty good.'

'I was average. Maybe, because of hunting and showing, all that, as a child, I was a bit more horseman than some jockeys. I don't know.'

'And now you can't ride at all?'

'Not if I don't want to end up on the lengthy roll of honour of dead fools, no. One bad knock on the head and I've had it, they say.'

'So – you mind talking about it?'

'Nope.' Micky shrugged.

'So, what happened?'

'What happened? Oh, it was Stratford, just before the festival at Cheltenham. I had a good chance in the Gold Cup too. Postman Pat. Anyhow, nothing very dramatic. An outside ride from a Northern trainer. Chestnut bitch. I'd never schooled her, never so much as been on her back before. Stratford was a bog, and as soon as I was mounted I knew I had trouble on my hands. First the bitch decided that she hated me and tried just about everything to get rid of me, then, on the way to

110

the start, she decided she loved me and wanted to get me away from all this. By the time we got there, we were both in a muck-sweat. So I soothe her a bit, lay into her a bit, but she's got other things on her mind, like she'd like to be covered by a cart-horse in Yorkshire and she doesn't want me around.

'One of the many subsections of sod's law. D'you know most skiers break their legs while standing still? 'S true. My mum, on the first day of the holiday in Verbier, she's trying on some new Kästels in her hotel-room – seriously – when somehow she goes over on one side, breaks her leg in three places and that's the end of her skiing career.

'It's the same race-riding. You always think death should wait for you beneath Becher's or something, but more often than not he's lurking in the wings of a plain fence at Devon and Exeter, Sedgefield, some pisspotical contest you haven't even got a chance of winning.

'What happened – you can see it on the video. Some weird people find it quite entertaining, matter of fact. This cow is tap-dancing, and occasionally whipping around because she's seen a particularly frightening leaf or another horse or a bird in the sky and she's feeling companionable. I've got her tucked in as far back as possible. Starter's hand moves to the lever. The other lads move forward. She rears.

'Now the thing about rearers – with a colt it's OK. He's not going to expose his belly and his *raison d'être* to the jackals. He knows, lose your footing, you're dead. With a filly, it's subtly, nastily different. The tapes go up. I can feel it coming. I'm reaching up her neck, trying to kick the irons away, but I never had a chance. It's not a rear. It's a backflip.

'So suddenly there's air beneath me where there ought to be horseflesh and horseflesh above me where there ought to be air. I'm falling backward, and she, companionable as ever, is falling with me. I remember I had a mouthful of mane and I remember screaming and then there's a lot of forked lightning, a lot of roaring in my skull, and that's your lot.'

'Eugh,' Jenny grimaced. 'What was the damage?'

'Enough. They mended the pelvis, patched up the spleen, but I lost one lung and one leg'll always be shorter than the other.'

'Ow.'

'Yup, it was rather, but I'd read the book, you know? I was going to confound the doctors. Headlines – *Brave Jockey Back in Saddle, Only His Determination Pulled Him from His Hospital Bed to Aintree Triumph*. That sort of thing. Then they put the cap on it. Did I happen to know as I'd broken my neck some time back? No, actually, I didn't. And if I fell again I'd be begging for a ride on the bottom weight in the Grand Celestial?

111

Thanks a million, Miracle Recovery Programme indefinitely postponed. Sub-editors scramble to re-set headlines. *Jockey Dies of Broken Heart. 'He Just lost the Will to Live,' says associate.*

'And that's when your wife rolled up.'

'Yeah,' Micky stared wearily ahead into the closing dusk. 'Look. Fox.'

'Where?'

'Missed it. Big dog. Yeah. That's when Nathalie rolled up.'

'What happened?' asked Jenny.

'Allowing it to really hurt. Refusing to get better, sulking you know? Along comes Nathalie makes it all all right. She was sweet. She worked for a bloodstock agency. Her father, old Sir Humphrey, a cardiologist, hunted with the Heythrop, owned a couple of 'chasers. I'd taken her out once or twice. Very proper. Discussed horses and Walt Disney. But she was the sort – sorry, but there are "sorts" in this regard – she was the sort you have a long relationship with, probably marry. The sort you need time for. I'd always been interested in the other sort. Now I had all the time in the world.'

'So she visited you in hospital?' Jenny nodded, 'I can see it. How'd she treat your other visitors?'

Micky turned to her, head cocked. He said. 'You're one bright woman. You know that?'

'I've been told.' She was po-faced. She changed gear and turned quickly to flash him a smile.

'Yeah, she visited me. Just happened to be passing first time, and I growled at her but said if she happened to be passing again. So she started to turn up with magazines and messages from the racecourse and quail's eggs and books about the South Seas. The books got rarer, more expensive. And she just slowly started to appropriate me. I didn't even notice it. First, I was too tired to complain. You know, Peter Straker would drop in, say. Nathalie'd say "Yes, well, thank you so much for coming. I think Micky's getting a bit tired now." Next thing I knew she was talking to my bank-manager. I had sixty grand or so. He'd advance another fifty. Then she talked to some of the people I'd ridden for. Sure, poor old chap, we'd send him a horse or two if he set up as a trainer. She didn't talk to me much. She'd kiss me on the cheek when she arrived, then she'd kiss me on the lips when she arrived, then she's hold my hand throughout the visit, then one day – I wasn't kissing anyone else at the time – I pulled her down on the bed and did the job properly. Christ it was agony. So then she goes and talks to her father. Marriage has just sort of worked its way into the plans. Not a bad idea, it seemed at the time. Easy. And old Sir Humphrey says he'll give us another hundred and fifty as a wedding present, and there we are. Horses, the yard, the lot.'

'Were you successful?'

'Yup,' he sounded surprised. 'At first. I was still in a wheelchair when we got wed. And – I don't know why, perhaps it's my bloody-mindedness – I got this reputation as racing's refuge of sinners. I'd get sent rogues, ungenuine pigs, and they'd go for me. Sanso was one of those. In a silly, adolescent way I'd always resented Cathy and Ed. You know, they were living in *my* home. They'd usurped me. But one day Cathy arrives with this, bred in the purple, but liked to run backward faster than forward when he came to the course. I stripped him down like a car, let him down, rebuilt him, gave away his whole three-year-old season, just persuading him that people were OK and that running is fun, you know? And is his fourth year under heaven he takes the lot. Brilliant. Used to amuse me. I was on bail "in the sum of £5,000" when Sanso retired to Kentucky, syndicated in the sum of $720,000.'

'Hm.' The fish-hook kinks deepened at the corners of Jenny's lips. 'Interesting really. You and Cathy both refuges of sinners. Me too. I was famous for it. Pick out a no-hoper from a crowd of thousands, me, and they'd see me coming a mile off, make a bee-line for me. So how come we're all rogues as far as the world's concerned?'

'Yeah', Micky said, 'And who's looking after who?'

Fergal had been sitting in his old Escort outside the Old Coach Inn for just three minutes when the passenger door opened. Outside sucked up the warm air and swallowed it. There was the rasp and the rustle of waxed cotton. The man grunted as he sat. The door clunked shut.

'Right.' The man was just a big black shape masking the blue light from the inn. His seething jacket aped his breathing. His tongue crackled in saliva, then he said, 'OK, so what's with you?'

'Mick Brennan,' Fergal said softly. He pushed his fingers back through his curls. His hands dropped back to slap the steering-wheel. 'He's OK. He's a friend of mine. He's at Ballysheenan now, running the show.'

The man said nothing, just swivelled his head to peer through the rear windscreen at the steady smoky rain.

Fergal said, 'Do we really need to bother them? I mean, one little old lady . . .'

113

'Living tax-free,' the man sighed. 'Sorry. Every human life is a sob-story to someone. Come one, come all.'

'Yeah. Well, . . . he's asked for time. He reckons he can persuade the old woman. She's just a little bit stubborn, you know? Mick's doing his best, trying to make her see sense. He wondered, is there any compromise he can offer, any way out? Face-saving, you know?'

'You say he's OK, Micky Brennan. He's had his troubles. You reckon we can rely on him?'

'To do his best, sure. Lord knows if he'll succeed.'

'One month,' the man or his coat sighed. 'No more.'

'OK, I'll tell him. But I was hoping . . . She couldn't do it in instalments or something, you know? Add a few punts to the feed bills and so on. We couldn't so something like that?'

The man had now turned to his left. He was ducking down to watch a young couple who stood giggling in the pub's porch. They draped a raincoat over their heads and made a scuttling run for the far end of the car-park. The man said, 'No.'

'Oh.'

'No, it won't wash: we'll have half the bastards asking for H.P. terms, if we do it for this lot. Nope. One month, then we'll have to give young Mick Brennan a helping hand.'

'I surely hope that won't be necessary.'

'Yup. Anything else?'

'No. No. Just . . . Margaret asked me to say . . . Oh, hell.'

'Yeah, well, you've said it.' The man reached for the door-handle.

'No, it's just . . . she says if there's any action, anything she can do . . . She wants to be in the thick of it, you know?'

The man gave a quick hard bark of laughter. 'The thick of it in County Carlow, and her a little slip of a thing with her head crammed full of the Che Guevara? There's no thick of it down here, Fergal, and she can thank God almighty for it. We quietly raise a few funds, give refuge when it's needed. That's it. We're the WI wing, knitting socks for the boys. She wants to play bang-bangs, silly bitch, she knows where to go. And let me tell you, Fergal, she goes up there, all the "let me perish for my beloved country and massacre the imperialist enemy", all that crap, that's just what they'll let her do. Perish. Loonies like that are useful for one thing and one thing only: cannon-fodder. Slaughter a pig and you make converts to vegetarianism. Keep a firm hand on her, Fergal. She's more use cooking your dinner.'

Fergal nodded several times, just in case his companion had not got the message. 'I'll tell her,' he murmured. 'She won't like it, but . . . Thanks, Colonel.'

'OK.' Again the man's hand moved to the door-handle. 'So one month right? And convince them we're serious, will you? I want young Mick Brennan working at this one.'

The door opened quietly. This time the outside sucked out the man's black bulk. The rain fizzed on the tarmac. 'I'll see you so,' he said. His black-leather gloved hand appeared for a second at the window, then the door swung shut and the whole car rocked.

'What we are plotting tonight,' Charlie announced grandly, 'is nothing less than the doom of the bookmaker.' He raised the port decanter and held its mouth over Eledi's glass. She shook her head. 'Mick?' Charlie filled his own glass and shoved the decanter towards Micky. 'Your plan. Tell the tale.'

There had been seven of them for dinner, all told. Georgie Blane had brought his daughter Joanna, a promising three-day-eventer now up at Cambridge.

Micky clasped his hands. He looked down on them for a while then he raised his eyes to Jenny, who sat almost opposite, and he said, 'Thing is, love, we gotta horse.'

'His name is Martindale.'

'Martin . . . You mean like those things round horses' necks, right?'

'No, that's martin*gale*. This is Martindale.'

'Never heard of him.'

'You wouldn't have, but he's a cracker. He's ten years old and he looked really good as a youngster. Good turn of foot, eager to jump, won a couple of sharp hurdle races in the North of England on the bridle. Then things started to go wrong. He still shows well on the gallops, but suddenly he freaks. His only two outings over fences, it was like someone'd slipped him acid and he was on a bad trip. He saw the people, the stands, all that, and he was scared shitless. First time; Doncaster, he's awash with sweat and he runs straight into the third fence. Second time; Thirsk, he got pulled up before the first all over the shop. Even tried to jump the rails.

'He belonged to a nice old boy called Billy Yeats; trained by Dominic Whelan up in Middleham. Anyhow, that time, all anyone knew was, he looked the part but he was bloody useless. So Billy gives up on him and takes him to Doncaster sales. Bloody lucky not to go to the knackers, but what saves him is, he's still got one thing going for him. He's a mover, a floater, you know? Beautiful extended trot. Hoverhorse. So he fetches three thousand guineas from some show woman or other.

'OK, so the idea was he was going to be a champion show-hack. But he kept doing the same thing. One minute he's going sweet as a nut, the next, he's turning himself inside out and reeling about the place like a drunk. They take him to a couple of shows. Saw all these people, heard the tannoys, had a complete brainstorm. Second time, Dunster, he damned near killed the girl riding him.

So, Mrs. Whatever isn't like us guys who just get rid of trouble like him. She loves her dear sweet Marty, so she calls in the vet, who just happens to be a bright young feller. He gives him a thorough screening, finds this brain tumor, right? And it's operable.

'All right, so this is where the necessary chunk of coincidence comes in. I just happen to know the girl works for the vet. She mentions this horse to me. Interesting. Brain tumor. Used to be a racehorse. Did I remember him or anything? I say no. Next thing. I run into Billy Yeats, and his ears are burning because Mrs Whosit has just rung him to give him an earful. "You sold me a pup, the horse was unsound. You cheated me out of three grand," and all that. Billy's been trying to explain to her about soundness. Tried to calm the silly bitch down, explain the meaning of *caveat emptor* in English words of one syllable, but she doesn't get it.

'So, he's telling me this story and he has a few drinks and he starts to get all wistful. Jesus, to think of it. This horse was so bloody talented. Sweet-tempered, great lepper. He remembers, at the time they all thought they had a worldbeater. And it's not till I've finished my drink and I'm actually stood up to say goodbye that he mentions the name. Says something like, "Ah, well. Fish, horses and women. We've all got a few Martindales in our lives, I suppose. The big ones that got away." So I put down my coat and prick up my ears.'

''Course he bloody does,' Charlie cheerfully broke in. 'Micky Brennan, the knacker's foe, the ultimate refuge of equine sinners, the ... See an animal going cheap 'cos it's only got three legs? Brennan's your man. Says, 'A minor handicap, I'll grant you,' and does the business.'

'Sod off, Charlie.' Micky smiled. 'So, Jenny. Get the picture? I am the only person in the world – save the vet's staff, none of whom gives a damn – who knows that this enormously talented animal has an operable physical defect. Far as the rest of the world's concerned, he's just a no-hoper.'

Jenny broke a small piece of leftover bread between her fingers. She placed one half against her lower lip and said, 'I like it,' before her tongue emerged to claim the fluffy fragment.

'So I talk to old moneybags over there,' Micky indicated Charlie, 'and he nips down an buys the beast.'

'S'right,' Charlie leaned forward. His forearms pushed spoons and forks rattling and chiming across the mahogany. 'So I took a trip down to darling little Rye, knock on Mrs Smith and Wesson's door and ask if she's got by any chance got a show-hack for my non-existent baby-brother. 'Oh, well,' says she, 'we hev ectually got this splindid enimal, Lord Vayun, es no doubt you've hard. Tharbrid, you know. Splindid animal. Quate splindid. But may daughter is so tirriibly, tirribly fond of him, so we'd be viry loath to part with him. Still, yis – no, please, don't go, Lord Vayun. Ay'm sure we could et least show him to you. Ebsolutely hate to think of you hevving a wasted trip.' Cow has the gall to ask me eight grand, would you believe. I told her fifteen hundred maximum. She said, 'Ay thought you were a chintleman, Lord Vayun, and would understand such things.' I told her I was and I did. Wished her good morning.'

'And?' Jenny grinned.

'Oh, she called me back.' Charlie tipped up the port decanter again. ''Will, ay must edmit, he is jest a trayfle hidstrong for Mirenda. Sech a fayn-boned gel. Ay do wish you could meet her. Ay'm sure your dear brother hes a farmer hend. Shall we say fayve?' 'One five,' says I. Well cut a long story short, we got him for two, had the operation done and he's going like a dream.'

Micky said, 'Yup. And we could hardly send the beast to Charlie's Newmarket trainers because the word'd get around in no time and he'd start odds on, so Georgie gets cut in as trainer . . .'

'Well, you do the training,' Georgie smiled.

'Well, both of us, but you're officially in charge, and Georgie can also ride a bit, case you hadn't heard, which is more than a little useful. Liam comes in as Martindale's jockey because he's the best amateur in Ireland and no one's heard of him in England. But we need extra manpower, for placing bets, driving, concealment and so on, so we agreed; each of us can choose one person we trust who'll be able to lend a hand. Charlie called Eledi in, Georgie has cut Joanna in, but as a sleeping partner because eighteen-year-olds talk, and I've elected you. Sorry.'

'Micky, what you mean, sorry?' Jenny half stood to lean across the table and grasp Micky's clasped hands. 'Thank you, thank you, Micky. I'm really honoured. Really.'

117

She sat back and swivelled her brandy glass slowly between finger and thumb. For a while she just blinked down at the oily amber patterns that it cast on the damask. The decanter clinked and gurgled.

Jenny looked up. She grinned. She said, 'OK. This is great. So, come on, what's the plan?'

The plan was, they entered the horse in a two and a half mile novice chase at Gowran Park just three weeks from now. No urgency, no eagerness to win. Just give him a nice, gentle hunt about the fences, to see how he gets on. Maybe a few of the others come a cropper and he is up there in the frame. It doesn't matter, but no one is going to bust a gut trying to get there.

Then Martindale moves over the water. He ceases to be 'trained G. Blane (Ire)'. That (Ire) would give off the smell of a raid. He would become 'trained D.F. Thomas, Camarthen'. Dave Thomas was a permit-holder. He had a scruffy little yard and two or three plodding point-to-pointers and hunter-chasers in Wales. Opinion of Dave Thomas did not run high. Georgie said that Dave Thomas could not train a clematis. Charlie maintained that Dave Thomas did not know his arsehole from breakfast-time. Georgie would go over and stay as Dave's honoured guest.

Jenny picked things up quickly. 'But hold on. If this animal's as good as you say, a few little dark eyebrows are going to be rising in the Welsh valleys, huh? And Georgie's there too. All a bit suggestive, isn't it?'

'Nope,' Gorgie grinned. 'See, my wife Claire is Dave's cousin, right? So there's no reason why he shouldn't do me a favour. So what's he doing, he's putting up a high-class animal called De Witt. Charlie bought De Witt last year. He's the same colour as our boy and he's good. Everyone knows that. So I tell them, De Witt's coming over to Ireland to be trained, and just while Charlie sorts out who's to train him, transportation and that, he's dossing down at dear old cousin Dave's place. Fact, De Witt's been let down and is grazing amongst sheep up in Border country. Now, same time, a ratty, cow-hocked animal called Simple Simon, shortly bound for the sausage factory, also arrives in the yard calling himself Martindale. So the lads and the curious visitors see Martindale and think he's De Witt, see poor old Simple Simon and think he's Martindale. Got it?'

'Got it,' Jenny smiled. 'Sounds good.'

'Right, then, come the day of the big race – and it is a biggy – it's time for De Witt to head off for Fishguard to be shipped over here, right?

So he gets all boxed up and drives off westward. Busy day all round. Martindale so-called gets into a box bound for Chepstow. Another animal from Dave's yard, Delightfully Still, bloody silly name, sets off for Kempton where he's to run in the fourth. De Witt goes westward for a few miles, then doubles back and takes the Scenic Route back to Junction of the M4. An exchange is made. Simple Simon, the so-called Martindale, goes off to meet a pieman. The real Martindale heads off for Chepstow. Meanwhile those of us that aren't toing and froing in horseboxes are fanning out all over London and the Home Counties laying bets.'

'That's right,' Charlie barked. 'Clever bets. Little bets. Single bets, some of them, and doubles with Delightfully Still. Delightfully Still won't start. Martindale runs – and wins, we hope, and just before Delightfully Still goes to start, the vet discovers that he's taken a knock. Unfit to race. That way all the doubles devolve on Martindale. Bookies invented the rule to make sure they get every penny going. We turn it on them.'

'Position is,' said Georgie through a mouthful of hazelnuts, 'we're all on for five grand apiece in the UK, plus whatever we can get here on account, so on. Charlie's staking me.'

'That's darned good of you,' Jenny raised her eyebrows. 'Thanks.'

'*De rien*,' Charlie squeezed her wrist and peered at her as though finding it hard to focus. 'Don't worry. You'll earn every penny. Right!' He pushed his chair back and stood up. 'Anyone for a spot of fives?'

Charlie's slapping shouts and high-pitched giggles arose from the billiard room above the simmering laughter and chatter of the others, above the thudding of the balls against the cushions. They were playing billiard fives, that peculiarly masochistic game in which billiard balls are propelled at high speed across the baize by hand.

Eledi and Jenny dragged their feet as they came up the stairs and into the drawing room. Eledi's hair was dishevelled. It sprayed out over the green wool of her dress like sunset on a glade. She carried a joint between her fingers. Both girls now held Waterford tumblers of sparkling water and ice. 'God,' Eledi groaned. She let herself fall back onto the sofa.

'Exhausting,' Jenny sat with a sigh at the other end of the sofa.

'Exhausting?' Eledi lay back, her eyes closed, 'God, a whole brood of screaming kids would be easier. Know what'll happen? Charlie'll come up with his hand all bleeding and he'll look brave, you know?' she mimicked pained bravado. Jenny giggled. 'And I'll say put something on that and he'll get all, oh, don't make a fuss, but really he wants nanny to put cream on it and kiss it better all along.' She laughed with real affection. 'I don't know. Is it all men that don't grow up, or just the filthy rich?'

'All of them, though being rich doesn't help.' Jenny reached out to take the proffered joint from Eledi. 'That's why, I suppose . . . Well, at least here it's just straightforward downright childish. Not like all these guys doing business or chucking bombs about, convincing themselves that this isn't a game.'

'Yeah. Like these big businessmen. Richard Heron, that type. It's attractive in some ways, but all it's really saying is, this can't be a game because games don't do so much damage and can't be this serious. Balls. They should take a look at billiard fives.'

'Or racing,' Jenny said thoughtfully.

Eledi turned her head against the cushions to look at Jenny. 'You thinking of Micky?'

'Yeah. S'pose so. Georgie seems to have been through the mill a bit too . . .' She drew deeply on the joint. 'But yes, Micky . . .' She exhaled through her nose and passed the joint back. 'Funny guy.'

'If you knew how Charlie hero-worshipped that man. Micky could do this. Micky could do that. If you had Micky here . . .'

'Yeah, but that's Charlie wanting to be someone else, isn't it? Charlie would like to know horses like Micky or fishing like Micky . . .'

'He'd like to be a fighter like Micky,' interposed Eledi. 'And that's one thing no one can deny our Mr. Brennan. Gets knocked down, bounces back for more.'

'Hmm,' Jenny brushed ash from her black velvet breeches. She rocked forward to pick up her glass. 'You ever going to put the poor guy out of his misery?'

'Charlie?' Eledi smiled, 'Oh, God, Jenny, I don't know. I mean, trouble is, you know, time comes you want to have children, you sort of go for the best that's around, don't you? Charlie's the best around.'

'Best friend, I grant you,' Jenny was playful. 'But I'd sooner marry a total shit than my best friend. They know too much about you. It's incest, for heaven's sakes.'

'Huh.' Eledi's shoulders rose and fell. 'Anyhow.' It was her turn to tease. 'What's with you and Micky, then?'

'Nothing.'

'Ah, come on, Jenny.'

'No. Really. Nothing. I mean, sure, we get on. He's a really funny guy, and he's sensitive and all that. Surprising guy.'

'But?'

'But ... I know Micky's had it tough in other ways, but far as relationships go, he's been spoiled. They all have. He's just had to give 'em a smile and a steak and they're flat on their backs. I've had all that.'

She looked up, then Georgie and Joanna appeared on the doorway, followed by Liam. Charlie's truculent voice came rattling up the stairs. 'No, for heaven's sake, I'm fine. Don't be such a bloody mother hen ...'

Eledi turned to Jenny. Her eyes rolled upward. She shrugged and wearily stood.

It was too late. They had jived a bit, smoked a bit, drunk a bit too much, worked up a healthy sheen, there would be no getting home tonight.

It did not matter. Screech and Michael were on duty tonight. Kevin would be keeping an eye on the yard.

Charlie had shown Jenny and Micky to adjacent rooms on the second floor. He had said, 'I hope this'll do you, Jenny.' And she had strolled in, seen the big inlaid mahogany bed, the fat white candlewick bedspread. There were red and green flowers on the white walls. There were twin Baccarat Schiaparelli Sleep candles on the mantel and fresh carmine and cream carnations.

Jenny said, 'Mmm, perfect,' and yawned like a treasure chest. She sat on the bed, then lay back and the velvet breeches had crept up, nestled and nuzzled in there. In the doorway, Micky gulped.

'The bathroom's just down on the right.' Charlie walked over to the window. He drew the curtains and returned rubbing his hands. 'I'm really delighted that you are in on this. Should be fun.'

'Mmm,' Jenny sighed luxuriantly. 'So'm I.' She sat up. 'Thanks, you guys.'

Charlie bent to kiss her cheek. 'Night, then, Jenny.'

'G'night,' she stretched. 'God, I'm beat.'

Micky stood irresolute in the doorway. She said, 'Micky,' and she held out her hands, arms straight, palms turned outward.

He stepped forward then took them and she stood and kissed him firmly on the lips. 'Thanks, Micky,' she murmured against his mouth and she kissed him again, softly this time, and her fingers trickled down his sleeve.

He said, 'Ah it'll be a gas. Night, love,' and he closed the door and followed Charlie to the next room along.

He lay flat on his back, staring at the slowly spinning darkness. He had drunk too much to sleep, too little to sleep. He had heard the chuckling of the tap in her basin, the squeaking of her bed-springs as she settled in. Hell, he could go down there, sit on the edge of her bed, kiss her ears, taste her hair, her eyelashes, let his hand roam over her body, feel it shifting – closer, receding, closer, receding, but always moving nearer like the tide.

He could. Maybe she would say, 'No Micky,' but she would say it softly. She would kiss him. She might say, 'No, not now,' or, 'No, not here,' or, 'No, I'm tired,' something like that. An excuse, not a rejection. He knew that.

Once upon a time, before he was married, he would have done it like a shot. He would have had the confidence. He had done it often enough back then. Now – hell, he would only make a mess of it, say the wrong thing, trip over the doorstop or something. For certain.

Tomorrow morning, seven o'clock, he would be sitting by Jenny in the front seat of the Peugeot. Eight-thirty, nine, she would be strolling into the office, as ever, with her forty JP Kingsize and her big gurgling bottle of Cherry Coke. She would say, 'How's it going?' and, 'Coffee?' as always.

No. If and when and God, it would be complicated if – if and when, it would be because they both made the decision in daylight.

All very well, but Jenny had made it clear in thought, word and deed that she was uninterested, not in Micky – he reckoned they got on well, that they were attracted even, each to the other – but in the easy erotic or romantic relationship. On the only occasion when he had eyed her with overt desire, she had briskly and coolly told him, 'Turn it off, Micky.'

He had said 'What?'

'The calf's eyes. Silly cocked eyebrow. God's sakes, I'm not one of your goddamned floozies.'

She was warm, she was funny, she was affectionate. Yielding, susceptible or passive, however, she was not.

From down here, the river sounded like a furious argument between the neighbours.

'So, that's it,' Fergal called above the burbling and the roar. 'One month, is all, they say.'

It was a fine clear night. The sky was deep tarnish blue. From where Micky stood, three or four yards upstream, Fergal was a cubist figure of black and blue planes. They stood waist-deep, staking out a net.

'I did try, Mick,' Fergal hollered, 'stuck my neck out, you know. But it's all PR, see? One exception, everyone tries it on. Can't allow special favours, you know?'

'Ah, hell, man,' Micky struck the water with an open palm, 'I'll never persuade Cathy. So – sorry – so what happens if – well, *if* we don't come up with the cash?'

'What usually happens?' Fergal passed Micky a length of the thick netting. 'I'm no expert, but with Shergar, in the first year they cut one of the stallions around, remember? Just a softener. Second year, well, you know what happened. But that's killing the goose, isn't it? I'd have thought – I mean, it's not like the Aga Khan off on the Costa Smeralda or something. Mrs Kramer's right here. I don't know. They'll not be messing around, though, that's for sure. See, the idea is, God leads your fish up here and we just put a curve on it here by the bank like so. And they just get stuck here. Potted. Read about it. Never tried it.'

'Should work,' said Micky, 'if there's enough water.'

'Ah, they've been coming up this last week all right. Not many, but they're here. Doesn't matter. Worth a crack.'

'OK, so what now?'

'Get out of this, sit down, have a cigarette. See what happens.'

'You'll not be wanting to take them out if this works, I trust?'

'Nah,' Fergal's teeth flashed. 'Well, maybe just one for the pot, like the old days, eh?'

Micky wiped his hands on the shoulders of his shirt and pulled his tobacco-pouch from the chest pocket of his waders. 'You know, this is bloody ridiculous, mate. I mean, look at us. Here we sit, happily messing about on the river together, and you're saying four weeks time, your mob are going to do something pretty unpleasant to me. It's – I don't know – weird.'

'Not to you, Mick.' Fergal flicked his paraffin lighter. His beard seemed to shake in the wavering blue and yellow light. 'Not your battle. Not my mob either.' He swung around to offer Micky a light. His left hand sheltered the flame.

Micky plucked tobacco from either end of the cigarette. 'No, but it is in some ways, isn't it?' He leaned into the light of the flame, then lay back and exhaled. 'Both. Really. It's your mob because at least you support them, and it's my battle because – I don't know. Sure, I could just walk away from it. I didn't choose to get involved, but, you know, overall I agree with Cathy. OK, I wouldn't mind paying up. Anything for a quiet life, me. But I haven't got the money to pay or refuse to pay. I don't know about the Republican cause. I don't even care. It's as good as any other cause. It's as good and imperfect a solution to the problem as any. Hell, I'm lucky. The original white nigger, me. No one ever kicked me around, called me a fucking pig-ignorant Mick or barred me from a pub or refused me a job 'cos I'm Irish. If they had, I'd want to do a bit of kicking back myself. But I don't approve of violence, I don't approve of extortion, I don't approve of the uses you guys put the money to. I reckon, you can't win the argument without a bomb, there's got to be something wrong with your argument. And anyhow – I don't know – another thing. Sounds stupid, but I suppose I'm loyal to my paymaster.'

Fergal lay back on his elbow. He watched the winking water. 'Whatever,' he sighed. 'We once won that way, didn't we? Still, there's no point in fighting it. At the moment, it's just a small local thing. Routine. You guys actually resist, try making a big thing of it, it becomes a point of pride. You get the big fellers involved then, and that means trouble, real big trouble. She's just got to pay the bill, you know?'

'Sure. But I don't think she will,' said Micky sadly. 'I don't know. It always happens. Everything looks good and suddenly . . .'

'Well, if you can't persuade her, someone else'll do it. You just keep out of it.'

'How the hell am I going to do that?' Micky spat out strands of tobacco. 'If I don't resign, that is? I come across some arsehole creeping about the yard, I'm meant to say, "Be my guest. Slash my horses about at will!"?'

'No . . .' Fergal sat forward now. He clasped his hands about his shins. 'Ah, I don't know, Micky. It's not my problem, thank the Lord.'

'So what'd you do in my place?'

'Well, you know me and horses, but sure, I know what you mean. I'd probably fight my corner, defend my patch, but it's just not worth it this time, Mick.' He flicked his cigarette away. It flew in a fizzing parabola into the water. 'It's just not worth it. Hold up,' he frowned. 'Something's got into our little trap. Doesn't look much like a salmon to me.'

Micky sat up. He snatched up the landing-net and jumped to his feet. Fergal had already jumped down the bank. Micky slithered down behind him, dislodging soil and pattering scree. Something struggled underwater in the net, chucking up handfuls of moonstones.

'What is it?' Micky asked Fergal's bent back.

'No fish that,' Fergal panted. He reached down until his beard spread on the surface of the water. 'Come here,' he breathed, then, 'ah, gotcha.' He straightened. An otter dangled from his fist. Its slick coat was pearled and phosphorescent.

'Poor little sod.'

'Ah, he's OK,' Fergal leaned over the net.

'Going to let him go?' Micky was surprised. He had never known Fergal to spare fish, fur or feather.

'Ah, sure. Why not? All poachers together, aren't we? There you go, feller,' he purred. He pushed the otter out into the sparkling stream. Micky reached out a hand to help him up onto the bank. Fergal's palm was as rough as salmon-skin.

Together the two men watched in silence as the little round head sped into the centre of the river at the point of three quicksilver Vs. It ducked suddenly and soundlessly, leaving nothing but a string of seed-pearl bubbles where it dived.

Fergal clapped his wet hands. 'Time to kill, time to let go, eh?'

''Sright.'

'Come on, Micky.' Fergal threw an arm around Micky's shoulders and quickly hugged him to his side. 'Let's go up to the beeches, see if the badger's young have arrived.'

'Listen, Fergal . . .'

'Hmm?'

'Say I'm likely to have a windfall in June. Say I promise to pay them then?'

'Uh uh. They say no delay. One month max. That's it. I don't know if they'd take a post-dated cheque. Maybe. You'd have to be pretty sure about that windfall though. You write a bouncing cheque to these boys, they're not just going to write you rude letters. You'd better start counting your testicles, feeling your pulse when you wake up in the morning, just making sure you've still got one.'

'OK. Yup. Maybe, just maybe, if Cathy doesn't come through, I'll have a proposition to make to them.'

'Yeah. They'll have one to make to you an' all. Meanwhile, just work at knocking some sense into her head.'

'Fuck it,' said Cathy succinctly.

Micky was pushing her over the frost-fused leaves on the track to the yearlings' paddock. The air was sharp as aquavit. He said, 'Cathy . . .'

'Nope, Micky. OK. You leave, Jen leaves, you can all piss off. I'll not hold it against you, but me, I've decided. Jee swee and Jee darned well rest. OK, so I should have told you. I'm sorry, right? But no way ... Shit, I thought we had like an international agreement. We don't give in to blackmail and terrorism, that right? So we hand over Rushdie, huh? Give Ulster to the bombers, the Malvinas to the Argentinians, just 'cos they're on the muscle, huh? To hell with it. Leave that to the French. I'll not do it, and that's my last word.'

'Yeah,' Micky sang, bored. He parked the wheelchair and walked past it to open a five-bar-gate which had sunk on its hinges. 'Fact of the matter is, you're honest, it's got damn all to do with all that high-blown principle stuff, you know that, Cathy?' He leaned for a second on the top bar of the gate. He could not resist grinning at her. 'What it is, it's just you're a stubborn old bat, is all.'

'Sure, OK,' Cathy nodded proudly. 'Never claimed anything else. I get pushed around enough in this damn thing without some brainless thugs push me where I don't want to go. So? So how many heroes majored in political philosophy? Know what a hero is? A common or garden, stubborn semi-psychopath, something gets on their tits. Wimp gets sand kicked in his face once too often, gets up and buries the muscle-man.'

Micky was behind her again. He tipped up the chair. Her voice softened. She said, 'And listen, Micky. You ever play daydream games? What if?'

'Sure. I've been on *Desert Island Discs* a thousand times, thought is it better to be deaf or blind, been to my own funeral – God, how the ladies wept – ridden the National winner, saved maidens from dragons – who hasn't?'

'How about the one goes, what if I only had – I don't know – months, say, a year to live?'

'Yup,' Micky admitted, 'OK.'

'And?'

'And I think, I don't know. I think I'd get all the pretty HIV positive porn stars together, go off to the South Seas and read RLS and drink kava and screw myself into oblivion. How's that?'

'Yeah, well. I ain't got much use for pretty porn stars and I don't like swimming. I used to think, "What if I had only months to live?" and you know how my mind goes? It goes, "OK, You've got a life to sell. What sort of bargain can you get?" I mean, someone who's not worried about hopping the perch, you can do a hell of a lot, right? It's kind of liberating. Assassinate Qadaffi, blow up the National Theatre, ski down Mount Everest and no turns . . .'

'Sounds like a good programme.'

'Yeah, but I got this damn disease. It may not kill me for a while, but it's in there worming away, and maybe tomorrow, maybe a few years' time, it bores through the castle walls, hits the right spot and it's lullaby time. And the thing pisses me off is, you don't make much of an international assassin in a wheelchair.'

Micky laughed. He said, 'Nice idea for a thriller, though. The gun's built into the arm, of course.'

'Yeah. The angel of death grounded and then some. But see . . .' she leaned back to look at Micky, '. . . see, here I can sell myself dear. I can use this disease as a weapon. Thing I could never take is impotence. Here I got a fight on my hands. You get me?'

At the gate of the yearlings' paddock, Micky let down the chair. He pushed the hair back off his brow. He said, 'I get you.'

For a while, then, they watched the two colts, one bay, one washy chestnut, as they played at being stallions, boxing, rearing, racing. Practising, because somewhere out there it was not all My Little Pony.

'Which one d'ye fancy?' Cathy asked.

'The little feller,' Micky hummed. 'The bay. He wants to win.'

'Listen,' Cathy croaked, 'like you said, it's my party. I'll not ask you to get involved, Micky.'

'I am bloody involved, Cath. Can't help it.'

'Up to you,' she shrugged. 'but don't blame me.'

'I won't,' he sighed. 'Same time, don't you blame me if I try to cheat you of your last blaze of glory. Me, I'm planning on staying on this earth for a good long while yet.'

'Here?'

Micky leaned on the gate. He watched the yearlings galloping on the glistening grass. He raised his eyes to the naked limbs of the lindens where the rooks held their contentious parliament – 'Order! Order!'

'You hear me?' Cathy called at his back. 'You planning on staying here?'

'Ah, hell,' Micky murmured. 'Where else 'd I go?'

April

Michael Ryan felt good. At first he had been surprised, suspicious even, when this lean, young fellow with his thin, floppy, mud-coloured hair had come up to him at the bar and offered him a drink.

The fellow had very clear, very pale blue eyes which shifted this way and that. He wore a sharp, blue-grey suit with a metallic sheen to it. The fellow said in his soft, up-country voice that his name was Frank and he knew no one down here, and would Michael honour him by accepting a jar?

People just did not buy drinks for Michael: he had no illusions. He was no sparkling wit, no ladies' man with tales to tell – Michael had thought at once, 'What's he after?' But he had accepted, because it seemed polite and because Michael's mam only let him have three pounds of an evening, and that just to get him out from under her feet. If she paid for his sins and his foolishness, she said, would she not be as great a sinner and a fool herself?

An extra pint of stout therefore, represented a fifty percent improvement on your average evening, and when your man came over with a large Paddy alongside the stout, Michael felt so guilty that this was a great night and a fine fellow altogether.

And usually down here at O'Brien's, people just nodded at Michael, said, 'Michael,' as though he might have forgotten, and carried their drinks to a table. Or they said, 'How you're keeping?' and turned towards the television before he could answer.

It took Michael a long time to answer. The thought was there, but it would not come out. Say he wanted to answer, 'Fine.' The embryonic 'F' of 'fine' sat there on his tongue, building up strength and size, causing his lips and cheeks to swell, and he had to go through all sorts of contractions before the word emerged all at once. The gestation period of such a word could be fifteen seconds or more. It could take longer than the tears to fill his eyes.

But this Frank fellow now, he was interested in Michael and his work. Michael even got to speak the names of the drugs and the antiseptics that he used up at the stud. He got to demonstrate his knowledge of breeding – how Fionnuola was out of Milesia by Troy and how this year she had gone to Be My Native up at Dowdstown . . .

Michael had all this stuff stored in his skull, but his mother was not interested and Screech and Micky knew it all already. It was good for once to let it all out for an airing, to see this chap nodding, smiling, asking questions, learning from him.

Once, Michael went to the toilet. He came back and Frank was no longer at their table. Michael thought, 'Oh God, I've driven the poor fellow away.' Then he saw him up at the bar beneath the strand of smoke which reflected the flickering blues of *Miami Vice*, and he thought, 'Ah, sure. He was just winding us up. He's up there mimicking us, telling them . . .' But no. Look. Here came Frank with his hands around two more pints of Uncle Arthur's best. He laid them on the table, said, 'Hold up,' and returned to the bar for another large Paddy.

Michael greeted him with, 'Ah, you shouldn't have. Ah-ah-ah-I haven't the money.'

'Don't worry about it,' Frank did not smile, but Michael had noticed that Frank just was not the smiling type. It might have had something to do with his teeth. From the glimpse that Michael had had of them, Frank had problems there. 'So, there's you, Micky Brennan in charge – that right? – and old Screech. That's the lot, is it?'

'Yep.' Michael rolled his head as he struggled for the next word, ''cept . . . Mrs Kramer and sometimes we . . . get a . . . couple of kids up for help. And there's . . . Annie Flynn works for M-M-Mrs Kramer up the house.'

'Ah, yes. Annie Flynn,' said Frank.

'C-comes in the mornings and . . . back again at . . . ten in the evening, put her to bed, p-poor old . . . lady.'

'You ever think of working elsewhere, Michael?'

With his muzzle deep in Guinness foam, Michael frowned and shook his head. He came up for air with a gasp and said, '. . . What'd . . .? Why'd I w-want to do that?'

'More money elsewhere, say the meat factory.'

'Nah,' Michael gave a broad sympathetic grin as though he thought that Frank must be soft in the head. 'Yuk. That place s-stinks. I like the horses, and now . . . M-M-M . . . M-Micky's back . . .'

'You like Micky Brennan, then?'

'Ah,' Michael grinned, 'he's a great lad, Micky. He . . . used to . . . take me out fishing with 'm when I was a child. T-talks to you . . .

straight, you know? And him a big jockey and all. You'd never know it. G-going out . . . fishing again this year. He said.'

'Did he?' Frank said drily. 'Nice guy. Well now, drink up, Michael. I'd like to show you something.'

Tuning forks were droning pleasantly in Michael's head when he had downed the Guinness and the Irish. He sat back and allowed himself the luxury of a loud sigh. 'Wonderful,' he said. 'Me mam'll kill me.'

'Come along now, Michael,' Frank stood and pushed back his chair. 'I'm going to show you something'll interest you. Come on. Up with you.'

Michael frowned irritably. He shook his head. 'Show us here,' he mumbled. 'It's nice and warm in here.'

Frank leaned over the table. He said softly and precisely, 'Get up, Michael. You're coming with me.'

'All right. All right.' Michael thumped the table. He lurched to his feet. 'It's . . . so important.'

Frank led Michael to the door. Michael turned and wished everyone, 'G'nigh!' Everyone chanted back, 'Night, Michael!'

Frank almost pushed him out into the street. 'Come along, now,' he said. He grasped Michael's elbow and bustled him down the street pavement. Michael lumbered at his side, trying to free his arm from Frank's grasp. 'All righ', all righ'. Don't rush us, will you? You ever notice? Sparkles in the air, gets cold like this. Sparkles.'

Frank steered him to the left now, into the car-park behind Delaney's lounge. As they turned the corner, the stiff icy breeze pounced out at them, pushing them back.

'Come on,' said Frank.

It was dark here, save for the flashing light of a small neon sign above Delaney's door. *Nite Bite*, it said, then it was extinguished, leaving an echo on the darkness, then *Nite Bite* again. It lit Delaney's station wagon and a small oblong of glistening tarmac, but if anything, merely served to deepen the darkness elsewhere. Michael could not even distinguish the colours of the three or four cars parked over there by the hedge. Frank breathed, 'Come on, come on,' and led him towards the cars. Beyond the hedge, some animals bumped and bustled.

'Hey,' Michael's habitual goodwill was waning in the chill. 'What's with you, man?'

'Right. Just stay here,' Frank ordered briskly.

So Michael stood still, adjusting himself to the gentle see-saw movement of the tarmac beneath his feet. He breathed deeply, and his breath bounced back at him off dark air cold as marble. Five foot away, Frank unlocked the Fiesta's door. No light came on as he pulled it open. He bent and reached in. He backed away from the car.

And suddenly Michael was stumbling backward from something invisible which whizzed towards him. Next thing, the pain hit, hot as a flamethrower's blast on his knees. He was off balance, going down.

He wanted to howl, but the breath had been knocked out of him. It came out as a high-pitched keening. The tears were hot in his eyes, cold as they rolled down his skin. He tumbled over onto his side in a foetal position, oblivious of the grit against his cheek. He clasped his knees and he tried to gasp 'God!' in prayer, not profanation, but it would not come out. It just got stuck in his gullet like a gargle. 'G-G-G . . .' then the pain hit again and he threw back his head, lips drawn back in a grotesque grin as still his throat convulsed, 'G-G-G- . . .'

There was a clang as the iron bar or whatever fell to the ground, then the Frank man was squatting over Michael. Cold steel was pressed into Michael's cheek, pressed upward so hard that a curve of flesh obscured his vision. He saw nonetheless the grim, thin face, faint crimson one moment, faint blue the next, and the shadows of Frank's nose and hair like Stanley blades. He saw too the soft glint from the steel thing in Frank's hand. He knew that it was a gun. He heard the crisp whisper of Frank's suit, the hissing of the icy breeze.

Red now, Frank said, 'Shut it.' Blue, he said, 'Sure, sure, it'll hurt for a while. Whole lot of nerves there, but you'll walk. Don't worry.'

He pushed the muzzle of the gun up harder. He said 'Michael, listen. Michael Ryan, 27: 3, Oliver Plunkett Close. Ballysheenan, mother Jennifer, 60, sister Maureen, 24.' Michael nodded and gasped, nodded and gasped. 'And a nice little dog, springer spaniel, your best friend, so they say, name of Heidi, right?'

'Ee . . .' Michael nodded.

'And at the moment you happen to be unemployed, d'ye hear? Maybe next few days you find work at the meat factory, who knows? But just for now you've got no job. You turn up at Ballysheenan again, you know what happens? Heidi gets it. Turn up again, it's Maureen's turn, all nice and slow. Then your mam. Then you. And you just say one word why, same thing, OK? Makes you feel better, you'll be doing your patriotic duty. You got it? You don't work at Ballysheenan any more, and they ask you why, you say just because. You got it? *You got it?*' Frank giritted his teeth and moved the gun-barrel to a point just three or four inches from the bridge of Michael's nose. 'I'm talking to you, Michael,' he sang, 'You got it?'

Michael shuddered. He blinked away the tears. 'Ee-ee-ee . . . b-b-b . . .'

'No buts, Michael. Michael. You got it?'

Michael nodded as though palsied.

'There's a good boy,' Frank caressed Michael's cheek with the gun. 'Oh, and did you know?' He stood. 'You're a terrible bore altogether, Michael Ryan.'

He giggled. His feet crunched on the tarmac. The car door clicked and creaked and clunked shut. Michael rolled over and pulled himself into a sitting position, still clutching his knees and quietly sobbing. The red reversing lights were giant asterisks. The car started up, swung back just three feet from where Michael sat. The gears changed, and he felt the wind as it passed him, kicking up a wake of grit. The headlight beams lighted the pub walls, then the pink cottage on the other side of the road.

Michael stroked his knees. He whined, 'Oh,' and then 'Oh?'

A sob jerked Michael's trunk. He said 'Oh?' again, only this time it extended, rising in pitch, and he curled up tight, rolled over onto his side again, and cried like a baby.

'We set then?' Liam O'Connell flashed a big white grin at Georgie Blane.

Georgie reined in. He screwed up his eyes against the icy waves of rain. He said, 'Ready when you are. Take it real easy, OK? Just concentrate on getting him back on his hocks, keeping him relaxed. Let him enjoy it.'

'Sure,' Liam nodded. 'Shame, though. I'd've loved to have hammered it out with one of the old guys.'

'Nah. What'd you be wanting to go through the rails for?'

'Yeah? You and whose army? They have rails in your day, did they?'

'Yep. Big hard ones. Big hard jocks to match.'

'Nancy boys.'

'Oh yeah?' Georgie wiped his eyes on a sodden sleeve, 'So who is it had the National fences cut down to gymkhana size 'cos they're too big and nasty and dangerous, eh? Today's heroes, isn't it; Lambo? 'Fraid of mucking up the mascara, is it?'

'Nope,' Liam chuckled, 'Just we've got brains to look after.'

'Ah, that'll explain the full cut of the breeches. Come on. Ready?'

'Let's do it. This boy's busting out of his skin.'

Georgie clicked his tongue and crouched forward, down, Chesterton moved into an easy back canter. Liam followed two lengths behind.

Martindale did not like this arrangement. He snorted and shook his head and strained against the bit. 'Easy, feller,' Liam soothed, 'easy.' The hooves grumbled. The saddles creaked. Liam's lips, as always when he was riding, were drawn back in an involuntary sardonic grin which had been known to displease losing punters.

One moment the first fence was yards away. The next, it seemed, they were right on top of it. Georgie shouted, 'Hup!' and Chesterton was over with a crackle of birch twigs and a squelch like a knife striking flesh as he landed.

Liam sat very still, dead centre. He counted the paces, checked the horse's striking stride, and now he pushed forward. 'Now!'

Martindale took it flat and fast, on the forehand like the hurdler that he once was. So soon as his forefeet broke the gossamer veil on the grass, Liam was gathering up the reins, urging, 'Come on, lad, come!' This, the stride away from the fence, was where races were won or lost.

Georgie called over his shoulder, 'All right?'

'Beauty!' Liam called, then, 'OK, feller. Ready?'

And the next. Liam saw Georgie kick on.

And.

Chesterton was still in the air as Martindale took off. Dear God almighty, but didn't the boy put in a short one to put himself right for the fence. Who was teaching whom, for the Lord's sake? And now, his memory jogged, Martindale was up and away on the landing side so fast that Liam was damned near thrown out the back door.

Too fast. Liam took in a reef. He was happy now. This horse was OK. He was going to win some day soon. He had the feel, the eagerness, the agression and the ability. No doubt. And here, at the last of the three fences, Martindale stood off and put in a huge one, just for the hell of it, clearing the fence by two feet or more.

Liam whooped. He drew upsides Georgie on Chesterton. 'Did it like a dream,' he called. 'I'd say we might have a squeak at Gowran.'

'Just let him enjoy it is all,' Georgie grinned at Liam's enthusiasm. Keep your eyes very firmly on the big one. 8th May at Chepstow. That's all that matters, OK?'

As the horses pulled up beneath them, Micky sighed deeply. He replaced the glasses in their case and he said, 'Charlie, mate, we've got trouble.'

'You're telling me. Mr Johnson of Tullow may make a beautiful suit, but it wasn't designed for synchronised swimming, believe it or not. Someone know about Martindale, or what?'

'No. This is serious.'

'All right,' Charlie sighed. 'Come on. Let's stroll. That rath looks like a suitable place for serious subjects. Come on. Let's go up there and cavort.'

They splashed down into the ditch, then clambered up the bank into the first millenium fortified farm. Charlie breathed deep, said, 'God, this air is good. OK, so . . .?'

'So. Someone turned up, demanded money from Cathy. Money or your life. Pretty much literally.'

'One nomination per season?' Charlie sadly shook his head.

'Jesus.' Micky's jaw dropped. 'How d'ye know?'

'I've heard. It's not shouted from the rooftops, but it's known.'

'OK, yup, you got it. And she refuses.'

'Damned old fool. Still, I suppose, she's not long for this earth, so why not? Do the extortionist bastards. 'Bout time someone did.'

'What she says. Only problem is – well, you remember Michael, Michael Ryan?'

'Yeah. Big bugger. Stammers. Your young protégé. Nice chap.'

''Sright. This morning he doesn't turn up for work. This afternoon I go down find out why. He says um er and he's thinking about going to the meat factory. Jesus, Michael'd kill sooner than leave Ballysheenan. He nurses those foals like he'd borne them himself.'

'So someone's leaned on him a trifle.'

'He implied that, as much as he dared. He was crying. And back in February someone tried to fire the yard. You remember I told you I had had an accident?' Micky held up his left hand to demonstrate the scar. 'It was the sort of accident happened when someone's walking around with a sharp blade.'

'God almighty, did you get him?'

'No. Will you lend me the nine grand?'

Charlie stopped. He frowned down at a spot six foot in front of him. Rain trickled from the peak of his tweed cap. He said, 'Hmm.' He then said, 'No, Micky. No.'

'No?'

'No. Sorry, Micky. Pain in the bum, but you've done it all arse about face. You come up to me and say 'Lend me nine grand, eighteen, sixty-three.' I'd say yes. No question. You know that. I've known you since David and the Shepherds were top of the hit parade and I – well, doesn't matter. I trust you. I'd give you the cash, no questions asked. But you come to me, say Cathy won't put up the money for the murder of some poor sod I've never met, how about you? So the answer's got to be no.

137

'Micky, I don't envy you your problem, but I don't want it passed on to me. I read in the paper tomorrow, 'Tracy Trotter was blown up because the Provos thought she was Field Marshal Witchetygrub' – normal procedure with the boyos – I have to think 'I've paid for that. I'm responsible.' I was in your position, God forbid, Lord knows what I'd do, but I'd like to think I'd tell the sods to get stuffed. Probably wouldn't have the balls, but no one's forced me to make the decision. Tell you what, you go outside again, knock on the door and start all over again. Say, 'Charlie, can I touch you for nine grand?' Make it eighteen. Start and these people go on. I'll say yes and problems solved.'

'No,' Micky shook his head. 'Don't bother. You're right.'

'No. Listen. Tell me it's for furniture, tell me it's for a stallion nomination, tell me you'd like to take Jenny off to Ceylon for a dirty weekend or something. In this context, it's polite to lie. Just don't force that filthy decision me. I couldn't live with it.'

'I understand. Don't worry about it.'

'God.' Charlie sniffed. 'I am sorry, Micky.'

'Forget it, mate.'

They walked on for a minute over the spangled tussocks. Micky sat down on the block of granite at the rath's centre. The rain was soft now. He said, 'How'd you feel if I use the coup to pay them off? I've got to do something.'

Charlie shrugged. 'Your coup, Micky. Do what you will. Just don't tell me about it. Sure. Seems sensible. Why not?'

'Yeah,' Micky said dully.

'You want to hear some good news?'

'Make a change.'

'Eledi's been taking some elocution lessons.'

'Yeah?' Micky raised his thick black eyebrows.

'Yep.' Charlie's cheeks were very red. He scanned the empty white sky. 'Er, yes. Um. Well, night before she left, she got as far as 'yes'. Hurrah for speech therapy, eh?'

Micky made a sound of satisfaction like a model in a soup advert, post-slurp. He stood and slapped Charlie's shoulder. 'Really? A wedding? Well, glory, glory. Well done, mate. I really am glad. Well done. Well done!'

'Yeah, well. Persistence pays.'

'So when's the announcement?' Micky held his hands.

'Next week. She's off sorting it all out, telling her parents, all that. I'm flying over to Cirencester tomorrow, talk to dad. Do the deed in June, with any luck.'

'Martindale better do his stuff, then. Buy you a wedding-present. Should be a hell of a binge. I'm delighted, Charlie. Best news I've heard in years. Really.'

'Thanks. Yeah. Listen. You and Gerard Monteith – I've asked him to be best man, he's there, you know – are the only ones know at the moment. Strictly hush hush.'

'OK. God!' Micky squeaked, 'that really is *wonderful* news.'

They returned to the barn where Jenny awaited them, and Micky was beaming so broadly that Jenny too smiled, happy to see him looking so young and carefree.

Her first remark as they climbed into the car was, 'Hey, what's up with you? Charlie said he'd pay, right?'

'Nope,' Micky's smile vanished. 'Nope. He said no. Worst of it, he's dead right. No one should pay the bastards. They're not us. They're not Irish. They're fucking traitors. No one should pay them.'

'But you've got to, haven't you? You're going to?'

'Yes,' Micky's voice was deep. 'Good damn me, God forgive me. Yes. I am going to.'

She laid a hand on his thigh. The hand squeezed.

Richard Heron was dancing in the firelight in the salon of his Loire chateau.

The girl in his arms could have been no more than twenty. Her loins were pressed hard against his, her head thrown back. She looked up at him with wide soft eyes. Her long brown hair was lustrous and tangled. Heron's hands clasped her buttocks tight beneath the crimson silk mini-dress.

Behind them, Sabrina Heron lay on the gilt and brocade sofa in purple and gold Lacroix. She looked at the twin half moons of flesh beneath her husband's thick fingers, the straining pink satin knickers. She reached across to pour herself a glass of champagne. It overflowed onto the marquetry table-top.

She leaned back again. She drank. Heron had pulled his right hand away from the girl. He beckoned Sabrina to them. Sabrina's lips twitched. She turned away.

Heron frowned. He said softly, *'Excuse nous.'* He released the girl. *'Deux minutes, c'est tout.'*

'OK,' the girl spoke dreamily. She pirouetted uncertainly and threw herself back onto the pile of cushions before the fire.

Heron grasped Sabrina's hand and led her out into the pale blue and white hall. He whispered. 'Come on, Sabrina, what's the matter?'

'I don't want to,' she said, 'that's all.'

'Come on, you can't tell me you don't like it. I saw you.'

'Sure,' Sabrina said sourly. 'OK. I liked it. I came. It can be fun. But the way I felt in the morning . . .'

'Oh, hell, so you had a guilt spasm. Big deal. Bloody ridiculous anyhow. It's the most natural thing in the world.'

'Not for me it's not. OK. I like the fantasy, but only as a fantasy. I'm not a bloody dyke.'

'Well, you were going down like a good 'un on Celeste.'

'Yuk. A one off. You engineered it. I was coked out of my head. I got turned on.'

'So? You'll get turned on again. Jesus, it's just a bit of fun we're talking about.'

'No, Richard.'

'Come on. Isn't she pretty enough?'

'Sure, she's pretty. She's gorgeous, but that's not the point. I don't want to do it. Why can't we just be normal?'

'We can, for Christ's sakes!' his voice strained against restraint. 'It's just once in a while it's fun to party. For variety. Jesus, I'd never have married you if I thought you were a fucking prude.'

'Me? A prude?'

'Well, really,' Heron smoothly changed tack. He put an arm around her shoulders and propelled her back against the wall. His right hand rucked up her brocade skirt and worked roughly at her quim. 'Come on,' he breathed into her ear. 'Come on . . .'

'Oh, damn it,' she moaned. 'Damn you. I don't want . . .' But he silenced her protests with his fierce kiss.

Without another word he led her back into the salon.

The girl lay sprawled on her bed of velvet cushions. Her arms were raised high above her head. Her crimson dress had ridden up to reveal a plush purse of pink satin.

Sabrina walked briskly over to the table. She poured another glass of champagne and knocked it back in one. She turned and clicked over to the marble-topped commode by the fireplace. She opened one of three little foil envelopes and tipped out its contents. She cut six long lines. She snorted two through a ready-rolled English £20 note.

Behind her she heard the girl say, *'Tu veux danser?'* And Richard, *'Non. Baiser.'* and the girl's deep laugh as the cushions sighed.

Sabrina was unbuttoning her dress even as she straightened and turned.

Richard, she knew from experience, was no respecter of dresses.

Frank did not like this job. He did not like the silence in the stable-yard. He did not like the darkness. His nature abhorred a vacuum.

He had seen Micky Brennan and the girl go in. He had waited for an hour. The lights up at the house had been extinguished one by one.

At home in the city, there would have been stimulus. People would have strolled by, kicking cans, out for something: money, a pizza, pussy, the pictures, a fight. The cars would have swept by, ventriloquist's dummies, growling Frank's anger for him. There would have been the constant jousting of the headlight beams, the shrieking of brakes, the rapid heart-beat of music from the bars. Here, there was nothing. Only the occasional baby squawk from somewhere out there, the maternal cooing of the breeze. Anything could come at you from the hollow darkness.

It would be better in a minute, when he had some action, when he had drawn blood.

Very quietly, he stepped out from behind the water butt and padded to the third box down. He teased the bolts open and slipped around the door. The animals inside stirred and jostled on the thick straw. Frank did not know horses. He was nervous, but he steeled himself to wait until the door was once more closed before pulling out the pen-torch. Even as it came on, something pushed at his arm. He started back.

The mare stood with her head just inches from his chest. She puffed slowly. Her eyes were big blue bubbles in this faint light. She snorted. Frank said 'Sh. It's all right, damn you.'

His shirt was sticking to his sides. Best do this quickly, get the hell out. With his left hand he pulled the flick-knife from his jacket-pocket. The foal stood at the mare's near side. Frank grabbed the mare's headcollar and pushed her around towards the manger. The foal tottered shivering around with her, keeping its position like a sidecar.

Now the foal was between him and the mare.

Now, Flick the blade open and . . .

One, Two. Lovely. Not too deep. Not too shallow. And go. Go.

Jesus, the foal sounded like an airlock in the drains. Frank found a nervous giggle seeping from him. He was back in control.

The mare squealed her protest. Hooves thudded on the floor as he forced the doors shut again and sucked up the fresh air. He switched off the torch and wiped his brow. The blade. Hell. There was nothing to clean it with. Frank was fastidious about such things. He returned to the water butt and plunged it in, keeping an eye always on the waiting-up room. Nothing stirred.

Right. He smiled. He pushed the blade shut and replaced it in his pocket. He straightened his jacket, adjusted the knot of his tie.

Time for the interview.

Billy Iceton had telephoned from Tara Stud at six o'clock to announce that Barbauld had been scanned in foal to Head for Heights. Micky had replaced the receiver and declared to Jenny that he was a genius and a *bone fide* wizard. He had dragged her protesting up to the house and opened a bottle of Cathy's champagne. Even as he had crowed and filled tumblers and accepted congratulations from Cathy and Jenny, he had known that his elation was a mistake.

Now night had fallen. The hangover had set in.

Jenny was in the armchair. A cup of coffee steamed on its arm. Micky sat at the table chewing a pen. He said, 'We need *someone*.'

'No one'll do it,' Jenny yawned. 'I told you. O'Brien said, 'I wouldn't even bother asking if I was you, miss.' And hell, I mean, you couldn't take someone on without telling them what was going down. Looks like you an' me are gonna be here a fair while. I still don't get it – I mean, whyn't you let me do it alone? OK, I don't know beans about horses, but you're right next door if I need you.'

'Nope,' Micky tapped the table with his pen. 'It's not that. It's not just you. I'm not having just one person here at night. I mean, how long'd it take to tie you up – or me – while someone else takes Sanso out of the yard?'

'S'pose so.'

'I don't know. We're just going to have to keep long hours. Play Scrabble a lot.'

'I don't mind. I'm good at nights. It's mornings I can't hack.'

It was now that the latch jerked up and the door swung inward. Micky was behind the door, so he could not see who stood there. He could see Jenny, though, as she stared and pulled herself upright in her chair and gasped slowly, 'Oh, Jesus God in heaven . . .'

Micky pushed back his chair and moved around to stand beside her. He said, 'God,' and sank onto the arm chair. Something very heavy had just shifted downward from his stomach to his colon.

Frank liked the effect of his entry. He said, 'Hello there.' He stepped in and pushed the door shut behind him, all the while keeping the gun pointed at Jenny's stomach.

'Who the hell are you?' Jenny's question was bold, but her voice was high-pitched and quavering.

'Put that damned thing away,' said Micky hoarsely. 'Where d'ye think we are, *Starsky and Hutch* or something?' He realised as he spoke that this was less than coherent. It just came out that way.

'They said we had a month,' Jenny grasped Micky's hand. 'You've made a mistake.'

'No mistake,' Frank said coolly.

'But you – they said a month!'

'That's right. My job's just to remind you. Oh, and the gardai. Tell them, thank you, it's all sorted, would you? I don't want to see them round again. If I do, I might lose my temper and call in the debt, OK?'

Micky swallowed. 'OK.' He nodded. He was learning things. A gun-barrel pointed at you, he had discovered, was pregnant with uncertainties. Take a fence wrong, you knew what was happening all the way to the ground. A gun occasioned a whole new type of fear.

'No,' Frank strolled around them, pausing at the calendar to pull a face of disgust. 'Just a friendly visit to make you aware that we are and that we're serious, you know what I mean?'

'Yeah, we got that message, thanks. We're doing our best. So just piss off out of here, would you?'

'In a minute, in a minute,' Frank was enjoying himself.

'God, you are revolting,' Jenny murmured. 'Thick as shit triggerman. Big deal.'

'Hey, now, I've got nothing against you!' Frank squatted at Jenny's feet. 'We're all in this together. You want to persuade Mrs Kramer, I want to persuade Mrs Kramer. I left her a little reminder in the third box down over there. You'll be wanting to patch it up, so I'll leave you be. In a minute, in a minute. Just looking round . . .'

Micky squeezed Jenny's hand. He released it and stood. 'What have you done?'

'Oh, just a little drawing,' Frank straightened, 'with a switch-blade. She'll get the message.'

Micky was no longer looking at the gun. His mouth was set in a thin straight line. His eyebrows meshed at the centre. 'Get the fuck out of my way, arsehole.'

'Don't move,' Frank grabbed Micky's arm. He shoved the gun into the flesh of his stomach. 'I don't want to have to use this.'

143

'You can't use it, you stupid little fart,' Micky snarled. 'You're just a little yob likes frightening people. You take orders, and your orders are, "give them two weeks". Your masters are going to be really pleased with you if you murder me and it's all over the papers, huh? Irish citizen killed by Provo bully boy? Great publicity. And you'll have to kill her too because she's seen you. That'll help the Noraid cause, huh? They'll tear you limb from limb. So, you're not a pathetic little jerk with a gun any more, are you? The gun is negated. It doesn't exist. Know what I do to pathetic little jerks who hurt my animals . . .?'

This was not strictly true. He had seen it done, received instruction from his friend Nick in prison, but he had never done it himself largely because to do it was to risk his life. Still. For a beginner, he reckoned that he did OK. He jerked forward from the waist, keeping his eyes on Frank's mouth. His forehead smashed into the bridge of that long thin nose. It hurt, but it seemed to hurt Frank a great deal more. He staggered backward. His right hand clasped his nose and rapidly filled with bright blood. He said, 'You bastard!'

His stomach was exposed. Micky thought well, why not, not that he knew much about this sort of thing. He followed up and drove his fist in hard just to see the kid bend the other way. It worked quite well. Frank doubled up and slowly dropped to his knees. Blood splashed over his mouth and chin and dripped onto the threadbare rug.

'Give us that,' Micky knelt and grabbed the hand holding the gun.

Frank said, 'Nnnng.' He tried to pull his hand away.

Micky prised the fingers off the butt. 'Now,' he stood. 'Jen, will you take this? Just keep him here while I see what damage the little punk's done. Don't help him if he begs you. Keep him right there on his knees. And you, unlike him, *can* shoot if he tries anything. And welcome.'

'I'll do it if he so much as looks at me.' Jenny took the gun in both hands. She held it at the full extent of her arms.

'Good,' Micky panted. He picked up a bucket, and quickly threw in antiseptic, dressings, syringes and phials. 'I'll be right across the yard.' He left both doors open as he left.

Jenny heard his clattering footfalls. She let out a sigh, rested her left buttock on the arm of the chair and pointed the gun at the kneeling man's head.

'Bastard,' the man whimpered. 'Fucking bastard.'

'You better learn some manners.' Jenny was agreeably surprised at the evenness of her voice. 'You say that once more and I'll see if this thing works. I never fired one of these, but I reckon even I couldn't miss at

144

this range. So it's, "Yes, miss" and "No, miss" and "If you please, Mr Brennan, sir." You got it?'

Frank looked up at her with narrowed eyes full of hatred. He sneered, but he said nothing. Jenny thought, 'Come on, Micky, come on . . .'

Micky returned in twenty minutes. His face was pale. He looked at Jenny, then down at Frank. 'Good. He behave himself?'

'He's been a good boy, haven't you, Frank? Says his name's Frank. He doesn't like you. Thinks I'm great. And my arms are dropping off.'

Micky laid down the bucket. He took the gun from Jenny. Again he walked over and knelt at Frank's head. He grasped a handful of his hair and pulled his head back hard. Frank wheezed. Micky shoved the gun barrel up between Frank's jawbones. 'Listen, Frank,' he crooned. 'You ever, ever, ever touch one of my animals again, I'll kill you; d'you hear me?'

With each 'ever', he had twisted the gun barrel deeper into Frank's throat, which made it difficult for Frank to say or nod, 'Yes.' But he managed a sort of 'Ghee' sound.

Micky released his hair and stepped back. 'Good.'

'What'd he do?' Jenny sat.

'You know Millamant's foal?'

'Yup.'

'Slashed him. Not too bad. Two long cuts, 'quarters and shoulder. I've dressed them and sedated both of them. Poor bloody animal. Hell of a state. He'll be OK. Distinctive markings for life, and I just hope he'll learn that not all humans are sadistic little bastards like this.'

'You going to call the gardai?'

'Nope. I'd like to, but I believe him. They wouldn't like that, might even get nastier. Anyhow, Frank here's going to run messages for me, aren't you, Frank?'

Frank spat.

Jenny said, 'Now, Frank. What did I tell you?'

'What you tell him?' Micky sat at the table.

'He'll show you himself, won't you, Frankie?'

'Fuck off,' Frank was sullen. He started to pull himself up. 'I'm not having this. I'm going to . . .'

'What's this do?' Jenny took up the gun from Micky's hand. 'I put it, say, right on a guy's hand and let it off?'

'Make a mess, I guess.'

'Yeah. Guess so.' Jenny strolled over to Frank. 'So, Frankie boy, what do you say to Mr Brennan when he asks you to run messages? You say . . .?'

Frank eyed the gun in her hand. He knew what that thing could do. He had seen. Somehow it would have been easier if she had known better what she was doing. He went down on his hands again.

Jenny squatted down in front of him. She squinted down the barrel at his forehead. 'You say what?'

'Go on.'

'Bitch,' Frank snarled, but she had her finger right there on the trigger. Dear Lord, but she could blow him away by *accident*. 'OK. OK!' he called, then he muttered down at the rug. 'Yes, sir.'

'Hey, you know something?' Jenny laughed as she straightened. 'You can have a lot of fun with these things, and they're educational too. Can we keep it?'

'Yeah,' Micky said absent-mindedly, 'Why not? Seems to improve these guys' manners. Good idea.'

He was writing '. . . *may concern. You keep your punks away from my animals if you want my assistance. I'll do better than pay one year's rent. I'll include you in something that'll pay out thirty years at once. How say you?*'

He was about to sign it, but thought better of it. He folded the paper. 'Right, Frank. You take this to your masters. I'll be sending it through another contact too, so don't fool me, or they might want to know why valuable documents are getting lost in the post. You can get up now.'

Frank clambered to his feet. He was sniffing a lot now, and his lips were rusty with blood. 'I've – I've got to warn you, Brennan. I'll not . . . You'd best watch your back. I think when all this is over, I'm going to kill you, just for myself. I'm serious.'

'Nah,' Micky grinned up at him. 'You're never man enough for the job. All you've got to learn is, don't threaten what you can't deliver, and lay off the muscle. And leave my animals alone. Now, like I said in the first place, sod off back to your gutter and leave us alone.'

Frank's tongue crackled like cellophane. 'I've warned you, Brennan,' he said softly and through clenched teeth. 'No one does this to me. You're dead. Whatever happens, just remember that. You are *dead*, d'ye hear?'

Micky wanted to say something, but his mouth was too dry and his stomach was gulping. He shivered as he watched the man go.

Eledi was trying to meditate. She sat in a moulded plastic chair in a quite corner of the rehearsal room while Eric and Peter, her "co-stars", worked through some business with the director.

Already she knew that this was going to be a disaster. She could feel it. She tried now to banish all thoughts from her brain. She closed her eyes, attempted to regulate her breathing. She needed just a moment's peace in which to compose herself, restore herself. But no sooner had she attained a blank screen behind her eyelids than jumbled, angry thoughts flashed onto it, flickers of resentment and frustration distorted it, then the countdown started, the inexorable countdown, 10–9–8–7– . . .

In two days, they moved to Bath. In two days, the show opened.

'Hi, Eledi!'

She shook herself. Her eyes snapped open. 'Hmm?'

Trish, the ASM, a tall blonde girl with bubbly fair hair gestured with a thumb over her shoulder. 'Telephone,' she said, 'I think it's his Lordship.' She was arch.

His Lordship. Eledi grimaced. She stretched and stood and very slowly padded through the double doors and down the corridor to the public telephone in the lobby. She picked up the received and sank onto the stool with exaggerated casualness. 'Yeah? Hi. Charlie.'

'Hi, darling. How's it going?' Charlie's voice was cheery.

'Fine. Well, not fine, actually, but there's nothing to be done. I'm OK.'

'Great. Well, listen, everything's going well with our horse, you'll be pleased to hear . . .'

'Charlie,' she broke in, 'I'm at rehearsals! This can wait till later, for God's sake. I'm working.'

'Oh, sorry. It can't matter for just a few minutes. Tell them to hang on to their handbags for just a second.'

'Charlie, I've told you . . .' she was menacing.

'OK, OK,' Charlie said hastily, 'they're not like that. Sorry. Listen. It's important. Thing is, how important is this opening night business? I mean, do you really want me there, or will I just make you more nervous?'

She closed her eyes. Tears were rising. How important was this opening night business? Only, for the moment, the centre point of her existence, the night when she would go out before hundreds of people dressed for protection only in her skills and her lines and her character. Which meant, the way she felt, that the production was negating her skills, emasculating her lines and diminishing her rôle, that she would go out there naked. She could not explain that to Charlie. She just said,

'Well, it would be nice if you could be here, but if there's something . . .'

'Well, darling, it's just – Tony Lamarque has suggested that a few of us – Georgie, me, Bernard, Toby, that lot – might go out to the West Coast for a few days for some fishing and a lot of oysters. He's taken some castle out there. But I'm perfectly happy to give it a miss. I just thought, if you were just being polite and would rather I wasn't there . . .'

'No, Charlie,' she hummed patiently, 'no, of course it doesn't matter. You go.'

'No, look, don't worry. Much more important that I should be there.'

'No, go, Charlie,' her voice came out high and plaintive. 'It really doesn't matter. It's going to be a total fuck-up anyhow. Better you catch it later. Look, love, I've got to go. You tell me about it later. Sorry, they're calling me.'

'OK. You're sure . . .?'

'I'm sure, Charlie. Bye,' she said rapidly. Eledi stood up. Her torso shook and tears were choking her. She found it difficult to stand upright because crabs were clawing at her belly. She raised the receiver to shoulder-level and slammed it down with all the force that she could muster. 'Stupid, fucking *bastard*!' she screeched, then, quieter, 'Child, bloody . . . God!' she blinked up at the lights and bit her lower lip. She panted fast and her fists clenched and unclenched at her hips.

Then she took a deep breath and it was over. She wiped her eyes and forced a smile. She swaggered back through the double doors like a Western gunslinger.

Richard Heron was breakfasting in the conservatory. He flicked away the *Racing Post*. So far, he had found nine references to himself in the English language papers, not including the runners' listings. He scanned the papers eagerly wherever he might be, seeking awe, resentment or, best of all, libel. Richard Heron liked a libel.

Sabrina walked in clad in a long white cotton robe. She swept past him without a greeting, cast a quick disdainful glance at him, and sat down. She picked up the discarded *Times* and poured herself coffee.

'Morning!' Heron was jolly.

Sabrina sipped her coffee. She said, 'This is cold.' She had been sulking for forty-eight hours now, since the girl had left.

'You know the origin of the croissant? I'll tell you. There was a pastry-cook in Vienna when it was being besieged by the Turks. And late one night the pastry-cook heard the Turks mining the walls and raised the alarm. Saved the city, see? So as a reward he was given

148

permission to patent a pastry, and he made it in the shape of the Turkish crescent. Marie Antoinette brought him with her to Paris as part of her household, *et voilà.*'

'Jöelle?' Sabrina called, then a mere second later, 'Jöelle!'

The maid scampered in. Sabrina snapped in ungainly French, '*Plus de café. Et chaud, cette fois.*'

Heron pulled across the *Daily Mail.* He flicked over the front page, picked up the telephone and tapped out a number. He used his left hand to raise the coffee cup to his lips.

'Hello?' he called. 'Hello? John? Richard. What's the story? Sorry . . .? Seven winners – that include Penny Plain? Great . . . Yup. So when's Wayland leave for Europe? Right, I'll be over there by then actually. Yup, popping over Friday morning. Scheduled. Arriving . . . hold . . . yes, arrives Sydney 0745 local. Angela'll be coming over the day before. Let you know, but I'd like to go straight down to the new place when I arrive. Get me whatisname, the architect guy. We'll go over the plans on the helicopter. Yes, the party's on Saturday. Fiona send you a guest list? Good.' Heron turned another page of the newspaper. He frowned and shifted forward in his chair to read. He licked his lips. 'Yes,' he said, 'Yes, hold it, John. Just a second . . . Listen, John, I may have to cancel. Something's just come up . . . Sorry about this. I may have to go to England . . . I'll take your advice on that one. OK, have the party anyhow. Look, I'll get back to you. Give me an hour, OK?'

He replaced the receiver without a goodbye. He picked up the newspaper now, hiding from Sabrina's bored gaze.

He saw a grainy chiaroscuro flash picture of a young man in a double-breasted dinner-jacket. His arm was linked with that of a girl – a slender, a beautiful, confident, smiling girl in a pale evening dress. The caption was '*Charlie and Eledi, Drowning in Romance.*'

My congratulations, and not before time, to Viscount Vane, 37, heir to racing supremo Lord Kilcannon, and actress Eledi Donovan, 34, who yesterday announced their engagement. Charlie has been single-mindedly wooing Eledi for sixteen years since they met at Cambridge.

'I think I first proposed to her in Christ College Gardens five minutes after I first met her,' recalls Eton-educated Charlie from his Gloucestershire home. 'I was twenty-one and had just seen her in a production of Comus. She said 'no' and has been saying, 'no' biennially ever since. Actresses get used to saying the same thing over and over again, but as last even she got bored and thought she'd like a challenge. She said, 'yes' beautifully. Pity it has to be one night only.'

Charlie, who will one day inherit 1500 acres of prime land near Cirencester at present runs the ancestral demesne and stud in Co Kilkenny and is a well-known figure on the racecourse. Eledi, daughter of banker Ivo Donovan and one-time bullfighter Clarissa, was most recently on our screens as Bessie in An International Episode. *She opens next week at the Theatre Royal, Bath in a revival of Peter Shaffer's classic farce,* Black Comedy.

'I am delighted,' she told me from rehearsals, 'I've always adored Charlie, but first my politics, then my career persuaded me to stay on my own. It's like drowning, really. You fight the inevitable for as long as you can. It's quite nice to give up in the end.'

Heron studied the girl in the picture again. He looked across at his wife, who gazed dolefully past him. He closed the paper and tapped just three numbers on the telephone. 'Angela? I want to fly to Bristol this afternoon. Yes. What's the name of the hotel near Bath where . . . Ston Easton. Yes. OK, book me a suite. Oh, and forget the Australian trip. No, some business has come up. No . . .' he smiled sweetly at Sabrina. 'No, Mrs Heron will be doing her own thing.'

The designers of Gowran Park economised. You drive up through the trees and park in a boggy field. Below you lies the course, essentially another, bigger field with scattered fences and hurdles, a few running rails. All the business of the course is done in a narrow, jerry-built street behind the stands. On the right, there are the loos and the weighing room, brick blocks barely distinguishable the one from the other, and the Tote counters. On the left beneath the grandstand, are the three bars and more Tote counters. There are the avenue of bookies' pitches, and the paddock which doubles as a winners' enclosure. That, more or less, is your lot.

Liam was already in the paddock in the green and crimson of Charlie's colours. He stood in the classic casual jockeys' pose, leaning back, one foot ahead of the other, arms folded as he apparently received instructions from Georgie.

'Going's perfect,' Liam announced. 'Lord, I am a bit worried at the thought we might eat this lot for breakfast.'

'Not to worry.' Georgie shrugged. 'So he wins at Gowran. It's not going to make 'em clutch their balls in terror over at Chepstow. Go for it. But a length or two, not a distance.'

'Oh, I don't believe it!' Charlie chortled to Micky in the avenue of book-makers. 'It's straight out of the Irish RM. And Jenny! What's she meant to be? That is too much.'

'What's that?' Micky's head swivelled. He saw Martindale trot in. Jenny led him. She wore cavalry twill trousers five sizes too broad and three inches too short, and a baggy old Arran prickly with straw. The horse was alert. His ears were pricked. His coat was dark and wet and flecked with foam.

'Ah, that. Yeah, I said, 'Look mucky. Look as if you came from a small permit holder cattle farmer's yard.' I think she got a little carried away. she has a highly developed sense of theatre.'

'Jesus, she looks like a Vaudeville scarecrow. *We're a Couple of Swells*. But the muck sweat, that's classic stuff.'

'Liam's work, needless to say. Text-book stuff. He says, "Stergene's your only man. Stergene or Swarfega, only Swarfega can leave bloody great green gobs of gunk, if you're not careful". Your man knows these things! So, now, he loses, comes in by twenty lengths next time out, he's already known to be erratic and everyone saw he'd sweated up, your honour. Beautiful.'

Charlie drank his hot whiskey and turned to the bookie behind him who was busy chalking, licking his fingers, erasing, chalking. 'Hey! Hello! What's with the 20–1 Martindale, Rory Coogan or whatever your name is? I want three hundred to ten and I'll not brook argument . . .'

Georgie flicked Liam up in the saddle and stepped back as the horse circled on a tight off-side rein. 'See you soon,' he said.

'Soonest,' Liam grinned and saluted.

Jenny led Martindale through the milling men in their tweed caps, and Fermoys, and onto the course. 'Luck,' she smiled up at Liam. She released the clip.

Martindale bounded away, and Liam was suddenly a comma on a dash, and the divots of turf flew back from the horse's hooves like anti-aircraft shells.

''Scuse us, sir,' Jenny turned back to Georgie and touched her cap. 'Where do us lowly stable-girls go to watch the contest?'

'Ah, it's all right,' Georgie grinned. 'You're in democratic old Ireland. You can go anywhere provided it's muddy and uncomfortable. Me, I'm going up to the stand. You'd best hang around here and look fetchingly downtrodden, in case you have to go and catch our boy if he falls.'

'You mean I have to run around making a damn fool of myself in front of everyone?'

'Well, you don't expect the distinguished trainer to do it, do you?'

'Hell, and I thought Micky was doing us a favour inviting me in. You just needed a yokel to do the dirty work.'

'That's right,' Georgie patted her back, 'and you do it as to the manner born.'

'Thank you, kind sir.'

'And if we win today, you get a fifty percent pay-rise. So who's the lucky girl?'

'Fifty percent of damn all. Great.'

Georgie waved as he moved off through the crowds, nodding this way and that as he went, touching his trilby, stopping to exchange a quick word here and there. Jenny strolled down to the rails. 'Don't let him fall,' she murmured. 'Please.'

'He'll be OK,' Micky was behind her. She felt his hand on her shoulder. 'Thought I'd come and share the agony with you.'

She smiled. Without averting her eyes from the course, she fumbled for his hand and squeezed it tight.

Liam O'Connell lazily moved Martindale up to the start.

At his right, Dessie Canavan clicked his tongue and rode his black-stockinged dun in an imaginary hands and heels finish at the walk. 'Hear yours is a rogue.'

'Crazy,' Liam grinned. 'Last time he ran, he got fed up with the fences and jumped the rails instead. That was years ago. It's just that Georgie's only got old Chesterton and about two cattle, and you know these old fellers, get a clapped-out nag and they think they'll work a miracle, win the National or something.'

'Yeah. Still, he looks the part. Sooner you'n me.'

'Ah, he's OK. I hope. Mellowed with age. Uh oh. Here we go.'

He pulled up the goggles from around his throat. He barely had time to adjust them. They were under orders for a second before the flag dropped. Liam had intended to tuck Martindale in at the back and get him settled, but the field moved off at funereal pace. There were nine of them in all, tightly bunched and clinging to the inside rail at a rocking-horse canter. Martindale was at the centre of the pack, three from the front.

'Ah, the hell with this,' Liam murmured, 'we're here for the race. Let's race.' Martindale was bowling along, striking out with his near fore, straining against the bit, so Liam just let out a reef. He muttered into the horse's ear, 'Come on then, feller.'

Martindale gave one big nod as though in agreement, and smoothly, easily drew away from the pack. No sooner was he clear of Fred Moody on the lead horse than the tumbling sound of the horses behind them thickened in texture. Martindale was still hitting out at invisible enemies, but he was going a little too freely. 'Easy, fellow,' Liam breathed, 'Keep your eyes on that minor obstruction up ahead, would you?'

But Martindale was too busy playing the Leader of the Pack. The fence, when it came, seemed to come as a complete surprise to him. He braked and skidded, forefeet planted, rear end sinking, and the thunder of the pursuers' hooves drew nearer. Liam gave him a crack with the whip and the other runners and riders were upon them and the air was full of creaking and slapping and rough exhortations as at last Martindale projected himself upward and lurched through the top of the fence.

There was a hard jolt as his hind legs dragged through the brush. If he had not been a gelding already, he would certainly have been one now, and he was descending steeply, far, far too steeply. Liam lay back, hoping to God that he could pull the horse's neck up, hoping to God that Martindale would find a safe footfall. Already all around him hooves squelched into the turf and the beech twigs crackled like bushfire. Liam grasped the pommel of the saddle with his left hand, the back with his right. It was the ancient cowards' way. He could do no more, save pray.

The jerk still came as a shock. Liam was flung forward and his right shoulder was damned near dislocated. Even after landing, Martindale was still going down. His right knee buckled. For a second, there was no reassuring equine neck between Liam and the sod. Then somehow the horse was pulling himself upward and forward again, three lengths behind the rest of the field, but running, falteringly at first, muddied but unbowed.

'All bloody right,' Liam said fiercely as he gathered the reins. 'That's your one freeby, son. Now on, it's concentration all the way. Shit!'

For now, he was not worried about their position. He worked at steadying the horse and giving him a breather. By the time that they reached the second, they were six lengths tailed off.

To this one, however, Martindale rose like a champion and flew over with barely a scratch to the girth-straps.

He had enjoyed that one. He was beginning to feel resentful again of those animals up ahead of him. That's the way, old son. You're getting the idea, but steady, steady . . .

Liam just hacked him about for the remainder of the first circuit, the rest of the field was strung out now. By the time that Martindale swung into the straight he had overtaken three of them and was perhaps, nine, ten lengths behind the leader. Each time that he passed a horse, he wanted a duel to the death. He swung towards his opponent, ears flat on his head, spoiling for a fight. Full marks for aggression, all right, and no problems with stamina. As they galloped out into the country for the second time, he still had plenty in the tank. Jumping? Well, apart from that first cock-up, he had done OK. Bold, brilliant if a little careless. Say seventy percent. Now, courage.

Liam wanted to give him a taste of the rough and tumble of jumping upsides.

The grey immediately in front of them stumbled on landing at the first in the back straight and his jockey tumbled over his head. That left four still standing ahead of Martindale. Of these, two were a good five lengths ahead of the others who were bunched together on the inside rail. Now that Martindale's back was down, Liam was sufficiently confident to yield to his straining, to urge him on.

And there it was; the overdrive, that sudden surge of power as the length of the stride increased and the ground was swept smoothly back beneath them. Martindale took the next, an open ditch, flat and fast, and suddenly they were occupying a nice broad space which had opened up between Dessie Canavan, on the rails, and an amateur called Pat Royston who rode like a randy dog. Liam panted across at Dessie, 'Just stay with us for this one, would you?'

Dessie did not bother to answer. Liam took the silence for assent. The horses took off at precisely the same moment. Liam's off stirrup hit Pat's saddle. Martindale landed with a puffing sound a split second after the other two and two feet ahead of them. Dessie's animal had pecked badly on landing and had lost ground. Martindale was back in his stride fast. He did not like to have travelling companions.

'OK,' Liam panted and wiped his nose with his sleeve. 'Pat, mate. How's about you lean on us gently at the next?'

'Yeah,' Pat grinned through mud-spattered goggles. 'You bet.'

'Gently, I said.'

'You got it, don't worry.'

Liam checked Martindale's free stride. 'Easy feller. You're about to learn a thing or two.'

Martindale was still straining to pull ahead of Pat's orange bay, and now, just four strides off the fence, the other horse suddenly veered towards him. Martindale grunted as the weight hit him broadside, knocking him almost onto the wings, but his stride did not falter. 'Yah!' Liam gave him a crack down the near flank and urged him hard to the right, clouting the other horse hard on the rump just as both animals went back onto their hocks and kicked.

'Hey!' yelled Pat. Liam grinned as Martindale, apparently undisturbed, leaped the fence like a bridge. Behind them there was a thump, an 'ouff' like that of a fighter when a good punch gets through, a tell-tale clatter.

The leader, Freddy Holmes, was alone up there now. The other horse cantered riderless across the centre of the course towards the racecourse stables, whilst its rider trudged slowly back towards the stands, whipping the turf. Xerxes Murphy.

As Freddy turned into the straight, he had ten lengths and more on Martindale. That was all right. Liam was in no hurry. Still, may as well test that supercharge again. Liam shook the horse up and rode him out. At last given his head, Martindale went for home as though he had just seen his long lost mama at the post. He swung into the straight just as Freddy took the second last, and – Glory Hallelujah – the yellow cap did not reappear. Liam looked back over his shoulder and bellowed his laughter. There was not a ridden horse to be seen back there. He slapped Martindale's neck. 'Walkover, my old son! You're a winner! Would you credit it?'

But as they arose over the second last, it was to see Freddy standing, the reins already gathered in his gloved left hand as he prepared to remount. His horse was circling, but that would not hold him up for long. 'Go on. Go on . . .' Liam sat down and the wind punched the words back into his grinning mouth, and Martindale, infected by his reckless urgency, went.

He went hurtling at last, hurdling at the last, on the forehand, taking the leap in his stride, and Liam knew, two strides off, that he was wrong, all wrong. Oh, he would have cleared any hurdle in the world by two feet or more. If he had not, the hurdle would just have fallen over. This, alas, was no hurdle.

His forelegs clipped the top and he ploughed at speed into the soggy turf. He skidded on his knees. Liam, meanwhile, found himself upside down on the horse's head, then somersaulting to land on his back. Martindale's breath was hot on his face. Liam looked up at him and said, 'Oh, God. Sorry, old chap. I forgot you were only a babby.'

They were playing jigs inside his head and beating complex rhythms on his ear-drums. His wrist played a hot counterpoint and his bum was bruised. He wanted to lie there for a while, stretch out on the grass and go to sleep, but Martindale was up and, a couple of yards away, Freddy slowly scraped over the fence and swerved away from them.

Martindale snorted and threw up his head. Liam found his left hand arising and falling. The reins were about his wrist. He said, 'Oh, shit,' and he clambered groggily to his feet. For a moment he rested his head on the animal's neck, breathing in the familiar hot meadowsweet smell of sweat. Then he heard the racecourse commentator's voice '. . . and it's Red Partridge, Red Partridge all alone . . .' and the rasp of the racegoers' cries as the favourite came in, and he somehow pulled himself up onto the horse's back. 'All right,' he slurred, 'get on with you.'

Martindale bounded forward.

'Micky', said a pleasant voice behind him as the crowd's chatter died.

Micky turned. He saw a familiar weatherbeaten face and sparkling grey eyes beneath a brown trilby. The Colonel. Micky had not seen him since the party at Newmarket a world and a century ago. He said 'Hello, how're you doing, sir?'

'Fine,' the man's deep, soft voice reverberated like a *legato* 'cello. 'A word?'

Micky looked quickly at Charlie, then, 'Sure. Where?'

'Let's walk,' the Colonel smiled with thin dry lips.

Micky frowned. 'You?' he whispered.

'Me,' the Colonel growled. 'Come on. Let's walk.'

The Colonel was a large and heavy man, but he moved fast, with a thick, gravelly growl on each breath. He walked in step with Micky towards the entrance turnstiles. 'So, Micky Brennan. Tell me about it. They've left me to make the decision, so you'd better pitch it to me clear and strong. What's the deal?'

'I . . .' Micky gulped, 'I want to get Ballysheenan free and clear, I want . . .'

'You want?' the Colonel's eyebrows arose. His high brow wrinkled. 'We know what you want, Micky. The point is, have you got anything we want?'

'Sure, OK.' Micky knew that he could blow it with just one word out of place. 'I-I think we have. But how do we work this, for God's sake? I mean, I can't just put up half the information as an ante. If I'm to persuade you, I'm going to have to give you the lot. It's valuable information. What – I mean, what are you guys laying on the table in return?'

'Ah, well, now,' the older man sighed, 'I'm afraid that must remain your problem. After all, you're the one wants something from us.'

'That sounds kind of paradoxical, doesn't it?'

'Maybe. But that we are going to get something from you is a stone-cold certainty, Micky. Like a death sentence, say. You're asking for a stay of execution. You're the one who's got to give us a good reason, aren't you? I don't even have to bargain with you, hmm?'

'Can I even . . .?' Micky shook his right hand as though to rid it of something irritating. 'Look,' he said, 'it's a coup.'

'I assumed as much.'

'So if I tell you and you decide you don't let us off the hook, will you at least promise not to use the information?'

'You have my word,' the Colonel nodded slowly. 'You will tell me and me alone your plan. If I counsel them not to accept your proposal, I promise that I will not pass on any details. Whatever is done here is done on my authority alone. All right?'

Micky sighed. He had no choice. He said 'OK.'

'Not,' the Colonel added, 'that I will not have a tenner on the Tote.'

'Yeah, yeah. Fair enough.'

Off the course now, the Colonel rested his bulk against a tall Irish yew. With the heel of his hand, he polished his steely skullcap of hair. He crossed his hands in front of him. A lad led a dejected-looking brown animal down the avenue. 'So. Tell me.'

'Wait, now, listen.' Micky held up his hand. 'If you like it, what are you offering in return?'

'How much can the market take?'

'I don't know. You probably have ways and means, but normally – well, there are seven of us in for five grand plus a bit of credit stuff this side of the water. Say we've got – I don't know – fifty grand invested in all. It would be part of your side of the deal that you'd do everything in your power to keep the odds long.'

'We'd do that anyhow, out of self-interest.' There was still a slight County Tyrone harshness in the soft Dublin accent.

'Is the market a big one?'

'Big enough to make real money.'

'OK. This thing works, Mrs Kramer gets a fool's pardon.'

'For good?'

'For her lifetime.'

'Uh uh. Ballysheenan gets honorary Irish status for as long as the Kramers or their heirs own the place.'

'For that,' Micky,' the Colonel picked at his pipe-bowl, 'it will have to be very good indeed.'

'It's good,' Micky nodded, 'and it's all or nothing. You accept any part of this, it's exemption for good and all.'

157

The Colonel sighed. 'All very well, Micky,' he mumbled through teeth clamped on his pipe-stem, 'but you've got to understand. We're dealing. You want something extra, we want something extra if it fails. At the moment, we're only talking about nine grand. You persuade us, we're talking about tens of thousands of pounds. The cost of failure will be proportionately high. You understand? Hmm?'

Micky urgently wanted to sit down. Instead he jiggled from foot to foot as the Colonel bent forward to shelter his match. Micky took a deep breath. 'Yeah,' he said. His voice faltered. He cleared his throat and tried again. 'Yeah. I understand.'

'All right, Micky Brennan,' the older man puffed contentedly on his pipe. 'We have a deal. Now sell it to me.'

Eledi Donovan slouched slope-shouldered through the wings and down the steps, round to the staircase which led up to her dressing-room.

She had been in more depressing situations, she supposed, though right now it was hard to remember them. Everything – and everyone here – seemed to conspire to make her job and her life more difficult.

And another thing. Maybe just because she asked questions here and there, maybe because of the announcement of her engagement to Charlie, Viscount Vane, the inevitable little clique had formed, and she had been firmly shut out. They went to supper together and were *so* surprised when she didn't come too, though they had never bothered to tell her where or when. They sniggered and whispered in huddles, fell silent when she drew near. Oh, it was all childish stuff. She should ignore it, but it got to her all the same.

For *this*, she had waited all these years to say 'yes' to Charlie? She wished that she were back in soggy green Ireland now, safe from petty bitchiness and ambition.

Oh yeah? And how long would that last?

Charlie had told the journalists, 'Oh, 'course she'll go on working, what am I to live on?' Ha ha.

But if it was always going to be like this – if her peers in the theatre were always going to resent her – what chance had she of reconciling Eledi Donovan, actress, and Eledi, Lady Vane, later Countess Kilcannon, mistress of demesnes and of millions of pounds and of all the responsibilities which millions entail?

Oh sure, there would be producers who loved a lord. They would give her – what? Drawing-room comedies? Coward? Thrill for the sponsors: 'You've met our star. *Lady* Eledi Vane? Eledi, darling, this is . . .'

Just look at her, in an A-line pale blue mini-dress with a whorl of sequins on the bodice, a border of sequins at the hem. Her hair was puffed up in a beehive. She looked bloody ridiculous.

And the director, Kenny, wanted her to bray like a donkey to demonstrate that she was a debby type. Could he not let the author's lines and her mannerisms do the job?

And – and this was the worst of it, he had blocked her like a superfluous bit of furniture. 'You'll be in the way, Eledi, dear. You stand over there beneath the stairs.' As far as dear Kenny was concerned, what she did mattered not a jot, provided that she kept out of the way of his stars and did not distract the audience from them.

Great.

And tomorrow it went up.

She walked into her dressing-room and pushed the door back, not caring that it scraped along the carpet and remained ajar. She sat at her dressing-table and looked at herself. Lady Vane, in her warpaint. She stuck two fingers in the pot of white cream and almost slapped it onto her cheeks, then she worked it in at the hairline, about her eyes.

She had known the problems when she had told Charlie 'yes', but they had never been so manifest until now. Thing was, sure, she could play Charlie's wife and the good mother for a while, but after – what? Five years? Ten? – she would fret, and then – she knew herself well enough – then she would be cruel, and she could not stand to be cruel. Not to Charlie.

'Eledi, darling?' A clogged, straining voice. Eledi raised smarting eyes to the mirror. She reached for the towel. Between blinks, she saw Hazel Woddis, veteran of a thousand provincial tours; pink plush face, hair like piss-streaked snow.

Eledi said. 'Hi!'

'I do hope that you don't mind me disturbing you, darling,' Hazel drawled.

'No, no . . .'

'It's just, I wanted you to meet a dear old friend of mine. We thought you might like to come with us for a little supper. Cheer us all up on the night before the opening.'

'Oh, Hazel,' Eledi swung round and summoned a smile from somewhere. 'That is sweet of you.'

Hazel pushed the door open and stepped in. She extended a hand behind her: the conjurer's assistant. Here he comes. 'One of my dearest, dearest friends,' she said sorrowfully, and a vaguely familiar tall figure stepped forward. 'I think you've met. Eledi Donovan. This is Richard, Richard Heron.'

'No, Hazel,' Heron's broad smile was like an incision in a water-melon, 'the problem is – and Lord knows why, what I've done – but Eledi's intended – he – for some reason, I don't know, he's got it in for me.'

'Oh, I'm sure he hasn't really,' Eledi chewed on partridge, drank Beaune, mopped her pale pink lips. 'No. He's not the sort to bear a grudge. Probably just some damn silly misunderstanding.'

'No, I think to be honest it's his father. I admire Charlie for that. Loyalty. But I think – old Benet has always disapproved of me. You know, I'm business, not quite respectable as far as these old guys are concerned. The racecourse is their patch. Don't blame 'em, but ... It's a pity. I mean, how did they make their fortunes, after all? The thing is, they forget. Not just their own origins, but also that racing's an entertainment industry. It serves the public. It's no longer, it can't be just the preserve of a small aristocratic club, you know? Must've been lovely when it was, but now ... So I understand why Benet doesn't like the new regime, the commercial angle. He thinks I'm some jumped up oik'll ruin the old sport, but of course in reality ... Well, times are changing.'

Heron raised a hand to summon the waiter. He indicated the bottle and drew a circle with his finger. When the waiter leaned over Eledi's shoulder, however, she covered the glass with her hand.

'Come on, Eledi,' Heron coaxed. 'Best thing you can do, on the eve of the big day. Put it all out of your mind, have a few drinks. Relax. Blow out a few cobwebs.'

'Oh absolutely ... Richard's absolutely right, darling ...'

'Oh, what the hell.' Eledi shrugged and removed her hand. She watched as the gouts of crimson liquid spurted into her glass. 'It's going to be a bloody disaster anyway. So, Richard, what are you doing here? Bit off your usual track, isn't it?'

'Hmm, Yes, Usually. But there's a little business I'd quite like to get hold of down here. It'll take some time. I'll certainly be able to see the show tomorrow.'

'Don't.'

'Eledi's having slight ego problems,' said Hazel sweetly.

Eledi's lips narrowed for a second, became a straight wound. She emptied her glass in a gulp, then, smiling, asked, 'So, how do you know one another, for heaven's sake?'

Hazel was fumbling in her bag. She pulled out a packet of Marlborough Lights, a tiny gold and red enamel lighter. 'Oh, I've known Richard for *ages*, darling. Long before he was a millionaire.'

'We've been friends for a long time.' Heron was looking into Eledi's eyes.

She said quickly, 'Where on earth did you meet?'

'Oh . . .' Hazel lit the cigarette, blinked and exhaled through her nose. 'Where was it, Richard?'

Heron's eyes were still fixed on Eledi.

'Hazel was a friend of my mother's.'

Hazel's eyebrows arose. She inhaled again. Her right hand shook a little. She purred, 'Such a sweet old lady.'

'So most of our acquaintance has been like this,' Heron continued. 'Hazel's touring, I happen to bump into a production. Leeds, Bradford, wherever I happen to be. It's happened several times, hasn't it? Now. Pudding. I know what *I'm* having.'

'I've been looking at your ring.' Heron helped Eledi into her coat. 'It's lovely. What is it, for God's sake?'

'Sapphire,' Eledi flicked her hair back over her collar. 'Star sapphire. I got a shock when Charlie produced it. It's an heirloom. One of his ancestors acquired in in India. I was expecting – I don't know, the usual faceted stones, lots of diamonds and glitter. Poor Charlie. I didn't even know what it was. Thought it must be an amethyst or something. I mean, this size. I said, "Oh," then, "Dear God." Poor Charlie. No, but I love it now.' She looked down at her hand. 'You can get lost in it. My crystal ball.'

'It's very lovely.' Heron held open the door into the hotel's hall. Hazel was off somewhere 'powdering her nose'. 'Tell you what. I'm having a dull time down here, don't know anyone around . . . I suppose Charlie'll be coming down for the first night tomorrow, will he?'

'Nope,' Eledi said sourly.

'No?' Heron's eyebrows leaped.

'No. Charlie's very sweet, but it's not his thing, really.' Eledi brushed nothing from her skirt. 'I can't expect him to understand. Acting for him is just . . . I mean, for me, it may be silly, but it is something serious. It's all I ever wanted to do. But he's got – oh, I don't know, something to do with the horses or something. Takes precedence.'

'Oh, that is unfair,' Heron looked distressed. 'I know how much it means, what it takes out of you being up there in front of the world. You know that I'm an angel?'

'Yeah?'

'Yup. Backed a fair number of plays and films now. It's fun as investments go and it's nice to make work for actors. I enjoy it.'

'Hmm,' Eledi extended a foot and studied it as she described a circle with her pointed patent toe. 'Probably for the best,' she shrugged. 'Charlie, I mean. He can catch it later on when we've ironed out all the problems. First nights on tour are usually surefire disasters, particularly a thing like this. Lighting and so on.'

'Ah. No. What was I going to say? I mean you and I at least can be civilised. Why don't you let me give you dinner tomorrow, after the show? If you don't think Charlie'd object, that is?'

'It has nothing to do with Charlie objecting,' Eledi said as he had known that she would. 'I make my own decisions, but . . .'

'Well, I'll leave it up to you. I must say it'd make my life a lot more fun. Think about it, I'll be at the show anyhow. Drop in after the curtain falls and see how you feel. Be fun.'

'I'll think about it, but I'll probably be absolutely dead on my feet. Thanks, Richard.'

'It's nice for me. Oh, and Eledi, for the Lord's sake, don't tell the old bat. I have to see her when I'm around because it's always in the bloody papers and she'd be on to mother in seconds, but another night of 'Sir John always told me' and 'Dear Larry' and I'll scream. 'Ah!' he cried as Hazel swaggered into the hall in her black velvet cape. 'Hazel, dear. Your carriage awaits. So nice to see you again.' He kissed her hand and threw open the front door. The night was clear and fine. A long dark car stood waiting on the floodlit carriage-sweep. The driver jumped out and opened the offside rear door.

'I can't wait for the show tomorrow,' Heron said gleefully, then, 'Eledi, thank you. Wonderful evening.' He kissed her cheek. For a split second his hands squeezed her shoulders. 'I'm so glad to have the chance to meet you away from all that pettiness and silliness. Hey, and don't worry about tomorrow. You'll be great.'

She was naked in bed that night when the telephone rang. She picked it up and groaned, 'Charlie.'

'Hi. Did I wake you?'

'No. I was just nodding off.'

'Just wanted to say hello and remember to be brilliant tomorrow and good night. Oh, and I love you somewhat.'

'Thank you, Charlie.' She reached for the discarded pillows and stacked them against the headboard. She punched them hard. 'Everything OK over there?'

'Fine. Our horse is coming over tomorrow, you'll be glad to hear. You sound pissed.'

'So do you. No, I just went out to dinner, that's all. Few glasses of wine. Unwind before the horrors of tomorrow.'

'I'm sorry I can't be there love, but . . .'

'But the boys have first claim. Don't worry.'

'I bet it's not going to be that bad,' Charlie continued blithely. 'In fact I bet it'll be a triumph. Like exams, you know, you think you've done dreadfully, that's always when you get the best marks. Like with finals. I thought I'd done OK, got a 2:2. You thought you'd failed, wanted to fling yourself from the Senate House roof. 2:1. Typical.'

'No, it's seriously dreadful, Charlie. Some ways I wish I were back there with you. Nothing but horses and heating to worry about.'

'Nah. Kick the little shits. You're bloody good. Don't let anyone stop you being bloody good. And don't let them get to you. It's just resentment.'

'Hmm,' she nestled further down in the bed. 'Listen, Charlie. When am I going to see you?'

'Oh, soonish. I'm going to be pretty frantically busy with the sales and so on, but what I'll try to do, catch up with you the weekend before the race. Stay with you at Richmond on the Saturday, see the play, then we'll go on somewhere for the Sunday and Monday. Wherever you like. London, Alnwick, the Outer Hebrides, OK?'

'OK.'

'It's just – what? Three weeks from now? And any time you feel like it, you can always bomb over here. Have you done any nuptial organising yet awhile? Dress, invitations?'

'I . . . Not yet. I'll see Mum this weekend. Look, Charlie, love, I've got to sleep. I can't keep my eyes open. I'll talk to you tomorrow.'

'OK. Have a good lie-in tomorrow, then go out there a chorus-girl and come back a star. Right?'

'Right.'

'I do love you, you know.'

'I know you do. Must be crazy.'

There was a pause. Eledi just listened to the rasping of the line, then she said, 'Night, Charlie.' She replaced the receiver

She turned out the light above the bed and threw the pillows to the floor. A car soughed by below, and an oblong of yellow light slid across the ceiling.

She frowned. She could not quite work out why she had not mentioned Heron. Tomorrow, perhaps.

'I think we should take it,' the Colonel sang in that deep reverberating voice. 'It's a bloody good coup, and if we handle it right, there's a pile of money in it.'

'What sort of sum we talking?' asked the big man in the donkey jacket who sat opposite. He had black hair, a red bulbous nose and pocked cheeks.

'The sky's the limit,' the Colonel shrugged. 'All to do with how quiet we can keep it, how much muscle we can call in to help us.'

'Call in Army Council, you mean?' said the man who looked like a bank manager on the bench by the fire. Goldrimmed glasses, a soft, pale face. A suit and knitted tie.

'Yes, I think so. It's big enough.'

'Jesus,' grunted the man in the donkey jacket. 'And this started as a nine grand collection. Anyhow, if you say so.'

They sat in the dark back room of a bar in Glendalough in the Wicklow Mountains. Their man was posted on a bar-stool on the other side of the door, keeping the curious away.

The bank manager flung a peat briquette onto the fire. It sent up a flush of sparks. The men just sat and watched it.

Here, down South, there was not much to the business. A cocky little shit, a trigger-happy bastard from up Andytown had come down recently in need of shelter. The Colonel had disappeared him. But he had said, this Frank fellow, before he disappeared, 'Know what you lot remind me of? Dad's Army. You remember? Fighting the Germans with pitchforks. Jesus, you lot haven't got a clue.'

Big man. So if he was so clever, how come he came down here snivelling for their help?

But down here, their function was minimal. In the old days, they had done a few snatches; Galen Weston and Don Tidey back in '83, and, of course, Shergar, but all three had proved fiascos and had caused bad feeling amongst the ordinary people in the Republic, and Army Council had vetoed further kidnaps. Now it was just a matter of safe houses, gentle propaganda, storage and occasional transport of arms and, above all, fund-raising. The Provos were not popular down here, though the cause inspired some sympathy, so it was softly, softly. Don't tread on Irish toes.

But the foreign stallion-owners, the blow-ins who lived here tax-free they were a valuable source of revenue. God in heaven, and weren't there stallions up Kildare and Meath standing at £100,000 a throw? That was big business.

Basically, the system ran itself. You just collected. Occasionally you encountered argument. Then, like with Micky Brennan and the Kramer woman, you called up some gouger who liked hurting people, told him to give them a bit of welly, make it clear. It's pay up or get out. Occasionally – there was a rock star not long back, a novelist – occasionally they chose to get out. Mostly they paid. Business like that did not concern Army Council. They had more serious matters to attend to.

'All right?' the Colonel said at last. 'You're happy to leave it with me?'

'You know the horses,' Donkey Jacket nodded. 'And you're the boss in these parts. Sure. But if it goes wrong, on your head be it. I'd not like to have Army Council's wrath depending on a bet on a horse, I must say.'

'Ah, well,' the Colonel smiled slowly. 'That's the crack, isn't it? Always wager just a little more than you can afford.'

'Yeah,' the bigger man snorted, 'Like in this instance, your head.'

'Could there be a finer bet?' the Colonel laughed. 'Could there be a finer bet?'

The producer had sent the bouquet of carnations, irises and daffodils which lay on the dressing-table. Charlie had sent the huge one of lilies and red roses which stood in a vase by the door. Richard's had arrived bang on the half, when Eledi was in bra and knickers, chewing on hairpins. Trish, the ASM, had come up looking very impressed. A maroon Roller pulls up at the stage-door. Out gets this enormous guy in uniform copper tan, flashing white teeth, looks like a film star. Special delivery from Mr Heron to Miss Eledi Donovan.

A nineteenth century long-handled basket, Kate Greenaway style, filled with violets; a large bar of Cadbury's Dairy Milk; a half-bottle of Clicquot; a note: just, *All the best, Richard*, and, with the note, a tiny envelope of white powder. Charlie did not like her doing drugs, but it was welcome there, then, about to go on stage and make a fool of herself in front of six hundred people.

Because that was what she had just done, and that was why now, having held it in check as she sighed programmes for schoolgirls, she was in tears as she sat at her dressing table and pulled down her hair.

Oh, the audience had enjoyed it all right. They had enjoyed Eric's clowning. They had liked the glimpse of Eledi's knickers as she clambered up the stairs. Yes, and Hazel, envious bitch, had stormed through all Eledi's best laughs and ruined the drinks-table business. God, whatever hapened to ensemble work? Everyone had to be a star. Try this. On one of the few occasions that she was allowed downstage, she had been speaking her lines when the audience had started roaring with laughter. She was meant to be in pitch darkness, so she could not turn and look at whatever was going on behind her, she had just had to carry on braying in that absurd exaggerated voice whilst Eric and Polly did some bit of lewd business that they had worked out by themselves.

She cried for all that, but above all she cried for loneliness, because in this company there was no one to talk to. She was too grand for them. And because those to whom she could talk – Charlie, her parents – would regard her problems with a play as trivial, worthy of a 'there there' or a 'what's it matter anyway?'

So it was only natural that she was crying. And it was only natural that, when Richard arrived, arms extended, she should seek shelter there.

'It is going to be all right,' Fergal Doherty announced. He sat and unlaced his heavy boots. 'Mick's given them a deal.'

'Big deal.' At the table, Margaret licked an envelope and pounded it shut with a closed fist. 'Dunno why that should make you so happy. Fucking Micky Brennan. Do him some good to find his precious horse kidnapped or something.'

'He's a friend, Margaret,' Fergal shook his head. 'My oldest friend.'

'Oh, sure. So how often are we invited to dine at Micky Brennan's house, eh? Eh? Big friend.'

'It's not like that . . .'

'No, it's not like that because Micky Brennan's no more Irish than the Queen of England. What's his father? A major in the British army. Lah di-bloody-dah. Soon as he's in long trousers, where's Micky go? Britain. So he's got an Irish name. So's Denis Healey, so's Ronald Reagan. Doesn't make them one of us, does it? Just come back when it suits and exploit poor simple Fergal O Dochartaigh same as the Brit landowners've been doing for centuries. Old friend. Buying the natives for a string of beads or a glass of Guinness. Great.'

'Ah, come on,' Fergal stood in his stockinged feet. He placed his boots before the stove. 'So every Irishman goes to the UK for work is a renegade, is that it? By that reckoning, there are more renegades than true Irishmen in Ireland. As for Major Brennan, sure he fought in the war. So did the Colonel. You know that? The Colonel made captain in the British army? True. 'Cos he didn't like Nazis doesn't mean he loves the Brits, does it?'

Margaret sighed, 'You've gone soft, Fergal Doherty, so you have.'

'Called growing up,' Fergal objected. 'I mean, sure, the old days working up North, you'd see things make your blood boil. I knew fellers killed. Bullet in the back of the head. No trial. Imprisoned. Five years for possession of a shotgun cartridge. Brit bastards calling you fucking Taig, get out of my way. You're young, you'd be crazy you didn't want to kill a few of them, sure. But then you look at it. What's it achieve? And all the factions. We're being exploited, you know that? We want a united Ireland. We want the soldiers out. But the big boys up there now, they don't give a fuck for the Irish. They are just international terrorists same as the Red Brigade, Baader Meinhof. They *want* the army there. They *want* division. They *want* brutality. Justify the revolution. And they exploit our old grievances, tell us it's all in the historic cause, and it's all so much shit. Kids are going out there and dying for Ireland, so they think, only they're not. They're dying for Libya, killing for the bloody Brigata Rossa. It's not what it was.'

Margaret opened the table drawer, principally, Fergal suspected, in order to slam it shut.

'Great, so it's cuddle up to England time, is it?'

'No, Chrissakes. It's just – separate the two things. The Brits were shits back in colonial days, so remember, honour the dead, make sure it never hapens again. And injustices today – the Maguire seven, the Birmingham six – fight and lobby till something gets done. But assassination squads and bombs in pubs – they've done Ireland more bloody harm that even the Brits did. What I reckon.'

'What you reckon, is it?' Margaret sneered. 'I've heard it all before. Must be something in the glands. Happens to men at a certain age, just like puberty or something. Suddenly they lose their balls and start spouting crap. So, how's Micky Brennan managed to wriggle out, then?'

'I don't know the details,' Fergal wandered over to the rusty fridge. He stopped and pulled out a chicken leg. 'Just some race or something. Long as it works, Ballysheenan's in the clear.'

'And if it doesn't?'

'If it doesn't . . .' Fergal chewed, gulped. 'If it doesn't, Ballysheenan is in deep deep shit.'

Margaret scratched her crotch through her skirt. She smiled. She said, 'I-can't-wait.'

'You know who's been around a bit?' Eledi asked casually. 'Richard, Richard Heron.'

'What's the little bastard want?' Charlie snapped on the other end of the line. 'What's he doing down there anyhow?'

'He's here on business. He saw that I was in the play and he paid a call. I think he's just trying to get rid of the bad blood between you. He's really very sweet.'

'Sweet?' Charlie yelped, 'Sweet? Heron? Sweet as a bloody black mamba. Keep well clear of that man, Eledi. He's poison.'

'Oh, come on, What's he ever done to you?'

'Nothing – to me, so far, but he hates my guts.'

'He doesn't, Charlie. Honestly. He really hates all this enmity and squabbling. He told me so. Congratulated me on the engagement, helped to cheer me up after the first night. He's been really nice.'

'If Heron's nice it's for a bloody good reason. Don't you have anything to do with him, love.'

'Charlie, I see whom I want when I want. You don't regulate my life, right?'

'OK. OK. I'm sorry. I'm asking you then. Please steer clear.'

'I would if you'd tell me why. You've done nothing to him and he's done nothing to you. So why the animosity?'

'I can't tell you that. Just believe me. He's got it in for me.'

'He hasn't. Why would he?'

Charlie hesitated, then, 'I can't tell you. Just believe me.'

'It's just snobbery, isn't it?' she heard her voice rising. 'Just because he's a self-made man and he's got more horses than everyone else, you all close ranks. Nasty, jumped-up little man, right?'

'No, Eledi,' Charlie intoned, 'it's more than that.'

'So tell me.'

'I can't,' he repeated, 'I really can't. It's a family affair, but for God's sake, just look at his marriage record.'

'So he's been divorced. It happens.'

'Twice, and each time he's busted up another marriage.'

Eledi was shivering now. 'OK, so he's not an Irish plaster saint. But at least he's trying to be pleasant. I don't see why you can't make the effort. It's so bloody childish.'

'I've never been less than polite to the little man.'

'There you go. The little man. Charlie, that sort of snobbery makes me sick. So Richard's stepped onto your precious turf and he wasn't at school with you. Grow up, will you?'

'I'm coming over.'

'What to protect your possession from nasty common little Richard Heron? Don't bother, Charlie. I can look after myself, and I'm not your possession. Richard's been nothing but kind and helpful. You could try taking a leaf out of his book. I've got to go.'

'Eledi, I love you.'

'I'll call you sometime soon.'

'Eledi . . .'

'Bye, Charlie.'

She depressed the tits on the telephone. Her teeth were clenched. Her eyes were cold and angry. She tapped out a number. 'Richard? Hi. Listen, your offer for this weekend. Is it still open? Great. No, I'd love to . . . He's got no right to object. Yup. OK. I'll meet you in the bar about – what? Twenty minutes after curtain down?'

'I don't know about "good",' said Micky, 'but I enjoy it. Had a lot of practice. There's some Sancerre in the fridge.'

'Didn't Nathalie cook, then?' asked Jenny.

'Burnt everything she touched. You need an orderly brain for this business. And she didn't have the energy. She was always sitting doing nothing, flicking through magazines.'

'Where's the corkscrew?'

'Over . . . Hang on, I'll find it.' Micky left the stove and rummaged in the kitchen table drawer. 'Here you go.'

'Thanks.' Jenny sat in the rocking-chair. She applied herself to the bottle between her feet. 'You don't think much of marriage, do you?'

'No, I think it's fine as a contract. You know, gives children security, organises the transfer of property from one generation to another, all that, but it's crazy that it's got anything to do with love. I mean sure, love can develop, you live with someone, share everything over the years, but it's a bloody silly motive for marriage.'

'Yeah, I think I agree with you. That fat's smoking, you know.'

'I know.'

'Sorry. Back seat cooking.'

'No; me, I reckon we're communal creatures. I don't think it's natural or right, one person having to be everything to another. The nuclear family. I mean, it's only an industrial invention, isn't it? Late nineteenth century. Factories mean breaking up communities and extended families, cooping people up in convenient, isolated units. It doesn't work. And if you're in love with someone, you're possessive, demanding, all that. The only way it can go is downhill. I reckon you marry someone you like for convenience, and keep love for discreet affairs. Govern your married life by courtesy. There's no courtesy between lovers.'

Jenny poured the wine. She carried a glass over to Micky. She said, 'Maybe I ought to marry you.'

Micky smiled into her clear still eyes. 'Good idea. Only problem is, I'm not convenient. Difficult bugger, me.'

'Oh, I don't know. You cook. That's convenient. You like your own space. So do I. You know how to run a stud, and it looks as though I'm going to inherit this one. You're not totally repulsive physically. I reckon you're about as convenient as they come. And you want children, don't you?'

'Relatively desperately.'

'Right. So do I. So.' She sat gingerly in the rocking-chair, leaned back and crossed her legs. She grinned up at him. 'Why not?'

'This is so sudden,' Micky trilled, then, letting his eyes wander frankly over her body, 'I must admit, I like the look of the fringe benefits.'

'Uh uh. No fringe benefits unless you marry me. We fringe benefit first, we might fall in love, then we're fucked, if you see what I mean.'

'I snore when I've drunk too much.'

'So we have two bedrooms.'

'I like seducing people and being seduced.'

'So do I. So use a condom and don't tell me about it.'

'You're crazy.'

'I don't think so,' she rocked contentedly. 'I don't think so.'

Micky cooked steaks.

The curtain had gone down at half past ten. Five curtain calls, take off make-up and that damn fool dress, put Charlie's ring back on, pick up the grip and run down to the bar.

Richard had been waiting in a dark suit and a red silk tie. He had handed her a large malt whisky and said, 'Hi. Drink up. We've got a long way to go.'

The Rolls had been parked outside the theatre. Sean, Richard's driver, who looked like an overgrown and barely animated academy award, bowed low from the waist as he had shown her in. He had driven them out to Ston Easton, where the helicopter waited. Heron had taken the pilot's seat. The floodlit hotel had dropped away beneath them, then there was the orange flush of the city, the bejewelled black counterpane of the fields, the creeping white strips of surf. They landed on the lawn before Heron's Jersey house at a quarter to twelve.

'Dear God,' Eledi thought, 'riches can shrink the world to a library globe.'

It was a long white clifftop villa, three sides of a square, five miles to the south-east of St Helier. Its wings enclosed a swimming-pool. Eledi had climbed out of the helicopter and there it was above her, glowing in yellow light which made the surrounding darkness absolute. Corkscrews of reflected light glimmered in the water. The main part of the house was of two storeys, the wings of one. A statue of a crouching faun stood at the centre of the pool.

'This is familiar,' Eledi mused at the pool's edge. 'I've been here.'

'Would you believe *High Society*?' Heron laughed. 'Not me. Guy who lived here before. Jimmy Taylor, investment broker, decamped with twenty-four million, he loved those old movies. You remember? Grace Kelly sailing the model of *True Love*? 'Boy, she was yar'. This is it. Must say, I like it. Keep thinking I'm going to hear Satchmo striking up with *Little One*. 'Right song, wrong girl', remember?'

I remember. God, Gas. I can play Grace Kelly. Well, could, if we had a little Rhode Island sunshine.'

'Later, in summer, you can do it to your heart's content.' Heron pulled open a French window and followed her into the drawing-room. The fire was lit and throbbing.

'Uh uh. I'll be married by then.'

'Well, we'll just have to persuade Charlie that I'm OK, won't we?' Heron flicked on a lamp.

'Be difficult. Still. Yes. I'm doing my best.'

'So. When's he coming over?'

'Couple of weeks. We've got a little scam going at Chepstow.'

'Sounds interesting.' Heron led her into the Valentino-tiled hall and up the curving staircase. 'A raid, is it?'

'Sort of, but it's very hush hush.'

'I wouldn't have thought old Charlie needed the dough.' Heron pushed open a white door.

'He doesn't,' she said surprised. 'It's for the crack. Not that a few of us couldn't do with a few grand extra. Georgie Blane already bought himself a pedigree bull in his mind. God,' she sighed as he entered the huge white and pink bedroom with plate glass windows overlooking the sea,

171

'this is wonderful. It's so good to be miles away from the bloody theatre. Thank you, Richard.'

'Don't mention it. Look, just take your time, have a bath, whatever, come down when you're ready. We'll have a little dinner and try and get you an early night.'

Eledi walked over to the dressing-table. She fingered the Penhaligon bottles, the drum of Arpège talc. She asked Heron's reflection in the mirror, 'Is your wife here?'

'My wife,' Heron shook his head sadly, 'chooses not to be my wife anymore. That's hush hush too, so don't tell Charlie just yet. We're getting a divorce. It's a mess.'

'Oh, Richard,' she turned with a groan, 'I am sorry.'

'What can you do?' Heron shrugged. 'Believe it or not, there are disadvantages to being rich, like you never know if people are sincere. I'm afraid she wasn't. Out for the main chance. In fact – I shouldn't be telling you this, but – I didn't know until it was too late – the fact of the matter is, dear Sabrina is a lesbian. What can you do?'

Heron prided himself on the unobtrusiveness of his staff. He had given orders, and his personal assistant, Angela, had seen to it that they were been carried out to the letter. He cast an eye quickly over the dining-room. The fire was blazing. The table was laid. The Waterford glasses threw out teazles of reflected light. The claret had been decanted into a silver and crystal jug. The white burgundy lay in a Baccarat ice-bucket. Consommé steamed on the hot-plate. Two cooked and cracked lobsters lay side by side in a bed of salad on the sideboard by a bowl of fresh fruit salad. Good. Simple, unpretentious, perfect.

He walked briskly back to the drawing room and out into the chill air. He clicked along the poolside, stopped at a door on the left, knocked once and walked in. 'Angela?'

There was rustling and groaning. The bedside lamp filled the room with soft pink light. Angela Bishop lay naked in bed. She had very long dark hair and eyes bright brown as horse-chestnuts. Her face and her breasts, which she made no move to cover, were uniformly tanned.

'Hi, Richard,' Her voice was very deep. 'Everything OK?'

'Everything's fine. No little playmates today?'

'Not tonight. I'm exhausted. Anyhow, period.'

'Oh. Listen. I want you to check something first thing tomorrow morning. Top priority. Chepstow. A fortnight's time. Any runner connected with Georgie Blane or Charlie Vane. If you don't see a connection at first, keep hunting. They definitely have a runner. Find it for me OK? Oh, and see if you can get Robin Halliwell over here tomorrow.'

'It's Sunday.'

'I know it's Sunday, Angela. But he's a solicitor and solicitors like money. Get him. Oh, and I'll want the full catalogue of those pretty pictures of Sabrina and the girls. All the ones without me in them. I want this to be the cheapest divorce in history.'

'Richard,' Angela's eyes shone with amusement, 'you are a total shit.'

'Sweet of you,' Heron smiled. 'I've got to go. There is business to do tonight.'

Georgie Blane was counting as he urged Martindale towards the log. 'One, two, three and hup!' Martindale stood off and sailed over the obstacle in a perfect parabola. 'OK, feller,' Georgie murmured, 'now for the big one. Take it easy.' He held him at a gentle canter as he approached the open ditch. This horse was a natural. He put himself right without human intervention. Only trouble with naturals was, they were apt to lose concentration in their eagerness to display their flair. This was just one last school to restore any confidence that he might have lost in taking that purler at Gowran. Georgie collected him, then, 'garn!' he yelled, and Martindale surged up beneath him like a great wave, over the eighteen inch bar, over the six foot ditch, over the four and a half foot of unyielding birch, and as soon as he was down, Georgie was scrubbing him on. It was a good feeling. A real double-handful. It had been a long time since Georgie had felt that thrill.

He pulled Martindale up very slowly. The horse shook its head. It wanted more action. That was good. Three miles on Chepstow's hills would be a hell of a lot more action. Georgie trotted him over to where Dave Thomas sat on his bay hack watching the four horses in his string.

'I don't get it,' Dave frowned. 'It'll be the drugs, I suppose. Brain damage. Bloody Charlie Vane, what's he up to? He's got this animal could win a bloody fortune and he's sending it off to the bog and he wants to race that little bugger at Chepstow.' He nodded towards the washy bay which cantered laboriously up the muddy hill. 'Is he suffering from a mental imbalance, is it? All the bloody money in the world and he buys bloody Martindale. Three mile chase? He couldn't win a bloody donkey-derby. Shamed to have him coming out of my yard.'

'Ah, well,' Georgie consoled, 'these millionaires are eccentric, you know.'

'And how long's he bloody boarding this creature with us, I'd like to know? Why can't I run him instead? He's fit and he's good. He'd win bloody races. Know how long it is since I had a winner? Four bloody years it is, and that was a bloody two horse novice hurdle, and the other chap fell. And this beautiful De Witt; "No," says Charlie, bloody twerp, "He's not to bloody race. He's to go to bloody bogland." Mad as a bloody March hare.'

'Not to worry. He's to sail from Fishguard on May 8th. Not long now.'

'May 8th,' Dave's eyebrows were horizontal dabs of flake white. They slanted now. 'That's the day bloody Martindale makes a bloody fool of us at Chepstow. I'll not be there to see it, that's for sure. I've got Delightfully Still running at Haydock. At least he can run a bit. Not fast, but he can bloody run. Come on. Let's get back to the house. Have a bloody drink.'

He turned the hack into the wind which swooped up at them from the valley below. He was still frowning. 'You don't think . . .' he started, then, 'No, bloody Charlie Vane's not that clever.'

May

Jenny winked at Micky as she pushed Cathy into the office. Cathy's cheeks were red. Her pointing finger shook. She said, 'Micky, what are all these men doing here?'

'Hmm?' Micky, at his desk, casually picked up a sheaf of papers and banged them into shape. 'What men are those, then?'

'All over the goddamned yard. Don't play the innocent with me. What are they doing?'

'Oh, *those* men. Yes, they're installing a security system. Closed circuit in all the boxes, floodlighting comes if anyone comes into the yard. I tried to get electronic gates but they can't install them for six weeks, so we'll just have to make do with alarms.'

'And who's paying for all this?'

'You are,' Micky said simply.

'I'm damn well not.' A sulky snarl.

'Well, then, I'll suppose they'll sue you.'

'Got them out of here, Micky. This isn't a joke. Get them out. Now.'

'Sorry.'

'Well, I'll get them out. I can't afford these bloody toys.'

'Cathy,' Jenny sat at her desk. 'You're a curmudgeonly old skinflint. You've got a simple choice. Either you pay for these very basic security measures or Micky and I move out. Got it? No way are we sitting up at night without some protection, some indication as to who's prowling out here. Already, thanks to you, we're understaffed. You've already had one foal carved up and damn near had the whole yard burned down, and we've been threatened with a gun. That's it. Oh, and Screech agrees. He's not hanging about either.'

Cathy looked from Jenny to Micky. 'What's going on here?'

'Security here is a joke,' Micky sighed. 'We've got Sansovino, who's probably worth a million or more, and perhaps five, six hundred thousand pounds' worth more in mares. You leave that sort of cash around in an unprotected farmyard? Anyhow, closed circuit helps with foaling. Just about every other stud in the world has it. This system can scan every box in the yard at will or at random. I'm also having an alarm system put in connects direct with the Garda station.'

Cathy's fist hit the arm of her chair. 'And where am I meant to find the money for all this?'

'In amongst the fluff and the mothballs in your own pockets, Cathy,' Micky said harshly. 'It's the price of your conscience. You may not remember this, but Jenny and I are shareholders in Sanso, and our vote is to pay these buggers. You refuse. OK, that's your business, but you have to protect your employees and your horses. And something else you've forgotten. I manage this stud, and I say we introduce these measures, every darned one of them, or I resign. And I don't expect any additions to my annual shareholder's bill, either.'

'Oh, yeah?' Cathy yapped, 'So you're a shareholder and you're so darned keen I should pay these murdering bastards, whyn't you just give them your share? That'd solve all our problems, wouldn't it?'

'That is a very stupid question,' Micky said quietly, 'and I think you know it.'

But Cathy was affronted now. Her face puckered. 'No, come on, Micky. Tell us. You're so full of good ideas at my expense, you're so ready to tell me to pay these finks, so OK, pay them, why not?'

Micky sighed. He wandered over to the window and peered out at the pale green beech trees, the blue scyllas which grew between the yard's cobbles.

'Because that share is my only asset,' he murmured on a monotone, 'and because if you want your shareholders to pay up, you should ask us all to share the cost, like we said, not just the one nearest you. I'm not going to subsidise all the other shareholders sooner than let them make their own decisions. You've settled for one course of action, Cathy. An admirable one, no doubt, but I think a bloody stupid one. You pay for it, or I'll call an extraordinary shareholders' meeting and explain that our property is not being adequately protected, OK?'

'So'll I,' put in Jenny.

'Look, what's with you two?' Cathy growled. 'All this lovey-dovey stuff all of a sudden? She sighed. 'OK. OK. You get your toys. I've got no damn choice, have I?'

'Nope,' Jenny grinned. 'None.'

It had rained almost all day in Jersey. Once, it had cleared up sufficiently for them to take a walk on the deserted damp beach, but otherwise they had been cooped up indoors. They had talked about Eledi's play, about

178

Heron's marriage, about marriage in general. After lunch, Heron spent an hour closeted with his solicitor in his study whilst Eledi lay on the sunbed and took a sauna. Heron had emerged from his meeting looking depressed, though he made an effort, laughed, said what the hell, he wasn't going to allow all this bloody divorce business to mess up their weekend.

They had played ping-pong and watched the new Spielberg video, and Eledi was happy and relaxed because she was miles away from Eric and Kenny and all that strutting crowd.

Last night as he had said goodnight, Heron had made a sort of inept fumbling pass. Nothing serious or aggressive, just the sort of thing that she would expect from an affectionate and lonely man. He had been hugging her, kissing her warmly, and then his right hand had moved down to hold her left buttock. She had just sidestepped, said, 'uh uh,' and kissed him briskly, said pointedly, 'Good night, Richard.'

And now the cocaine had started before dinner. Angela had joined them. A nice girl. There had been a couple of bottles of champagne somewhere in there. Then they had moved onto frozen vodka. Every time that Eledi felt a little woozy, she just cut another couple of lines and the trickling heat down her throat made her body feel alive, It made her skin tingle and her nipples tauten. She felt clear-headed and happy and companionable.

She wore a dress of blue silk jersey, black stockings, black patent courts. She had kicked off the shoes now to jive with Heron, then with Angela, showing them some new moves. Now, out of breath, she lay sprawled on the sofa, another glass of vodka in her hand, and Heron was saying wickedly, 'D'ye know Angela is an actress?'

'You are?' panted Eledi.

'No, Richard!' Angela protested. She laughed and hit him on the shoulder.

He said, 'Yup. Our Angela has been in several movies in her time. You like to see one?'

'No, Richard.'

'Yes,' Eledi caught their laughter. 'Come on. Let's see.'

'No, you don't want to. They're – Richard keeps them to embarrass me. They're from ages ago. They're – rude.'

'Come on, I want to see. Where are they, Richard?'

'No, Richard . . .'

'Da dah!' Heron held aloft a videotape.

'No,' Angela giggled. She jumped up and down in a half-hearted bid to wrest it from him. 'Put it away! Burn it!'

179

'Put it on. Come on. Don't be a spoilsport, Angela.' Eledi drained her glass and pulled herself unsteadily to her feet. She grabbed Angela's hand.

Angela was resigned but coy. 'But they're *rude*.'

'Good.'

'They're *very* rude,' Heron walked over to the television cabinet. He knelt and inserted the tape. He picked up the remote control and pressed Rewind. The video purred, 'Cocaine!' Heron ordered. 'Angela, darling, cut us six monster toots.'

Angela shrugged. 'Well, don't say I didn't warn you,' she grinned. She flounced over to the smoked glass table where the bag of cocaine and the razor blade lay. 'Richard, you're a pig.'

The razor-blade tapped and scraped, tapped and scraped. Eledi poured more vodka into the three Waterford tumblers. First Heron, then Eledi, then Angela snorted the thick lines on the tabletop. 'God,' Eledi gasped, 'Mmm, that is *good*.'

'Right. Showtime!' song Heron from the sofa.

'Oh no!'

'Yes,' Eledi sat on the carpet crosslegged. 'Showtime. Show and tell-time.'

Angela perched on the sofa above her. 'Oh, all right. Get on with it.'

Heron picked up the remote control again. The video clicked and groaned.

The picture was clear, almost professional quality. Angela was lying on a lounger by a swimming-pool. Not this one. Somewhere foreign. France, perhaps, Italy. She wore a skimpy black bikini with white spots on it. She had a great body.

A well muscled man with bleached light brown hair emerged from somewhere and dived into the pool. He crawled a couple of lengths, then pulled himself up from the water. He dried himself, then lay on an airbed beside Angela. He said something to her. She smiled. She clambered off the lounger and picked up a bottle of sun-oil. She knelt by the man and started to smooth the oil into his chest, his stomach, then his shins, his thighs. The guy, not unnaturally, was getting a hard-on as her fingers barely touched the pouch which was his scrotum. Eledi laughed, 'Wey hey! You've got him going.'

'Oh, turn it off, Richard. Eledi's going to be shocked.'

'Pah!' Eledi was scornful. 'Take more than this to shock me.'

On the screen, the man's left hand had crept across to stroke Angela's quim through the thin black fabric. It plunged in, then, his forefinger hooked and dabbled. Angela leaned back for a while and kissed him.

Her hand pulled at the broad cock which had sprung from his trunks. Then she sat up, unhooked her bra and kissed her way down his oily body to take him in her mouth.

Eledi watched the bobbing black head, the flickering pink tongue, and suddenly her mouth was very dry. She gulped and crossed her legs, enclosing the pulsing warmth there. 'God,' she said, and her voice quavered. 'I could never do it with an audience. Who was filming?'

'Oh, a friend.'

'Our Angela is a slut,' Richard said, keeping it light. 'Just you wait.'

Angela hit him again. 'Well, don't say you don't enjoy it.'

Eledi could not resist looking up at those smiling lips, those long hands, long legs ... She turned back to the screen. Her vision blurred. She blinked.

Angela had removed the black and white panties now, and was straddling the man's face whilst continuing her tender ministrations to his cock. She swivelled around. Her hand reached back between her legs. She closed her eyes and sank onto the upright penis.

Eledi involuntarily said, 'Mmm.' She pressed her legs tighter together. Water filled her eyes. Sweat trickled down her back.

Heron had got up now, keeping the pressure off her. He had walked over to the glass table. She heard him cutting more lines. She heard him say, 'That, I will have you know, is my place in France. What the help get up to when the master's away, huh?'

Soon the man was on top of Angela, buttocks clenching and loosening as he pounded into her. His lips nuzzled at her throat, her breasts. Then there was someone else on the screen. A girl with a Pre-Raphaelite curls and white skin. The man stopped thrusting, just lay there supported by his straight arms, his cock still in Angela's heaving body. He said something. The girl smiled. Angela too grinned at her, extended a long arm. And suddenly the girl was down there with them, oiling Angela's body, kissing it, going down on her.

All the combinations.

Every time that Eledi opened her eyes, it was to see that thrusting cock, oily limbs entangled, breasts man-handled, russet hair, black hair, bleached hair ...

Her eyelids were very heavy now. The room was lurching. The heat in her loins was growing like some sort of slow motion explosion. She wanted to put her hand down there, to ease it.

Then somewhere far away Angela was saying, 'I've had enough of this. Good night.'

Eledi said, 'G'nigh'.' The lights went out. She turned over on her side and curled up, a little girl tucked in. The screen kept flickering, filling the room with a soft flush of light. It was strange. Her mind was half asleep but her body was alive and hard and eager and she watched with something like ferocity in her eyes the twining bodies on the screen. She groaned, alone now in the darkness. Her hand at last was clamped between her thighs.

Then another hand was there, warm and gentle, and there were soft kisses on her neck, her ears, a hard cock pressing at her buttocks, the tears were hot in her eyes and she keened, 'Oh God,' but her hips were shifting rhythmically against the pressure of his hand as she turned to him and clasped his head fiercely to her breasts.

Tuesday 8th May started bright and beautiful with a clear baby blue sky and pure white light at the horizon.

In the Welsh valleys, Georgie Blane was up before the smog of night had fully cleared. He dressed quickly in cavalry twill trousers, polo-neck and a tweed hacking-jacket. He padded down the stairs. In the kitchen, a room of grey bulging walls and coal-stains and piles of *Weekend* and the *Daily Mirror*, he made tea and put the soaking porridge on the slow plate of the Aga. He wandered out into the yard.

It might be a ragman's yard, a Steptoe yard, with its scruffy strutting chickens, its old tractors and wheel-less cars. Georgie squelched past boxes filled with furniture and hurdles to the four boxes from which horses peered.

He wished Martindale a cheerful good morning, gave him a double handful of oats, then tied him up on the rack chains. He mucked out, whistling as he banked the clean dry straw around the box and forked the wet stuff into his muck sack. He swept the floor meticulously.

He walked out into the yard again, bolting the door behind him. Sparrows chattered and martins swooped above his head as he fetched a bale of new straw. He spread it and tossed it about the box.

Now he applied himself to the horse. He picked out each of the hooves in turn, then oiled them. He sponged the eyes, the nostrils and the dock. He then unfastened the straps on the rug and rolled it back onto the horse's quarters. He groomed him thoroughly, sponging, drying, brushing and curry-combing, all the while making a soft horse-snorting sound with his lips, at once to calm the animal and to keep the flying hair from his nose and mouth. He threw the rug forward over the withers and repeated the performance on the rear end, this time adorning its rump with check quarter-marks. He pulled the mane, banged the tail with the scissors, and plaited both.

'There you go, feller,' he straightened and pulled the rug back. 'Beautiful.' Then he jumped.

Over the horse's back, he saw Dave Thomas standing in the doorway.

'Um,' he said, then, 'Oh, mornin', Dave.'

'You're a bastard, Georgie Blane,' Dave Thomas announced. 'You and Charlie Vane both.'

'What are you on about, Dave?' Georgie smiled.

'You use me and pay me a peppercorn keep, but you'll not tell old Dave Thomas the truth of it. Oh, no.'

'Dunno what you're banging on about.'

'So you doll an animal up like that to go to the ferry, do you? I thought it was bloody so all along. This is bloody Martindale, isn't it?'

'No, no!' Georgie ducked back under the horse's neck. 'This is De Witt. I'm dolling him up 'cos he's a present. It's nice, you know, the lady who's getting him . . .'

'Bloody crap you talk,' Dave stamped. 'This is bloody Martindale. This is the one runs at Chepstow today. It's a con is what it is. You thought you'd pull the wool over my bloody eyes. Poor old bloody Dave Thomas, he'll never know the difference. That's it, isn't it?'

Georgie glanced over Dave's shoulder. At any moment the lads would be arriving. They might be in the yard already. Dave was not whispering. Georgie made up his mind.

'OK, Dave,' Georgie laid a hand on his arm, 'you've outwitted us. Yup. This is Martindale. We were going to tell you just before the off, but for Christ's sakes keep your voice down if you don't want the odds cut to nothing.'

'You were going to tell me? Ha!' Dave removed his blue Lennon cap and pushed his fingers back through his white hair. Georgie was glad at least to notice that he had lowered his voice. 'If you could've got away with it, you'd not so much as bloody mentioned it. Well, I'm going to Chepstow today and I am going to have a bloody good punt and there's bloody bugger all as you can do about it. I bloody deserve it.'

'Yes, Dave,' Georgie sighed. 'Of course you do. But for God's sake keep quiet about it, OK?'

'Oh, I can keep a secret as well as the next fellow, thank you. Better than some, I'd say.'

'Come on,' Georgie appeased, 'I'll tell you all about it over breakfast.'

'I've got to take the horses out.'

'Oh, they'll keep twenty minutes or so. Come on. This is important. It's big money we're talking here. And anyhow. I'll be gone by the time you get back. I'd best put you in the picture.'

The phrase 'big money' appeared to exercise a persuasive power over Dave, who suffered himself to be led back to the kitchen and sat down at the table. Georgie served porridge and made more tea whilst he very slowly explained the rudiments of the plot. He was working out his options as he did so.

It said in Georgie's Badminton Diary that, if you shoe a horse with thirty-two nails, and the first nail costs a farthing, the second halfpence and so on, the entire shoe will cost something over four million pounds. With the likes of Dave and his cronies, information too spread exponentially. There was no way that Dave would not tell a chum at the sports that he was onto a good thing today. Say he told three good drinking-pals. They would each tell three more. The secret of Martindale would spread faster than 'flu at Harrod's sale.

'So what we plan is this,' George said as he reached for a mug. An idea came to him then. Not a sure-fire one, but there was a chance. He opened the cupboard beneath the work-surface and pulled out a large breakfast-cup decorated with a hunting-scene. He filled it to the brim with tea. 'I drive Martindale towards Fishguard so the lads don't know. Here. Drink up. Only I only get as far as St Clears and then I double back and meet Simple Simon's box at the service area at the end of the M4. We swap over and we arrive at the course about eleven-thirty, right?'

'You think I'd've told the bloody lads, don't you?' Dave was hurt.

'No, 'course not, 'course not. It's just, we didn't want you to have to worry about letting it slip out. Need to know, you know? Hang on, Dave, I'm desperate for a pee. Have to be quick. The box'll be arriving any minute. Here. Have a top up.' He tipped up the pot and filled the cup again. 'Won't be half a second.'

Georgie was pulling his Swiss Army penknife from his pocket even as he walked down the narrow flagged corridor to the downstairs loo.

The loo was, in effect, no more than a cupboard beneath the stairs. The door opened inward. When it was open, there was precious little room for a man to sit in here. There were photographs of Dave riding point-to-points on the walls. There was a hunting-horn. A couple of Giles annuals. Nothing that would serve as an improvised screw-driver.

Good.

Georgie pushed the door open. He bent and quickly unscrewed the arc of chrome which served as a door handle inside. He removed the key from the hole, dropped both the handle and the key in his jacket

184

pocket, flushed the loo, left the door open and strolled back down the corridor to the kitchen.

'Sorry about that, Dave. So yes, that's basically it. Liam O'Connell rides. No one knows him over here. Best bumper rider in Ireland, and pretty mean over fences too. Any luck, the horse wins and we all clean up.'

'Who's placing the bloody bets, then?'

'A gang down in London, the Home Counties. We can't let you have more than five hundred on. Account and on course.'

'Five bloody hundred?' Dave poured himself more tea. Georgie smiled, and prayed. 'And me the trainer? You must be crazy. I'll have a bloody thousand on. I'm owed that at least.'

'Let's compromise, Dave. Seven-fifty.'

'Eight hundred, I'm due that, Georgie. Nothing to stop me going and laying five grand on him if I choose. Remember, I sussed you.'

'Yes,' Georgie nodded. 'You sussed us. It was clever of you. Stupid of me to get so over enthusiastic about the horse too. Still. OK, eight hundred, but carefully, Dave. Scatter it about a bit, OK?'

'You think I'm a bloody fool?'

Dave pushed himself to his feet. He wiped his arm on his sleeve. 'Right. I'll see you at the races, Georgie boy. Thought you could pull the wool over my eyes, didn't you? Ha! I've been around too bloody long for that.'

He turned towards the door into the yard, reached for the handle, then stopped. 'Bloody tea,' He shuffled back towards the corridor.

Georgie smiled contentedly as he heard the loo door click shut. He strolled over to the window and sipped his own tea. He waited for the roar.

'Oh, God that's a bummer,' Joanna Blane piped in the dining-room of the Tara Hotel on Kensington Gore. 'So what happened?'

'I don't know,' Micky unfolded his napkin. 'Apparently she said doing the play made her aware she couldn't combine acting and being Charlie's wife. She chose acting. Charlie said she was cut up about it. She also said something about she'd learned that she didn't love Charlie enough. I mean, she loved him more than anyone as a friend sort of thing, but the man she married she'd have to be so in love with she'd never look at anyone else and she wouldn't mind sacrificing acting. That sort of crap.'

'Oh, lawks. Meaning she has been looking at somebody else. Who? The star of the show?'

'Not according to Charlie. Know how she turned up in Ireland? In a private jet. Owner, one Richard Heron. Said her piece, cried a bit, climbed back into the plane. Nice touch, eh? The sod of it is, there's damn all we can do.'

'Poor Charlie,' Joanna twiddled her glass of orange-juice between forefinger and thumb. 'He's such a sweet guy. Do you think he'll be up today?'

'Yeah, I reckon. He's been laughing the whole thing off for the past couple of days. Until late at night when the first half bottle of brandy's gone and he starts thinking. Then it takes another half to knock him out. I don't blame him.'

'Oh, poor Charlie. I remember when daddy used to be like that.' Joanna raised her yards of dark straight hair and tossed it into floss.

'Hush up. Here he comes,' Micky pushed back his chair, 'Charlie, mate, good to see you. How's it going?'

'Don't be so fucking solicitous, Micky,' Charlie pulled out a chair and sat heavily. He was very white and the flesh about his eyes and at his jawbone was puffed up like that of a drowned man. He drew his hand across his forehead. 'Sorry. I've got the high priest of heads and I'm fed up with every bugger being sorry for me. Come on. Let's make a hearty breakfast. Today's the big day, for heaven's sake. Come on. Let's at least have some fun today. Smash the bookies. That'll brighten the horizon a damned sight more than you chaps and your long faces.'

'Show you something else that'll cheer you up,' Micky unfolded a copy of the nation's biggest-selling tabloid. He stabbed at it with his finger.

Charlie picked it up and squinted at it. 'Whassat?'

Micky leaned over his shoulder. 'Look. There,' he pointed.

Charlie read from the foot of the horoscope column; '*Estella's Tips from the Stars: Martindale, 3.30, Chepstow. Delightfully Still, 4.15 Haydock.* Dear God in heaven. No, I'll amend that. Dear gods. I shall be a pantheist ever more.'

'Nope, don't bother converting.' Micky laughed softly, 'It's Jenny's clever wheeze, isn't it? Estella used to be in fashion, but Richard Moreton needed an astrologer, so now she's an expert on the stars. She also happens to be an old schoolfriend of Jenny's. So Jen rings, says, 'Do us a favour', and behold!'

'I'm not sure I see the point,' Joanna frowned. 'It'll just shorten the odds needlessly, won't it?'

'No, for heavens sakes! Don't you see? A few not-very-serious astrology buffs may have a fiver each way, sure, but the bookies will have seen this. They don't believe in the stars; they believe in the

186

form-book, so when the odd double bet comes in, they don't panic. If anything, they lengthen the odds to attract more mug bets. It's brilliant. At least at first, they'll see a load of stargazers, not a coup.'

'You were right,' Charlie cackled, 'that has cheered me up very much indeed. Come on. Breakfast! Eggs, bacon, tomatoes, Cumberland sausages, kidneys, black pudding and fried bread. Every last porcine portion. I want to get out on the streets!'

Liam O'Connell arrived at Chepstow racecourse at midday, just twenty minutes after Georgie had led Martindale down the ramp into the racecourse stables. The race would not start until half past three. Nonetheless, Liam's first destination as ever, was the weighing-room.

The weighing-room was unfurnished save for the scales, but much of the space was taken up by jockeys, officials, trainers and so on who stood around gossiping, plotting and swapping stories.

Liam knew some of the faces here – Irish emigrés and fellow-amateurs mostly – but his job today was to be unobtrusive, so he nodded or waved to one or two, but walked briskly through to the changing-room.

There were four jockeys already on the benches. Liam knew their faces from the press and television, but he knew none of them personally. They nodded at him and continued with their conversation, laconic, cryptic, at once typically English and typically professional. One of them wore trousers but was bare-chested. One slouched in a string vest and jockey shorts. Another was naked save for a towel slung around his neck. The last was already in his colours, though his feet were stockinged, his head bare.

They were veterans. You could tell by the thick ridges of muscle in their necks, shoulders and backs. You could tell by their many scars.

'Poor bastard. First time treads on a broken hurdle which flips back. Collarbone, crushed vertebrae, the lot. Ride again maybe, but strapped up to the eyes. Twenty-two and a canvas robot. Jeez.'

'Yeah. They say buy Saatchi, by the way. Everyone's knocking it, but the gearing's good and they've cleared the decks. They're dirt cheap.'

'Oh yes? Listen, you know that horse you ride . . .?'

'Try a name.'

'Oh, you know the bugger. Brown thing. Quick to come into himself . . .?'

'Nice trick.'

'Always there or thereabouts first time out. Feet like dinner-plates.'

187

'Night Train!' – a unison chant.

'Yeah, that's the boy. So, what's going to happen to him now, Mrs Maxwell's croaked an'all?'

Liam strolled over to his valet who was busy laying out neatly folded breeches on the table.

The valets go from racecourse to racecourse. Every evening they take home the dirty clothes, boots and tack and return with them clean and mended. This valet was a short, gypsy-faced fellow who looked more like a music-hall jockey than did the jockeys. Liam held out a hand. 'Liam O'Connell.' He grinned.

'Oh, yeah. Thomas's mad horse in the fourth, right? Nine seven with breastplate. Should do that easy enough.'

'Yeah, no problem. Listen, a friend of mine, Georgie Blane . . .'

'Old Georgie. How's he?'

'Fine. Great. He's been staying a few days at Dave's. Dave's gone off to Haydock, so Georgie'll be dropping off the colours and the kit. Can you furnish us with a helmet?'

'No problem. Don't worry. We'll have everything ready. You just relax, Mr O'Connell. What I hear, you're not going to have a very relaxing afternoon exactly.'

Liam shuddered. 'No,' he breathed, 'Too right I'm not.'

Slowly the course and the car-parks filled. Jenny watched the barking men and the droning women as they laid their picnics or greeted their friends in the car-park. In her red loden, she strolled down through the members' gate, admiring the green and purple hills which enclosed the racecourse.

She had had a busy morning. First she had had to load up Simple Simon, the erstwhile Martindale, and drive him to a vet who was to dispatch him to a better world which he had done little to deserve. Then she had to drive down to the motorway service station, where Georgie had transferred Martindale to her horsebox and had taken over the driving-seat.

She had told Georgie briefly about Charlie over a cup of coffee there. He had grown as angry as she had ever seen a man, so angry that he became quite still. Nothing moved, not his mouth, his eyes or his hands. She could just feel the hatred pulsing out of him. Jenny had been suddenly aware of his mind as a muscle, a great taut, straining thing, hurling laser rays of wrath through the ether. Jesus, she thought, I wouldn't like this man for an enemy. And I hope his aim is good.

And then it had been over for now, and back to business. Georgie had told her about Dave Thomas reluctantly emulating the three old ladies of song. He had apparently told all the lads – well, farmhands – to go home, he said, save old deaf Owen, who was to drive Delightfully Still to Haydock. Jenny, therefore, must take the horsebox back to Dave's place, see Delightfully Still safely loaded up, and come on to Chepstow in the car.

'But I thought Delightfully Still wasn't to race,' Jenny had objected. 'I thought the idea was, we bet in doubles, so they don't notice, then Delightfully Still – damn silly name – scratches, and all the bets devolve on Martindale.'

'That's right. So what we have to do, is you get back to Chepstow quick as you can and turn into the stable-girl. Soon as you arrive, I drive the car to Haydock armed with cold spray and a small hammer.'

'You're not really going to hurt him, are you?'

'Nah. Same as stumbling and grazing your knee. A slight swelling is enough for the vet to insist he's unfit to race. It's going to be a push, Jen. I think we'd best be moving.'

So far, so good. Except for Dave Thomas's lucky discovery, everything had gone according to plan. Martindale was in his box, keyed up and raring to go. Georgie must be well on his way to Haydock by now. All she had to do was to grab some lunch. And pray.

Micky had had a leisurely sort of morning. He had travelled by taxi, placing the odd bet here or there about Fulham, Battersea, Wandsworth, Clapham and Putney. Now he had instructed his curious driver to take him to Paddington.

Charlie has insisted from the outset, 'You do the morning-run, then get up there and see the contest. It's your plan. You damn well deserve to be there. We'll do the rest, and we'll all meet up at the Tara in the evening.'

His plan, God save him, made so many moons ago in that little labourer's cottage in Suffolk, and now come to fruition. All this money, all these people, all going to fulfil *his* plan. It must come out right. It *must*. So much depended on it now.

The taxi braked hard. Micky had to extend a hand to stop himself from falling into the partition. The driver growled 'Arsehole. You see that?' He slammed his hand down on the horn.

Funny. Once Micky had thought this place great crack. Now he developed a headache within five minutes of arrival.

Was that just because he was growing old? Oh, partially, perhaps, but it was not just that. He developed a headache as soon as he arrived in England these days.

Because? Because the priceless chalk downland on which he used to train had been ripped up to make unyielding prairies, because you could no longer take a dog for a walk without being challenged, because hunting and shooting were judged by the number of kills and the smallest children by the clothes that they wore, because buildings were only seen in terms of their value, because mortgages constituted the only topic of conversation, because everyone, both here and in the country, seemed brash and loud and in a hurry. Because vice and spirituality and communality and games had all been subsumed by the urge to possess. No energy must be wasted. Nothing was done simply for the crack.

He looked at his watch, then leaned forward. Goddamned mobile confessional. 'Sorry, can we just pop down to the Oratory for a minute or two?'

'You're the boss, guv,' the taxi-driver hummed. 'Trying to get God to fix the odds, are you?'

'Something like that.'

'Why so many bookies, then? You've got a scam on, haven't you? A coup.'

'Something like that.'

'Mum's the word, eh?'

'Mum, I'm afraid, is the word.'

The driver was now eager to impress Micky. With a deal of cursing, he executed a U-turn across Brompton Road, so that the near door opened onto the pavement outside Brompton Oratory.

'Just be a couple of minutes,' Micky told him.

He stepped from the snarling and the growling of the street into the cool stillness of the church. He thought, Jesus, this site must be worth millions, and look at it, empty save for one woman arranging flowers up by the altar, one man praying at the left of the nave. Oh, and God up there in the tabernacle. Criminal waste.

Micky dipped his fingers in the font. He crossed himself. He genuflected quickly and slipped into a pew at the very back. He knelt.

His prayer was less than formal. 'Please let this work. Please. Oh, damn, I'm no good at this. Real opportunistic praying, huh? Yeah, well, I've been caught in the trap too. Watching my back all the time, trying to fill time, never stopping like this. Hell, there's millions of people rushing past outside, and in here, an absence, an absence that feels strong – stronger than any presence, an absence which is worth a building like this, a building worth billions even, because here there is sanctuary, and there's room to think about all the damn fool meaningless things, the constant, unmoving things in the middle of all this meaningful, purposeful change and movement. God, I'm gibbering, but it feels good. Yeah, well, listen. Whoever. Help us today if you can. Right? Nice seeing you. Um, amen.'

He crossed himself and stood with a rueful smile. Once again in the nave, he genuflected. Then he frowned.

The man ahead of him, the man with his face in his hands – it was Charlie. 'Oh, and please help Charlie,' Micky appended. 'He deserves better. A whole lot better.'

He turned and tiptoed back towards the door. Then he heard a voice like that of a sick cow. It echoed in the vault. 'Micky?'

Micky swung round. Charlie was pulling himself slowly to his feet. He shuffled sideways into the nave, all the time looking towards the altar. He knelt and got up, his eyes turned downward.

As he approached, Micky said, 'Sorry.'

'Be bloody silly,' Charlie rested a hand on Micky's sleeve. Still he did not look up. 'Just dropped in. Still got three hours more. Got to get going.' He raised his eyes then. They were wet and red-rimmed. He said, 'Micky . . .' His face crumpled. His voice cracked, and then Micky was hugging him close, whispering, 'Oh, God, Charlie, I am so sorry. So sorry,' and although he tried to swallow them back, the tears were running down his cheeks too. It was all right. they were expatriate fellow citizens, in their own embassy.

'Gor,' Charlie laughed at last. He wiped his eyes, 'Cop us two, would you? You're as bad as I am. Come on, Micky, mate. You've got to get to your triumph, and I've got to get to those betting-shops. Just over three hours to go. Let's go for it.'

Joanna scrawled in as ill-formed a hand as she could contrive, *£5 win, 3.30, Chepstow, £5 double, Martindale, 3.30 Chepstow, Delightfully Still, 4.15 Haydock*. She pushed aside the curtain of smoke and walked up to the counter. It was a quarter past two. She was at Ladbroke's, Shepherd's Bush Green. From here her map led her to shops in Acton, Willesden, Ealing, Northolt and Uxbridge, then down to West Drayton, Slough and Windsor. No shops of the same chain within a five mile radius, they had resolved, for fear of too rapidly discernible a pattern. Perhaps a twenty or a fifty here or there, but mostly tenners and fivers.

The cashier was looking up an ante-post Derby price on the computer-screen. 'Come on,' Joanna shifted from foot to foot, 'Come on . . .'

She still had two thousand, five hundred pounds in various pockets. She wanted to get rid of the lot.

Georgie strode into the parade ring just behind the jockeys. He was panting. 'Liam,' he called, 'Liam . . .'

Liam turned with his usual broad grin. His cap was pushed back onto the back of his head. His orange hair sprouted from beneath his cap. 'Ah, there you are. The trainer's meant to arrive first, you know. It is important to observe the proprieties in these little matters.'

You're bloody lucky I'm here at all,' Georgie panted. 'That bloody Owen wouldn't leave me alone for a second, then the vet took hours, then the traffic out of Manchester . . . He stared 'God in heaven, man, what do you look like?'

'Like what I am, an unknown, ignorant Irish peasant. Look at your horse and his custodian, while you're at it. Aren't they a thing of beauty?'

'Lawks,' Georgie grinned at Martindale, who was once more coated in thick foaming sweat flecked with straw, 'to think that I groomed him this morning. And Jenny's back in costume, I see. I hope we're not overdoing it.'

'Not a bit of it. See the odds?'

'I saw what I thought was 10–1 quoted on the way over.'

'According to Micky, you could get tens to twelves in the ring. He came in from fifties and then someone started laying against him. He's moving out again now.'

'Odd. So Micky made it?'

'Yup. He saddled him in your absence. Look. Over there.' He pointed with his whip at the stands end of the paddock where Micky stood watching Martindale and Jenny as they circled. 'Your only man.'

'Good,' Georgie smiled.

'All well at Haydock?'

'Yeah, yeah, Delightfully Still very unfortunately had to be withdrawn owing to an injury sustained in transit. Now, listen. You've walked the course?'

'Twice. Last night and this morning.'

'And?'

'Hilly. Easy bends. Decent size fences. Well built. I like it.'

'Good, so do I. Hilly is right, but it's the sort of switchback ride they seem to enjoy. It's a good galloping course, strangely enough, but for God's sake hold something in reserve. He'll need it in the shake-up. It's not a bad novice field, but if you get round OK, you've got their measure. Just keep him out of trouble, that's the main thing.'

'Sure. I've already had a sermon from Micky. I'll not be looking for trouble, I can tell you.'

There was silence between them then. Liam tapped his boot with his whip. George whistled silently and watched Jenny leading the horse. The crowd all around them buzzed. At last, the horses were turned inward.

'Well,' Georgie swallowed. 'This is it, eh? All these months.'

'I'll be back before you know it.' Liam assured him.

Jenny came up with the horse. She said, 'Well, here we go. God, this is terrifying. Everything OK, Georgie?'

'Everything's fine.'

Once again he bent to give Liam a leg-up. To his astonishment he found that the leathers had been let down by five or six holes, so that Liam sat his mount like an eighteenth century farmer out hunting. 'I don't hold with all this riding short,' Liam laughed down to him. 'New-fangled stuff. Like a monkey on a thistle.'

Georgie tried hard to keep a straight face. He just said, 'God speed, Liam.'

'Yeah, well.' Liam turned the horse away. 'Be seeing you.'

'Well, big day, eh, Micky?' the Colonel joined him as he walked back to the stand.

'Yup. Should I be seen talking to you?'

'And why not? I'm a respectable fellow, you know.'

'So what's with the odds?' Micky sounded puzzled. 'How come they're still wandering out? Your doing?'

'Nope. We've done nothing to shorten them, but . . . There must be another steamer.'

'With that much support? It doesn't make sense.'

'Not to worry,' the Colonel stepped up onto the stand ahead of Micky. 'You've done a good job, Micky. Now let us pray that the horse delivers.'

'Oh, he will,' Micky said as the Colonel climbed the steps away from him. 'Don't worry. He will.'

'Know who I just saw?' Georgie Blane unwound the strap of his binoculars and took up a position on Micky's right. 'That bastard Heron. I damn near walked over and pushed that smug bloody nose to the other side of his face.'

'Don't,' Micky said softly. He was watching the animals up at the start. 'a) Charlie'll not thank you and b) Heron would ensure you got put away for a long time. One thing I've learned. Bide your time and the chance for revenge will come. One of these days, we'll get the bugger.' He frowned. He pulled the binoculars away from his eyes. 'Hold up. What's he doing here? Heron doesn't go jumping. Oh, Christ. Oh, Christ Jesus,' he moaned, 'Oh dear holy God almighty. Please let it not be.'

'What are you thinking?' Georgie turned to him.

'Someone's been laying heavily against Martindale. Who would that be?'

'Heron,' Georgie said in a voice like a funeral drum. 'You think Eledi . . ?'

'Our ex-co-conspirator. And Heron doesn't throw away that sort of cash on a petty gesture. Oh, God help us . . .'

The course commentator twanged, 'They're off.'

At three twenty-five exactly, twelve men walked into betting-shops in Belfast and placed five thousand apiece in readies on an unknown animal named Martindale. At the same time, the main telephone exchange, which had been evacuated after an anonymous telephone call, was shaken by an explosion. The caller had said that there would be two bombs. No one could go in there to sort things out until the Bomb Squad had searched the entire building and neutralised any devices that they might find.

Gregory McCabe, Hoyle's Bookmakers' Regional director, Northern Ireland, had given up smoking two weeks ago. He had smoked four cigarettes in the past ten minutes. Yesterday, five of his shops had had the day's takings, ripped off at gunpoint. Today he stood to lose the better part of a million pounds.

He had a pretty shrewd idea who was responsible. With people like that, you did not argue. You paid up.

Gregory McCabe had not much hair – just a clump of black above each ear. Nor did he ever believe that people ever really tore their hair when in distress. Nonetheless, when he heard 'They're off' on the satellite television he looked down on his hands to find precious strands in both.

They had set off at a fair old pace for a three mile chase. Martindale was content to bowl along with it. Liam too was unconcerned. They were lying four lengths fifth of twelve, and the favourite, a bright grey, was on their inside. The fellow up front, a dull chestnut with no form and a poor sense of balance when tired, would come back to them in time. For now, he was working at getting his name mentioned by the commentator, moving up another couple of lengths before reaching the first.

Liam stopped thinking about him. He had other things to worry about. Nineteen of them, to be exact.

The first of them was fine. Martindale saw it clearly and put himself right without breaking his enormous stride. He and the grey flowed over it, and – thank God for Georgie's schooling – Martindale was the quickest away. Perhaps these old boys did know a thing or two.

God. Good feeling. The warm sun on your back, the winey breeze wriggling around you, the going good, the grass dry, the horse beneath you powerful and responsive. Hell, so you broke a limb from time to time, but this was the best; a battalion of fellows around you, the divots spurting from heels ahead, the reverberating rattle of hooves all around and a battle in prospect.

The second was easy, the third, the fourth, the fifth; at each, a ragged chorus of exhortations, the moment of silence, the wildfire crackle, the drumfire landing, the sighs from the horses, grunts from the men, and on, feller, on.

At the sixth, they encountered a problem. They were still lying fourth or fifth, and Martindale was galloping a touch too freely, so Liam pulled in a reef, collected him, put him right. As Martindale kicked to project himself upwards and over, the bay heels of the horse ahead, just a yard to their right, skewed and dropped with tell-tale suddenness. The jockey's hand arose, clutching for puppeteers' strings which had suddenly been cut. Liam had to steel himself not to hook his horse up. Beneath them, the bay had stumbled sprawled and rolled. His legs flailed in Martindale's path. His jockey lay curled and clutched his head.

Martindale came down steeply. He jinked to the left so smartly that Liam was nearly unseated on the off side, then swung back again, weaving around the stiff swinging legs. Other horses landed and galloped by. Martindale put in an ungainly little skip over the curled up jockey but caught him in the back, rolling him over.

Liam had been leaning backward. Now he was jerked forward and down, then Martindale was up again and running. He leaped off in pursuit and Liam was flung inelegantly back into the middle of the saddle.

'Nasty,' muttered Georgie.

'Lost a lot of ground,' Micky agreed. 'Still. Going well.'

'Where is he?' Jenny, her stablegirl disguise once more covered by her coat, had climbed up onto the steps beneath them.

'"Bout nine lengths back, jumping like a stag. Eighth or ninth. Plenty of time. The favourite's looking good too.'

'Oh, God.' Jenny jumped up and down. 'How can you guys stay so calm?'

'Calm?' Micky smiled, 'God, Gene Kruper should try beating as fast as my heart. Nice one. He's moved up a couple of lengths, and Poison Ivy's gone.' He held the glasses in his left hand. His right moved forward to clasp Jenny's shoulder. Briefly her cheek was cool on the back of his hand. 'Well done, Liam,' he hummed. 'Come on, my old son . . .'

Martindale liked waterjumps best of all, because he could stretch out and skim them, flat and fast. He must have gained two lengths there. And now it was out into the country again. The field was spread out. There were five to catch. The chestnut which had led from the off was coming back to them. They took him on the turn into the back straight.

Martindale felt all the way a winner. He was jumping intelligently, stylishly, and every inch of him was giving out the message; nothing beats me today.

Liam tried to recall the names. The leader was Lezard, ears back, jumping like a show-jumper that has been rapped once too often. The Comma, two lengths back, a burly black, then Woodbrook and Barnard Castle upsides three lengths further back. A quick glance over his shoulder told Liam that only one of the other fancied runners, Random Harvest, was still standing, another three lengths or so behind.

At the open ditch, The Comma pecked badly on landing and dropped out of contention, for now at least. Liam clicked his tongue. Martindale moved upsides with Woodbrook and Barnard Castle. The jockey on the grey, a tall, blond fellow with a round pink and white face, turned. 'Thought yours was crazy, Paddy.'

'Sure and that was only a phase he was going through.'

'He looks good.'

'Just you wait. Excuse us. Something in our way.'

All three horses took the plain fence side by side. Again, Martindale stole half a length on his opponents. Liam smiled as he heard Barnard Castle's jockey shaking his mount up. He came up on Martindale's outside. 'Bastard's good,' he panted grudgingly. 'There been some punting going on?'

'Oh, sure and would a good Catholic boy indulge in the terrible sin of gambling?'

'Would he ever? Fucking Paddies.'

Both men sat down and concentrated on the next fence. Lezard was just two lengths ahead of them now. He arose, but his stomach hit the birch so hard that his rider was flung forward. The poor fellow was doubled up over his horse's ears as Martindale and Barnard Castle galloped past. He would recover.

They were running downhill now. Random Harvest was breathing down their necks, ready to make his move as they entered the straight. The Comma was back there too, plodding relentlessly on. This, then, was the shake-up.

Martindale was still enjoying himself, still full of running. Liam leaned forward and whispered into his prick ears, 'You've got 'em, you old bastard. You've got 'em cold.'

In the smoke-filled betting-shop, men just kept on writing slips and carrying them up to the cashier as though nothing out of the ordinary were happening. Charlie sat at the table and his fingers scrabbled at the knee of his suit-trousers. He would have liked to shout, 'Silence! Don't you realise? The most important race of the season is nearing its climax! Extinguish your Woodbines. Stop your wittering! Remove your hands from your donkey-jacket pockets. Chest out, stomach in, thumbs by the seam of your trousers. That's my horse that's winning, Listen!'

But the burbling went on, and the commentator droned in that familiar disinterested tone, 'And as they turn into the straight, it's Martindale, Martindale by a neck from Barnard Castle, with Random Harvest coming with a strong challenge. And it's Martindale and Barnard Castle as they come to the second last, and they're neck and neck with Random Harvest struggling to get on terms and The Comma closing. Martindale and Barnard Castle as they approach the last . . .'

As they approached the last. Liam kicked on, and Martindale easily put a length between him and the other two. Random Harvest was at his near side, Barnard Castle at his off. 'Eeny-meeny-miney-mo,' Liam muttered. Then he made up his mind.

Two strides off, he swung Martindale hard to his left, stealing Random Harvest's ground. 'Hey!' called a hoarse voice behind him. Liam gave Martindale a quick urgent slap. He arose steeply, scraped through the top of the fence and descended so steeply that Liam was almost lying on the horse's back, then he was rocked forward and his teeth smashed into the horse's neck.

'OK,' he spat as Martindale set off towards the finishing post. 'The dog will have its day all right.' But Barnard Castle was still at his right. Just to make doubly sure, Liam pulled the whip through to his left hand.

'And it's Martindale,' the commentator was still unexcited, 'Martindale, the outsider, going away now from Barnard Castle. Martindale by five, six lengths, and Martindale passes the post with six lengths to spare over Barnard Castle, with the Comma and Diamondback in a battle for third.'

Charlie smiled slowly. He stood. A moment ago he had thought that he would whoop and holler when the moment came, but now that it was over, he just felt very tired. Satisfied, sure, but strangely sad.

He should have been celebrating with Eledi. That was part of it, of course. And then, damn it, the excitement had kept him going all this time. Now it was all over.

He wandered out into the dingy grey street, and just stood on the pavement watching the shuddering buses, the jerking cars. Now that it was over, he did not know where to go.

'We did it!' Jenny clapped and jumped. 'We did it!' She flung her arms around Micky and kissed him again and again. 'Oh, Micky, well done! Well done, Georgie. We did it! We're rich! Martindale – Oh, God, I thought I was going to have a coronary . . .' She stopped then. She frowned. She said, 'What's up?'

Micky had his eyes closed. He was breathing very slowly as though to calm himself. His teeth were clenched.

'What is it?'

'Excuse me,' said Georgie. He too looked grim. He jumped down the concrete steps and wove quickly through the crowd which traipsed its way to the winners' enclosure or to the bars.

'What is it, Micky?' Jenny shook him. Her face was just inches from him. He put an arm around her and drew her close. She felt him shaking, his cheek against hers. He said quietly, 'Liam threw it. There's no way we can keep it. Liam bumped that poor bastard halfway along the straight. He threw it. Oh, God, Jenny, he threw it. We've had it.' He opened his eyes. Through the mist, he saw the Colonel further along on the same step. The older man was glaring at him, and breathing very heavily. His face was white.

'I don't understand,' Jenny stroked Micky's hair. 'He won.'

Micky shook his head, and above them the tannoy farted and the course-commentator announced 'Stewards' Enquiry. Stewards' Enquiry. All betting tickets should be retained until the results of the enquiry are known.'

Georgie strode into the Winners' Enclosure as Liam rode in from the far side, the usual broad grin on his face. There was a half-hearted patter of applause.

Georgie took Martindale's bridle. He patted the horse's neck. 'That's a fine boy,' he crooned.

'Gave us a great ride,' Liam said chirpily. He dismounted and undid the girths. 'Bit rough at the last, but a great ride.'

'Liam . . .' said Georgie.

'Yup?' Liam turned, one hand on the saddle.

Georgie did not telegraph it. One moment his hand was by his side, the next it had curled into a fist and smashed straight into Liam's grinning face. Liam sat down eight feet away with a thump which shook the turf.

There was a gratifying gasp from the crowds. Someone shouted, 'Hey!' Hands grasped at Georgie's arms and pulled him back, but Liam shook his head and flapped the hand which was not covering his face. 'It's OK,' he waffled, 'fair play to him.'

He stood and returned to the horse. He pulled off the saddle. 'I had that coming,' he snuffled to Georgie. 'Sorry, mate.'

'What did the bastard offer you?' Georgie breathed heavily through his nose.

'My own stables.'

'Enjoy them.'

'Thanks.' Liam nodded. And he shuffled unsteadily into the sanctuary of the weighing-room.

'What are we doing here?' Jenny suddenly giggled, then, 'I mean really. What the hell . . .?' She wrapped her fingers around the mug. She shuddered. 'Crazy,' she sighed, 'crazy, crazy, crazy.' She sipped and threw herself back in the waiting-up room's over-ripe leather chair.

199

Micky did not look away from the closed circuit television screens. 'Today I am a Bulgarian Minister of Education,' he hummed, 'tomorrow I shall be Helen of Troy.'

'What?'

'Or try "Peculiar travel suggestions are dancing lessons from God".'

'Oh, great,' she mumbled into her mug. When she looked up she was grinning. Her teeth steamed. 'Just fantastic. Now I am facing death and destruction all alone with a gibbering idiot. Just great.'

Micky glanced quickly back over his shoulder, 'It's your friend Vonnegut, isn't it? Good an answer as any. Or you could try an old English song. Sing it in rugby coaches. Very philosophical. Goes *"We're here because we're here because we're because we're here."* Just to be witty, we sing it to the tune of *Auld Lang Syne*.'

'Thanks. That helps a lot. No, but I mean here. Now. It just seems so – unreal. I mean, in Ireland, for God's sake, out here in the quiet and cutesie countryside. Things like this just don't happen. In a *stable*.'

'I know,' Micky nodded, 'but it's for real all right, girl. They're out there. Fergal told me. Just a matter of what they do and when they'll do it.' He plucked a bent roll-up from the Pernod ashtray and placed it between his lips. He shook a matchbox. 'Mind,' he said and the cigarette waggled, 'lot of momentous things get to happen in stables.'

'You ever get laid in one?'

'Yup. Lost my virginity in one, actually.'

'Tell me.'

'Not now,' he exhaled smoke through his nostrils. He grinned. His teeth caught the grey glare from the screens.

'Did it prickle?'

'Uh huh. Thought all dire warnings had proved true first time. Got myself shriven and prepared to die. Seriously,' he said above her laugh. 'Got in the bath, saw this rash, thought, 'so this is God's punishment for fornication. Tomorrow I go blind, next day I go mad, Friday I die!'

Jenny whooped. 'You Catholics. And?'

'And I didn't. Die, I mean. Got off scot free. Been chancing my arm ever since. Look, shut up, will you? I've got to keep watching, you've got to keep listening. They could be out there right now.'

'It's not happening,' Jenny's shoulders shook again. Her voice was small as she repeated the words, this time to herself. 'It's just not happening.'

There had been no celebration on the night of the race. Micky and Jenny had flown directly back from Heathrow. Charlie, Georgie and Joanna had got very seriously, very morosely drunk.

Micky and Jenny had consoled themselves in a no more original way. That night, Jenny had stayed down at the bungalow. When Micky had joined her in bed, she had said, 'I'm no damn good at this lark. Don't know why you bother.'

She had proved nervous, uptight and unresponsive, while Micky was impatient, filled with the urgency at once of frustration and of fear.

'I liked the cuddles,' Jenny announced in the morning, 'but I was lousy when it came to what your compatriots call "the Bold Thing", wasn't I?'

'Terrible,' Micky kidded her.

'Told you so.'

'Yeah, but I reckon you'll learn. Nothing wrong with the raw materials.'

'Thanks,' she had shrugged. But learn she had, as night after night her quick flashes of affection became lengthier and less self-conscious and her shyness evaporated. Micky learned too – not to stop so soon as she made a joke, not to insist upon those parts which were said to be the principal triggers of orgasm, not, indeed to insist upon orgasm. It was never earth-shattering, but it was, as Jenny would say, 'really quite nice'.

The morning after that first night, Micky had informed each of the staff in turn that, within a week, some unpleasantness might be expected. From what quarter he did not say. To his surprise, it seemed, there was no need.

Annie Flynn had said, 'Oh, stop.' She could not hold with those people and they needed a darn good spanking, and did Micky really think as she'd leave poor old Mrs Kramer because of a few masquerading madmen in Halloween hoods? No, Micky had had to admit, he didn't. And anyhow, she had appended, how was she to pay for her Shane's leather jacket if she were not to work here, she'd like to know.

Screech said 'Hmph,' kept his own council and stayed on.

It was mid-afternoon on the Thursday when Fergal rang.

'Mick?' He spoke very quietly.

'Fergal. Hi, mate. How's it goin'?'

'Not so hot. Listen. You alone?'

'Yup. I'm working in the office. Why?'

'Listen. I'm going to tell you something 'cos you're a friend. You've got to promise not to tell Mrs Kramer, OK? Or the gardai. You've got to swear.'

'Tell them what?'

201

'I am doing something as I shouldn't. I've been told when someone – when they're sending someone in. I want your word that you'll not tell Mrs Kramer.'

'What are they going for? Her or the horse?'

'Dunno. Wouldn't tell you if I did. Maybe neither, like I said. Maybe just a scare, a gesture of some sorts. I don't know. But you've got to give me your word. You don't tell the old girl. It's either that or you don't get to know either.'

'OK, OK,' Micky sighed. 'You've got my word.'

'Well, shit, Mick, I don't have to tell you a blind thing. I'm sticking my neck out enough as it is.'

'OK. Sorry, mate. Just . . . Bit fraught, that's all. No. It's good of you.'

'Right. Listen. It's tomorrow night. Dunno what time, dunno what they're proposing. All I know is, someone's coming over tomorrow, so get the hell out or – I dunno. Just look out for yourself. I don't want to see you getting hurt, Mick. It's not your battle.'

'Maybe not,' Micky mused. 'Is it yours, then?'

'No, thank Christ. I don't want to have to fight you, Mick. Of all people.'

'I'm glad to hear it. Be honest, I'd rather not fight anyone at all. Just have to hope no silly bugger gets in my way.'

There was silence now, save for the prolonged gasp of the Calor-gas heater, the occasional rustle of Micky's leather jacket or of straw as a horse moved in one of the adjacent boxes.

Micky suddenly leaned forward. He narrowed his eyes and frowned at the screen. 'That is Screech, isn't it?'

Jenny jumped up. She peered over his shoulder. Her fair hair touched his cheek. There was an overhead view of a horse on each of the screens. A foreshortened human figure had walked into the bottom left-hand corner of the middle screen. 'Yeah,' Jenny's voice vibrated in her breastbone, and hummed down Micky's jaw. 'Yeah,' she stabbed with a forefinger at the screen, 'that's him. No one else got a pate like that.' She turned away and slumped back into the chair, banging open a *Daily Mail* on her thighs. Jenny combed back her hair with her fingers. 'I'm hungry. You?'

Micky shook his head. 'Couldn't eat a bloody thing. What were you thinking of?'

'Dunno,' she shrugged, 'Could go up to the house, grab a corpse or two from the 'fridge. Some beer, something.'

'Uh uh. Sorry. Have to wait. No way you are going up that yard on your own, and someone's got to stay down here. Perhaps when Screech gets back. There's tea and biscuits.'

'So you can walk up there, right? Not me, right?'

'Nope,' Micky sang and sighed. With both palms outstretched, he slapped the table twice. 'Nope, I'd not go up there alone either. Not if – not if Isabella Rosselini were out there with her skirt above her waist and a pound of foie gras between her lips.'

'Micky Brennan, I am always astounded by the scope and range of your imagery. Extends from the head of the bed to its foot. OK, so it's biscuits.' She got up and shambled slowly around the room. She ran a finger along the back of the chair, the edge of the sink. 'God,' she said to the calendar, 'Isn't it time you got rid of this damned thing? It's gross.'

'Screech likes it. Probably reminds him of a favourite mare. Will you not leave an old man his dreams?'

'Yuk.' She wandered on. 'Seriously, Micky,' she was suddenly subdued, 'what are we doing here? I mean, we could get actually hurt – killed doing this, right? Really dead! For a horse? We got to be mad.' She leaned back against the draining-board. Her hands hung crossed over the denim welts at her crotch.

She glimpsed the ghost of Micky's smile in the screen. 'Try a principle,' he said.

'Nah. A principle's bigger than this, isn't it? A principle makes you feel all noble. Those guys out there, they got principles.'

'For Cathy, then.'

'Ha! Not me. Stupid, stubborn, opinionated old cow. Why'd I want to get shot at just for her bloody-mindedness?'

'Maybe we're just that sort. Won't concede to bullying.'

'But we're the ones did all the arguing for concession!' she squealed. She raised her hands and let them slap back onto her thighs. 'All the guys so full of "we must fight them on the beaches, never surrender," all that horseshit, where the fuck are they now, I'd like to know?'

'They've changed,' Micky shrugged. 'We've changed, I suppose. Faltering?'

She sighed, and walked over to him, placing her hands on his shoulders and massaging the muscles through the leather. 'No,' she said, and her voice was low. She bent, kissed the top of his head, then scrubbed the kiss away. 'No. I suppose it's like, you're born somewhere, brothers and sisters. I mean, you can't choose it, but it's yours. Got to do your best for it. Not exactly heroic as motives go. Still.' She slapped his right shoulder hard. 'I just wish to God they'd get on with it. I suppose – well, when it comes to it, we'll just have to give in, won't we?'

Micky reached up to grasp the hand on his shoulder. 'S'pose so. I'm not martyr material. Nah, we can only go so far. See what happens. Don't worry, doll. We'll be OK.'

'Yeah, sure.'

Micky swung round. He quickly kissed her stomach and her pubis through the denim. 'Don't worry,' he breathed. 'Everything'll be OK.' And he clasped her left buttock and pulled her loins against his face so hard that his arm trembled. For a moment her long fingers held his crown. He closed his eyes. He looked very tired.

A shuffling footfall sounded outside. The latch arose with a rap which made the walls ring. Jenny's hand sprang up as though burned. 'Er, yes . . .' she said in a conversational tone as she strolled away.

Micky turned back to the screens. He blinked. 'It's all right,' he said, then had to clear his throat, 'it's all right. It's only Screech.' He took a deep breath. 'How's it going, mate?'

Screech did not look up. 'All quiet enough,' he mumbled into the front of his tan kennel coat, 'so far.' He shuffled over to the kettle like a blind old dog intent on a routine. 'Whasstime?'

'Just after midnight,' Micky told him, 'Long time to go yet. I'll just dash up to the house, check on Cathy now you're back. Grab some supplies from the fridge.'

'Ah, maybe they'll not come after all,' croaked Screech. 'Maybe they'll not bother.'

'Oh, they'll come, Screech,' Micky said casually, 'More'n their job's worth not to. God knows what they'll want. You can count on that.'

'They' were already here as a matter of fact.

In dark cords and trainers and a dark nylon blouson which rasped as he moved, Frank crouched between the wall and the rhododendrons. He did not like any of it. The stillness made him angry and uneasy. He felt like a child ignored.

Even the dog here had been old and mild-mannered; an Alsatian with cloudy eyes, a shaggy black and tan coat and black and tan teeth, she had hobbled gape-legged toward him, growling uncertainly. Frank had said, 'Whoah now, come along, now,' and he had swung the gun like an axe. He had smashed the butt harder than necessary into her skull, just above the bridge of her nose. She had grunted, teetered for a second and crashed into the undergrowth.

She was probably dead as soon as she hit the ground, but her stiff legs had still shuddered and twitched. He had pulled out the flick-knife, the one from Milan, and plunged it deep into her throat before drawing it upward and out. The blood had pulsed out for a matter of seconds only. Frank had cleaned the blade on the grass.

And now he was just waiting. He would know when the moment came, when the house was fully asleep and he was fully awake. For now, the house was settling. The machines which had operated today would still be warm. The old woman might still be lying awake, staring up at the oily blue shadows on the ceiling. Soon would come the chill and the stillness of deep sleep. And then, when this fury in his brain had filtered down to suffuse his body, then he would move in.

He wanted Micky Brennan.

He glanced down towards the yard. He could see only the wall, the faint flush of light from beyond. He would have to think hard, fix on a fantasy, if tonight was to go well. Here, death seemed a commonplace. Its angel was diminished by the breadth of the sky and the silence.

A cool breeze followed the rain like a shuffling dog at heel. Frank shivered. Absently he clasped and released, clasped and released the damp fur of the dog beneath him. He must think. He needed to summon the avenging spirit which would stiffen in his body like lust.

Down in Fergal's cottage, Margaret was shrieking above the trilling falsetto of the Queen of the Night.

'You did *what?*'

The big dog got up and retreated trembling into the corner.

Fergal looked apprehensively up from his fly tying. He shrugged. 'I just told him to expect trouble tonight. Nothing else. Give him a chance to get out of the way. Jesus, woman, he's a friend. No need for him to be involved. He's one of us.'

'A friend?' Margaret gaped. 'One of us? What are you . . .?' She gave up. She strode across the room and ripped the stylus across the vinyl. Fergal groaned. He clutched his head.

'Do you realise what you've done?' Margaret returned to bend over Fergal. 'You've betrayed us! Every goddamned one of us! They're up there risking their lives for us, for Ireland, for you and me, and you've only given them away! I don't believe you! I don't believe you! I mean, Christ!' she prodded his temple with a stiff finger, 'What do you have in that thick head of yours? What chance have they got without the element of surprise? So for him, a fucking half-Brit, you're prepared to sacrifice your own people? You're mad, Fergal Doherty! Mad, mad, mad!'

'He promised not to tell the old woman,' Fergal mumbled into his hand. 'It'll be all right.'

'All right?' With one broad sweep of her arm, Margaret cleared the table of hook-boxes, fly-boxes, feathers and silk. 'How can they be all right? Micky's probably got a fucking army waiting for them. Jesus!'

She sniffed and walked haughtily out of the room. Fergal shook his head and fell into his knees to collect the hooks.

Margaret returned. She sat, kicked off her trainers, pulled on suede boots. Fergal watched the performance through the table-legs. 'Where are you going?' his voice plaintive. 'No, Fianna! Back!' he pushed the black and tan bitch away from the scattered fish-hooks.

Margaret laced up the boots without a word. She stood and stamped. 'Where are you going?' Fergal raised his head above the table.

She gave him a look which would ripen, wither and rot a cucumber within seconds. 'Where d'ye fucking think?' she snarled. 'I'm going to warn the *men*, the real men up there doing a job while you just . . . Fact, I'd stay there if I was you. Right where you are. It's the right position for such as you, isn't it? Among the dogs. On your fucking knees!'

It was one o'clock now. The rain had passed on. The moon was no more than a paring occasionally visible through a shifting caul of cloud.

Up in her room, Cathy was sleeping. The lamp was still on, and she had not made use of the giant mechanical harness set in the ceiling. Only the double-barrelled shotgun and an open copy of *Sires* occupied the bed. She was still in her wheel-chair, still fully dressed in a brown tweed skirt and a purple cashmere sweater. Her chin had sunk down onto her breast. Her legs had swung apart. She snored like a riffled pack of cards. Her right arm hung over the arm of the chair. The hand slowly opened and closed, opened and closed . . . Occasionally a shudder corkscrewed through her, and then her whole torso twitched and trembled. She mumbled something to herself as a mother might to her baby, and her shoulders sank once more in sleep.

Micky watched her from the doorway for a minute. He smiled and slowly shook his head. 'Night night, Cathy,' he whispered. He pushed the door quietly too, crept down the landing, down the stairs and down, yet again, into the kitchen. He gathered together half a chicken, a bowl of cold cauliflower cheese and two cans of beer. And because he was down there, he left by the kitchen door and hurried back to the yard.

Frank had glanced at his watch and over his shoulder. Now he stood and stretched. He bent to pick up the shotgun. He broke it and checked both cartridges.

Outside, he knew, there were men from Donegal, maybe even from the North, expert men with firepower and horsepower aplenty, ready to storm in, blitzkrieg-style, and remove the precious stallion. But Frank had volunteered. Frank had insisted. Frank had pressed them. He wanted Micky Brennan. He wanted him squirming. He wanted him whimpering. He wanted to see real abject terror in his eyes. Stick a gun in his mouth, tell him, 'Suck it'. Frank had spent a lot of time imagining it.

But they had not cared about Micky Brennan. Only about the bloody horse. If they could kidnap the horse, they reckoned, they could recoup some of their losses from the insurance company. 'Keep out of it,' one of the hicks had said, and Frank had snarled.

But he was here. He was here because the men had been discussing the new security at Ballysheenan. They had had all the details, of course, from the company that had installed it. And suddenly they had come upon a hitch. They had huddled together then and spoken very low. Occasionally one of them had glanced at Frank and returned to the quiet discussion with a nod. And at length, the older man with the gut had separated himself from the pack and strolled towards Frank. 'So you want to be of assistance, hmmm?'

'I want to do fucking Micky Brennan,' Frank had answered.

'Know how to do Micky Brennan?' the big man had smiled, 'Know how to really hurt him? Take that horse away. You know that? Micky loves that horse, right? And it's his only livelihood. Killing him isn't going to do any good, now is it? Get that horse and we make a lot of money and Micky suffers for a long, long time. So. You can help us there. There's an alarm, connects to the gardai station. We'll want someone to go in early, alone, neutralise that alarm, can you do that?'

'I should be able to,' Frank had sneered, 'Done it often enough before, haven't I? I guess you've never seen such a thing these parts. Fucking bumpkins.'

The man had sighed a deep, rumbling sigh. 'Well, Frank,' he had said, 'you are going to get your heart's desire. You go in and take that alarm out. That's all.'

'I get a gun?' Frank had been eager.

'No,' the man had said firmly. 'No need. You just go in, neutralise the alarm, and my men do their business.'

Frank had gone along with the old fool. He had nodded and taken his orders like a good little schoolboy. Then earlier this evening he had 'borrowed' the shotgun, with suitable threats to keep him quiet, from a farmer down the way. It was a primitive weapon, but it would serve.

And lo and behold, here the little bastard was, Micky Brennan himself, striding briskly across the gravel and up to the front door of the house. He let himself in, and Frank could have danced for excitement. There were no alarms in the house, just one little old lady. Micky Brennan was his.

OK. The time had come.

Frank felt great. It always came, you waited for it. This weird sort of feeling when your heart was thudding and your stomach sounded like submarine sonar and your brain was peopled by a thousand tangled images, yet somewhere within you, there was stillness. You felt strong then, invulnerable.

Once Frank saw a darts player on TV. Big gut. All around him there was ragged shouting from the men and squealing from the women. The commentator feller twanged 'And John, you need one hundred and fourteen!' And this man, for all the kerfuffle around him, he had just stepped forward and his eyes had glazed over and his right hand had come up like a suspicious cobra, and Frank had just looked at him and said, 'He's got it.'

Time to move.

'Hey!' whispered someone behind him.

Frank nearly doubled up. He gulped down a gallon of air. He said 'Shit!' Alarms sounded in his temple like dissonant, shrill funing-forks. His sphincter contracted. The gun swung round.

'No!' gasped the voice from behind the wall. 'I'm here to help.'

'Who the fuck . . .?' Frank panted. 'Stand back from that wall. I'm coming out. I want to see you. Hands out.'

Anger clutched at his diaphragm and blurred his vision. A whore. For Christ's sake, what's a whore doing out here in the middle of the night? Who's she think she is, anyhow? What'd he have to do? Smash her skull in like the dog's? Hell, no. That'd leave a hell of a mess . . .

He peered around the gatepost. She stood with her arms extended at her sides. Jesus, but there was nothing to her at all. She was wearing tight jeans or something. He could see all of her silhouetted against the light from the main road down below. She was slender as a sprat.

He stepped out onto the road, his finger on the trigger-guard. 'Right.' He glanced up the lane over his shoulder. He circled her cautiously, prodded her from the rear with the gun-barrel. 'Get up that bank, into the field. Move!'

She nodded. She walked obediently across the lane. The bank was steep. Twice she gasped, once she cursed as a thorn or something punctured her skin. He just said, 'Get a move on.' He wanted to be off the road.

She stood at the top now. Following her, Frank said, 'Through the fence, and down.'

She obeyed. She ducked below the top strand of barbed wire and cautiously lay down. It was a ploughed field planted with young grass or wheat. The crop afforded no cover, but it was cool and quiet.

'Right,' Frank knelt. He held the gun in the crook of his right arm, the muzzles pressed against her left cheek. His left hand ran fast over her body. 'Turn over.' She rolled and now he knelt astride her, pushing the gun-barrels against the base of her skull. Her breathing was quick and shallow. Her buttocks shifted beneath him. 'Still!' he ordered. His left hand grasped the back of her neck and pushed her face hard against the earth. That felt good.

He hated this woman as an adolescent hates his mother when she interrupts his lustful progress. He lusted after Micky Brennan at this moment. He was curt.

'All right,' he climbed off her and knelt on one leg by her head. 'Turn over, what are you doing here, who are you?'

'Margaret Sheehy,' the girl panted. She wiped her face with her palm. She spat. 'I had to come up here. Help you. You don't know . . .'

'Help me what?'

'You know, the horse, the old woman . . .'

'What the fuck do you know about that?' Frank hissed.

'It's my bloody man. Was anyhow. Fergal Doherty. He has contacts with your lot, right? Thing is, they know.'

'Who . . .?' What the fuck are you talking about, woman?'

'Them in there, the Kramer woman. Micky Brennan, all of them.'

'Well?'

'They know you're coming, I mean someone's coming.'

'So?'

'No, they know it's tonight. Fergal told Micky Brennan. They're waiting for you.'

'Still!' Frank spat as Margaret raised her trunk on her elbows. 'This bastard told them?'

'Yes, damn him to hell. It's old pals time. Him and Micky, you know the sort of thing. Thought he'd spare him. Says Micky promised he'd not tell the old woman but, God knows, the place could be crawling with cops.'

'It's not,' said Frank simply, 'I've been here ages. Maybe your friend Micky Brennan kept his word.'

'They've got alarms and God knows what else down the yard, lights come on as soon as you walk in, that sort of thing.'

'I know,' Frank's voice was thin. 'I'm not aiming to go to the yard.'

'So, you're still going in?' she breathed. This time when she propped herself up and turned her body towards him, he did not object. 'You can't.'

'I don't know,' he snapped, 'just shut it, will you? I'm thinking.'

'You can't,' she said softly. She reached out for the cold gun-barrels. Very gently she pushed them away from her.

'Shut it!' He did not move the gun back.

'Come home with me,' she soothed. 'I'll make you comfortable. You can come back some other time, another night, they're not prepared. Come on.' Her hand grasped his and squeezed.

Frank's fingers closed about hers. Slowly they pushed them backward so hard that she whimpered. 'Get your filthy hands off me, whore,' he snarled. He pushed her back onto the cold earth.

The wind smelled of pine. Frank said, 'I'm going in.'

'All right,' she said in a small voice. 'What do I do?'

'Have to come with me,' said Frank, 'Keep my eye on you. Not having you running around here while I'm in there. But you shut it and you do as you're told, right?'

'Sure. Of course. I promise.'

She was good as gold now. All she had needed to get the girlish nonsense out of her head was a quick slap-down.

'Right,' Frank stood. 'Come with me, and not a fuckin' word I say so, got it?'

'Got it,' she hugged herself as she stood. Her mouth was extended in a broad, excited grin.

In the waiting-up room, the whiskey was out. Screech had a mug of it. He sat morosely on a hard-backed chair beneath the calender. Occasionally he drank with a noisy equine slurp. Jenny still lay in the armchair, nursing a Duralex glass and chewing on chicken. Micky was back at his screens.

'God, I wish we could have a radio or something,' Jenny stretched her arms towards the ceiling, her legs towards Micky. 'Lucky Cathy, sleeping the sleep of the just and we're the ones awake and it's all her doing. Great.'

Screech did nothing noisily or dramatically. He grunted and suddenly stood. He laid down his mug and folded his hands. He said, 'I'm going.'

'What?' Micky swivelled his chair round. 'What d'ye mean, Screech? Going where?'

'Going home,' Screech mumbled.

'Hey, Screech . . .' Jenny coaxed. 'I thought you were with us!'

'How'n I be with you? I'm with the horses, sure. You 'n Mrs Kramer, you're 'kay, s'pose. Micky Bren . . . But I got to live here, haven't I? Who'm I say you're right, they're right. Look what happened to Michael. 'Srumours. 'Speople won't talk to him. I got to live here. I can't fly off to New York or London. You try it.'

'But, Screech,' Jenny sauntered across to him, barred his way. She placed a hand on his shoulder and looked into his eyes, but Screech looked downward at the threadbare orange rug, at his old boots patched with Form-book bindings. Jenny said, 'The horses. Sanso. They've been your life. You saw what they did to Millamant's foal. You want to help these sort of people?'

Screech chomped like a ruminant. He shook his head. 'No truck with people like that,' he muttered, 'but one fights something. Win or lose. This one it's only lose, 'n it goes on the rest of your life. Sorry.'

Jenny turned her head to Micky. Her eyebrows arose at the centre. Her eyes were bemused. Micky stood. He put his hands in his pockets and strolled over. Screech looked from Jenny to Micky and back again like a cornered animal.

'That's all right, Screech,' Micky said cheerfully. 'Don't worry about it. I'd have done the same in your position. Don't know why I'm not doing it now. Truth to tell. You're probably in the right of it, and I admire your courage. I know it must be bloody difficult. We see you tomorrow?'

'Dunno,' Screech mumbled. 'You need me.'

'Ballysheenan will always need you, Screech,' Micky said softly.

Screech shuffled between them, halt and gape-legged like an old man taken short. 'Goin' home,' he said. It came out like a husky whine. Then he hurried for the door latch, hurried to get through, hurried up the little passageway to the fresh air and the dripping starlight.

Micky and Jenny stood still. They watched the door banging in the breeze. 'Poor old sod,' Micky's voice was hollow. 'Must have been the hardest decision of his life. It's easier to stay once you're here.'

'Is that why we're here?'

'Maybe,' Micky sighed. 'Who knows?'

211

'Fat lot of good we're going to do all alone against the big battalions.'

'Yeah.'

Micky looked up into Jenny's sad eyes. He mustered a smile from somewhere, and saw her lips wriggle in a small sideways grin. He reached up, touched her hair, her cheek, her throat. 'Is kissing you a bad idea?'

'Nope. It's kind of a distraction thought.'

'What the hell,' he took her hand and led her to the armchair. He pushed her gently down. 'Five minutes distraction after this lot seems fair enough for me.'

Getting in had been a doddle. Frank had found a basement window at the back of the house. Its frame had been rotten and one pane had already been broken and patched with soggy cardboard. All he had had to do was cut out the cardboard, reach in for the latch and raise the little window.

He climbed in first, keeping a hold on Margaret's right foot as he did so. The drop was not so great as he had imagined because a chest deep freeze stood beneath the window. Margaret followed him through. It was colder in there than outside.

Together they slid off the deep-freeze and onto the undulating flagged floor. Frank flashed on his pen-torch. The walls were of bare stone streaked with damp. There were old wine boxes and piles of newspaper, a couple of pairs of skis propped up in the corner, a tangle of picture frames, some empty, some surrounding Lalla Rookh-style engravings of insipid Oriental women.

The plank door led onto a bare passageway, past other cellar rooms, and so on into the L-shaped kitchen.

This was a surprise to Margaret. All this money, this dirty great house, and all the old woman had was rough old painted wooden cupboards, a rusted wire vegetable rack, a wooden clothes horse on a pulley hanging from a central beam, an antedeluvian Kenwood mixer and a chipped old stone sinks Not a modern machine in the place. What was she, some kind of miser or something?

Frank opened the fridge. He peered in. It started to hum and Margaret started, covered her mouth with her hand, Frank pulled out a bottle of milk and a plate on which one complete sausage and one half-eaten, some broccoli and some boiled potatoes lay sweating beneath a mask of cling film. The sausages were fat ones, English style.

Frank perched on the table corner. He chewed on the sausage. He washed it down with deep gulps of milk. Margaret watched fascinated as his very prominent Adam's apple bobbed in the light from the 'fridge. 'What are you doing?' she whispered.

He leaned forward and gasped, 'Shut it.' He wiped the milk from his lips on his sleeve. He laid down the milkbottle and picked up the gun. 'Right. Stay behind me and keep quiet.'

He led the way up the stairs and into the hall. The tiny beam of light was turned downward. It showed only the carpet, the shadows of furniture which seemed massive and menacing as standing stones. It led round to the left. She saw his hand on the banister, his trainers rocking, toe to heel, on the stairs. She extended her arms and felt her way. She kicked the first step and stumbled forward. A hissing punctured sound burst from between her teeth. She clambered up the remaining stairs to the landing.

Frank grabbed her arm and dug his nails in, squeezing tight. 'I said keep quiet, bitch,' he hissed. 'Think this is a game or something, do you?'

'No!' she yelped under her breath. 'No, sorry.'

'Stay here.'

'What?'

'Stay here. Don't move an inch. Just stay here. Still.'

'I want to go with you.'

'Fuck it, do you hear me? I said stay here. You move, I'll blast you, hear me, whore?'

'OK. OK!'

Frank turned and padded up the stairs. The light wobbled, then was extinguished. The floor boards on the upper landing croaked once. Frank's jerkin rustled slightly, then the soft footfalls stopped.

Margaret rubbed her arm. Now alone in the darkness, she could hear the drumming of her heart, the rapid rasp of her breathing. She licked her lips. She tried to stop her chest from rising and falling so fast, but her efforts merely seemed to make her breathing sound louder. She saw the silhouettes of the trees against the gun-metal blue sky through the windows on either side of the front door. Anyone came from there, switched on the light, she was centre stage, bang in the gold. She could smell the sweat from her armpits, hear the slight click as she moved her arms from her sides. And now, up to her left, the voices started up. They rumbled like threatening thunder.

Cathy had heard their soft progress through the hall and up the stairs. She was waiting. So she was only momentarily nonplussed by the sight of this lean, white-faced young man in the doorway. She said 'Er . . .' just once, and she shook a little more, then her culture came to the rescue. 'All right, punk,' she growled. 'Come in. So what's your business, huh, punk?'

Frank took it all in: the absence of Brennan, the glitter in the woman's eyes, the pippin blush in her cheeks, the steady shaking of the gun at her hip. The old biddy couldn't miss even if she pulled the trigger by mistake. Old shotgun, mind, all autumn shadows and fancy chased metal. Maybe it was her husband's. Maybe it had not been cleaned or oiled for years. It did not look like it. She didn't look like the sort of woman.

He glanced down at the gun which hung from his right hand. Shit. No bloody chance.

Frank said casually, 'Ah, just wanted a word.' He tossed his shotgun onto the bed.

'All right, now get away from there,' Cathy jerked the gun barrels in a persuasive gesture learned from a thousand movies. It worked. With her left hand she swivelled the wheelchair so that her eyes and the gun barrels could follow him. 'Over there,' she ordered. 'That stool by the desk. And don't move. Case you didn't know, these things make a mess of human guts at this range.'

Frank knew. He nodded and moved easily over to the pale blue velvet upholstered stool in front of the bureau. 'I sit?' he asked.

'You sit.' Cathy nodded.

'OK.' Frank tugged up the thighs of his trouser-legs and sat cautiously. He spread his hands 'So, what now?'

'What the hell you think?' Cathy's voice barely trembled. She swallowed quite a lot. 'Two options. I get sick of you and I shoot your balls off or I feel charitable and all I do is call the guards and get you locked up for a long time. You see any other way?'

'Ah, but hold it right here.'

Frank held up his hands. 'First, you let that thing go off, it's you that'll get locked up, you know. There'll be a witness or two, I can promise you that, girl, and that shooter of mine'll have disappeared. And anyway, sure, kill me, get me sent down, whatever you like. Where's that get you? There's plenty more outside there. Tractor blocking the lane out there, tree down in the other direction. I don't come out, I send a signal that you didn't co-operate, they move in. Take them a minute or so, deal with that horse of yours, get out. They'll not be so pleasant. Me, my job's just to talk, have a nice little chat, you know?'

'Oh, sure, yeah. You're here to talk. So why the artillery, huh?'

'Ah, now, surely that's obvious enough isn't it, Mrs Kramer?' Frank's voice was soft. 'I mean, look at you. D'ye think I expected a friendly welcome? Surely even I have a right to defend myself, same as you?'

'All right,' Cathy's lips worked. 'So, you want to talk, talk.'

'Well, now, what I'm here for, Mrs Kramer,' Frank was earnest, 'is to talk to you about a small contribution to your host country. The island where you've chosen to live, that's all. I mean, I think you'll admit, we in Ireland, we're a hospitable bunch, now aren't we? And that despite many centuries of poverty at the hands of the imperialist exploiters. No one'll deny that. Am I right? Well, now, thing is, you go to stay with someone, a lady like you, do you just expect that sort of hospitality, just take it for granted, do you? Or do you give you host some small something? Well, now, that's what we feel so, Mrs Kramer. We like guests. Keep open house. But – I am sure there's been some sort of misunderstanding here – when you were asked for a very small contribution, you refused! Now, you'll be the first to admit, that's not very gracious, now is it? And some of the Irish people are thinking – maybe they're wrong. I wouldn't know – "Well OK. She can't be bothered to help us, why should we put up with her? Why doesn't she just go back to where she came from?" You understand the reasoning?'

It was a well-prepared speech. Most people did not react as Cathy did. She simply said, 'You're full of shit, you know that? OK, so you're saying, I get a good deal here in Ireland. I agree, but the government hasn't waived tax in respect of bloodstock just for fun, you know. It's a big earner. I employ agrarian labour. My stallion brings in mares and money and prestige to this country. So, Mr Whatever-your-name-is, I am not a non-contributory guest. But OK. You're saying, the Irish people want a bit of cash in return for my staying here. Seems fair to me. I'll write out a cheque here and now. Nine thousand Irish punts, right? Made payable to – what? the *taoiseach* is it? Or the Dail? The Boys' Brigade? You just tell me – the charity or the government department of your choice. Name it and we'll have no more argument. You can scramble off out of here, and I can go to sleep. OK?'

Frank's smile said that he had heard all the dodges. 'We *can* take cheques, Mrs Kramer,' he said softly, 'though we'd prefer bank drafts or cash. If you'd just make it payable to Father S. Fisher, that'd be best.'

'And what's your Father Fisher to do with the Irish people?' Cathy sneered. 'At a guess, I'd say that Father S. Fisher is a little old priest in Boston or St Louis probably doesn't even know his name, somewhere a long, long way from Ireland. Maybe he's even a dead priest. Maybe he doesn't even exist, hmm? No, I'll tell you what I'll do, punk. I'll make

215

out the cheque to your *taoiseach*, even write him a covering note, why not? '*This is for the benefit of the Irish people from a grateful guest.*' How's that suit?'

She was angry now. Frank knew that she would not concede. Anger had melted her fear, and with it her caution. Like this, she would make more mistakes, but she was a damned sight more volatile and dangerous. There was one thing that he had not tried. Put a gun to her head. Tell Micky fucking Brennan, you do what I tell you or I blow her away . . .

'Now now, Mrs Kramer,' He placed his hands on his knees as though to rise. 'You're being downright bloody-minded here . . .'

At this moment the wind swept in like the tide. The curtains were sucked up. The pages of the book on the bed cackled. The door swung open on a gust and bounced back. Something banged downstairs. The Margaret woman yelped, and Frank was up and moving.

One stride and he threw himself forward. He was on top of the old woman now. She smelled of talcum. He saw the inside of her lower lip as her mouth dropped open, the oily film on her eyes as they swivelled upward, the flash of the diamond on her puckered pink hand. His right hand clamped down on it. His left swung back. Get her a good clout round the head, shake her brains up a bit.

Jesus. Jesus. Dear God in heaven, and those big black holes were still rising . . .

It was like a film camera zoomed out fast. The Kramer woman with her open mouth, her angry, orange-webbed eyes, was receding. The room rang and roared as though he had been underwater a long, long time. Frank was doubled up like a bull hit him dead centre. He was hurtling backward, flung over the bed, and still it was not over. Still he was pushed back, arms flailing, by this almighty invisible thing, until his back smashed into the wall and his teeth clunked shut.

He was aware of the salt blood filling his mouth. It bubbled as he gasped for air. He tried to move, but his limbs were dead as stone. The woman had wheeled her chair closer to the bed. She said something with a sneer, but he could not hear her. There were too many other sounds in his head. He just concentrated hard on focussing his eyes on the flowery fabric of the valance before him.

It had been the wrong hand. That was where he had gone wrong. Fucking ridiculous. Somehow that frail little creature had had power enough in her right forearm to raise the gun with the same hand that pulled the trigger.

His body was jerking strangely as though somebody was punching him. Liquid pumped from him. It was warm and sticky on his thighs. The pain

216

was intense, but he did not know where it lay. It was part of the noise in his head, part of the desperate heaving for oxygen, part of the cloying oily liquid which stuck and clicked in his throat.

The dark-haired whore was in here now. She was silently screaming at the old woman, beating her with her fists. She should not do that. Not a whore with an old woman a hundred times her better. Frank tried to raise a hand to stop her, but all that happened was that his fingers slowly scrabbled at the gritty soup which had been his hip.

The whore was bent over him now. Her black hair tickled his nose. Bitch should leave him alone. He wanted to concentrate on the flowers on the bed. They reminded him of something, only he could not think of what.

This wasn't it. He knew that, despite the compulsive shaking of all his limbs, the burning pain, all that. He had a higher destiny than this, to bleed to death on a thick beige carpet because of nothing more than an accident with a sporting gun, for Christ's sakes.

It, when it came, would be fine and exciting. Awe would mark his passing. The Frank Show closed on a theme tune of screams and curses above the rattle of the Stirling as the filthy fools realised, too late, that the high, fine, final truth was in their midst.

He had rehearsed that final scene too often to believe that it could end like this, with his nose pressed into the stinking breast of a whore, the blood welling in his mouth and spilling in great gouts down his front. Frank was young. It was all right. His show could not end on a slow melt, then a bright star contracting to a point in the darkness, which lingered for a moment. And went out.

'You bitch!' Margaret was sobbing. Her tone, however, was one of astonishment rather than grief. 'You bitch!'

'Shut your mouth,' Cathy ordered, but her own mouth was swollen and the consonants were soft. 'Fucking drama queen. Get a doctor, Chrissakes. What'm I meant to do, some bastard jumps me in the middle of the night? Get a doctor and stop playing Juliet, will you?'

Margaret looked down at the silky head in the crook of her arm. The trembling and the jerking had stopped. The blood which lay now in warm pools on the wetted denim in her lap, had stopped flowing. She released Frank suddenly. She said 'Oh!' She shuffled back on her knees. Her eyes were wide. 'He's dead!' she whispered, disgusted, incredulous. 'Jesus Christ Almighty. He's dead!'

'Probably.' Tears dripped from Cathy's jawbone. Her cheeks shuddered as she tried to control herself. Her shoulders bobbed up and down. 'That's what you get, isn't it, if you play with the guns?' She sniffed. 'So whyn't you call the doctor, child? The police? Do something useful, for God's sake!'

Margaret, however, was still transfixed by the thing beneath her. She stared. Frank just sat staring back at her. He looked almost as startled as she, only his mouth had dropped open to reveal twisted grey and rusty teeth. A little pool of blood still lay glistening on his tongue, and blood brighter than a parade soaked into his shirt and his blouson. His stomach was a bloated bulge now. He had held it in in life.

There were several reasons why he could not hold it any longer.

The charge had taken him low in the stomach, just left of the centre, pulverising the hip and much of the pelvis, bursting the stomach walls. Several gleaming, steaming things had made the most of their new found liberty. Even as she watched, something fat and veined and purple slithered into the light. Margaret yelped and turned her head away. Suddenly, almost absently, she opened her mouth and vomited. 'Oh, dear God,' she whimpered 'Oh. Jesus, no. It can't be . . .' She wiped her chin on a bloody forearm. She groaned. 'Jesus, Mary and Joseph, no. . . .'

Cathy had made her way to the telephone. 'Whyn't you think about a little prayer somewhat earlier?' she sobbed. 'That's what death is. Take a bloody good long look . . .' Her voice arose to a squeak and failed her. She picked up the receiver. Her trembling forefinger found the dial.

Margaret heard the dial turn once, then again, before she recognised the sound. She yapped, 'No!'

She jumped up and threw herself across the bed. She slammed her right hand hard down on the telephone. 'No, you don't, Mrs fucking Kramer,' she panted through gritted teeth. 'You're going to pay for this. You think he was alone? Oh, no. There are thousands of us. Millions. You think – you think you can just come into a country, exploit us like you do, kill a poor, brave Irish boy and just get away with it? Oh, no, Mrs Kramer. You're going to pay and pay and pay.'

She pulled herself across the bed, leaving a streak of brown blood on the counterpane. She stood above Cathy, and bent and jerked the telephone wire from its socket. 'There,' she said, 'you can't reach down there, can you?' She pinched Cathy's left cheek between finger and thumb. She shook it. 'You can't reach down there, can you?' She talked as though to an idiot child. 'You know what's going to happen? I'll tell you. I'm going to go down to tell them what's happened, and they're going to come back and take the body away, and while they're at it, they'll probably want to tear you and your precious little nag to tiny pieces, d'ye hear me?'

'Yes,' said Cathy simply.

She could not raise a hand to wipe away her tears.

'All right. You just stay there. Well, you've not much choice, have you?' Margaret laughed. 'You just stay there and enjoy the stink, Mrs Kramer, and think about what you've done, and *him* a poor boy barely out of his teens. Think and wait, and they'll be back. Oh, boy, will they be back.'

And just because she could and because she was summoning the anger she needed if she was to move, she caught Cathy a loud, open-handed smack across her plush pink cheek. Cathy barely seemed to notice. Her head jerked sideways. She puffed out air, then just sat there and carried on silently, uncontrollably crying.

Micky was still kissing Jenny when the boom of the shotgun blast came rattling down the row of boxes.

When it happened therefore, Jenny could not leap up as she would, while Micky, thanks to the angle at which he had wedged himself between the arm and the seat of the chair, had to flounder and scrabble and support himself on Jenny's stomach before he could stand. He pushed the hair from off his forehead and rushed to his bank of screens. He flicked the switches.

'I think it was the house.' Jenny pushed her right hand backward through her hair. She buttoned her shirt and strode over to the telephone. She snatched up the receiver and tapped out Cathy's number. 'Could be a decoy . . . Nothing. Unobtainable.'

'What do we do?' Micky's leg jiggled. 'What do we do?'

'We've got to go. Sanso OK?'

'So far.'

'OK.' She pushed down the latch.

'Right,' Micky followed her. 'Let's run and don't stop for anything.'

'Set?'

'Let's go.'

They ran, and a chorus of running ghosts followed as their feet slapped on the concrete and the cobbles. Jenny easily outstripped Micky. He was four yards behind her as her feet first crunched on gravel, ten yards behind as she humped up the stoop to the front door. He caught her as she fumbled in her tight jeans pocket for the key.

219

She unlocked the door at the second time of trying. She pushed it inward. Micky pushed past her. He switched on the main light. 'Cathy!' he called 'Cathy!'

Margaret had picked up the gun on the bed. She had hurried out onto the landing. She was in heroic mode. She had to tell them before the guards arrived. Your boy is dead. Move in.

Nonetheless, when she caught sight of her reflection in the Venetian gilt mirror at the top of the stairs, she paused for a second. All in all, she was pleased with the effect. The blood on her chin and arms was turning brown. On her shirt it was still bright red. On her jeans it was maroon and glistening still. What with the gun, she looked pretty formidable. She pushed back the hair which had fallen over her face. She pulled a handkerchief from her pocket, licked it and wiped away the sooty trickles of mascara beneath her eyes. She left the blood.

She turned away, head down, to go down the stairs.

She was just four or five steps down when she saw the slender pale blue denim legs, the crumpled white shirt, the girl's flushed cheek and glittering wide pale eyes. Behind the girl, Micky Brennan scurried across to stand at her side on the lowest step.

'Jesus Christ,' Jenny breathed, then, 'Well, if it isn't little Margaret. You the sort they're sending in these days, they're really in trouble. Cathy? Cathy! Are you all right?'

'She's fine,' Margaret was sullen. Her tiny breasts bobbed up and down as if a speedboat had just passed by. She steadied the gun on the banister.

'Cathy!' Micky bellowed.

'I'm here.' Cathy's voice wobbled and rang.

'You OK?' called Jenny.

'Yeah.'

'You'd better get out of the way.'

Margaret glared at Jenny but only took one step downward. 'There's been an accident. There's going to be trouble.'

'So we see.' Micky moved up a step. With a still arm he pushed Jenny behind him, but she stepped out and moved to his side.

'Jenny, Micky?' Cathy called.

Her voice strained as though she were wheeling her chair, yet still she was not visible at the head of the stairs. 'Punk broke in. Gun. Tried to get the money out of me or he'd kill Sanso. Jumped me. Poor stupid little fucker. Shot him. Had to.'

'He dead?' Micky still watched those blued gun-barrels. He placed a foot on the next step, but he did not transfer his weight.

'Yep!'

'Murdering bitch,' Margaret spat over her shoulder.

'So what's the foul-mouthed Mzzz Sheehy got to do with all this?'

'I don't know,' Cathy gulped. 'Seems to have come with the punk. Says there's men all round. She says the word, they'll come in, take Sanso. She hit me.'

'Did you now?' Jenny said slowly. Once more Micky held her back as she took a further upward step.

'Get out of my way.' Margaret gestured uncertainly with the gun. 'You want me to fire this?'

'No,' said Micky. 'Definitely not.'

'Have you called the police, Cathy?'

'Please, Micky.'

'What? I said have you called the gardai?'

'No! Bitch pulled out the 'phone. Can you do it? Micky? Please, Micky?'

'OK, love. Just a second. Come along, Margaret. You'd best put that silly thing down.'

'Not fucking likely, Micky fucking Brennan. You get out of my way or 'I'll fire. I've got nothing to be afraid of, you know. They'll protect me . . .'

All this time, as she called out her responses, Cathy had been sitting in the doorway of her room. She had been holding the picture which usually stood on the bedside table, the one of Ed leading Sansovino in after the Prince of Wales's stakes.

Ed, chubby little, beautiful Ed, was beaming. Micky was there on the other side of the horse, his binoculars hanging from his hand. He looked positively winsome, for once in his incongruous top hat and grey morning-coat. She had been holding that picture and keening and sobbing and just occasionally swallowing a deep breath in order to answer the shouted questions.

Now, she traced the contours of Ed's face with a trembling forefinger. She touched Sansovino's nose through the glass. She grinned and wiped the tears from her eyes with one of those damn fool little embroidered handkerchiefs. The mist was back and her shoulders were shaking before her hand had dropped back to her lap.

She laid the picture on her thighs, face down, and she wheeled the chair out onto the landing. 'My battle,' she murmured, 'My . . .'

Jenny, now just five steps below Margaret, saw Cathy first. She saw the stains of tears on her pearly pink skin, the deep red mark on the left cheek, the eyelids which were now the colour of tinned salmon. She said, 'Cathy.'

Margaret half turned.

Micky barked, 'Cathy!' then, 'No!'

Margaret looked back at Micky bemused. She swung round. She yelped.

Cathy had emerged on the landing at speed, swivelled the chair and wheeled it to the head of the stairs. And she simply kept wheeling.

With a gravelly 'Garn!' from the days when she would urge a hunter at a fence, she leaned back, clinging tight to the chair seat, as it hurtled over the edge.

Margaret had only seen a blur out of the corner of her eye. She had not even had time to define the danger as she flung herself hard against the wall. For all Cathy's efforts, of course, the chair must topple. Margaret saw the woman's livid face and triumphant red eyes swinging towards her, past her, like the corpse from the closet in the films, then the left wheel of the chair hit her knee, and Margaret was falling, caught up in the wirligig of aluminium and carpet and flesh.

It was less than a second perhaps, before the chair moved on, flinging the old woman forward onto her face and skittering on without her into the hall, but in that second Margaret's knee was slammed against the wall and twisted agonisingly, her face was burned by the carpet and something crushed the fingers of her right hand.

The first thing she said was, 'Ow.'

She was lying head downward. Her knee hurt more than anything that she had ever known. The drying blood made slabs of the cotton shirt. She slid down two more steps in the course of righting herself. She rolled over, sat up and clutched her knee. She groaned.

'Bitch,' she panted. 'Bitch! I'll kill her! I'll . . .' She reached up for the banister and pulled herself to her feet then her weight hit her knee and she howled, 'Ah!'

Beneath her, oblivious even of her presence, Jenny Farlow knelt over Cathy's twisted body. The old woman still breathed, but her eyes were closed. Her gross white legs had fallen open. Her golden hair had broken free to form a film over her face. Her neck was distended. Her head was flung back over the edge of a stair as though in a paraody of ecstacy.

Micky had snatched up the gun and broken it open. He held it under his arm as he too knelt, plucking the hair from the Kramer woman's face.

Margaret winced hobbling down the stairs. 'Bitch,' she drooled down at them. 'God in heaven, but I'll do her. Ah!'

Micky said quietly, 'Fuck off, Margaret.'

'Haven't you done enough damage?' Jenny said in a sing-song crooning tone, at once speaking to Margaret and soothing the old woman. 'Just go away, will you?'

Margaret pulled herself around them and staggered down into the hall. She did not understand how it could be like this. She stank, she hobbled and no one was frightened of her. It had never been like this in daydreams.

'You're all going to die, you know,' she mumbled as she dragged her lame leg painfully to the door. 'All of you, all of you! They've got the roads blocked. They're coming in for that precious horse. You'll see. You can't do this sort of thing in someone else's country. You think anyone's going to help you now? Poor stupid bloody . . .' The words burbled on, diminishing until they were merely a part of the wind's complaining.

'Micky,' Jenny piped quietly.

'Yeah?'

'Get out of here. Take that horse with you.'

Micky winced. 'What?'

Get out. Take Sansovino away.' I'm the boss now. I want Sansovino out of here. Now. He's our only asset. Get him out.'

'But you heard them. The roads are blocked. The word is out. We'll never get a box out. And then there's Customs. There's no way . . .'

Jenny looked up at him. She said nothing, just looked up at him with hard, inexpressive eyes.

'Oh, no, Jen,' he hit his forehead. 'Come on. I can't!'

'How do you get a horse cross-country, Micky?'

'I can't. Goddamn it, he hasn't been ridden for three years. I haven't . . .'

'Go, Micky, please.'

'What about you?'

'They'll not touch me. It's the horse they want. Go. Please.'

Micky stared at her, long and hard. He swallowed several times. Then he slowly nodded. 'You want me to ride him out of here.'

'General idea.' Jenny flashed him a quick, fraudulent grin. She leaned over. She closed his mouth with hers. 'That's not for doing it,' she said. 'And remember, he's half yours if you choose. That's convenient enough, isn't it? Get moving.'

Micky stood. He looked down at the open door. He shuddered. 'Fuck you, Jenny.'

Without looking back, he clattered across the hall and out into the darkness. At the end of the drive, Margaret jumped, expecting pursuit, but Micky Brennan turned left. He was headed for the yard.

Margaret was lucky. She had not far to go.

All evening since she had left, Fergal had been feeling sick. He felt sick at her disdain, sick with remorse, sick with worry and fear. It was not in his nature to allow his woman to take risks while he sat safe at home.

Margaret was his life. She was the one fine, delicate, incomprehensible thing in his existence. His conviction of his own rightness had crumbled rapidly over these past few hours.

So as last he had whistled up Balor and climbed into the van. He drove up toward Ballysheenan. He had known to expect the road-block – the tractor, the Escort, the motorbike, the men sitting above the ditch on the bank. He knew the procedure. So he had pulled up short, identified himself. He could not barge through, of course, but at least he could wait in the rear.

The blue tractor stood across the lane. He had turned the van so that it too formed a barrier, then he had climbed from the van and leaned on the roof. He had chewed his thumbnail, and waited.

By the time that Micky reached the yard, Fergal was already hugging the shadow that was Margaret, breathing in the scent of her hair, begging her forgiveness.

Three men stood around them, arms folded. Their outlines were soft in the dull headlight beams from the van, the brilliant quartz glare from the big, silver bike. Margaret, the shadow, said only, 'Leave me alone.'

'I'm sorry,' Fergal whined into her hair, 'I was a blasted fool, a damn stupid fool. Oh, thank the Lord that you're all right.'

She pushed hard at his chest. She shook her hair, 'Just leave me *alone*, I want to talk to these *men*. Let me *go*, you stupid little *shit*.'

Fergal sounded like a musical saw. He stepped back. Margaret limped deliberately into the full blast of the light. Her bloodied shirt was unbuttoned now to reveal the twin curling shadows of her cleavage. Her crotch was a frayed fan of dark stains. Fergal moaned. 'Oh, God no. Are you hurt?'

'Shut your mouth.'

'But, God almighty, woman . . .'

'Shut it,' she shrieked, 'Damn you to hell!'

Fergal swallowed. He recoiled two steps further back into the shadows. He pulled at the fingers of his left hand, one by one.

'And yes, since you ask,' she continued, cooly now, 'I am hurt. But this, this is the blood of a young man was in there doing his duty, a good young Irishman that you killed. You and your old chum, your only man, the main man, the good feller, all that crap. You, and stinking Micky Brennan.'

'What?' Fergal squeaked, 'Ah, come on, would you, Meg. No one got killed.'

'Oh, didn't they?' she laughed just once. 'Did they not? Oh, good to know, Fergal Doherty. Good to know. So what's all this then? Ketchup, is it? So I imagined it, did I? I just imagined I saw him blown apart with a shotgun, did I? And who was responsible for that, I'd like to know? For a young man bleeding out his life-blood in my arms? They were waiting for him, Fergal, and all thanks to you. They were waiting with guns and broad grins on their faces. He's dead, do you understand that?' She dragged her leg over and screamed in his face, so close that each word moved his moustache, 'Dead, dead, *dead*!'

One of the silent men stepped up now, asked briskly, 'Which room was it?'

'The old woman's room. Up the stairs on the left.'

'Right,' he ordered, 'Clean up, then get down to the horse fast.' He nodded to his companions. One climbed onto the motorbike, one into the car. The bike's *basso profondo* simply ripped up the scale like a punctured balloon. The car throbbed back and screeched forward in pursuit.

Fergal was gulping down a lot of air yet still he struggled for more. 'But . . . Oh, Christ Jesus, no!' he shrilled, 'He said . . . Micky promised . . . No. Not Mick. He wouldn't!'

'He did,' said Margaret, a monarch graciously granting a petition. 'Frank walks in there. Like you said, there's to be no killing, so he's all peaceful, not expecting trouble, and they were waiting for him with their guns and they just – blasted him away.' She shrugged, then thought better of the casual approach. She covered her face with her hands. Her shoulders bounced. Her voice was thin. 'I saw it, damn it. They – just – blasted – him – away.'

Fergal's world had just turned upside down. 'But he couldn't . . .'

'He fucking did! He did,' she sobbed, then she uncovered her face. She pointed. 'Go up there. Take a look. Your good, trusted old chum, see what he did. Because of you.' In the remaining light, her face was ripped by lines and streaks of shadow. 'Micky Brennan's up there in that yard right now, laughing his fucking head off at you, Fergal, and there's a lad lying up there too, guts all over the floor, and Micky Brennan killed

225

him, Fergal, Micky Brennan killed him and tried to kill me too. Now do you understand?'

'I understand,' Fergal breathed.

'Hold it,' the senior man stepped forward again. 'You say Micky Brennan's in the yard?'

'I saw him going there,' Margaret wailed.

'Don't worry,' Fergal's voice was husky. 'I'll hold Micky Brennan till you come.'

He started to move forward, slowly at first, uncertainly lumbering like a wounded animal, then faster, faster, more decisively as he neared the gates of Ballysheenan, ducked beneath a low-hanging chestnut branch, and marched in.

The lights in the yard were full on. Micky had left the box light off, however, and shut the doors, so he had to work in the sparse light from between the doors, the soft moonlight from the skylight.

Sanso resented the bridle, but, after a lot of shoving with his head accepted the bit. He did not like the neckstrap much, but since Micky reckoned that to be the one essential bit of tack, he persisted and won the day.

Now, the saddle. Some of Ireland's stallions, like Sure Blade at Kildangan, were ridden regularly. Sanso had not been ridden since the Arc. He had no saddle of his own, therefore, and Micky chose from the stock in the tackroom a heavy, creaking old hunting-saddle with a sheepskin roller. The saddle was received with a lot of twitching and deep, aggrieved grunting. There was a deal more protesting as Micky looped the crupper over the tail.

He knew that he would not, could not do this. He knew that the battle, such as it was, had been fought and lost up there in the house. He knew – he suspected at least – that Cathy would not recover and that any second now the men would arrive to claim the horse. There was nothing more that he could do, save stand in – and be shoved out of – their way. Sansovino, old rogue, international superstar, an animal whose name would be known long after Micky's was forgotten; Sansovino, worth more money than Micky had earned in his lifetime, was now forfeit.

Micky tightened the girth as hard as he could. Still he could not pull it closer than the fourth hole. Jesus, the size of this animal.

He hoped that they would come soon. He hoped that they would spare him the necessity of leading Sanso out, making to mount him, all that charade. But the horse was ready, so Micky puffed out air a bit, opened and shut his sweaty hands.

Now, only now came the voice. 'Micky Brennan?' and a roar, 'Micky Brennan!'

Micky said quietly 'Fergal!' He called 'Fergal? Hi. What's going on, mate?'

He pushed open the door. Fergal stood on the cobbles. He cast a shadow which ran the whole length of the yard.

'Christ, give us a hand,' Micky raised an arm to protect his eyes from the dazzle. 'What are you doing up here, mate? We've got trouble.'

'You better believe it.' Fergal stepped towards him, and only then did Micky see the dull glint in his hand, the sharp flash in his eyes. 'Bring out that horse, Micky.'

Micky backed towards the stable door. 'What . . .? Hey, Fergal, steady on. Take it easy.'

'Bring him out.'

'Come in and get him.' Micky shrugged.

'I'm not going in there. You're bringing him out. Now. I want to watch your fucking complacent Brit face as I kill your darling gee-gee.'

Micky made the decision before he knew it. It surprised him. Fergal was moving towards him now. Micky knew that low-shouldered walk. He had seen it in prison. It was the gait of the fighter.

Micky scurried back round the stable door and into the thick darkness. 'Look, Fergal,' he called, 'what's got into you . . .?'

The response was so unexpected that at first Micky did not know what was happening. The lower door smacked against the jamb. Something rustled the straw. Something chimed and whined around the cement walls. Only then did the sharp, rapidly dissipated 'crack!' from outside permeate Micky's confusion. The horse neighed and angrily stamped. Micky crouched like a suppliant.

He opened his mouth to call again, but nothing came out. His whole body was shaking. He said 'F-F-Fergal! Jesus! Was that you?'

Feet rapped and shuffled. The gun out there snapped again, this time closer and deeper. Again the door jerked and something breathed round the box. This time, the horse's reaction was immediate. He reared and trumpeted his pain and outrage. The rein was pulled from Micky's hand. The hooves thumped down into the shavings. Sansovino reared again, screamed again, reared and screamed, reared and screamed.

Micky instinctively grabbed the rein. His already tremulous voice was shaken further by the horse's movements. He said, 'No, Fergal! What the hell are you *doing*? Stop! Take the horse but don't shoot him! God in heaven, man, you could've killed *me*.'

Again Fergal's footfalls drew nearer. He said something. Only when he repeated it louder, did Micky know what that something was.

'Wouldn't I like to, Micky Brennan?' Fergal snarled. 'You shat on me, Micky. You told them. You broke your word.' His voice arose in pitch, and the sharp edge of pain rang like a lathe long after the echo of the word was gone.'

'I didn't!' Micky pleaded. There were tears now in his eyes. He reached across, feeling the stallion's smooth, waxy coat. His fingertips touched moisture at the muscular chest. 'Oh God,' Micky breathed. 'Oh God, oh God.'

He did not know what to do, where to go. He was trapped in here in the darkness of the stable with an animal angry and in pain. Outside, a man with a gun stood waiting for him. Shaking feverishly, Micky pulled Sansovino to the left hand side of the door. He crouched at the horse's near side. His stomach whimpered. So did he. 'I didn't!' he called again. 'Really, Fergal.'

'You fucking liar! You hurt Margaret,' Fergal yelled, 'You lied to me, you *fucker*.'

Again a bullet punctured the wood of the door and slapped into the back wall. Again it twanged and skittered around the box. Micky cowered and covered his head. With a trembling left hand he pulled the reins to the saddle's pommel. He closed his eyes and felt for the iron. He raised his foot. He pulled himself up onto the broad shuddering back.

At once the horse stiffened and strained forward. A racehorse, first and always.

Micky was crying now, swallowing giant sobs which would not stay down. He was almost frozen by terror and would have welcomed death just so as to end this anguish.

He ran a shivering hand consolingly down Sansovino's neck. He leaned forward so that his cheek lay against the horse's mane. He grasped the neckstrap, sure that he must topple off at the slightest movement. He took a deep breath, then he shook the stallion up, kicked once, hard, and the darkness rushed over him like a blanket pulled back by an impatient mother.

Floodlight was harsh as a scream. And Fergal was there in the brilliant blur of it all, and a small gun with a big nozzle was raised. Amidst the clattering and slithering of hooves on the cobbles there was the bark of a gunshot. Sansovino stopped dead and reared. Micky just hid his head and clung on like a monkey as he felt the upward surge. There was a jolt, a weird banshee shriek, then Sansovino was down again. Micky opened his eyes.

Fergal was no longer there. He had simply vanished. Micky looked beneath him, at where Sansovino pawed and stamped. Then he closed his eyes again and a huge sob, bigger than all the rest, broke from him.

He remembered Fergal's smiling face. He had to remember it. On the huge body which lay stiff on the cobbles, it did not exist any more.

Micky looked up toward the house. The lights were on up there, and soon the men would be coming. He soothed the stamping, puffing stallion. 'Come on, my old son,' he said wearily, 'Oh, God in heaven, come on.'

And Micky rode.

He rode trembling down the gently sloping field and down to the five bar gate onto the road. Sansovino was dancing a bit, and Micky actually dismounted to open the gate. Then from up at the yard he heard doors thudding, voices raised and an engine starting up. He saw the solitary headlight beam of a motorbike swinging like a lance though the dark sky, then dipping towards him as the machine bounced down the track.

'Oh, merciful heaven,' Micky breathed. He clambered onto Sansovino's back again. Another engine approached from up the road. Headlights scanned the hedgerow at the bend. Micky took a deep breath. He clutched the neckstrap as though there were hundreds of feet of emptiness beneath him. He said, 'Go on,' and he kicked.

Sansovino crossed the lane at a trot. The headlight beams were full on them now – the one behind, the two above and to the right. 'Go on!' Micky yelled and he kicked again, harder, more urgently, and Sansovino leaped up through the brambles on the steep bank and into the cornfield above.

Infected by Micky's urgency, Sansovino galloped, reckless of potholes or obstructions, and Micky clung on for dear life, his teeth chattering with the horse's every giant stride as the cold night air flattened his hair and made his eyes sting and the thick black mass of Brennan's Beeches loomed closer and closer. Micky whispered 'Whoah,' but Sansovino now had no thought of stopping. The trees rushed past them, brushing them as they went. A blackthorn branch lashed Micky's face and twice he saw a thicker branch and ducked only seconds before it would have smashed into his face and broken his neck once and for all. But he made no effort now to stop the horse as they hurtled up towards the moon.

And then, out in the open, down again over a field of barley thick enough to slow even Sansovino. He pulled up at a bank of granite rocks and snorted angrily.

'OK, boy, OK,' Micky soothed and stroked, soothed and stroked. He rode Sansovino along the bank to another gate. As soon as it was opened, Sansovino darted through. Micky clutched his mane and cried 'No!' then 'No, boy. No, please . . .'

They were on the riverside road now. To their right, the water shone brilliant in the moonlight, whispering softly to itself.

Micky told himself fear travels down the reins. If you are frightened, your mount will be disturbed. *Ergo*, don't be frightened. QED.

Some neat formulae just do not work in practice. He was frightened of falling, frightened of the sudden burst of speed from this churning monster beneath him, the sudden buck, or stumble, of fear. He was frightened of headlights and engine sounds. He was frightened of men in black with guns in their hands. And fear, so they said, travelled down the reins.

But Sansovino took charge, trotting fast towards Micky's chosen sanctuary.

Once, long ago, Fergal and Micky had built a shelter in the woods just fifty yards above the river. It was a primitive construction of stray planks, branches and beams, sheets of corrugated iron and laurel branches beneath an outcrop of rock in the steep slope. There they would talk through the night. Micky would pass on to Fergal all that he had learned at school, while Fergal would show him knots and new poaching tools and would speak of the heroes of Irish history with such familiarity that Micky sometimes thought that he was gossiping about the inhabitants of Ballysheenan today. From there, too, they would creep out to kill fish or fowl or simply to observe the foxes, the otters and the badgers.

Micky rode towards that shelter almost without thinking. It was there. It was where he had always gone for escape. That was all.

The ripping sound of an engine behind him made him start awake. He looked to his left. There was a barbed wire fence beneath the woods. To his right the ground plunged steeply into laurels and rhododendrons. Quickly, he steered Sansovino down there. The horse half-slithered, half leaped down the bank and into the thick laurel bushes. Micky crouched down. 'Shhh,' he said, 'Shhh,' and he stroked Sansovino's heaving neck.

The motorbike screamed by like an angry cat. Off to alert – whom? Everyone. The whole of Ireland. 'If you should happen to see a man on a horse, just let us know . . .'

Micky's heart was doing strange convulsive things of its own invention as he straightened and urged the horse back up onto the road. Quickly now. Before the motorcycle came back.

The old track seemed little used now. It was overgrown with low brambles and ferns. Micky kicked Sansovino through it, dismounted and led the horse to the shelter of the overhanging rock. He could see little, but by groping his way around the ramshackle little house, he discovered that brambles had renedered one of its three sides impregnable. At the front, the laurels had grown right up to the wall. On the southern side, however, the structure had collapsed. Micky peered into the musty darkness. He called, 'Hello?' The shelter echoed reassuringly. He led a reluctant Sansovino in, and, still clutching the reins, he slumped down onto the dirt floor.

He could not stay here. It was too close to Ballysheenan, and he had no way of tethering the horse whilst keeping him hidden. He would have to go on. But for now, weariness anaesthetised his fear. He just sat there for a while and allowed his eyelids to sink, his limbs to become heavy. Once or twice a car passed along the road below, and Micky groaned and roused himself, only to sag back again.

Occasionally too an image returned of Fergal lying in the yellow flood of light with his face ripped off as if by giant teeth, his head stove in by stamping hooves. Then Micky's eyes snapped open as in a falling dream and he muttered a prayer that this night might be undone or, at least, that his mind should be washed clean of the memory.

And all this for a horse.

But that was in accordance with tradition. Great Celtic tombs have been found. Archaeologists open them, thinking to find a warrior king within, but they find only the honoured bones of a horse and his ornamental trappings. And somewhere around Ballinamore there is a more recent, unmarked grave in which a Derby-winner lies.

It might have been an hour later that Micky heard the voices. He was suddenly fully awake, and scrambling to his feet he told Sansovino, 'Steady. Please. Keep quiet . . .'

There were two male voices, soft and low. Micky could not hear what they were saying, but they were close, perhaps fifty yards away, and they were coming closer.

Only now did Micky think to look at his shelter. He pulled out his lighter. In its dull light he saw the remains of a log fire on the floor, a recent log fire, and a damp and yellowing Page 3 girl beamed vacuously out at him from the rear wall. Page 3 girls had not existed in Micky's and Fergal's time.

It was time to be moving.

Sadly, Micky led Sansovino out into the damp night air. Again he mounted, more confidently now, or more resigned. The male voices laughed. They were very close. Micky leaned back as Sansovino scrabbled down the track, clopped quickly across the road and onto the towpath. The voices were to the south. Micky wanted to go southward. He said, 'Come on, boy,' and urged Sansovino into a trot, a canter, a gallop – and still the voices were to the south of him. Micky had forgotten the way in which sound can travel over water.

Then suddenly, he was on top of them, two teenage boys squatting down by the river bank. The water exploded shockingly with a flash and a dull bang, and Sansovino swung violently sideways and reared.

Micky closed his eyes and keened, 'No ...' He clutched onto Sansovino's neck. 'No ...'

Then the horse was down again and snorting, galloping onward smooth and fast, and two startled boys were left gaping on the bank. When they returned to the village, they would have their own contribution to make to the legends of the land.

There was more traffic then usual. Micky was sure of that.

From his vantage point high on a heather-topped hill, he saw car after car cruising the narrow lanes below. Occasionally one car stopped next to another which had come in the opposite direction. He could hear on the wriggling wind – or imagined that he heard – words, the thump of car doors, then the cars set off again, headlight beams scanning the still sleeping fields.

Dawn came slow and lustrous: black velvet to blue brocade unfurling to show its white satin lining. Then suddenly the larks and the pipits were up and the sky was a uniform pallid blue and the crows were off on the day's business.

Micky steered Sansovino to a copse of oaks and beeches five miles above Kilkenny. He said, 'Whoah, there,' and slid from the horse's back. He wanted to sleep, but there was still much to be done.

He examined the horse's wounds. The first, low down on the chest, must have been a ricochet, or maybe the door had taken the power out of the bullet. It could not have penetrated more than an inch, and already it was encrusted with black scab tissue. The second, the consequence of the shot fired in the yard, was a diagonal streak of red along the horse's neck, stretching from the throat to the crest. The bullet had seared along the side of the neck, ripping a shallow glistening trench in the wall of muscle. It was still slowly bleeding. Sansovino's coat was thickly caked with dried blood.

Micky let the horse graze for half an hour, then led him to the little winding track through the wood. He found a puddle, and soaked two handsful of clay dirt in the water. He found comfrey leaves too, and mixed them into the wattle. He sealed the wound with this poultice. Sansovino shuddered and pawed a bit, but otherwise did not object. Micky unbuckled the reins then, and tied them together as best as he could. He tethered the horse to a small silver birch. It was all that he could do. He knew well enough that, should Sansovino become fractious, he could break away from his tether with one hard tug. He was too tired to care, too urgently in need of forgetfulness divine. He lay down on the short cropped grass and breathed in the wet-dog scent of the earth. The horse cropped above him. The birds chattered and creaked. Everything about him rustled and sighed. He lay on his side, curled up like a comma. He slept.

The pattering applause of an old tractor awoke him. He blinked up through the net of the birch leaves, the thicker filigree of the beeches above. The sun was past the meridian. He rolled over onto his stomach. Sansovino was still there.

Micky looked at his watch. It was ten past two. To his left, out in the field, the tractor slowly rattled down the hill, pursued by circling seagulls. Micky cautiously stood and stretched.

It was absurd, but in his own country even that tractor driver might prove an enemy, or, at least, a garrulous and innocent informer. Better to wait here until dusk at least. But his throat was dry and his mouth was full of bitter saliva. He was hungry and thirsty. He plucked sorrel and comfrey and hawthorn and chewed on them. They did nothing for his thirst, and little for his stomach, but at least they staved off the worst pangs for now.

Now he set about his work – the very opposite of all that he had done throughout the years. As a stable-lad he had cleaned and strapped and groomed. Here he dirtied and hacked and brushed against the grain. He would never succeed in disguising Sansovino from the man or woman who knew horses, but maybe, just maybe, the cursory glance from the passing motorist would take in no more than a penknife, scissors and his hands, it took time to attain the desired effect – desired that is, given that Sansovino could not be shrunk to a New Forest pony. By four o'clock the stallion looked – well, like a very dirty, unkempt thoroughbred stallion. It would have to do.

Micky rode on through the darkness past raths and rivers, farms and castles. He avoided major roads. Often he spent up to ten minutes at the time in looking for a gap or gate in hedges and banks. He might be willing to sit this brute, but he was damned if he was going to set him at a jump.

Now numbness seeped like a embalming fluid into his limbs. Every rustle in the hedgerows, every screech or chirrup or scream recalled Fergal, only Fergal.

The big man had given him another pair of ears and eyes.

It was Fergal who, wealthy beyond measure as a monarch of this wild world, had taught Micky to recognise living creatures where once there had just been scrub or ferns. He had taught Micky so to emulate those creatures as to anticipate their every movement. He had taught him to read the many complex riddles which constitute the land. He had taught him to be still and receptive in body and mind to the point where wild creatures would treat him as no more alien than the trees.

He had been, God save him, the only man to whom Micky could talk of such things, the only man who had known Micky the Irish boy, before he had been forced into racing and England. Suddenly Micky felt terribly alone. Now, he had no witnesses to what he still felt to be his real life, his real identity.

All his friends were English at heart, or, like Charlie, rich – and the rich have no nation. Charlie, confronted by those same men who yesterday had threatened Ballysheenan, would simply have said, 'Bloody thugs,' and caught the first flight out, to London to Tuscany, to New York. Home for him was a matter of bricks and mortar.

To Micky however, through the many years abroad, it had always meant these valleys, these smells, these animals, these people. And the boy – the long-haired songwriter, the hunter, the damned fool dreamer, had at last come home and, in doing so, had, however indirectly, killed his brother.

He told himself that he could not, should not feel guilt. He had almost persuaded himself on that score, but he could not talk away his grief – for the man, for the years missed, for all the many more years that he had promised himself on his return home.

Nor could he escape the resentment. Why could he and Fergal not have continued to work and to hunt and to love their land without the bloody rich and the bloody English, the bloody soldiers and the bloody Libyans making capital of the very bracken and bogs, the hills and the rivers?

For all these musings, Micky rode towards Kilcannon House. Now that Fergal was gone, where else should he go?

He arrived at the big gateposts soon after eleven. He dismounted as soon as he was on the drive. Stumbling on unseen brambles, he led Sansovino into the trees on his right. Once deep in shadow, he tethered him to a beech tree and turned away. The horse appeared to have been infected by Micky's depression. He was listless and uncomplaining. He hung his head.

Micky stayed in the shelter of the trees. On the verge of the lawn, he crouched and watched. There were five or six cars parked outside the house. Lights were on inside, but they were too high to light more than a few yards of the gravel. Anything might lurk in the surrounding darkness.

But these was music in there, and warmth, and the sound of laughter. Micky straightened. Precisely because anything might be lurking out there, there was no point in further attempts at hiding. He jogged quickly across the gravel, took the steps at a jump and let himself in through the big front door. As soon as it closed behind him, warmth and relief enveloped him. It would be all right now. He was back on his own territory. Back home.

The hall was lit but empty. The noise came from the morning-room at his right. Charlie was entertaining. Micky could not just walk in there. God knew who might be there or what their sympathies. He crept tiptoe instead to Charlie's study and quietly shut the door. By the light of his lighter, he located a bottle of whiskey and a bag of Spillers' Shapes. He cleared a space for himself on the big sofa, ate three of the dog biscuits and washed them down with the whiskey. He waited.

The party across the hall sounded like someone fiddling with the tuning of an old wireless. There was distant chat and the occasional burst of laughter or of shouts. They made Micky feel sorry for himself. Once he even allowed himself the luxury of weeping. He awoke surprised that he had slept. It was pitch dark now. The light in the hall had been turned off. He groped for his lighter amongst the cushions. He found it at length at his feet. He looked at his watch again. It was half past three.

Micky stood up and stretched. By the flickering light from the lighter, which was three times extinguished by Kilcannon's many and mysterious draughts, he crept across the hall and up the staircase. Mrs Halloran, he knew, was as deaf as a post, but there would be guests. Few people drove home after one of Charlie's dinners.

Charlie slept in the same room that he had occupied since boyhood. It was small, but he preferred it to the many larger rooms – for sentimental reasons, he said, and because of the view. Micky reckoned that the principal reason was that it was easily kept warm. Water by guests' beds had been known to freeze by morning.

Micky pushed open the panelled door and slid around it. He closed it and whispered, 'Charlie? Charlie?'

There was no response. Micky flicked his lighter. By its light he saw Charlie sprawled fully clothed on the bed. Micky reached down and turned on the bedside lamp. He sat on the bed. 'Charlie?' he said, louder now. 'Charlie? Wake up.'

Charlie groaned, 'Gway.' He covered his eyes with his arm.

'Charlie,' Micky shook him hard. 'Come on, damn it. Wake up. It's important. Come on. Wake *up*.'

Charlie lowered his arm at last and blinked wet, yellow-edged eyes at the ceiling. 'Micky!' he drooled affectionately.

'Charlie, you're pissed. Come on, man. I need your help. Quickly.'

''m not pissed,' Charlie pulled himself up on the bed and blinked very seriously at the basin in the corner. 'I'm fine.'

'Good. Now, listen. I've got Sansovino here.'

'No you haven't.' Charlie sounded surprised.

'Yes, I have, arsehole. Not *here*, God's sakes. He's out in the drive.'

'Sansovino?' Charlie frowned. 'He won the Eclipse. What's he doing in the drive?'

'Christ,' Micky sighed. 'Come on, Charlie. You're getting up and you're coming downstairs. I need you sober.'

With much loud protest, Charlie suffered himself to be escorted down the stairs and into the kitchen. Micky insisted that he drink instant coffee, milk and orange juice. Meanwhile, he made himself a makeshift meal of cheese and bread and cold sea-trout.

'So, what's all this about?' Charlie said at last, 'You look bloody awful.'

'You don't look so great yourself, mate. Listen. You know what I was discussing with you the other day? These people demanding cash?'

'Cash. Yup.'

'One nomination per year.'

'Nomination. Sure. I know about that.' Charlie struggled with the information, but Micky could see that he was getting there in the end.

'Danegeld,' Charlie said.

'Well, they came last night. Cath got hurt, badly hurt. They came for the horse. I rode him away.'

236

'Dear God,' Charlie stared. 'They must be after you.'

'They must be.'

'Christ, they could be here. Place might be blown up. Jesus.'

'That's why I need your help, Charlie. I've got to get the horse out of the country. Can you arrange it?'

'Jesus, man,' Charlie gulped coffee and exhaled noisily. 'You know what you're getting me into? If those buggers caught up with us, if they knew I'd helped you to dodge 'em, they'd have this place burned to the ground in seconds. No. Look. Best thing. Whyn't I just write you the cheque? God, I mean, it's just nine grand. I write the cheque, the whole thing over. No problem. This has gone too bloody far.'

Micky shook his head sadly. 'That's the point, Charlie. It's gone too far. I don't want to pay them any more. Don't ask me why. I'm not sure myself. They've bullied me and I'll not fucking knuckle under any more. That's all.'

'Oh, come on, Micky.' The bluster had re-entered Charlie's voice. 'Very heroic and all that, and I approve, but you say Cathy's already been hurt, and that's enough unpleasantness.'

'If you knew the half of it,' Micky murmured.

'No, really, Mick. I'm your oldest friend and I'm as Irish as you. I know the situation well enough, but write the whole thing off as a bad debt, for God's sake. A necessary evil. Here. Come on.' He stood and walked from the room. He lurched into the doorframe and bounced off it. Micky heard his footfalls as he crossed the hall.

Micky just placed his face in his hands and waited. 'I'm your oldest friend . . .' No, Charlie. Not quite. 'I'm as Irish as you . . .' No, Charlie. Not quite. There's a difference. Not a big one perhaps. Just a few million pounds and a few thousand acres. It never seems much to those who have it.

And yet Charlie was right. Where was the point in continuing the fight? Why risk more bloodshed, all for the sake of nine thousand pounds? To be Irish was to live with compromise. It was a skill acquired over millennia. But to be Irish too was to be individualistic, and fierce in defence of the least patch of land, and if it was blood which affected Micky's reasoning English mind now, it was that fighting blood. No bullying invader, whatever his nation, whatever his cause, was going to force Micky Brennan's hand. That, at the last, was all there was to it. Bloodymindedness, no more. He was fighting for his land now. His and Fergal's.

Charlie returned. He slapped the cheque down on the table. 'There,' he boomed, 'I've left the payee bit blank. I hate to do it as much as you do, thinking where that bloody money goes, but if the buggers are shooting now . . .'

Micky looked down at the cheque then up at Charlie. He said, 'No, thanks, Charlie. Keep your money. I told you. I'm getting Sanso out. Are you going to help me or not?'

'You're mad!' Charlie squealed. 'These people are big and powerful, Micky! They'd kill both of us, like as not. The Colonel was saying only this evening – you know the Colonel?'

'I know him,' Micky said grimly. 'He was here?'

'Yes. He *is* here. He's staying. I mean, he's just trying to mediate, Micky. He's just trying to help. He was saying . . .'

'Are you going to help me or not?' Micky asked.

'I have helped you, damn it. Look.'

'To get the horse out.'

'I can't!' Charlie spread his right hand over his eyes. 'Just think, Micky . . .'

'Yeah,' Micky stood. He let his hand rest for a moment on Charlie's shoulder. 'I have thought. Don't worry, mate. I'll see you.'

Micky picked up a chunk of bread and cheese. 'Thanks for the meal, Charlie.' He turned and walked wearily out of the house.

As Micky remounted and steered Sansovino in the vague direction of Cork in hope of hitching a ride on a cattle-board, Ward Kramer slept in the Shelbourne Hotel in Dublin. As Micky once more unsaddled and tethered the horse and settled down to sleep in a wood for the rest of the night, Ward breakfasted and climbed into a hired Vauxhall Viva to drive the sixty or so miles to Ballysheenan.

Ward was a tall, handsome man who kept himself fit by regular swimming, squash and weight-training. He ate well, drank little and had never smoked. All this was clearly advertised by his tanned and glowing skin, his glossy blond curls and the limpidness of his pale blue eyes.

He was a man who thought much and spoke still more of duty. He regarded his work as a lawyer and a politician as duty to the public. He was surprised and aggrieved that the public did not always see it that way. He was dutiful too to his family and to his investments and to the Catholic church. When, therefore, the call had come from Ireland, his duty had been clear. He had cancelled all but his breakfast meeting and flown out almost immediately. There were obviously things to take care of in Ireland.

He reached Ballysheenan just after ten. He found nobody at the house, so he walked down to the yard, where for all his delicacy in pulling up his trousers at the knees, their cuffs were swiftly muddied and his polished moccasins were spattered with dilute manure.

He stood at the entrance to the yard and called, 'Hello?' and, on three notes, 'Hello?' To his horror, two monsters from Irish legend shot from one of the open loose-boxes and flew at him, slavering. Ward stepped backward. He raised his arm to protect himself. He yelled, but they were on him, their breath hot and foetid on his face, their muddy paws working at his lightweight jacket.

'Muddler!' he heard a woman's voice, 'Memphis! No! Down!' And the worst of it was, there was laughter in the voice.

The dogs descended, panting and sniffing at his alien legs. Ward surveyed the damage. His jacket and trousers were adorned now with ornate muddy runes. His shirt was streaked. His cheeks were hot. His hair had fallen over his forehead. His heart palpitated fast.

'Goddamned curs,' he fumed. 'Goddamned filthy curs. Look what they've done!' He looked up. He saw Jenny looking fit and high-coloured in filthy jeans and a man's shirt. She was smiling. She was actually smiling.

'Sorry 'bout that, Wardy,' she stroked one of the monsters. 'Didn't know you were coming. We just can't stop them jumping up. Good trip?'

Ward swallowed a good deal before trusting himself to speak. 'Fine. Up till now. I only brought the two suits. Where did those hell-hounds come from?'

'Oh, they're Micky's,' Jenny grinned. 'Come on. I'm afraid we're pretty busy at the moment. Still, there's some coffee in the office.'

'Who is Micky?' Ward tiptoed after her.

'Micky Brennan. Stud manager.'

'Brennan? I thought he was Mom's trainer?'

'He was. Now he's her stud manager. Oh, and I'm going to marry him.'

'You're going to . . .' he swallowed, 'm-marry a stud groom?'

''Sright,' Jenny pushed open he office door. 'Seemed sensible. I mean I don't know anything about horses and he's quite fun in bed, so.'

'Dear God,' Ward reached for the desk for support. 'Everyone in this country is crazy. Has he got any money, this Brennan?'

'Not a dime.'

'Dear God,' Ward slumped into a chair. 'Well, on your own head be it.'

'That's right,' Jenny poured coffee.

'So, where's this Micky Brennan?' Ward demanded.

'Oh, he's away at the moment.' Jenny was magnificently vague. 'Have you been to see Cathy?'

'No. I thought I'd come here first, find out what was happening. Some people came to see me in Boston. Seems Cathy's been behaving amazingly irresponsibly. Is the horse being well looked after?'

'Mmm? What horse?'

'Sansovino, of course.'

'Oh, yes, he's being well looked after.'

'I'll want to check him over.'

'What on earth for, Wardy? You don't know one end of a horse from the other, for God's sake.'

'Nonetheless. He's a valuable asset.'

'Yeah, well. He's away at the moment, too.'

'Away?' Ward arose from his chair like a wave, 'Where's away?'

'Be honest, I'm not quite sure.' Jenny admitted. 'But he's with Micky. It's a long story.'

'I'll call the police.' Ward was outraged. 'You can't have a million dollars just "away". What the hell is going on here?'

'Everything's just fine,' Jenny soothed. 'Stop worrying. Screech and I are managing just great. Look, why don't you go and see Cathy? You'll be a lot more use there. Unless you fancy joining us in the mucking out.'

'Dear God,' Ward muttered again. He shuddered from head to toe. 'Dear God, the whole place is crazy.'

Aware now that he was going to get little sense out of the Farlow girl and shying from the prospect of "mucking out", Ward took Jenny's directions and gratefully clambered back into the car.

He was greeted at the hospital in Kilkenny by a sister who smiled up on him and said, 'God save us, but what sort of trouble have you been getting into? You sit down. The doctor'll be along presently.'

Ward explained patiently that he was not here for treatment but to visit. The sister was at first sceptical but at least consented to show him to Cathy's ward. 'Poor old thing,' she cooed in the lift, 'but she's tough as they come. It's a terrible accident and her in that state, but she may yet pull through, God willing. And, oh, the mouth on her for an old woman. You've never heard the like for the cursing and swearing.'

Ward had been brought up on the like. It affronted him to the core, but he kept his silence. He was shown into the private room. Cathy lay on a black truckle bed beneath an open window. The light through the flapping curtain was the same pale cream as the walls. The floor was covered with brown linoleum. There were three vases of flowers and that old picture of Sansovino on the side. The glass in the picture was cracked.

The sister bustled rustling in ahead of Ward. 'Now, who left the window open?' she scolded, 'you'll be after catching your death, Mrs Kramer.'

She reached up for the window-latch, but Cathy mumbled, 'Leave the fucking thing alone, sister.'

The sister started. She turned to Ward with a despairing shrug. 'There,' she shook her head, 'She won't be told.'

Ward dismissed her. 'Thank you, sister. I'll see you on my way out.'

'Now,' he sat on the edge of Cathy's bed, 'I told you you should have stayed in care. You were bound to have an accident over here on your own. And look at this. It's hardly luxury, is it?'

Cathy groaned. She mumbled her words almost entirely without vowels. 'Nuns are bloody good. 'M fine. Don't fucking fuss. Dunno why you bothered to come.'

'Good thing I did, mother. The stud's in chaos. God knows what you've been up to. I had complaints even in Boston. Jenny doesn't seem to know what's going on, and where the hell is our stallion?'

'Not our stallion,' Cathy moaned. ''Smine.'

'All right, all right, but it's still my duty to protect the animal. He's a family asset.'

'Bollocks. 'Smine. Jenny. Good girl.'

'And I hear she's going to marry this stud groom feller.'

'Yup. Planned it all along. Worked too. Good thing.'

'I dont know what Aunt Helena will have to say about that.'

'Fuck Aunt Helena.'

Ward considered this statement. He decided to change the subject. 'So,' he said with a cheeriness reserved for children and invalids, 'what exactly is the matter?'

'Fell downstairs. Hip's gone. Left leg broken. Concussion. Few other bits and pieces. I'll be OK. Get back to Boston. Why're you such a mess?'

'Two goddamned big dogs at the stud,' Ward flicked fastidiously at his lapels. 'They attacked me. Should have those animals destroyed.'

'They bite you?'

'No.'

''N they didn't attack you, did they?'

Cathy's body was shaking beneath the blankets. Ward leaned forward. 'Are you OK, mother?'

241

Cathy didn't answer. Her body still seemed to be convulsing violently. A tear had appeared at the corner of her left eye. 'Shall I call the sister, mother?' he whispered anxiously. This caused an even greater convulsion, so Ward got up and strode purposefully to the door. 'Sister!' he called 'Sister!'

The little nun came promptly. 'What's the matter?' She clicked across the room.

'I'm not sure,' Ward announced. 'She seems to be in some pain.'

'What's the matter, dote?' the sister leaned over Cathy. Ward stood anxiously by.

Cathy drew a deep wheezing breath. 'Sister mother,' she said, then 'those dogs. Oh, God. Take him away, nurse. It *hurts*.'

'There now,' the sister turned smiling, 'You've been and gone and made her laugh. You'll be wearing her out, poor dear. You just say goodbye now and come back another day.'

'Oh.' Ward was stupefied. He had never understood his mother. He dutifully bent and kissed her. He said, 'I'll be back tomorrow.' And Cathy still shook and wept with silent, agonising laughter.

An elderly but upright man stood up as Ward re-entered the hospital's vestibule. He wore a long waxed green coat with a corduroy collar. He held out a hand. 'Mr Kramer would it be?' he asked with a smile.

'That's right.'

'Colonel Murphy. Might I have a quick word?'

'Er, sure.' Ward shrugged.

'It's a private matter. Shall we find a quiet corner somewhere?'

It took five minutes. Ward agreed that the cause of the Irish people was just. Ward agreed that it was perfectly fair that Ballysheenan should do its bit. Ward agreed that his mother had behaved disgracefully. Ward thought of the many Irish voters in Boston, and, warmed by this thought, wrote a cheque made payable to Father S. Fisher for $20,000 and handed it to the Colonel.

He had only had twenty-three pounds in the back-pocket of his jeans. Only now in a bar four miles to the north of Cork city, did Micky dare to call Ballysheenan.

He had ridden for four days and four nights; four days of sleeping rough, four nights of dodging cars and lorries as he made his way down through the foothills of the Knockmealdown Mountains to cross the

Blackwater at Ballyhooley and so on through the Nagles and down to Cork.

His beard had grown thick and strong. He smelled bad even to himself. He was tired beyond thought and his every muscle ached, but he rode on, almost mechanically making the calculations as to how to ford this stream, how cross this main road. He had eaten rarely, and always at small roadside cafes, having found a sheltered spot up to a mile away in which to tether the horse. He had no longer felt anger or fear, just the firm, if imprecise conviction that he must keep riding until he reached Cork and that then everything would be all right.

Sansovino had seemed strangely unconcerned by the radical change in lifestyle. At times he even seemed to enjoy the journey. On occasion he was coltish, but familiarity had overcome Micky's fear. He had lived in the saddle forever. It was his natural home. And there had been nothing to be frightened of now. All that had mattered was Cork. It had become a Grail.

He had no thought as to what he would do as at last he arrived there. He had just ridden on because he had not known what else to do, where else to go.

Now he dialled the number of the house with a shaking finger. There was no reply. He rang the office. Screech answered almost immediately with a husky, 'Ballysheenan.'

''Lo Screech,' Micky said softly. 'Jenny there?'

There was a bit of a scuffing sound as the receiver changed hands. 'Micky? Oh, God, thank the Lord, where the hell are you? God, you don't know . . . What's been happening? Are you OK? Where are you?'

'Hush, darling,' he said quickly. 'Just listen. Are you OK?'

'I'm fine. What about you, for God's sake?'

'I'm OK, but don't ask me where I am.'

'But listen, Micky . . .'

'I've got to be quick. They'll trace this . . .'

'But listen, Micky. They've been *paid*!'

It took a second or two to sink in, then, 'Oh, God,' Micky moaned. 'No. Please. Not after all this. Not bloody Charlie, was it?'

'No, love. Ward. Came back and paid like a shot. He thought he was protecting his votes in Boston and his investment. Case you'd like to know, Sanso's never going to be his. Cathy's given him to me – well, to us, if you go along with my masterplan. She says it was her masterplan actually.'

Micky's chest walls heaved, yet he found that he could not get a good lungful of air. He gasped, 'How is she?'

'She's fine, but she's probably going to need clinical care from now on. Certainly for the next few months, maybe longer. Micky, look, in case you hadn't noticed, I'm proposing to you, and you've got to accept anyway because then the owner of the stud will be Irish.'

'OK, Jenny,' Micky wiped tears away on his sleeve. 'Look – I can't talk now. I'll – I'll think about . . . Listen. I'm down in Cork. Please send a horse-box and . . .' he rested his head against the glass. 'Get me home, please, Jenny. Please. Get me home.'